A HUNDRED HOURS OF NIGHT

A HUNDRED HOURS OF NIGHT

ANNA WOLTZ

Translated from the Dutch by LAURA WATKINSON

ARTHUR A. LEVINE BOOKS *An Imprint of Scholastic Inc.*

Originally published in Dutch as *Honderd uur nacht* by Em. Querido's Uitgeverij BV in 2014.

Library of Congress Cataloging-in-Publication Data

Names: Woltz, Anna, author. | Watkinson, Laura, translator.
Title: A hundred hours of night / Anna Woltz ; translated from the Dutch by Laura Watkinson.
Other titles: Honderd uur nacht. English
Description: First American edition. | New York : Arthur A. Levine Books, an imprint of Scholastic Inc., 2016. | Summary: Furious at her father, who is caught up in a sex scandal, and suffering from panic attacks and obsessive-compulsive disorder, fifteen-year-old Emilia December de Wit runs away from Amsterdam to New York City, where she meets sixteen-year-old Seth, and his eleven-year old sister Abby—and then Hurricane Sandy hits and the lights go out.
Identifiers: LCCN 2015039412| ISBN 9780545848282 (hardcover : alk. paper) |
Subjects: LCSH: Runaway teenagers—Juvenile fiction. | Fathers and daughters—Juvenile fiction. | Hurricane Sandy, 2012—Juvenile fiction. | Panic disorders—Juvenile fiction. | Obsessive-compulsive disorder—Juvenile fiction. | Friendship—Juvenile fiction. | New York (N.Y.)—Juvenile fiction. | CYAC: Runaways—Fiction. | Fathers and daughters—Fiction. | Hurricane Sandy, 2012—Fiction. | Panic disorders—Fiction. | Obsessive-compulsive disorder—Fiction. | Friendship—Fiction. | New York (N.Y.)—Fiction.
Classification: LCC PZ7.W8373 Hu 2016 | DDC [Fic]—dc23 LC record available at http://lccn.loc.gov/2015039412

10 9 8 7 6 5 4 3 2 1   16 17 18 19 20
Printed in the U.S.A. 23

First American edition, May 2016

Book design by Yaffa Jaskoll

The publisher gratefully acknowledges the support of the Dutch Foundation for Literature.

Nederlands letterenfonds
dutch foundation for literature

"We hold these truths to be self-evident, that all men are created equal, that they are endowed by their Creator with certain unalienable Rights, that among these are Life, Liberty and the pursuit of Happiness."

United States Declaration of Independence, July 4, 1776

That shocking story on the Internet is not me.

The fairy tale I'm about to tell the American officials is a lie.

Do I still have a story of my own? I don't know.

I'm fifteen and I'm from the Netherlands. My dad wears corduroy pants and likes stargazing more than anything else. And, oh yeah, I almost forgot—last Tuesday he destroyed the world. My mother is Nora Quinn. She was born in Ireland, and now and then she speaks to me in English.

I mean: She speaks to me now and then. Always in English.

She's an artist. Her paintings are in museums all over the world, and if she feels like taking off all her clothes and starting a new painting up on our roof, stark-naked, she does exactly that.

I'm their daughter. That was my story.

But now I have nothing at all.

1

I'm the only person in the world who knows what I'm going to do today. That is, if I actually go through with it . . .

My boots wait, perfectly still, on the smooth tiles of the departure hall. Whenever someone glances at me, my heart stops beating for an instant. Do they recognize me from the Internet? Are they about to start yelling at me?

But nothing happens. Everyone at the airport looks right through me. Yesterday they were all reading about my dad and what he did, but today they're off on vacation. They're dragging around suitcases and screaming toddlers and they've already forgotten all about their tweets.

I certainly haven't forgotten the threats on Twitter, though.

My breathing has felt shallow since Tuesday evening. My mouth is dry. Somewhere inside my head, an alarm's ringing, over and over. *Danger*, it says. *Run! Get away!*

I act like it's perfectly normal for me to be standing here all alone at Schiphol Airport. The information boards flicker above my head; I smell men's sweat; a dog the size of a small horse is pushed past inside a plastic cage.

Every thirty seconds, my hand reaches for my bag to grab my cell phone—but every time, my arm stops halfway. For the first time ever, I've actually turned off my phone.

I take out my passport and flick through the blank, stampless pages. When I get to my photo, I pause. I don't like looking at pictures of myself. My hair's too straight, my eyes are too big, and my face is too pale. I look like I'm fading away into nothing.

But the photo in my passport is different: It was taken four years ago when I was still in elementary school. I'm looking out of the photo fearlessly, as if I'm *superexcited* about the rest of my life. I was eleven and I liked to grow sprouts in empty eggshells.

I'm not that girl anymore.

My name is next to my passport photo: Emilia December de Wit. Seriously, that's my name.

The middle name was my mom's bright idea, and even when I arrived late and wasn't born until January 2, she still thought calling me December was an excellent plan.

My dad could easily have said, "Maybe Susanne would suit her better. Or Margriet." Then again, he could also have said, "How about we call her Cosine Isosceles Triangle de Wit?" Then my mom might have realized that incorporating your own insanity into your child's name really isn't such a great idea after all.

But my dad just kept his mouth shut. Of course he did. Even fifteen years ago, the guy was already a selfish jerk.

He simply didn't give a damn about the name of his only child.

Finally, it's my turn. I put my passport on the desk and desperately try to work up a little moisture in my mouth.

"And what's your destination today?" asks the desk clerk in her bright blue suit.

"New York."

I stand up straighter. I'm scared, but at the same time, I feel something new and exciting running through my veins as I say the name of the city: I'm going to *New York*. My friends all have posters on their bedroom walls of boys they've never seen in real life. But above my bed, I have the New York City skyline. Okay, I've never been there, but I'm in love with it all the same.

"Are you flying alone?" the desk clerk asks.

I nod. Breathlessly, I answer her questions.

Yes, I packed my own bag.

No, I don't have any hazardous substances in my carry-on.

I'm just taking my shoulder bag onto the flight.

The woman looks at me, but she doesn't seem to recognize me from the Internet. And thank God she doesn't suddenly remember seeing a disgusting man on the news last night who had the same last name as me.

My bulging suitcase gets a label and disappears from sight. And I get a boarding pass. Boarding will begin in ninety minutes.

All alone, I walk to the line for passport control. I don't belong with anyone and I feel strangely light without my luggage. My blood is tingling. I still can't quite believe it: I'm really going to do this. Two days ago, it was no more than an idea. Just a thought: If I were a completely different person, I'd give the world the finger and fly to New York.

It's Friday, October 26. In ten and a half hours, I'll be there.

2

Everything is so different when you're on your own. Colors are brighter, noises sound louder, plans can go wrong at any moment. As I walk through the echoing terminal after the passport check, I tell myself to be tough. A girl who steals her dad's credit card in the middle of the night so she can buy a plane ticket isn't going to sit crying in the airport restroom. A girl like that isn't going to start screaming, and she's certainly not going to turn on her cell phone to call her mom.

I buy a cappuccino even though I don't like coffee; I need to stay alert. The cut on my left hand is still painful. Blood's seeping through the bandage now, but I can't do anything about it. I'd rather bleed out than change the bandage in a public restroom.

And then suddenly I stop walking.

I stare at a girl in the store that sells impossibly expensive bags. She has blond curls, tight jeans, and Uggs. It's Juno—it must be. She's standing with her back to me, so I can't see her face. Heart pounding, I wait for her to turn around.

It's someone else.

Shaking, I walk to the nearest row of seats. I sit down, clench my hands together, but stop as soon as I feel the cut. How could I have ever thought I was brave?

With trembling fingers, I take out my folder full of papers. I printed out absolutely everything. My flight times. The bus I have to take when I arrive. The dollar exchange rate. How much of a tip I should give. Which museum has the most Impressionist paintings. I keep reading until I get my breath back, and then finally I dare to look up again.

Outside, through huge panes of glass, I can see seventeen airplanes. They're about to let their engines roar, soar away, and transform into swans, high in the sky.

It's over now, I tell myself. I can't bump into Juno in the hallways anymore. Her friends won't be able to yell at me in the school yard. My gym bag is safe from their lighters, and that locker with all the stuff written on it isn't mine anymore.

I'm never going back to that school.

In the waiting area by the gate, I have to turn my phone on, just for a moment. I wait anxiously to see if any messages arrive, but there's nothing. My mom and dad think I'm at school and everyone in my class naturally assumes I'm under the covers at home, crying my eyes out.

Well, it just so happens that they're wrong. And it just so happens that the time has come to flip off the world—or at least my mom and dad. The email's been ready and waiting to be sent since last night:

To the losers who created me,

I thought we had a deal. I'd do my homework, set the table, and not get my navel pierced. You'd feed me and not do anything that might get you sent to prison.

The deal's over now. That much is clear.

You think I'm doing some monster physics test, but I'm actually on the train to Germany. I'm going to stay with Klara. I'm going crazy here, so I'm off to a country where my dad isn't the latest news. You have no idea what it's been like at school and on Facebook and Twitter and everywhere else.

You don't have a clue what it's like to be me.

Don't come after me. And don't call either—I won't pick up. Neither will Klara, and, anyway, she changed her number ages ago.

I'll send another email tomorrow to let you know I'm still alive.

That is, if I am *still alive . . .*

E.

My thumb hovers over the SEND button. At this point, I can still go back. I could just get up and walk from here to Arrivals, through the baggage claim, where the suitcases dizzily spin around in circles, and out into the hall, where no one's waiting for me. I could catch the train back home as if I'd never planned to escape.

And then I remember Tuesday evening again.

I was sitting in our quiet, cozy living room, doing my history homework. It was about the American Declaration of

Independence. Which is, without a doubt, one of the best things ever written, but that's not the point right now.

Mom was working in her studio—she hadn't even stopped to eat—and my dad was upstairs in his office, fiddling with his scientific instruments.

Outside in the dusk, people walked past our window. I looked out at those unfamiliar shadows as the first, shining lines of the Declaration of Independence marched through my head, and I was happy. For one brief moment, everything felt just right.

And then the phone rang.

Not my cell, but the landline. I walked to the phone, pulled my sleeve down over my hand, and picked up the receiver.

On the other end of the line I could hear a hysterical woman sobbing and choking.

She said she was Juno's mother.

And she wanted to speak to my dad.

I press SEND and my email flies away. I don't want to go back.

More people die in car accidents than in plane crashes. That's what I tell myself as I walk through the gray tunnel to the airplane. The alarm bell in my head is still ringing, but I try to ignore it.

I have an article in my bag, which I memorized last night. A plane's air-conditioning system filters out no less than 99.97 percent of all bacteria and viruses from the air. If you keep strictly to the Ten Golden Rules for Plane Journeys, you'll be fine.

As soon as I'm sitting in my seat by the window, I put Golden Rule Number One into action. I take a packet of disinfectant wipes from my bag and I start scrubbing. The plastic tray table, my armrests, and the buckle of my seat belt all need to be clean. Luckily, the people around me are focused on their magazines and earplugs and on flattening other people's luggage by ramming their own bags into the overhead bins. They barely even look at me.

During takeoff, I stare at the bandage on my left hand. I can feel the plane jolting in the wind, the sky tugging at our wings, the engines racing to keep us alive.

To be honest, though, for more than an hour, I actually feel pretty fine inside that Boeing.

Unfortunately, I then have the brilliant idea of asking a flight attendant how many people are on board.

"Three hundred," she says cheerfully as she hands me a plastic cup of apple juice.

I look around. I'm hanging up here above the ocean inside a vibrating cocoon with *three hundred* other living creatures. Three hundred slimy, snotty creatures who are sniffing and coughing and *breathing* the entire time. A large man closes the restroom door, and suddenly I wonder how many people would be crazy enough to poop eleven kilometers in the air, high above the clouds. No one at all, I'd have thought. But clearly I must be wrong. After all, some people poop at school, or at the fairground, or when they're visiting someone else's house . . .

Then it starts.

Sometimes, when I think too hard about my PIN code, I suddenly can't remember it. And it's the same with breathing. As soon as I start paying attention to my breathing, my lungs forget how to act normally.

God, this is so embarrassing.

I'm hyperventilating.

No one notices at first, because I'm trying to suffocate quietly. But after a couple of minutes I can't hide it anymore. My chest is going up and down, faster and faster. I can feel sweat on my forehead and my throat is burning. I gag and a kind of whining sound comes out.

The whole plane is looking at me. Five people press their bells. A little girl starts crying.

Soon there are three flight attendants standing beside my row of seats, discussing me in whispers. Then a call goes out through the airplane to ask if there's a doctor on board.

I don't really notice what's going on because I'm too busy dying, but a Russian doctor appears from business class. He confers in broken English with the flight attendants and with about fifteen passengers, who are all butting in. While the consultation is still in full swing, a woman who is clearly a fully qualified mother tells me to breathe into a paper bag. Then the Russian doctor gives me something to calm me down.

It's a long time before they all stop looking at me.

Tears roll quietly down my cheeks and onto my neck, because I obviously got it all wrong. I'm not giving the world the finger. The world is giving me the finger.

Yet again.

Dazed, I stare out the window. The sunny clouds beneath the plane look like they're made of whipped egg whites. It's a frozen world with no people in it. With no plans and no disappointments.

Then I fall asleep and dream about my dad's orrery, his model of the solar system.

It's an old-fashioned contraption that stands in the middle of his office. When you crank a brass handle, the planets creakily turn around the sun. I was six when he let me operate it for the first time. It was magical. With just one hand, I could make the planets move. As I slowly turned the handle, my dad explained what makes it light in the daytime and dark at night. And why it doesn't get dark all over the world at the same time.

In my dream I'm standing in the darkness outside his office door. Inside, I can hear the planets quietly squeaking. I hesitate for a moment before opening the door. The light of a streetlamp comes in through the windows. The instruments are gleaming: the big electrostatic generator by the window, the barometers on the wall, the microscopes under their glass domes.

In the middle of the room is the orrery with its brass handle. But it's not my dad who's turning it.

It's Juno.

Her blond curls are shining more brightly than all the instruments combined. She looks at me.

And then she laughs.

As the wheels of the plane touch the ground, I feel a lump in my throat.

I am Columbus. For the first time in my life, I am in America.

As soon as I'm inside Newark Airport, I look eagerly around. But all I can see is a gray corridor with dirty carpet on the floor and threatening signs with pictures of cell phones crossed out in red. I'd imagined America would gleam. That everything would be spotlessly clean and modern. Which sounded great to me.

After the corridor, we enter a room the size of a church. A long line of people zigzags silently through a collection of poles and cordons. It's like an amusement park, but without any signs to tell you how long the wait is.

A tense silence fills the hall. America isn't a country you can just walk into. If the immigration people think you're secretly planning to stay for longer, or if they suspect that you're lying, they put you on the next flight home.

And yes, I'm planning to lie.

My stomach feels like I'm right at the top of a roller coaster. I can see the large man from the plane looking at me. The mother with the paper bag is keeping an eye on me too. Do they hope I'm about to start panicking again?

Well, if I have to stand here for another thirty minutes, their wish will come true.

Finally, a man in a uniform sends me to desk number seven, where a woman with deep-set eyes and scraped-back hair is waiting for me.

"Good afternoon," she says gloomily. She takes my passport. "How are you today?"

I look at her. This woman, someone I've never met before, will decide, in less than ten minutes, if I'm allowed to enter America.

"What is the purpose of your visit to the United States?" she asks.

I gulp. The airport here feels different than the one at home. English is my second mother tongue, but I'm not sure if I've memorized the right lies.

"Just a vacation," I say. "I want to see New York."

"How long are you staying?"

"Two weeks."

On Wednesday night, when I booked the flight, I wanted to buy a one-way ticket at first. But then I started to read all the horror stories about the American immigration system, and I soon realized that I'd never, ever be allowed into the country without a return ticket. They only let you in if they're sure you're going to clear off again before too long.

"Where will you be staying for the next two weeks?" asks the woman.

I take the folder of printouts from my bag. It contains all the information about my room and the emails that the owner sent me. The paper seems to be shaking even worse than my hand.

The woman takes a good, long look at everything, leafs through my passport, and then frowns.

"You're fifteen?"

I nod.

"And you're here on your own?"

This is the big moment. Of course this woman doesn't need to hear all about my real life. She just wants a story that sounds right, a fairy tale she can listen to without becoming concerned.

"My friend Klara's coming too," I say. My voice sounds like cold oatmeal. "We rented the apartment together. Klara's twenty-one and she used to be my family's au pair. She's landing at John F. Kennedy Airport on a flight from Frankfurt this evening. I have her telephone number right here." I push another piece of paper over to the woman. "But she's still on the plane right now . . ."

With one hand, I hold on tightly to the counter, even though it's sticky. If I don't, I know I'll fall over.

The woman flips through my passport again and looks up at me.

"Do you have written permission from your parents for this trip?"

I offer up silent thanks to the Internet. I knew I was going to need a letter. I take it out of the folder, along with the copies of my parents' passports. I snagged half the letter from the Internet and made up the rest myself. And I copied the signatures from their passports, so they should be right.

I slide the documents across to the woman and wait anxiously. She studies the letter and the photocopies for a long time. If I believed in God, I'd be praying now. Constantly, pleadingly. But I don't believe in God.

I used to believe in grown-ups. And now I don't believe in anything.

Finally, she nods. Gravely, as if she's decided I can go straight to hell.

"Okay. Place your left thumb on the scanner."

I hesitate at the sight of the greasy glass plate. But I'd do anything for America. I think as hard as I can about the antibacterial gel in my bag and I put my thumb on the scanner.

5

This is incredible! I made it! Emilia December de Wit is in America.

My first stop was an ATM. Then I used my first-ever dollars to buy a ticket for the bus into the city. Which is where I am now. On the bus. Right at the front, almost next to the driver, so I can look out through the windshield. It was the only way to see out, because there are advertisements stuck all over the side windows, from top to bottom.

As we wait for more passengers to get on, my self-control fails me: I have to turn on my cell phone. The messages come pinging in. Nine missed calls from "Dad" and three from "Mom's cell." As I stare at the glowing screen, I start to feel sick. Ever since Tuesday, the Netherlands has been just one big stinking swamp, and I can smell the stench even from here.

There's no way I want to listen to whatever those voice mails have to say, but I make myself read the text messages. Dad sent the first one just after I'd boarded the plane.

Damn it, Emilia! Just saw the broken glass in my office. I understand why you're angry, but this is unforgivable. I know you skipped school today. Call me ASAP.

I look down at the bandage on my hand before opening the next text message.

Pick up the phone! If you don't call back, I'm getting into the car and coming to fetch you from Frankfurt. We need to talk. Now!

The last message was sent an hour ago.

If we don't hear from you by midnight, we're calling the police and reporting you missing.

My hands are shaking. I knew he'd be mad. That's exactly what I wanted. But "unforgivable"? He's never said that before.

Don't call the police, I text back. *Do you really want to mess things up even more? Klara and I just ate schnitzel and I'm fine. Will call tomorrow.*

As I hit SEND, the bus starts moving. I put my phone on silent and bury it in the bottom of my bag. I have to forget about the swamp, or I might as well not have bothered to escape.

Look outside, I say to myself. *You're Columbus!*

I focus on the details. The traffic signs above the road are bright green. The sky is cloudy, and the cars are the size of tanks. Americans build their roads with big slabs of concrete, and the old bus shudders every time we bump onto a new one. We make a slow curve. The concrete road becomes an overpass. And then I stop breathing.

There, in the gray distance, is New York City.

I recognize the skyline immediately from the poster over my bed: Hundreds of gray, brown, and glistening glass buildings combine to form the most beautiful bar graph in the world. As I gaze at it, one word dances and spins around inside my head: *finally*.

All those movies and photos and TV shows and news items have prepared me for this moment. But now I'm seeing it for real. And it feels just like when I made the planets move for the first time.

Suddenly, I realize why American immigration wanted my story to be just right. As I see that world-famous skyline with my own eyes, I understand.

America is the ultimate story. It's like stepping onto a life-size movie screen. If you want to play your part, you have to fit in.

The bus drives into a tunnel that seems too narrow. Tiled walls whizz past. Car lights flash by in the darkness. I see an orange traffic cone lying in the middle of our half of the road, and I close my eyes for a moment.

Then we emerge from the tunnel and we're in Manhattan. A handful of Native Americans once lived on this small island between two rivers. Now it has 1.6 million inhabitants, and it's crammed full of skyscrapers.

From the bus, I can't see where the buildings stop. The Friday-afternoon traffic is insane. Yellow cabs everywhere. They're honking their horns in a hundred different ways, as if every taxi is speaking a different language.

We drive past oceans of people gazing up at gigantic neon signs. Flashing advertisements for *The Lion King* and the latest Samsung phone and the "Biggest Burger Ever!" dance across the buildings.

The world around me is sparkling. Everything is gleaming and glittering away.

• • •

And suddenly I wonder if I really fit in here.

As New York roars outside, I look down at my hands. The skin is dry and cracked, like the surface of an old painting. I wash my hands constantly, and it's ruined my fingers.

What would this city want with me?

I am Emilia December de Wit, and I'm too scared even to touch the metal bar in front of me. I'm too scared to eat a hot dog from a food cart. I'm too scared to use the subway at rush hour.

I don't know what would happen to us if my dad had to go to jail.

I have no idea how I would look after my mom. Or if I'd even want to.

I wonder . . .

But then I stop.

We're driving past a singing, jingling, laughing park. Around the edges, beneath the red and yellow trees, are glass stalls with little stores inside. In the middle of the park, there's an ice rink full of skaters in brightly colored hats. As I hear the first Christmas song of the year, I feel happiness in my veins.

Do I fit in?

Hey, this is New York City. You only have to look at all the girls who live here in the movies. If the stories are even a little bit true, this place is teeming with lonely, hung-up control freaks like me. Women who write down everything in their bulging diaries. Who can't stand surprises. Who constantly clean their apartments, wearing an oversize sweater that once belonged to their ex or their dead father, and who have only a cat to talk to, and eat takeout every night from one of those cardboard boxes, and have piles of teddy bears gazing up at them from their perfectly made beds . . .

It's beginning to look a lot like Christmas.

My collection of dusty teddy bears is a big, fat zero, and I definitely don't have a fluffy cat. But if there's anywhere in the world I should feel at home, it's here, in this glittering city.

The bus gasps to a halt at the last stop.

"Grand Central," calls the bus driver without looking around. "Last stop. Everyone out." He throws our bags onto the sidewalk, and the rattling bus drives away.

And so here I am. With my boots on the flat gray sidewalk of New York. Everyone else knows where they need to go. They disappear, along with their suitcases and bags.

All on my own, I stand on a sidewalk that's as wide as an entire Dutch street. Enormous buildings tower all around me. I tilt my head to look up at them. A few streets away, a silver skyscraper shimmers like the spire of a fairy-tale church. High in the sky, eagles' heads stretch out from the metallic building. As I gaze at them, I fall in love.

I just wish I could actually see Grand Central station . . . Where could it be?

It's a lot colder here than in the Netherlands, so I button my winter coat all the way to the top. My head's spinning. The sky's still light, but to me it feels like eleven thirty at night. If I stay here forever, I'll have seen six extra hours of sunlight by the time I die. And my dad will have lived in the dark for six hours longer.

A yellow cab pulls up. The driver smiles at me through his open window. "Need a ride?"

I was planning to take the subway to my room. My print-out says I need to take the green line, number 6, downtown, but suddenly I feel like I'm about to keel over with jet lag. My psychologist—I saw her for a while, but thankfully that's over now—always said an occasional change of plan isn't a bad thing.

So I nod.

My bag goes in the trunk, and soon we're zooming south down Lexington Avenue. You only have to study the map of New York once to see how the city fits together. It's like someone arranged a box of building blocks on a sheet of graph paper. The wide routes from north to south are called avenues, and the ones from east to west are streets. The streets all have a number, so you always know exactly where you are.

If only my life were that simple.

I sit in silence, looking out the cab window. The buildings are starting to shrink, and the sharply dressed businessmen turn into kids in skinny jeans.

I found my room online just yesterday morning, on craigslist. My finger was sore from hours of scrolling and my eyes were burning. I'd just about given up. It wasn't going to work. I'd have to resign myself to life in the swamp. America didn't want me. But then, hidden among five hundred dingy broom closets and seven hundred insanely expensive apartments, I suddenly spotted my "studio."

The photographs showed sunlight streaming in through two large windows, and the description said those windows had a view of the Empire State Building. I felt like Goldilocks: This room was just right. It was available for the next couple of weeks. And all I had to do was pay in advance with my dad's credit card.

6

It's like stepping out of the cab and onto a movie set, a set that fifty people have worked on for weeks to make it obvious to even the dumbest of viewers: This story takes place in New York.

But this isn't a set; it's for real.

As the taxi pulls away, I gaze around. My street's lined with tall trees in flaming fall colors. Most of the buildings are five stories high. They're reddish-brown and ocher and gray, with flat roofs and elegant metal fire escapes. Two girls walk past. I can tell just by looking at them that they're runway models. Their legs are so long and thin. They have bored looks on their faces and big cups of coffee in their hands. With those little plastic lids on top.

I look at the house numbers. My room must be on the top floor of that bloodred building. Beside the front door, there's a messy line of buzzers. There are more buzzers than stories, so it takes me a while to find the name I'm looking for. There it is, in faded letters: Greenberg.

I'm too tired to be nervous, so I pull my sleeve over my finger and press the button.

Nothing happens.

I ring again, but there's still no sound from behind the front door. All around me, though, the city is insanely loud. Sirens wail from three different directions and there's honking everywhere: long blares and short beeps and whole stretches of uninterrupted noise. Then a truck rumbles down the narrow street, engine growling and black clouds pumping from the rattling muffler.

As I start coughing, the front door opens. I was expecting a guy with a goatee. On the website, Mr. Greenberg was a grown man with two Chihuahuas, a big grin, and a blond beard.

But the guy in the doorway isn't an adult. He can't be much older than me. His short dark hair is ruffled, his T-shirt's inside out, and he's not wearing any shoes.

He's not smiling either.

"Okay," he says. "What is it this time?"

I stare at him.

"I know Abby sent you." He sounds mad. "My aunt already called." He holds up an iPhone. "Abby's disappeared, and when that kid goes missing, she's always up to no good."

"I . . ."

"You got a banana with a note hidden inside?" He doesn't even wait for me to answer. "No, of course not. Abby never does the same thing twice." He sighs. "So are you going to act something out for me? Or do you have a video clip? Do I need to go somewhere?"

I shake my head. I seem to have forgotten how to speak.

"Okay, I get it," the boy says. His eyes are very dark brown. "You're not going to answer until I say exactly the right thing. Like a kind of password." He frowns and looks down at the ground. His cheeks are slowly turning red.

"Abby wants me to talk to you. To have an actual conversation with you, just like that, out of nowhere. That's it, isn't it?" He wipes his hand across his face. "That's why she chose you. A pretty girl, the kind of girl I normally wouldn't talk to. But she doesn't get it. It doesn't work that way. I mean, there's a reason why I don't talk to pretty girls. Pretty girls and me . . ."

He stops and I stare at him. *A pretty girl?*

The boy sighs. "You can tell Abby I blew it. This challenge was too difficult." He starts to shut the door.

"Wait!" I say. "Who's Abby?"

The door swings open again.

"My little sister," he says. "But you already know that . . ."

As he looks at me, I can see it slowly dawning on him.

"Really?" he says, in that feeble little cold oatmeal voice that I so often hear myself using. "You don't know who Abby is?"

"No."

"So you have nothing to do with one of her challenges? She didn't tell you to wait here until I started flirting with you?"

"Sorry," I say. "My name's Emilia. I come from the Netherlands and I've rented a room here."

He's about to say something, but then he shakes his head and remains silent.

"So Abby's missing?" I ask.

"She was supposed to stay with my aunt this weekend, but she ran away." He still can't quite meet my eyes. "Abby's eleven, and that seriously is a terrible age. She has no idea how dangerous the world can be. She thinks she's James Bond and that she can solve all the problems in New York."

"And that she can find you a girlfriend . . ."

I immediately wish I hadn't said anything, because the red glow in his cheeks had just started to fade.

"I talk too much," he says.

"Me too," I blurt.

That's not true, because usually I keep my mouth tightly shut. I'm always scared of saying the wrong thing. Fifteen years old and I still feel like I don't know the rules.

It's a while before we pluck up the courage to make another sound. The sirens go on screaming in the background; the taxis keep blowing their horns; the city still races and gleams.

Finally, he breaks the silence. "Hi. I'm Seth Greenberg," he says. Like a well-programmed American robot, he shoots out his hand. "Nice to meet you, Emilia . . ." But his hand isn't part of a clean and polished robot arm. His fingers are covered with black smudges, as if he's just changed the cartridge of a printer from the Stone Age. Or maybe he repaired his bike, like, a week ago, and he hasn't washed his hands since.

I know it's dumb, but I can't handle it right now. I can't touch that dirty hand. I'm too tired. I just can't bring myself to do it.

So I say, "Sorry." I clench my right hand into a fist behind my back. "I have a cold. I don't want you to catch it."

He shrugs. "But if Abby didn't send you, why are you here?"

"Because of the room!"

He looks puzzled.

"I just told you, didn't I? I rented your studio." I take the printout from my bag. "I was in touch with Mr. Greenberg. I guess that must be your dad?"

"I don't think so," says Seth. "My dad's been dead for two years."

I leaf through the papers. My hand with the cut is shaking again. I pretend not to have heard what he just said about his dead dad. Right now, all I want is for Seth to take me to my room. I want to pee and to shower and to sleep.

"Look." I hold the papers in front of his face and he begins to read. The information about the studio. The emails I sent to Mr. Greenberg. His replies.

"So you're here all alone?" Seth asks after a while. "You've come from the Netherlands and you rented a room off craigslist?"

I nod.

"Holy crap!" He shakes his head. Not just a quick shake, but a really slow, long one. "You're even worse than an eleven-year-old."

"What's that supposed to mean?"

"I honestly thought things would get easier with Abby. I thought, sooner or later, that she'd quit her secret missions and going AWOL and causing trouble. But then I see this . . ." He looks at me. "This room doesn't even exist."

"Of course it does!"

"No, it doesn't. This so-called Mr. Greenberg of yours is a scammer. There's no studio for rent here. The guy's just used photos of some other room. Like you could see the Empire State Building from here!"

"But look!" My voice sounds shrill. "His name's in the ad. That's right, isn't it? Greenberg. That's your last name."

Seth shrugs. "He must have copied it from the nameplate by the buzzer."

He doesn't say anything else, just looks at me. He's giving my brain time to absorb what he said.

These past few days, every disaster that happened since the big bang has gone through my mind. And all the disasters that are yet to come. Train collisions, plane crashes—I was prepared for anything.

But I never would have imagined that the room I paid for simply doesn't exist.

Seth's cell phone starts ringing. An irritating, tinny jingle. He answers.

"Abby!" he cries. "Where are you? I just spoke to Aunt Leah. She was in tears . . ." He listens for what seems like ages. "You're crazy! Stay where you are. I'll come get you."

He puts his phone in his pocket. "Got to go. The kid's a disaster area."

"But . . ."

"Hey, I'm sorry. Abby's arranged to meet someone off the Internet. I've got to get to her as quickly as possible. You'll have to find somewhere else to stay. Lucky there are plenty of hotels in New York."

"Wait!" I call, but the front door's already closed.

I hear his feet racing up the stairs. And then . . . silence. Just my heart, pounding in my head. And the blood rushing past my ears.

7

I stand there, looking at the closed door.

And I'm still there, motionless, when Seth comes back out of his building with his bike. He's wearing worn-out sneakers and a black hooded sweatshirt, and he has a neon-green helmet on his head.

"Good luck!" he calls, and then he leaps onto his bike and races away.

I want to yell at him that he has to stay with me. That I'm fifteen and I have no idea what to do next. He's the only New Yorker I know even just a little bit. The only one who actually counts, anyway, because otherwise I only know celebrities: Taylor Swift and Beyoncé and Daniel Radcliffe. But I don't yell and Seth goes zooming around a corner in the distance.

OH MY GOD! I say furiously to myself. *How dumb can you be? You know you can't trust the Internet!* At school last year we even had these stupid lessons in "social media awareness," taught by a very prim and proper lady who knew ten times less about computers than we did.

Why did I believe for even a second that Mr. Greenberg, with his smile and his blond goatee, would be so kind as to rent such a wonderful room to me for hardly any money at all?

Or, yeah, well, for five hundred dollars a week.

Compared to the other rooms, though, that *was* cheap. And yesterday I'd been stupidly naive and transferred a thousand dollars to Russia or to Nigeria or to God knows where that guy and his Chihuahuas actually live. If the mutts even exist . . .

I clench my fists—including my left hand, the one with the cut—until my eyes fill with tears.

Finally, for the first time in my life, I'm in my favorite city in the world.

But with no faucet.

With no mattress.

And with no credit card.

I look at my phone. Three more missed calls from my dad. An astonishingly large number of the cells that make up my body want to call him back, sobbing, but I ignore them.

It's six in the evening and it's getting dark fast. Then the lights come on and suddenly my street looks like a street in a play. First I was walking across a movie set, now I'm standing on a stage with fire escapes made of cardboard and fake trees made of plastic. Every now and then someone throws down a few fall leaves. Every leaf is the shape of two little hearts stuck together.

I stare at them for a long time. Then I put my foot on two hearts and slowly twist my boot back and forth.

With great determination, I put up fences inside my mind. I'm only allowed to think about the next quarter of an hour. What to do next—that's all that matters. Thoughts about murderers and rapists are off-limits. Calling my parents is out of the question. *Shaking*, *shivering*, *trembling*—those words aren't part of my vocabulary.

Okay. The facts. I don't have a bed in this city.

So how does a person get a bed here?

By paying money.

What do I need to do first?

Withdraw more cash.

And what do I need for that?

An ATM.

I extend the handle of my suitcase and start walking. The wheels make a dull rattle on the concrete sidewalk. As I go past the colorful houses, from spotlight to spotlight, I think about a guy in this documentary I once saw on TV. He was about twenty, but ever since he was thirteen, he'd felt like he was in a movie. He wasn't *real*, that's how he put it. And he thought his mom and dad and friends and teachers were all actors too.

I felt sorry for him. No one wants to be an actor forever. But at the same time I wondered if he was the only one saying out loud what everyone feels. Maybe it was different in elementary school. But I know that everyone at my high school is playing a role. Seriously. Our whole building is just one big theater.

I hope that's all going to change when I'm older. But sometimes, when I lie awake and the night is at its darkest, I'm scared it'll never stop. And I worry that people can't give up acting even when they're adults. That we're never free. That the performance will go on forever.

• • •

At the end of the street is a six-lane road that cuts straight through the city. The traffic is blocked solid and—of course—everyone is beeping and honking away. At least half the cars are taxicabs. Cabs going nowhere.

On the broad sidewalk, people with all kinds of different plans in their heads are crossing paths. Professionals in designer clothes are leaving work and rushing to the subway. There's a group of boys in secondhand coats and glasses with thick frames who have to be students. And girls in ultrashort, shiny minidresses who are wobbling their way to couches, cocktails, and blond rich guys with names like James Howard III.

Those guys really do exist. I've seen them in the movies.

As I'm thinking about numbered heirs, I spot the brightly illuminated window of a Bank of America. Pulling my heavy suitcase behind me, I half jog to the bank. I rattle the door.

Locked.

Feeling kind of stunned, I stare at the ATMs inside their bare box and suddenly a man with a beard appears beside me. Not a white Santa Claus beard, but one of those hipster beards that are suddenly so popular.

"You want to go in?" he asks.

I just nod.

He swipes his credit card through a slit beside the door. The light turns green and the door opens.

"Thank you!" I say, surprised.

The man gives me a grin and then walks on. I pull my suitcase into the bright box and put my card into the machine.

But it doesn't work. It seems I can only withdraw cash once a day when I'm abroad. But all I took out at the airport was fifty dollars—nowhere near enough for a hotel.

I drag my suitcase back outside. The fences inside my head are still upright. But they're shaking. It won't take much to make them fall.

"Excuse me!" I call to a woman in a hilarious outfit that looks like something straight out of *Sex and the City*. "Do you know where I can get free Wi-Fi?"

I can't tell how old she is. Her skin is pulled tight and her face is heavily made up. She's like some scarily realistic mannequin from a window display.

"They got Wi-Fi at Starbucks," she says in a sugary voice like a little girl's. "Go straight and take a right onto Broadway."

I wheel my suitcase through the honking and the neon lights toward the green-and-white logo with the mermaid. Inside, it's warm and smells like coffee. I go to the bathroom first, which—thank God!—is clean. Then I buy a cup of tea and a blueberry muffin. I sit at a table by the window and, before even removing my coat or having a bite of my muffin, I take out my phone.

I know that I quickly need to find a hotel where I won't have to pay until tomorrow, but first I Google "how to treat cuts." The wound in my hand is a constant throb. And I also want to know how polluted the air in New York is and I have to check if Daniel Radcliffe really does live here.

I deliberately don't look at my email. Or at any news sites. And I can't even sneak a peek at Facebook or Twitter, because I deleted my accounts yesterday.

The muffin is sweet and gooey, with juicy blueberries and a faint vanilla flavor. Finally, I feel warm again, and fewer of the cells in my body want to phone home and sob.

But then I look at a forum for tips about hotels—and it's all over.

As a minor in America, you can't rent a hotel room on your own. Apparently it's a liability thing. And you can't lie about your age, because everyone always asks for your passport.

I keep on looking, but I can't find a solution. An hour later, there's only one thing I can think of: Go to the police. Hand myself in.

And they'll put me on the first plane home tomorrow morning.

Starbucks closes at eleven at night. I put on my coat, pick up my flowery bag and my suitcase, and head outside. I stand on the ice-cold sidewalk.

New York loves to celebrate the fact that it's Friday night. A stretch limo drives by, a group of men in tiaras and boas is yelling that Mitchell's getting married, two giggling girls walk past in glittery skirts—but I'm just not interested. In the Netherlands, it's five in the morning. I've never, ever been awake for such a long stretch of time. My head feels muzzy and my body's shaking.

I know exactly where the nearest police station is now. But I walk in the opposite direction.

I spent a long time thinking about it at my little table by the window. I imagined what it would be like to report myself to the police. How it would feel when they called my parents. And then, later, what it would be like sitting around the kitchen table, the three of us.

So I'm walking back to Seth and Abby's place. If I turn up on their doorstep at eleven thirty at night, they're sure to let me in, aren't they? They'll have to, won't they?

Exhausted, I trudge along the six-lane street, past the ATMs inside their bare box, back to the narrow street with the trees. A bunch of drunk people go by. A few men call out something, but I look down at the ground and walk on.

I don't know if I'm scared.

No, of course I'm scared, but I've got bigger problems than a bunch of drunk guys. That's what I tell myself. I try to think about movies and imagine I'm walking across a stage again, but I'm too tired.

All I can think about is my dad's solar system. I can see planet Earth in front of me, and I feel as if I'm walking at an angle. All that time in the Netherlands I was walking upright. Now I've flown to an entirely different part of the globe. That has to affect your head somehow, doesn't it? Surely your blood must stop flowing normally?

Feeling dizzy, I stand in front of the red building again. I pull my sleeve down over my finger and press the button next to "Greenberg." I put my ear to the door and listen. I ring again and wait.

After seventeen rings, I give up. Seth must be sleeping like a mammoth, or maybe he never came back.

I drop down onto the stoop and lean my head against the red-painted bricks. My hands were already cold, and now I can feel the ice creaking inside my legs. I look longingly at my bulging suitcase. Neatly folded inside that suitcase is a wonderful sleeping bag that I always take with me because I don't like other people's blankets and quilts.

I think about taking out the sleeping bag, but I don't. It would get dirty out here on the street. And what if the police see me lying there in a sleeping bag on the sidewalk like a homeless person? Then I won't have to walk to the station on my own. They'll just ask me to accompany them.

I take my phone out of my bag and see that my dad's finally answered my text message.

Okay, we won't go to the police yet. But I want to talk to you and Klara tomorrow.

I immediately hide the message behind the fences inside my head. Tomorrow I'll decide how I'm going to answer him.

A group of men walks past singing. One of them yells that I'm cute. Another stands right in front of me and asks if I want to go with them to a bar on a hotel roof in the Meatpacking District. I tell them I'm staying here, that I'm waiting for friends who are stuck in traffic.

He asks if I'm from Ireland. I say no.

He asks for my number. I say no again. The whole group laughs. They nudge one another, but then walk on.

My teeth start chattering.

All those heart-shaped fall leaves lie withering on the ground around me. Most of them are yellow, but there's a red one among them. I stare at it. I'm used to feeling lonely. Whenever I hear my mom talking about what it was like to be pregnant, I know that even then, inside her tummy, I must have been a little bit lonely.

But being this lonely—that's something new.

I open my eyes again when I hear a boy's voice. For a moment I think it's Seth. But this voice is different. Louder. Angrier.

I sit up straight. My bones are chilled through. My eyes are stinging. It's a blond boy and he's coming closer. He's walking down the middle of the street, kicking an empty beer can and cursing wholeheartedly.

"Those fucking arrogant bastards!" He gives the can another kick and almost loses his balance, but manages to stay upright. "I hate those rich fuckers!"

And then he sees me. He stops.

I don't think I've ever seen anyone so handsome before. His faded jeans are fraying and the laces of his black high-tops are loose. Under his jacket he's wearing a white T-shirt with splashes that look black in the streetlight. But I can tell they're bloodstains. His right hand is bandaged.

He takes a swig from a bottle in a brown paper bag and looks at me.

I'm so tired now that the whole world seems like a movie. Slowly I hold up my own bandaged hand—a kind of salute from one wounded soldier to another.

"Vietnam?" he asks, pointing his brown bag at my bandage.

"War of Independence," I say. "How about you?"

"Me?" It's a while before he answers. "I'm having the worst fucking day of my life. I've only got nine fingers left and I got fired."

His blond hair hangs over his ears. I can't work out quite how old he is. Older than me in any case. Older than Seth too.

He takes another swig. Then he frowns. "Are you part of my worst ever day too? Or are you just sitting here?"

"I think I'm just sitting here," I reply. "I'm already part of other people's worst day."

My teeth have started chattering again and I know I'm going to get sick. Not a cold, but double pneumonia. Acute meningitis. Or, quite simply, dead.

"What are you doing?" he asks.

"Just waiting for some friends."

"Friends? You mean those little square pictures on Facebook?"

I nod. "That's what I'm waiting for."

"And what if . . ."

He stops talking and sways. I watch as his eyes roll back into his head. The bottle falls clattering onto the street.

I'm too late to catch him, but I manage to grab his shoulders and make sure his head doesn't hit the curb. Together, we collapse onto the ground.

I can feel the roughness of his jacket and the warmth of his skin against my bare hands, and I shiver. How filthy does a leather jacket get if it's never washed? Can dried blood make you sick?

I look at his pale face. My breathing is fast.

Should I scream for help?

Start banging at random on nearby doors?

Call 911?

I'm going to do all of that. I really am. I'm not going to let this guy die on the street. Of course not. But I'll wait just a moment. Because I don't want to call the police. I don't want to go back to Amsterdam.

Carefully, I lay him on the cold sidewalk. His head has to be low, so the blood can flow to it. I check his pulse. I know how to do it because I check my own heartbeat every day. Something's beating away, inside his body. He's still alive.

And then he moves. I instantly let go of his hand.

"Jesus." He groans. "What . . ."

"You fainted," I say.

"Wow." He rubs his hand across his face. Slowly, he shakes

his head. "Maybe I shouldn't have had a drink after those painkillers at the hospital . . ."

I'm kneeling beside him. The street's deserted. I feel like having a quick cry, but of course I can't.

He looks up at the starless sky. "Maybe I should just go to bed," he says, without moving.

"Do you live far from here?"

"No. I'm nearly home. I live just over there." He points at an off-white building with a rusty fire escape. "Pretty handy." He's still lying there.

"Come on, then," I say. I'm worried he's going to get pneumonia too.

Between the two of us, we get him to his feet. He's still swaying, so I don't say anything when he puts his arm around my shoulders. I've never felt such a heavy arm before. He can't get the door open, so he hands the keys to me.

"Sorry," he says. "Now I've just got to get up these three flights of stairs . . ."

I sigh. Looks like I have no choice. "Wait a moment," I say. "I'll just put my suitcase here in the hallway, or it'll disappear."

I discover that there's one advantage to dragging a drunk guy up three flights of stairs: It's a great way to warm up. It's been a long time since another body was so close to mine. My dad hasn't been allowed to touch me for years. My mom's never liked the feeling of anyone else's skin against her own.

And then, halfway up the second flight of stairs, I suddenly have an idea. What if this crazy drunken boy has a guest room?

It's insane and I know it. Normally, I wouldn't even dream of sleeping at a strange guy's place. Well, at Seth's, yeah, but that was different. Seth's even more awkward and shy than me, plus he's got an eleven-year-old sister. Staying with a big brother is fine.

But the person who's hanging around my neck right now doesn't seem at all shy. He looks like a rich guy who's fallen on hard times, and he curses like the heroes in American movies. From the point of view of a potential houseguest, he actually has just one thing going for him: He's only semiconscious.

It's not much, I admit. But the streets of New York are bitter tonight. And how badly can you be assaulted by someone who's keeling over?

After three steep flights of stairs we're standing in front of a mint-green door.

"Not my choice of color," he says as I turn the key in the lock. "I took over the room from a friend of mine."

He heads inside, but I stand in the doorway. I didn't know jaws really could drop in surprise.

In the middle of the room is a double mattress piled up with blankets. And that's the full extent of the furnishings. Literally. No chairs. No table. No closets. Just brown linoleum, bare walls, and a lumpy ceiling with water spots and a lightbulb hanging from a wire.

"He gave me the mattress too." He kicks off his shoes. "Had no time to get anything else yet. And, of course, no money."

He throws his jacket on the floor, pulls the bloodstained T-shirt over his head, and drops his pants. I stare at the ceiling, but can't help noticing the smiling Cookie Monster on his boxer shorts.

"Where's my phone?" he mumbles. He picks up his pants. "I need to set the alarm. Those fuckers at the hospital say I might have a concussion. Because I crashed to the floor when I saw all that blood." He sighs. "They said my mom has to wake me up every two hours tonight."

I raise my eyebrows. "So where's your mom?"

"At home, in Detroit."

"Did you tell that to your doctor?"

"None of his business. Why should I tell some asshole where my mom lives?"

He lies down on the thin mattress, places the bandaged hand on his chest, and pulls a blanket over himself. I stand in the doorway, looking at him. His eyes are almost closed.

"And what if you're unconscious two hours from now?" I ask. "Then you won't even hear your phone."

"Oh yes," he says drowsily. "Then I'm screwed. Oh well, nothing I can do about that."

The bare lightbulb throws a pale light on his face. In one corner of the room is a cardboard box full of clothes. In the other is a stack of fifth-hand books.

I'm so tired that I'm almost falling over, but I need to think.

That mattress was probably already there when dinosaurs were roaming New York. God knows how filthy it is. God knows what could fall onto your face while you're sleeping here. And God alone knows how many cockroaches there are . . .

I want to turn around and race back down all those stairs. But if I can't sleep for a few hours, soon I won't be capable of doing anything at all. And there's another thing. This stranger is on painkillers and beer, and he just fainted not so long ago. He could end up in a coma tonight.

I'm still hesitating. I weigh the cold against the bacteria. The sidewalk against a double mattress with a half-naked boy on it.

And then I think about my parents. I picture their faces. My dad with the wrinkles across his forehead like lines on a graph. My mom with her gray-green eyes that look straight through everyone and everything.

How about that? Those pathetic swamp dwellers think I've run away to Frankfurt, but I'm really in New York. This is most definitely a good thing.

But it could be even better.

They think that right now I'm safe inside Klara's spotless little apartment. But one day I'll tell them I spent my first night in New York lying next to a half-drunk, almost completely naked, blood-spattered boy on an ancient mattress in a moldy room in the middle of the city.

I'm looking forward to it already.

10

When an unfamiliar ringtone wakes me up at three fifteen in the morning, I lie there, frozen.

I really did it. I stayed and I slept beside him. And no one in the world knows where I am. He could murder me and dissolve my body in hydrochloric acid without anyone noticing.

There are no curtains, so I can vaguely see him. The cell phone beside him is still ringing, but he's just lying there, motionless.

I have to reach over him to grab the phone.

"Are you awake?" I whisper. He smells of beer. And coconut.

He mumbles something.

"Do you know what city we're in?"

"New York," he says hoarsely.

"What's your name?"

"Jim."

And suddenly he sits upright. "What the . . . ?" He stares at me.

"Sorry," I whisper. "I stayed the night. I was going to tell you, but you were already asleep by then."

"So you just lay down beside me in bed?" He shakes his head. "I could sue you for indecent assault."

"I've still got all my clothes on!"

"But I don't." He lies back down. "Just make sure you stay on your own side. I don't like girls in my bed." And then he's asleep again.

I'm boiling hot when I hear the alarm again two hours later. As soon as I turn it off, I hear him groaning.

"Jesus, this hurts."

"Your four-fingered hand?"

"Like it's exploding. And then imploding. And then bursting apart all over again. Seriously, I . . ." He makes a noise that sounds a lot like a whimper.

"Didn't the hospital give you any painkillers?" I ask quietly.

"God yes, and antibiotics! Cost a fucking fortune. But they said I couldn't do without them."

I feel dizzy when I stand up. I turn on the light, squint through my half-shut eyelids, and search the pockets of his leather jacket. I find two boxes of pills and read the instructions on the front.

"There's some Coke on the floor in the corner," he says gruffly.

I hand him the half-full bottle and an orange pill and try not to notice how good-looking he is. At school, the boys who look like that are the worst of all. And every single one of them is friends with Juno. Last week their posts online actually made me vomit.

• • •

"Jim!" I whisper two hours later. "How old are you?"

"Seventeen," he mumbles without opening his eyes. "And it doesn't matter what you say. If I want to move to New York, then I will. I don't have to go to school. I hate it there."

"I know what you mean," I say.

He opens his eyes. "Jesus!" His blond hair is sticking to his forehead. "I thought you were my mom."

It's starting to get light outside. I can tell it's already midday in the Netherlands, because I'm finding it harder to sleep. I was just dreaming about Jim. So it's pretty weird to wake up and to still be lying in bed beside him.

He turns onto his back. "All those adults have made such a fucking mess of things. And now I'm supposed to go to school forever and ever so I can learn how to keep their fiasco going? Yeah, right!"

I don't answer. I know all about fiascoes, but that doesn't matter right now. I listen to his breathing, which slowly becomes deeper again.

When I was little, and Mom was away, I was allowed to sleep in the big bed with my dad. He didn't like fairy tales, so before we went to sleep, he told me about things that were true. About the rings of Saturn. About air balloons, steam engines, and barometers. And about Benjamin Franklin, who flew a kite in a storm to catch the lightning.

Another hour later, I'm too hungry to keep sleeping. I get up and go looking for the bathroom. A shower's not an option, not with how hairy and filthy it is, but the bandage on my hand really needs to be changed. It can't wait any longer. With trembling hands, I clean the wound with disinfectant and two types of iodine.

In a way, I have to admit, the cut isn't that bad. It's not light-years deep. And it doesn't really look inflamed either.

"Jim?"

He groans.

"I'm going to get breakfast. I'm taking your keys, okay?"

He doesn't answer. I take that to mean, *Great. How very kind and thoughtful!*

11

Slowly, I walk down the stairs. Just the act of lifting my legs, thinking, looking around—there's something unreal about it all. My body is dirtier than it's ever been. My last shower was thirty-three hours ago, and I spent the night in a human-size rats' nest. But the situation is not entirely hopeless. Because I got through the darkness without the police. I haven't been dissolved in hydrochloric acid. And for the first time in my life I slept next to a boy.

The boy in question was an almost unconscious, nine-fingered high-school dropout who could sue me today for sexual assault. But if I can forget about that for a moment, it's going to make a great story for my friends.

That is, if I still have any friends. They didn't send me any threats over the past few days, not like the others. But they didn't do anything to help either.

As soon as I open the front door of Jim's building, a cold wind blasts my face. Dark and pale gray clouds ripple across the morning sky. I button up my coat and look around. Where can I find food as quickly as possible?

Then I spot the girl.

She's sitting on the steps in front of Seth's door, exactly where I was sitting last night with my teeth chattering. There's a chain around her neck, fastened to the stair railing with a shiny lock, and a piece of cardboard on the ground in front of her pink rain boots. I cross the street.

MY BROTHER IS KEEPING ME PRISONER.
DO YOU WANT TO HELP ME? THEN BUY ME
A CUPCAKE (ONLY IF YOU CAN AFFORD IT),
VOTE FOR OBAMA, AND MARRY MY MOM.
SINCERELY, ABBY GREENBERG

I look silently at her. So this is Seth's sister. Her eyes are the color of melted chocolate and she's almost as skinny as her brother.

"Hey, I was just thinking," she says, as if she's known me for years. "Justin Bieber and James Bond and SpongeBob and God are all men." She stops. "No, maybe SpongeBob isn't quite a man . . . But he's certainly a boy sponge. That's not very fair, is it?"

Even though she's chained up, she's moving constantly. She twists the end of her dark braid around her finger, scuffs her pink boots across the ground, and I notice that her face can smile and look serious all at the same time.

"Would you like to be a man?" she asks.

"No," I say immediately.

"Why not?"

"Men are dirty."

She nods. "I get it. You're gay. That's okay. Same-sex marriage is allowed here in New York. Everything's possible here."

"No, I'm not a lesbian," I say. "I just like things to be clean."

She frowns. "So what are you going to do? You can't get married to someone you think is dirty, can you? They'll say to your husband, 'You may now kiss the bride,' and you'll just go, 'Eeeww!' "

"You're right. That could be a problem."

Before Abby's had time to come up with a solution, the front door opens.

I know he lives here, of course, but it still feels weird to see Seth in the doorway again, the boy I spent so long waiting for last night.

He looks even more serious today than yesterday, but perhaps that's because now I'm comparing him to Jim.

"Hey, Seth," I say. I want him to think that it's completely normal for me to be standing here on his steps whenever he opens the front door.

But he ignores me. He looks at the chain around Abby's neck and, with one leap, he's down the steps. His eyes fly across the sign at her feet. Without saying a word, he picks up the cardboard from the sidewalk and rips it into pieces.

"Hey, watch it!" yells Abby. "Remember the Constitution! The First Amendment says we can say and write whatever we want. We did it last week at school."

But Seth is clearly not thinking about the Constitution. He grabs her arm and shakes it. " 'My brother's keeping me prisoner'? Do you really want people to call the police? Then I'll have to explain that Mom had to go to San Francisco and we're alone all weekend. And then they'll take you away."

"Ouch, don't tug at me!" she says angrily. "I'm all chained up. Can't you see?"

"Then undo the lock!" He lets go of her arm and takes a step back. "Where's the key?"

"I don't have it," says Abby. "I was going to swallow it, but I couldn't get it to go down. So I threw it away."

"You threw it away?" asks Seth. "What do you mean?"

"Oh, you know. I just threw it away," she says. "Over there somewhere." She waves her hand vaguely in the direction of the other side of the street.

I do my best not to laugh. As far as I'm concerned, eleven is actually a perfect age.

"I'll help you look," I say in a serious voice.

Seth and I cross the narrow street and silently begin our search operation.

"So how do you two know each other?" Abby calls from the stoop. She's following our efforts with great interest.

As my eyes roam over the sidewalk and the road, I tell her about the room that didn't exist.

"Seriously?" she asks. "And Seth just told you there are plenty of hotels around here?" She gives her brother a look of disgust. "Children aren't allowed to rent hotel rooms—you know that, don't you? I tried it when I ran away last year. And it didn't work."

He mumbles something.

"So where did you sleep last night?" Abby calls over to me.

I point at the off-white building. "Over there, at Jim's. I met him on the street in the middle of the night. He'd been injured and I made sure he didn't end up in a coma. But now I have to find somewhere else as soon as possible, because Jim has a bathroom full of bugs and a mattress stuffed with woolly mammoth hair."

Seth looks at me for the first time today. "You slept in a strange guy's bed last night?"

"Yeah. After you abandoned me on the street, it seemed like a pretty safe option."

"But that's perfect," cries Abby. She's dancing up and down on the sidewalk. The chain lies forgotten at her feet. "You can stay with us. Mom's not here and her room is superclean."

"You're not chained up at all!" Seth stares at her.

She nods. "I only had one padlock. So I could fasten the chain to the stairs, but not around my neck."

12

I can see Seth doesn't want me around, and that's a pain.

"There's no need, really," I say. "I can sleep at Jim's again."

"Of course you can't," he snaps. "You're staying with us. Didn't you have a ridiculously huge suitcase with you yesterday?"

I don't answer. He should try packing his entire life into a box. And last night I managed to drag that "ridiculously huge suitcase" up three steep flights of stairs all on my own. If you can carry a suitcase by yourself, it can't be that big.

"I'll be back in a minute," I say.

I open Jim's front door and head inside. But halfway up the first flight of stairs I stop. I turn around.

"Seriously?" I say. "You're both coming up there with me?"

"I may be only eleven," says Abby, "but it so happens that I like meeting new boys. Especially wounded ones."

"What about you?" I ask Seth.

"Safety precaution," he says.

As he stands there, with his skinny arms and serious eyes, part of me wants to laugh at him—and part of me doesn't.

On the stairs, the paint is flaking off the walls and it smells like seaweed. I can hear people yelling on the second floor and there's music thumping away on the floor above.

"He's probably still asleep," I whisper when we're standing in front of the mint-green door. "It must have been a pretty serious injury. I don't know what happened, but he's only got nine fingers left."

"Oh, that's so supersad!" But Abby looks like she's just heard it's her birthday tomorrow. "How old is this Jim, by the way?"

"Seventeen."

"Seth's sixteen," says Abby enthusiastically. She looks at her brother. "Mom's always saying you don't have enough friends, isn't she? Maybe you can be friends with Jim!"

Seth glares at her but doesn't say anything.

Cautiously, I open the door. A warm fug of sleepiness hits me in the face.

Jim is awake. He's sitting up in bed with my suitcase next to him.

The suitcase is open.

All around Jim, on the filthy mattress and the poop-brown linoleum, my clothes lie scattered. My pale pink bra is on top of a clump of blond hair. My wonderful sleeping bag is covered in dust bunnies. Three pairs of underpants are strung beside a few moldy crusts in a pizza box and my favorite sweater is half across Jim's hairy leg and half across a lump in the Cookie Monster.

I feel as if my head's about to short-circuit.

"Ah," says Jim. "So you're back? I woke up and didn't

know what the hell was going on. You'd taken off with my keys, and just left that shitty suitcase behind."

It's like looking through a microscope. With absolute clarity, I can see my clothes lying on the floor. And everything else is black.

"How about we put everything back into the suitcase?" I hear Abby ask. "I'll help."

And that's when I start screaming. I'm out of breath and completely hysterical. I can hear what I sound like, but there's nothing I can do about it.

The same thing happened to my laptop once. I opened a new screen and, without me doing anything, the computer started opening screens too, all by itself. Dozens, hundreds of screens, appearing faster than I could click them shut, until my whole laptop was jammed and my dad had to take it back to the store.

Jim, Seth, and Abby stare at me in amazement, but no one takes me back to the store. My fingers are tingling and there's sweat on my forehead. I know it's all gone disastrously wrong, and I'm terrified of what's going to happen next. Of how I'm going to feel. And what I'll be thinking. In a few minutes' time, I'm going to be sure I'm dying.

I don't mean "dying" in a manner of speaking. Not in the sense of: "Whew! I've been running so fast, I think I'm going to die." I mean literally. I'll think I'm dying.

• • •

"What's wrong with her?" I hear Abby ask in the distance.

"She's losing it." Jim sounds calm. "You can see that, can't you?"

My chest hurts. My lungs are gasping for air.

This is the end.

"We have to do something," Abby cries. "She's really not okay."

And then everything goes black.

"Jesus," says Jim. "I'm going to call an ambulance."

I'm never going to see my mom and dad again. I'm sure of it. I'm dying. And then, in the midst of all that blackness, I feel a calm arm around my shoulders.

"Come sit down." Seth's voice sounds very far away.

I don't want to sit down, because I'm dying and there are hairs and crumbs and dead flies on the floor. But he pulls me down anyway. In the darkness I feel his hand on my back.

And then he starts talking to me. My lungs are hurting and my throat is burning and my mouth is dry and everything in my body is thumping and racing and rasping and I know for sure that it's going to break. That I'm going to break.

But still I can hear him.

"You're having a panic attack," he says in a flat voice. "But it'll soon be over. You're coming to stay with us, remember? My mom's bed isn't stuffed with woolly mammoth hair. And we have furniture, like normal people. A table with chairs, three bookshelves, and a couch . . ."

All I can hear is the sound of my own breathing. And his voice.

"We have a washing machine too. You can wash all your

clothes at our place. And we can make breakfast for you. How do you like bagels with scrambled eggs?"

I can't answer. But I want him to go on talking. And to stay beside me. So at least there's someone with me when I break. I don't want to die with no one noticing.

"Slowly . . ." he says. "You have more than enough air."

I cup my hands and hold them over my mouth.

"That's right," he says, and his voice is still flat and calm. Like he's talking to an alien from outer space who's just landed here. "You see? It's getting better . . ."

Gradually, my lungs calm down. My heart's stopped pounding as if someone's in pursuit. The short circuit is over.

I look down at the floor. I can see the others again, but I wish I couldn't. I wipe my cheeks. Then, shakily, I get to my feet and start picking up my clothes. I need to get out of here as quickly as possible.

13

I am sitting in a silver subway train and racing along beneath skyscrapers and parks. My long line of seats is staring straight at the row of people on the other side of the aisle, so I look down at my lap.

Reality once again consists of more than a pile of clothes on the floor. The microscope has vanished. I can see everything again, and now I'm as embarrassed as hell. I always am, after it's happened. I'm not crazy. But I know how it looks to other people. I understand why Jim said I was losing it.

That doesn't mean I understand Jim, though. What possessed the idiot to open up my suitcase like that? I don't care if he looks like Brad Pitt at seventeen. He needs to keep his nine dirty, sticky fingers off of other people's belongings.

I still haven't said thank you to Seth.

As we walked out of the off-white building, I could tell he was expecting me to say thanks or something. But I couldn't do it. All I could do was act like nothing had happened. It turned out that Seth was pretty good at that too.

They let me shower for as long as I wanted, but after twenty-three minutes, food became more important than getting clean. The bagel with scrambled eggs that Seth made for me was fantastic, but I didn't even thank him for that. Because then it would have felt like I was thanking him for the other thing.

"And now I'm going to give you a tour of New York," Abby called out just as I was swallowing my last bite.

Seth shook his head, though, and said she was grounded. Because of the chain and the padlock and the key she'd thrown away.

"But we can't just let Emilia go wandering all over the city by herself!" Abby said indignantly. "She might almost die again."

"I'm sure she'll be fine," said Seth. "And if anything does go wrong, there'll be someone who knows what to do."

"How exactly did you know what to do?" asked Abby.

"A girl in my class gets panic attacks," he said. "She has to be brought back to life almost every day."

During this conversation I was standing right next to them in the green-and-white kitchen, apparently invisible.

And all that time I was in their home—while Seth fetched a clean towel for me and made scrambled eggs and showed me how to use the washing machine—he didn't look at me once. And his dirty hand didn't come anywhere near my back again for even a second.

I get out at Seventy-Seventh Street, and as I come back up aboveground, it feels as if I'm in a different city. I look around, excited. Here on the Upper East Side is where the multi-millionaires live. You can tell because of the buildings with the green canopies and uniformed doormen, and the blacked-out limos and the women with no wrinkles. A dog walker comes by with seven different kinds of dogs on seven tangled leashes, and everywhere I look there are babies in fancy strollers being pushed by women chattering in a flurry of foreign languages.

I look at the nannies' faces. I listen to their accents. And as I cut across to Central Park, I think about three years ago.

When I came home from school one sunny day in September, my mom was lying on the floor of her studio among the brushes and turpentine. She couldn't remember how to paint, she said. She just couldn't do it. Her head was empty.

I instantly knew that it was my fault. And my dad's. He'd recently been made school principal and I'd been at the school for just three weeks. We'd been too busy with our own stuff. And that wasn't the agreement.

It's crazy. I wasn't there when the agreement was made. No one ever told me about it—but I've always known how our life works. For my mom, her paintings come first. And she comes first for me and my dad.

The three of us stumbled on for a month. My mom lay on the floor of her studio. My dad had migraines and had to cancel meeting after meeting. I skipped classes so I could go home and shower in the middle of the day.

And then we found Klara on the Internet. She lived in Germany and wanted to come to Amsterdam for a year before starting a degree in art history. I was twelve and thought I was too old for a nanny, but Klara wasn't there just for me. She came for all of us, and she made sure our life didn't fall apart. She taught me how to whistle with two fingers and how to make apple strudel; she explained how kissing works and played German rock music.

And she got my mom to stand up again.

The Metropolitan Museum of Art lies gleaming at the edge of the park. It's just about the biggest museum in the world, and it looks like a temple. It's white and vast, with columns and wide steps full of tourists. I listen carefully as I walk through the crowd. Before I can enter the temple, there's one thing I need to do.

I stop beside a noisy family of Germans. I sit down about a meter away from them and take out my cell phone. My hands immediately start shaking. I'd rather lick an ice cream cone that Jim's already licked. But if I don't call my dad at this point, he's going to contact the police.

He answers almost instantly. "Emilia!"

I hold my cell phone so that he can hear the Germans talking in the background.

"How are you?" He sounds nervous. "Was the train journey okay? Did Klara come fetch you from the station?"

"*Alles ist wunderbar*," I say in German. "*Fantastisch.*"

It hurts to hate him. But I can't help it.

"We need to talk," he says. "I know you don't want to hear about it, but I have to explain what happened. It's absolutely essential that you listen to me."

"*Das ist absolut notwendig*," I say, quickly translating his last sentence into German. I don't want to have to think.

"Stop being silly," he yells.

"Silly? Christ!" I yell back at him. A few tourists look at me. "Why should I listen to you? Why should I listen to anything you say? Twitter and Facebook have been spouting crap about us for days. I've already heard way more than enough."

"But that's not the real story—you know that, don't you? It's all lies! You need to hear my side."

"No, thank you."

"Emilia, you're fifteen! You can't just disappear to another country. We're worried about you. And we miss you."

That swamp dweller just doesn't get it. He thinks he can still play the loving father.

"Well, boohoo," I shout. "But maybe you should have started worrying sooner. Before you destroyed my life, for example. Then half the Netherlands wouldn't be wishing we were dead. And then I could have stayed at school."

He's silent for, like, three eons.

"I resigned yesterday," he says. "Did you know that?"

No, I didn't know that. I immediately put up a fence around it.

"I've got to go," I say. "We're about to eat."

"I want to speak to Klara!"

"She's in the shower. I haven't told her what you did. I wanted to be someplace no one knows about it."

"Emilia . . ."

I cut my dad off and sit there on the cold steps for thirteen minutes, without moving. And then I head into the temple.

14

The museum feels like an oasis. The floors are spotless and there's not a trace of mold on the walls. It smells faintly of art, and the building is so huge that even when half the world is in here looking at the paintings, there are still some quiet galleries.

I wander past medieval altarpieces, faded tapestries, and Egyptian sphinxes. I'd hoped to be able to forget the real world here, just for a little while—but it doesn't work.

I see a statue of a Greek god and it reminds me of Jim. I see a silver globe and I know that my dad would think it was "magnificent." Every painting makes me think of my mom, of course. And I keep thinking about what I said to Abby: that men are dirty.

I basically grew up in museums and art galleries, so I've seen a lot of things. But wow, there's a lot of naked skin on display here. Grown-ups act all mature and as if it doesn't count—because, of course, it's *art*—but the walls of this place are actually covered with porn.

It makes me pretty mad.

Nearly all the artists in the olden days were men. Did they

really have to paint so many naked women? Are breasts really the most important parts of a person?

As I walk around the silent galleries, I realize I'm clenching my fists.

Stupid men. Dumb men. Sleazy, horny perverts.

Sorry.

But that's the only conclusion I can reach. This is the abbreviated history of men: First they painted museums full of naked women. Then they invented the computer. And then they filled the Internet with porn.

I stare at the painting in front of me.

I don't notice at first. But as soon as I see it, I turn around and walk away. Out of the gallery. And through another gallery. I can still see her in front of me, though. A young woman in pastel colors, looking back over her shoulder as she steps into the bath. Her blond hair ripples down her bare back and you can just catch a glimpse of one perfect breast.

I don't know about the breast. But her smile is exactly the same as Juno's.

The great glassed-in courtyard in the American Wing finally makes me forget everything for a few minutes. The white space has a wall of windows three stories high, and all those windows look out onto the fall colors of Central Park. The sun's broken through the clouds, just for a moment, and the yellow and red and orange of the trees glows more brightly than paint ever could. The white hall sparkles.

I feel a bit nauseated, so I buy a bottle of Diet Coke at the museum café. The tourists at the tables around me sigh deeply as they study the map of the immense museum. I drink my Coke and try not to think about my dad not having a job anymore.

At the table next to mine are two American women who obviously don't come from New York. They have Southern drawls and each of them is the size of three wide-screen TVs stacked together.

"I'm sure glad we didn't go for that hotel downtown," says the platinum blonde in a loud voice. "There's no way it's gonna flood where we are."

"You think the subway will still be workin'?" asks the woman with red hair. "You heard anything about that?"

The blonde shakes her head and sighs dramatically. "Would you believe it? The one time we go to New York—and there's a hurricane on the way!"

My glass of Coke stops in midair.

I look straight at the blonde woman. "A hurricane?"

"Didn't you hear?" she exclaims. "It's all they're talkin' about on TV."

The redhead nods. "Hurricane Sandy's on her way, darlin'. Half of Jamaica's already lost power, somethin' like fifty people have died in floods in Haiti, and Sandy caused havoc in the Bahamas yesterday."

"And the day after tomorrow she'll be in New York," says the blonde. She stands and picks up her tray from the table. "Good luck, honey. Make sure you've got enough food at home!"

I sit there, frozen, at my table. I don't panic, because I don't believe a word of it. I watched ten whole seasons of *Friends* last year, when I was sick for weeks. And in all those old episodes there was never, ever one single hurricane in New York.

Calmly, I take out my phone. The museum has free Wi-Fi.

I Google "hurricane sandy."

I read a few articles.

And then I start giggling. I can't stop. I'm having an actual, genuine fit of the giggles. Because Hurricane Sandy exists. And she's coming. There's some uncertainty about her path. It's possible that she'll race past New York on Monday, instead of plowing right through the middle of the city.

But it's true. There are hundreds and thousands of cities in the world. And I chose to run away to the city that's going to be hit by a hurricane in two days' time.

Of course, the giggling fit stops far too soon, and I can't just stay sitting there in the museum. I can't avoid reality any longer. I need to get to Seth and Abby. We have to prepare for a hurricane.

15

Come to the horse in the middle of Union Square. Tonight we're eating the best burritos in town!!!

Abby's text message arrives as I'm walking from the museum to the subway. I take a look at the map. If I get off three stops earlier, I'll be right at Union Square.

On vacations, my dad always retains absolute power over the map; every summer, I go running after him like a little sheep. But it turns out that I can actually do it myself. I can find my way from one place to another. I can explore a city all on my own.

Union Square is an island of trees and benches in a sea of traffic. Abby's "horse" is a statue of George Washington—granted, on a horse. I stand beside it and quickly take out my cell phone to make myself look busy. When I'm holding my phone in my hand, it feels okay to look around.

I soon see them coming: Abby in her pink rain boots, Seth with a striped knit cap on his head. They both have intense brown eyes and determined expressions. The difference is that

Abby looks like she's off to save the world while Seth looks as if he's preparing to face a long jail sentence.

"You're never going to believe this," I call out. "There's a hurricane on the way!"

"Oh yeah. We know," Abby calls back.

I stare at them. "Really? And you didn't think to mention it?"

Seth shrugs. "It won't be that bad. We have hundreds of TV channels here, so they have to exaggerate everything to make sure they have enough news. There was a hurricane last year too. The whole city prepared for a disaster and then hardly anything happened. Everyone was pretty disappointed." He sighs. "Come on, let's go."

I don't understand why he has to sigh so deeply and why he has to look like he's locked in a cage. He's out for a walk with his little sister and a girl he called "pretty" yesterday. And going out for a burrito on a Saturday evening can't be so bad, right?

Soon, I find out the answer to that question myself.

If you don't have much money but you're really hungry, then on a cloudy Saturday evening there's truly nothing better than eating a burrito at Dos Toros on Fourth Avenue.

Really. When I'm ninety and I'm in a retirement home, I'll still remember that meal.

It's warm inside the little restaurant. You have to pick up the food yourself; there's a long line of hipster students waiting. The interior is extremely simple. Almost minimal. Wooden benches, wooden tables. No art on the wall, just a story about two brothers who came to New York and couldn't find a good burrito anywhere. So they went into the burrito business themselves.

I don't know if it's the language or the city or my jet lag. At home I find restaurants' stories about sustainability and local products and little in-jokes irritating and totally phony. But here it works. I really do believe that those two brothers are doing their utmost to make sure I get the very best of burritos.

And as I finally sink my teeth into a hot parcel of black beans, salsa, sour cream, grated cheese, guacamole, and intensely juicy, tender grilled steak, I know it's true.

"Oh. My. God," I say with my mouth full. "This is the best burrito in the world. Seriously. This steak is so incredibly tender. Oh, and the guacamole!"

For the first time, I see a big grin on Seth's face. There's salsa on his chin, but right now I can even handle that.

"We come here at least once a week," he says. "We can't go without it any longer."

I look at Abby, who's licking sour cream off her fingers. Then at her brother, who's taking another bite. And I'm so jealous that it almost hurts. I want to eat here every week too.

I don't want to just be on the run here for a while. I want to live here.

As soon as we're back home, I put another load in the washing machine. I'm exhausted and I want to go to bed as soon as possible, but I hesitate when I see how disappointed Abby looks.

"What's wrong?" I ask.

She twists the tip of her braid around her finger and doesn't reply.

"Watch out!" Seth is sitting on the couch with his laptop. "She was digging around in the freezer this afternoon. I'm afraid she's seen it in the movies: When girls are home alone, they have to do 'girl things.' Like painting their nails. And crying into ice cream cartons."

"Not crying!" says Abby. "Just eating ice cream in front of the TV. I thought it'd be fun. I mean . . ." She looks at me shyly. "We've got cookie dough . . . And we could wear our pajamas . . ."

"Count me out," Seth calls from the couch.

"Hey!" says Abby, glaring at her brother. "I'd rather be a boy too. But I'm a girl. And I don't have a sister. And Mom's always working."

"Well, Mom has to earn enough money to take care of three people."

"I know that!" She sighs. "I'm not a baby." She walks off. "Forget about it. It's not like I care."

I look down at the floor. And then I go after her.

A quarter of an hour later, we're sitting together, watching *The Simpsons.* Abby wanted both of us to eat out of one gigantic tub, but I couldn't bring myself to do it.

"You think I'm gross," she said miserably. Her eyelashes were still wet with tears.

"That's not true!" I cried.

"Yes, it is. You don't want my spoon to touch your ice cream."

I sighed. "I'm sorry. It's not you. I mean . . . Did you know there are more bacteria living in your mouth than there are people on the planet? You've actually got more than seven billion bacteria in your mouth!"

"Really?" She looked a bit happier again. "I'm going to tell my friends that." She fetched two bowls from the cabinet. "So you wouldn't eat from the same tub as your mom? Or your dad?"

"No one. I swear."

When we sat down on the couch, Abby hesitated.

"Can my pajamas touch your pajamas? Or are there lots and lots of bacteria living on pajamas too?"

I didn't ask when her pajamas were last washed. I just said it was okay.

So now she's sitting ridiculously close to me, digging into her ice cream. I can see that Seth is secretly watching *The Simpsons* too, out of the corner of his eye.

"I'm pretending you're my sister," Abby whispers to me.

I don't tell her that I'm doing the same.

16

Six in the morning.

It's dark outside and the city is finally quiet, but I'm wide-awake. I'm sitting at the computer in Seth and Abby and their absent mom's chilly living room. My eyes are flying across the screen. My finger is clicking away like crazy. "Oh my God," I whisper very quietly. "Oh my God!"

Dozens, hundreds of pages, full of news about Hurricane Sandy. Tomorrow evening or tomorrow night, she's going to race across the city. Mayor Bloomberg is advising us to stock up on food. And bottles of water. And candles and matches and flashlights.

The weather sites explain that Sandy could be the worst storm in history. The hurricane that's approaching from the south is going to collide, above our heads, with ice-cold air from the north and a winter storm from the west. And it's also a full moon tomorrow. That means the water's extra high and there's an even greater chance of the city flooding.

I shiver. The lamp next to the computer throws a circle of light onto the keyboard, but the rest of the room is filled with shadows. When the wooden floor behind me creaks, it gives me the fright of my life. I turn around and see Seth standing in the middle of the room.

His hair is sticking up and he's not wearing a T-shirt.

"Jet lag?" he asks with a voice that's only just woken up.

I nod. He picks up his hoodie from the couch, walks to the open kitchen, and turns on the coffeemaker. Silently, he studies a newspaper on the counter. I wrap my robe more tightly around my bare legs, and suddenly I'm aware again just how strange it is that I'm here.

"Have you seen this?" I ask. He's not looking, but I still point at the computer screen. "They're shutting down the entire subway system tonight. As a safety precaution. And there are going to be shelters all over the city for people who have to be evacuated."

He doesn't reply, so I go on talking.

"Half of New York could flood. And there might be a power failure!"

Finally, he looks up. "And two airplanes can fly into two skyscrapers, fifteen minutes apart. But it doesn't usually happen."

It's like someone double-clicked a file inside my brain.

I instantly see the pictures in my head. They could have come from a movie, but they're real. A bright blue sky, two sunny white towers. An airplane crashing straight into the first tower. A ball of fire and black smoke, an airplane-shaped hole in the building. And then everything goes on repeat: another airplane. Another explosion. Another thousand deaths.

"Were you here?" I ask. "Were you living in New York on September eleventh?"

He nods. And then he sighs. "Coffee?"

No one's ever asked me if I wanted something to drink in that kind of tone before. It's practically screaming: *I don't want you in my home. If this hurricane weren't on the way, you'd be out on the street.*

"Yes, please," I say politely. I still don't like coffee, but that doesn't matter. "So?" I ask. "Do you remember the attacks?"

"I remember what it smelled like." He hands me a mug of inky black liquid and sits down next to his laptop on the couch. And then he suddenly shakes his head as if he's made up his mind. "You know what? I'm not in the mood for this. I've had it with pretending nothing's wrong."

I don't react.

"Don't you see how weird this all is? You appear out of nowhere. First you spend a night in that guy Jim's bed. Then you have a panic attack and you have to come wash all your clothes at our place. You jump at every sound and you look like it's the end of the world—except for when we're eating burritos, and then, for half an hour, we're best buddies. But no matter what happens, we're not allowed to ask you any questions. When Abby tried it yesterday, you totally froze."

I can feel it happening again. What he calls "freezing."

"Sorry," I say stiffly.

He runs his hand through his dark hair. "It's too bad I'm not nice, like Abby. But I had plans for this weekend. The website I'm working on has to be finished tomorrow. But then my little sister arranges to meet some psycho off the Internet, and we have to calm down Aunt Leah and so we stay overnight at her place, and then, to top it all off, you turn up . . ."

I don't answer and, after a while, he just shrugs. "Forget about it. It doesn't matter." He picks up his laptop and opens it.

I know exactly what he's doing now. People are right to give up. To give up on me. But it's not exactly fun.

Silently, I look down at my hands. At the white, split skin. At the cracks in my fingers and the rawness around my nails.

"Okay," I say. "What do you want to know?"

He looks up.

"Simple." His eyes are as black as the coffee. "What are you doing here?"

"I came to see New York."

"But why are you here alone? Where are your mom and dad?"

"In Amsterdam."

"Do they know you're here?"

"No."

It's a while before he says anything else.

"Did you run away?" he asks finally. He sees me nod. "Why?"

"Do you really want to know?"

"Yes," he says, and suddenly he's the boy who sat beside me in the darkness again. The boy who made sure I didn't die. "I really want to know."

I can feel something resisting inside my stomach. It hurts, but I need to stop paying attention to it.

I'm standing on the highest diving board. And I'm about to jump.

17

"Okay," I say. I don't look at him. And then I jump. "My totally messed-up father isn't just my dad. He's also my high-school principal." I stop again. He *was* the principal, I keep forgetting about that. Now he isn't anything.

"My school has a thousand students, so it's not like I know everyone there. But there's this one older girl who I do know. Everyone knows her. God knows why, because it's not as if she's funny or nice. But she *is* popular, and she always has been. You know, think of any high-school movie and imagine the prettiest cheerleader. Well, that's Juno."

Seth nods. "I can't stand her already."

Outside, New York stays silent as the earth slowly turns to the east. Hurricane Sandy is raging above the Atlantic right now. The city is waiting.

I clear my throat. "Juno's mom—who, incidentally, is a woman who thought it was a great idea to name her daughter after the Roman goddess of marriage . . . Well, last Tuesday, that mom found sixty-seven text messages on Juno's cell phone. The messages weren't sent by her friends or her aunts or a guy she'd met on vacation, but by *my father*."

"Jesus."

I nod. "My dad, the school principal, sent sixty-seven text messages to a seventeen-year-old girl. He started in April and sent the last one on Monday."

"What was he writing to her about for all those months?"

"You really want to know?"

Seth nods.

"Well, I don't." My hands are trembling. I clench my left hand, but I can't feel the cut anymore. "It wasn't just the messages either. They met up with each other. At a café. Can you picture it? My fifty-year-old dad in his scruffy sweater and corduroy pants. And Juno sitting there next to him. He says he was giving her extra math tutoring. And nothing else."

"Do you believe him?"

"The whole thing makes me sick." I shake my head. "So I don't want to hear what that man has to say about his 'side of the story.' It just makes me want to puke."

All the fences inside my head are flat on the ground. As I gaze out over the landscape, I feel sick.

For fifteen years I thought we were a family. But now I know that, all that time, my dad was just playacting. The thought of him sitting there for minutes—maybe even hours—with his cell phone in his hand, trying to decide what to say in his text messages. The thought of him looking at her for all those months. The thought of us sitting at home around the kitchen table and him thinking about her. It's driving me crazy.

• • •

And there's something else.

My mom spoke to me just once last week. Really spoke to me, I mean. And what she said was that I shouldn't take it so hard. That men sometimes forget their good sense—and that's just the way things are.

How messed up is that? My mom should be even more furious than me. She should be screaming and howling and threatening to leave my dad.

So why isn't she?

"What happened next?" asks Seth.

"All hell broke loose." I shrug. "I'm at the same school, and everyone knows I'm his daughter. Juno had kept it to herself for months, but as soon as her mom found the text messages, Juno told her best friend. Within a couple of hours, the whole school knew. And within a day, the whole country had heard the news. It was a nightmare."

"I'm so sorry."

He's trying to comfort me, but I'm not done yet. I jumped off the diving board, but I still haven't hit the water.

"You wanted to know, didn't you?" I ask. "Why I ran away?"

He nods.

"Well, that's just the half of it."

The other half really should be easier to talk about. And yet I hesitate.

"Did your dad do something else?"

"No." I pick up the pen from beside the keyboard and start scribbling on a yellow sticky note. "Other people did the rest. On the Internet. They heard about my dad and suddenly everyone had an opinion. They thought he was a sleazy asshole. Well, they're right about that. But they didn't stop there. Now they're calling him a rapist. A pedophile. And they're yelling that he should be sent to jail."

I take a swig of the coffee, which is way too strong for me, and I start coughing. Seth waits until I can breathe again.

"You wouldn't believe how disgusting people can be on the Internet. How cruel they are. Every hour there were more threats. I didn't even know some of the words they were using. Really. I had no idea there were people out there who sit at their computers dreaming up so many different ways to kill someone."

Seth looks down at his laptop and says nothing.

"They said they were going to come to our house. They wrote what they thought about my mom. And what they wanted to do to me. They were very clear about it. If our house went up in flames and we were burned alive, the world would be a better place."

I keep trying to remember they're only words. So far those people have done nothing. Not for real. Our house hasn't been set on fire. My dad hasn't been hanged. But still, those words *mean* something. Real, living people have written to say they wouldn't care if I burned to death.

"Did you report it to the police?"

"Yes. They're going to look into it. At least they said they were." One last scribble. The yellow sticky note is totally black now.

I put down the pen and look at him. "I had to get out of there. I had no choice."

He nods without saying anything.

I go on looking at him and suddenly wonder how many addresses there are in New York. Of all those millions of apartments, "Mr. Greenberg" picked Seth and Abby's for his scam.

He couldn't have made a better choice.

18

I've come back to bed.

I had no idea what was supposed to happen next, with Seth in the living room. But I couldn't just sit there as it got light outside, while he thought about the gaps in my story.

What was in those sixty-seven text messages.

How things started between Juno and my dad.

Where my mom is in all this.

What those men on Twitter wanted to do to me.

I'm lying in their mom's bed, but I don't close my eyes. A dark procession of Twitter handles is parading around inside my head. All those nicknames of people I don't know, people who say they hate me and my family.

What good are words when they no longer mean anything? Where do you stand when someone writes: *no wonder ur dad dont wanna fuck u. ur way 2 ugly*—and the police just tell you to ignore it?

19

"Where do you want to go?" says Abby in a serious voice. She's wearing a yellow hat with an orange duck's beak at the front. "Trader Joe's is the best, but it's also the farthest away. Kmart is cheap and it's usually total chaos there. I know the whole family at the cute little Korean food store. And Whole Foods is expensive and snooty and superyummy."

We're standing on the street with four empty shopping bags. Seth thinks it's dumb that I want to stock up on food, but I've told him I'll pay for everything. I can withdraw cash again now, so that's not a problem. All he has to provide is an empty kitchen cabinet.

"I'll take Abby with me," I whispered to him. "Then you'll have some peace and quiet to work on your website."

And he nodded. "Okay, then."

Our six a.m. conversation has, without any discussion, been placed on the "this didn't happen" list. Or maybe more like the "this *almost* didn't happen" list.

But Seth's stopped looking at me like he wishes I'd dissolve in hydrochloric acid.

And when he said it was okay for me to open a new jar of

Nutella even though the old one wasn't empty yet, I managed to say "thank you."

"You choose," I say to Abby. "I don't know the stores anyway."

She swings the shopping bags, looks up at the uniformly gray sky, and then starts laughing. "Let's go to all four of them!"

On our way to the first store, I still think that I'm making a fuss, with all our bags and our serious plans. But three hours later, I know that half of New York—and I mean *literally* half of New York—is stocking up on groceries today because there's a hurricane on the way.

I've never seen such long lines for the checkout before. They coil like snakes through the stores and never get any shorter. Some New Yorkers read a book while they're waiting; others just grin and look around. At Trader Joe's, a staff member is standing at the end of the snake with a big sign saying END OF LINE. Because otherwise you'd never believe a line could be that long.

I stand by the sign while Abby runs around fetching food. The "hurricane checklist" we picked up online is flapping in her hand. The power could fail, so we need to buy food that will keep without a refrigerator. Cans of soup, crackers, peanut butter, and also—it's on the list, right there in black and white—"comfort food." Food to make you feel better.

Abby and I both agree: Comfort food during a hurricane comes in big bags and crunches deliciously between your teeth. And it would seem that the rest of New York thinks the same, because the shelves of chips and snacks are almost empty.

Abby stares at them in horror. "I've never seen that before. The entire city's going to run out of food!" She dashes for the last two bags of salty popcorn and clutches them in her arms.

"Soda!" I cry. "We need something sweet and fizzy."

But Abby shakes her head. "We'll have to go to Kmart for that. They're way too green here for normal soda."

"Sorry?"

"They think soda's bad for us."

It's insane. On TV, I've seen hugely obese Americans who had to be hoisted out of their homes with cranes. But most New Yorkers seem to be really slim. You see gyms and yoga classes and runners wherever you go, and every meal tells you how many calories are in it.

"Look." Abby picks up a tub of dark green flakes. KALE CHIPS, it says on the packaging. "If you really want to belong, this is what you snack on. Chips made from raw, organically grown, freeze-dried kale. Seven dollars a tub."

"People are crazy."

"Every year," she says solemnly, "New York gets a different vegetable that's hip. This year it's kale. They mix raw kale in with salads too. And you can even buy tote bags with pictures of kale on them."

"People really are crazy."

"Not everyone. We don't have enough money to be crazy. But some rich New Yorkers are totally nuts."

• • •

Our final expedition takes us to Kmart. We stand in line to pay, with our four bottles of lethal soda. The line isn't long this time, but the woman at the register is moving more slowly than any human being I've ever seen. Sometimes she gives a deep sigh and then rests her arms for a while beside her gigantic breasts. And then she continues, still in slow motion.

"By the way," Abby says suddenly, "did you know Seth has been beaten up at school three times?"

"No," I say. "I've only known him two days."

"So? You can ask a lot of questions in two days." She tugs the hat with the beak down over her ears. "Did Seth tell you what happened on Friday? Why he raced off to get me and left you standing on the sidewalk?"

I shake my head and she looks at me sternly.

"Do you want to know or don't you care? Would you rather look at your phone, or at all those lists you have in your bag? I'll just shut up, then."

I swallow. "I'd like to know."

"Okay. So . . . I'd arranged to meet someone on Friday." She looks expectantly at me.

"Who?" I ask obediently.

She starts giggling. "A gentleman from a dating site."

"Abby!"

"It wasn't for me! Gross! The man was forty! He was for Mom."

The line isn't moving at all now. There's something wrong with the cash register and we have to wait for the manager, who has a special key.

"You had a date for your mom?"

"Yes! Dad's been dead for two years now and so . . ." She stops.

"You don't have to talk about it," I say quickly. "If you don't want to . . ."

"Duh, but I do want to talk about it! The whole thing's so dumb. Of course we all mega-miss him. More than mega. Supergigamega. But it's like Seth and Mom are stuck in some kind of time capsule. They act like he died last week. Which isn't true."

I don't say anything.

"And you know Seth builds websites as a part-time job? Well, recently he made this dating site. He showed me the home page, and I went back to take another look at it later. Girls can join for free, so I did. I put up a photo of Mom and she got responses right away. It was superfunny. Men are totally weird. But anyway, one man sent a nice email, so I made a date with him for Friday. To see if he might be good for Mom."

"And?"

"Seth turned up before 'talldarkandhandsome72' got there. He's so mean! If Mom never ever gets a boyfriend, then it's all Seth's fault." Abby sighs. "But of course that's exactly what he wants."

"Do you really think so?"

She nods. "They want to stay together in that time capsule of theirs. And they don't care that I'm not in there with them. They don't even notice."

20

We get home with four seriously heavy bags of food. Abby starts unpacking and I dash straight to the computer. Of course, I have better things to do, but I still want to take a quick look and see what those horrible swamp people are up to. To see if my dad's still an idiot. And if my mom's found the time to get in touch.

I open my dad's email, read the first couple of lines, and feel goose bumps on my arms.

"Emilia," Abby calls from the kitchen. "If you don't come quickly, I'm going to organize the kitchen cabinet without you!"

I stare at the screen. It's too late for fences inside my head.

"I'm putting the cans of chili con carne in their place right now!" shouts Abby.

I stand up. It's weird, but I can only think of one thing: I have to tell Seth. I walk to his room and knock on the door.

"Yeah?"

It's the first time I've seen his room. It's a small space with two computers, an overflowing toolbox, a tangle of colored electrical wires, and a model of a dinosaur. And then, above his bed, completely unexpectedly, a poster of one of

Picasso's paintings. A pale woman you can see in profile and from the front at the same time.

"What?" he asks.

He turns his desk chair to look at me. I feel like the woman in the poster. He's not just looking at the face I can see in the mirror. Ever since this morning, he's been able to see me from the side as well.

"My dad knows I'm in America!"

I notice that he stops breathing for a moment. My hands are tingling.

"He got suspicious after our conversation yesterday, so he did a bit of detective work. When he took a look at his credit card statements, my ticket to New York was on it, and now he says he's taking the first plane here tomorrow morning. He's told the police too. He says I'm not allowed to walk around the streets on my own for a second longer and that I have to report to a police station."

I'm out of breath. This city was mine. I was safe here. And now I'm not.

"But you're not on your own, are you?" says Seth. "You have us now."

I look at his dark brown eyes and feel my heart beating just a fraction more calmly.

"I've found a place for the soup too," Abby calls from the kitchen. "You're missing all the excitement!"

"I can't go back to the Netherlands," I whisper urgently to Seth. "Not this soon. Everyone on the Internet's still yelling way too loud."

"Then don't go to the police," he says calmly. "Send your dad an email to say you're safe and staying with sensible people, and then let's hope Sandy takes care of the rest. So that he can't fly."

"But what about the police? He emailed my photograph to them. They'll be looking for me." My fingers twitch anxiously. "I'm going to have to disguise myself. It's the only solution. I need another coat and I have to dye my hair."

He raises his eyebrows. "Seriously? You want to dye your hair because the police are looking for you, even though an actual hurricane's on the way? That is a total Abby plan!"

"But it could work." I look at him pleadingly and after seven seconds he lowers his eyes.

"You can borrow a coat from my mom. But hair dye . . ."

"We'll buy some! Right now, before the stores close."

"We?" he asks.

"Please? I don't want to go on my own."

And then Abby appears beside me.

"What have you two been up to all this time?" she asks indignantly. "I've already organized our entire kitchen cabinet!"

"We have to go out for a little while," says Seth. "You're staying home, okay? Mom's going to call on Skype soon."

"But I want to go with you," she says. "It's megafun outside. Just like when everyone's doing Christmas shopping, but it's hurricane shopping instead. I can talk to Mom later." Seth looks at me. I don't know why, but I don't want Abby to come with us.

"We're just going to buy some extra peanut butter," I say.

"It's going to be really boring," says Seth.

Abby looks at the floor. "Well, if you don't want me there . . ." She looks forlorn. As if she's not being allowed in the capsule again. I'm about to give in, but then Seth blurts out something.

"Emilia and I are going on a date. That's why you can't come."

We both stare at him in amazement.

"Really?" asks Abby. "Did you really, actually ask her? And she doesn't think you're dirty?" She looks at me. "Emilia, are you going on a date with Seth?"

I know it's not real. Of course I do. It's just the only way in the world to keep Abby at home—that was very smart of Seth.

But still I feel like someone's asked me out for the first time in my life.

I nod casually. "Yeah, we're going on a date."

"But what if he starts kissing you?" Abby cries out excitedly. "You'll get seven billion of his bacteria in your mouth!"

I can't help it. I shudder.

21

"Do you often go out on dates?" I ask Seth as we walk together down Broadway.

He stops. "You do know this isn't a date, right? I just said that to keep Abby home."

"Yeah, like I didn't get that already!" As I thrust my hands into my pockets, I feel my face turning red.

The sky above our heads is now the color of clay. There's the occasional gust of wind and I immediately think: Are these the first tentacles of Sandy?

Lots of the old-fashioned buildings along this part of Broadway are at least ten stories high. Everywhere I look, I see wrought-iron curlicues and designs in the stone: lilies with long stems, owls, peacock feathers, and wavy lines. Of course I don't mention that to Seth. I realized a long time ago that most fifteen-year-olds don't know anything about Jugendstil and Art Deco. It's no one else's business that they're my favorite decorative styles and that New York is full of them.

We stop in front of the wall of hair dyes at a huge drugstore. There are at least a hundred different kinds, and I have no idea which brand to choose. I haven't even decided which color I want.

"No," says Seth suddenly, his eyes wandering over the packaging, "I've never been on a date before. Why would I? Way too much hassle."

"Exactly," I say quickly. "Couldn't agree more. A complete waste of time."

"Do you know what color you want?"

I shake my head. He looks at my straight, light brown hair and frowns. "Not blond. That's not you."

"My mom has red hair. But I don't think . . ."

"Dark brown," he says. "Really dark, so that it's almost black. But not quite."

"Like yours?"

He runs his fingers through his rough hair. "More like Abby's. Glossy, I mean. And, um, a bit wavy."

I sigh. "I don't think a little dye is suddenly going to make my hair wavy."

As we leave the drugstore, Seth stops. He looks up at the sky and then at the people walking by, huddled into their winter coats.

"Come on," he says. "We'll take the subway. I want to show you something. Anyway, once Abby and Mom get Skyping, they can't stop."

I hesitate. The longer I'm outside, the more chance I'll be recognized by the police. I look at the plastic bag I'm holding, with the hair dye inside, and wonder if this is an

Abby kind of plan. Maybe I'm worrying about nothing. But maybe not.

"Okay," I say.

There are huge posters about Hurricane Sandy all over the subway station. Digital signs are warning that the last trains will leave the station at seven this evening.

"Poor tourists," I say. "Just imagine choosing this week of all weeks to see New York . . ."

As I say it, I realize that I'm actually one of those poor tourists.

When we come up aboveground from the South Ferry station, the wind's blowing harder than before. We walk through a park, step over a line of sandbags, and then we're standing by the water. Choppy gray waves with screeching seagulls above. On the left, an orange ferry sails by, and on the right . . .

It feels as if my heart grows a little bigger for a moment.

There, in the hazy distance, is the Statue of Liberty.

The giant woman made of gray-green metal stands on her own island, a crown on her head and a burning torch in her right hand, triumphantly raised aloft. As if she's just won some kind of contest.

"She was already there," says Seth, "when my great-great-grandparents arrived on the boat. They'd been persecuted in Russia, so they immigrated to America."

I feel a shiver run down my spine.

"Can you imagine what it must have been like?" he says. "There were no airplanes, so you had to travel by ship to America. You were at sea for, like, two weeks. Two weeks without land in sight, on the way to an unknown place. Movies didn't exist back then, and you couldn't just download a travel guide on your phone. Those people had absolutely no idea where they were going to end up. Then, after two weeks at sea, they sailed into the harbor of New York. And the first thing they saw was her."

He points at the Statue of Liberty. Seagulls skim across the water. My hair blows into my eyes.

"Lady Liberty," he says quietly. "All those Italians and Poles and Irish and Russians who were dreaming of becoming American saw her torch, high in the sky. They'd left behind their villages and families. Everything. Their entire lives. And then they started over again here."

I look at the Statue of Liberty and try to imagine it. Not what it's like to leave and then to email and call and send text messages every day. No. To leave and never hear anything else from each other for your entire life. Truly to start all over again.

Seth turns around. He leans with his back against the railing and looks at the gleaming skyscrapers around Wall Street, at the huge bronze eagle in the park nearby, and at the line of white sandbags on the waterfront walkway.

I don't know how many people have ever seen New York like this. Gray, abandoned, with a helpless little line of sandbags in the foreground.

"You probably think it's a load of crap," he says. "The whole story about the land of the free. The American dream. When we wage war all over the world. When people have been imprisoned without trial at Guantánamo Bay for ten years."

I shake my head. "No. Not at all. It's not crap."

"So what were you thinking about just then?" he asks. "You looked so . . ."

"I was thinking about all those people. What it must have been like to arrive here a century ago. What New York looked like back then. And what you'd have done if you didn't know anyone and had nowhere to sleep . . ."

I don't tell him what I thought after that.

That, if this really had been a first date, it would have been a pretty perfect one.

22

"Hey, you guys!" calls Abby when we get home. "I just saved someone's life!"

The living room smells like baked beans. The heating's up high and there's soft jazz music playing. And on the couch, under a flowery blanket, lies Jim.

Seriously. The nine-fingered movie star is back.

His eyes have a strange glint and his cheeks are red. Abby's eyes are gleaming too. She's put her hair up and she's found a purple party dress to wear.

"Oh . . . my . . . God," Seth says slowly. "You've gone crazy."

Abby laughs. "You say that every day. So it can't be true, can it? If I already went crazy yesterday, there's no need to act all surprised about it today."

I don't say anything. I don't want Jim to be lying there on the couch. I'm the one who's staying with Seth and Abby. Not him. That guy is way too good-looking to be just lying around here. This is going to end badly.

"I went over there to check up on him, and it's a good thing I did. He has a temperature," says Abby. "I felt his forehead." She looks at me. "I washed my hands after. With detergent." She picks up a cell phone that I recognize as Jim's. "And I've made a diagnosis. Those other doctors don't have a clue. Jim still has all ten fingers. Take a look."

She shows us an X-ray picture on the screen. A white-and-gray skeleton hand on a black background. Four intact fingers and one intact thumb, but there's a line running through the index finger that stops just before the end of the bone.

"He was cutting meat with one of those scary machines. At the restaurant where he was working. And then he slipped. A little bit more and he really would have only nine fingers left."

I sigh. I go out to take a quick look at the Statue of Liberty and suddenly this kid knows everything there is to know about Jim. Great. So he had all ten of his sticky fingers all over my clothes. That really doesn't make it any better.

"Abby," says Seth. "Hall. Now."

He doesn't look at me, but I follow them into the semi-dark hallway. There's no way Jim can stay here; that seems perfectly clear to me. And the two of us together should be able to stand up to an eleven-year-old girl, shouldn't we?

"Am I grounded again?" Abby asks happily as soon as the door to the living room is closed. "What a terrible punishment! Having to stay indoors during a hurricane!"

I look at that slender little girl, standing there defiantly with her chin in the air—and suddenly I understand what she's up to. She's trying to break open the capsule. Her mom and Seth have to come out of their isolation. All she cares about is making the two of them wake up.

"That guy," Seth whispers, "could be a murderer. Jesus, Abby, I can't believe you went over there to see him!"

"Your date was going on forever. So I thought: I'll just go take a look and see if Jim's still as handsome."

"You could have seen that at his place, couldn't you?" I whisper. "You didn't have to bring him home with you!"

"I most certainly did! He has a temperature. He keeps forgetting to take his medicine, and all he has in his room is Coke and a few cookies. I couldn't just leave him there, could I? There's a hurricane on the way!"

Seth's face is thunderous. "What do you think Mom's going to say tomorrow, when she gets home?"

"But Mom's not coming home tomorrow! Her flight's been canceled; she just told me."

I instantly think of my dad. And of the bed, which is now mine for one more night.

"Seriously," says Abby. "Jim has nowhere else to go. His family lives in Detroit, he's been fired from that restaurant because he can't work now, and he has no friends in New York." She looks at me. "You're allowed to stay here, aren't you? And you have an actual bed to sleep in. Jim has to sleep on the couch. We're running our own hurricane shelter right here. It's going to be fun!"

I look at the floor, because I still don't want to be in the same apartment as Jim. I don't know what to do when he looks at me. And he reminds me of Juno's friends. But there's absolutely nothing I can do about it. I get that now.

"Well, I'm not going to speak to him," mutters Seth. "He can stay until Sandy's over, but I don't want anything to do with him."

"And he has to stay away from my clothes," I say.

"Fine by me," says Abby chirpily. "Finally, I'll have someone all to myself. That's even better than a dachshund." She looks at me. "And it's better than a sister too."

Suddenly, everything is different inside our hurricane shelter.

I watch in silence as Jim drinks a cup of chamomile tea. As Abby plumps up the cushions. As Jim runs his feverish fingers through his hair. I really don't want to, but when there's a movie star lying on the couch, you can't help but look.

The movie star turns his head three centimeters to the left. "So you're obviously still in school . . ." he says to Abby.

She nods and beams at him. "I'm the best at spelling in the whole class."

He sighs. "You know, everyone should quit school as soon as they get the chance. The world is going to the dogs, and what is America teaching its children? That you have to make a career for yourself and earn as much money as possible."

Abby looks serious. "Really? You think I should quit school?"

"Of course he doesn't!" Seth yells from the kitchen.

Jim shrugs. "All those bankers who caused the financial crisis went to school. President Bush went to school . . ."

"Everyone went to school," says Seth. "What's your point?"

But Jim isn't listening. He's looking at Abby and talking about all the terrible things they teach you at school. I bite my lip. It's like I don't even exist.

Jim doesn't ask how I'm doing now. He doesn't want to know where I'm actually from. And of course he still hasn't apologized about my suitcase.

I get up. "I'm going to go dye my hair."

He doesn't even hear me.

Wearing nothing but a pair of underpants, I stand in front of the mirror in the bathroom. I put on rubber gloves and wrap the oldest of the five towels I had in my suitcase around my shoulders. Carefully, I mix the dye. As I shake the bottle, I think about those people who came to New York a century ago.

Two hours later, I finally dare to come out of the bathroom. On a scale that includes hurricanes and death threats, the color of your hair doesn't really register. But still I feel nervous.

Jim hasn't moved from the couch. He's gesturing violently with the hand that's not bandaged.

". . . like I ever voted for fucking capitalism! And now with this economic crisis . . ."

Abby is sitting in a chair opposite him. She looks like she's in a movie theater, watching a movie that she doesn't quite understand but still thinks is great. Seth has put his laptop on the kitchen counter and is watching the scene with simmering rage.

And then Jim stops talking and they all look at me. It feels like I just got off the boat. I'm stepping onto the waterfront and America is seeing me for the first time.

"Is it dumb?" I ask. "It looks weird, doesn't it?"

Seth slowly shakes his head. "I . . ."

"It's fabulous!" Abby yells excitedly. "Your eyes are kind of glowing."

"You should be careful," says Jim. "If you go out looking like that, everyone will be asking if you want to be a model."

"Don't be silly!" I try to sound cool.

He tilts his head and looks at me. But before he can say anything else, Abby starts rattling away again.

"They should ask *you* to be a model, Jim."

Jim shrugs. "They do."

"Really? And?"

"I think it's really fucked up, the amount of money that companies spend on advertising campaigns. And then they want me to pose in some tailor-made suit, or with a cell phone that no one really needs? No way."

"Not even if you can make loads of money doing it?" I ask.

He shakes his head. "That," he says, suddenly looking very serious, "is exactly what's wrong with the world. People doing things they don't really want to do, just because someone gives them loads of money to do it. Selling drugs. Making banks go bust. Prostituting themselves. I don't think anyone would do that stuff just for the sake of it. But they will do it for money."

The three of us stare at him. Seth is frowning. Abby still looks as if she's sitting in the movie theater. And me? I feel a little short of breath.

Jim nods. "I have a theory . . ."

"How about butternut squash soup this evening?" says Seth, cutting him off. "We've got some in the freezer downstairs. Emilia, do you want to see the basement?"

"Of course she doesn't want to see the basement!" snaps Jim. "Why would she want to do that?"

"Emilia?" asks Seth.

They both look at me. And they wait. Even Abby is quiet.

I can feel my heart pounding weirdly. Of course they're not really interested in me—I get that. They're just dumb adolescent boys who have to turn everything into a competition. Jim hardly even looked at me before Seth offered to show me the basement. And Seth never asked if I wanted to see the basement until Jim got here.

"Okay," I say, "show me this basement."

Seth looks triumphant, but he shouldn't think he's won. It just so happens that there's one thing I'd rather do now than listen to Jim. And that one thing is to talk about him.

Together we walk downstairs, past an old-fashioned balustrade with curls of metal. There's a smudge of hair dye on my wrist that will probably never come off, but oddly enough I'm not that bothered about it.

We stop at the door to the shared basement. Seth looks at me.

"This building," he says, "was constructed in . . ."

"Jim is so different than I thought," I whisper. "When you look at him, you think: That guy must be so superficial. But he really thinks about what's going on in the world! Don't you think it's cool that he doesn't want to be a model?"

"Nope," says Seth. "Whenever anyone asks me to be a model, I say no too. It's really nothing special."

"Seth!" I sigh. "Don't be so childish."

"I'm not being childish," he whispers angrily. "Believe me. If I were Jim, I'd kill myself. There are guys like that who ruin every school. They think they can do whatever they like and that it's perfectly natural for the world to fall at their feet. Just imagine Jim was at your school. Who do you think he'd be hanging out with?"

I don't have to think too hard.

"Yeah. Juno," he spits. "If she's the captain of the cheerleading squad in a movie, then Jim's her boyfriend. He's that kind of guy. An asshole."

"That's not true!" I'm still feeling a bit short of breath. "I thought the same at first. But all that stuff in the movies—it's not true. Because Juno, the most popular girl in school, doesn't have a good-looking boyfriend in real life. No, in real life she meets up in secret with my dad. And it turns out that Jim, who looks like a movie star, is thinking about a solution for the financial crisis . . ."

Seth just looks at me. Not as if I've just arrived on the boat, but as if I'm leaving.

"Why are you looking at me like that?"

"Like you care." He pulls open the heavy basement door and walks down the stairs. "I'll talk to you again in ten years," he calls up from below. "When Jim's still a loser without a high-school diploma. And I've just made my first million."

"Idiot!" I call after him. "You really don't get it. It's not about how much money you have."

"Ha!" His laughter echoes. "You can think that as long as you have enough. As long as you can use your dad's credit card to run away from him."

And then the door closes behind him.

23

Monday morning. The sun's only just come up, but we're ready and waiting for the storm. We've showered and had breakfast and brushed our teeth, and now we can't think of anything else to do.

This is insane. Here we are in our hurricane shelter, waiting for a storm that's "most likely" going to tear across the city. Along with eight million other people, we're watching the hurricane's every move. No one knows exactly what's going to happen. Maybe Sandy will swerve around New York and everything will be fine. But maybe half the city will end up in ruins.

Gray drizzle is falling outside. A strong wind's blowing, but I wouldn't call it a storm yet. Seth and Abby's mom is stuck in San Francisco, and now I know for sure that my dad hasn't been able to get a flight today. He'll have to wait, just like us.

The pathetic jerk's emailing me every hour now to ask how I'm doing, and I send him a short and carefully considered reply every three hours. Even the famous artist Nora Quinn has taken the time to send a message to her daughter before the deluge descends. She didn't write a single word about last week. Nothing about Juno. Nothing about the people who want to hang, draw, and quarter us, or the ones who want to rape us. She just told me that when she was twenty, back before she became scared of flying, she once went to New York. And that if I get the chance, I should definitely go see the Frick Collection. It's the most beautiful art museum in the whole city.

In the early afternoon, Abby and I go outside, because sitting around inside the apartment is driving us crazy. Nothing's happened yet, but New York is already a ghost town. It's like some deadly virus has hit the city, and we're the only two survivors.

Everything is closed: stores, restaurants, schools. The hospitals are the only places that are still open. There's hardly any traffic. Very occasionally, a wet cyclist rides by or we see someone dash outside to walk their dog.

"So what are you going to wear on Wednesday?" asks Abby as we go past a dark store full of Halloween costumes.

"I'm Dutch," I say, peering at the cobwebs and skeletons in the window display. "I don't do Halloween."

"Really? I'm going as a megascary zombie." She pulls off her yellow hat and lets the wind blow through her hair. "All the other girls have sexy costumes, but that's just dumb. Like monsters and witches would ever wear miniskirts and curl their hair. Monsters don't even have hair. Monsters have slime." And then she stops walking and turns to look at me. "Hey, do you think Jim likes sexy witches?"

I can't help laughing. "I'm sure Jim thinks sexy witches are 'corrupt and capitalist' in these times of economic crisis."

She looks puzzled.

"No," I say. "I don't think he likes sexy witches."

All the same, though, I wonder if Abby's mom might have some clothes I could borrow for a costume. Not really sexy clothes, of course. But not unsexy either. As sexy as is kind of believable for a witch.

When we get home, cold and wet, I discover that there's one place in the world that's weirder than the abandoned streets of New York—and that's the living room in our hurricane shelter. There are too few people out on the streets today, but inside the apartment there are obviously too many.

Seth has pulled his hood down over his head and is refusing to talk to Jim. Whereas I am saying as little as possible to Seth, because I think he's being childish. Abby's changed her clothes in the meantime and is now wearing a sky-blue party dress with patent leather shoes, and Jim is blissfully smiling at everyone. His fever's gone, and he and Abby have gone through two bags of tortilla chips.

Outside, the heart trees are waving their colorful arms, and Sandy's getting closer and closer as we watch her "live" out the window, but we're also following her on TV and on the computer and on our phones. The local networks have reporters in raincoats on standby throughout New York. The news keeps switching to them, but there's nothing to report. Every hour, they get colder and wetter and, every hour, they repeat that Sandy really is almost here now. But not quite . . .

Even the news sites in Holland are telling me how we're all doing over here. It's making my head spin. Far away, back at home, they're calling Sandy a "devastating superstorm." They say America is "trembling and quaking," and they're predicting dozens of deaths.

I can feel goose bumps on my arms beneath my sweater.

I look at Seth. I want to ask him if I should be frightened. Abby's just a kid, and all Jim ever talks about is the financial crisis. If anyone can tell me if we're really in danger, it's Seth. But he doesn't look up. He's slouched over the counter, frowning as he rips a yellow sticky note to pieces. I suddenly realize it's *my* sticky note. The one I scribbled all over in black.

By the end of the afternoon, the trees in front of the window are whipping back and forth, faster and faster. It's almost dark now, and the rain's pouring down. On the TV, Mayor Bloomberg advises us to close our curtains and blinds so the glass won't go flying across the room if the windows are blown in.

"I hadn't even thought about that," says Abby. She looks worried.

Seth lets down the blind. I'm secretly glad we don't have to look at those cold, reflective rectangles anymore.

The mayor announces that the schools will have to remain closed tomorrow. He repeats that it's not only people who are welcome at the emergency shelters, but also pets, and we see pictures of a scared-looking cat and a yellow dog pooping on the floor of a school gym.

Gravely, Mayor Bloomberg announces that lots of people have refused to leave their homes, even though they're in danger. He says they're being very selfish. If they have to be rescued by the fire department, they'll have knowingly put those firefighters' lives at risk.

"If you are in your home, or somewhere safe where you can remain—stay there," he says ominously. "The time for relocation or evacuation is over."

I feel a chill at the back of my neck.

Sitting in silence, we watch the reporters in their raincoats, who finally have some news. The rivers to our left and our right have risen and are beginning to wash over the edges of Manhattan. I spot the waterfront where Seth and I stood and looked at the Statue of Liberty only yesterday. Right where we were standing, it's now flooded. The water isn't over the sandbags yet, but the soaking-wet reporter is yelling into his microphone that he's been told to leave the waterfront. It's getting too dangerous.

I walk to the window and lift the blind. The rain's coming down in giant sheets of water that blow horizontally in the wind, slapping the windows, as if we're driving through a car wash. You can hardly see the streetlights now, and the branches of the heart trees are whipping wildly about.

I keep thinking: The wind can't blow any harder. It's impossible. Any harder and it'll tear the houses from the ground. But Sandy just keeps blasting away, harder and harder.

Now I can see the hurricane for myself and hear her hysterical shrieks. She howls around the buildings, pulling so furiously at the windows that I let go of the blind and back away. Suddenly, I can imagine how air really is capable of breaking glass.

We've abandoned the snacks. Sometimes comfort food is too distracting. We watch the TV and listen to the wind.

Abby's been sitting with Jim for a while now, and I quietly go sit beside her. Seth stops what he was doing at the counter and comes to join us on the couch. We know the worst is still to come. That's what the newscasters keep telling us. And that's what we can hear outside. Every crack of the whip is a little louder. Every punch of the storm hits a little harder.

Then the lights begin to flicker.

I hold my breath and I feel Abby stiffen next to me. But before anyone can say anything, it's already over and the lights are on again, as if everything's fine.

"What was that?" whispers Abby. "Why did that happen?"

No one answers her.

The voices on the TV get louder and shriller. The waiting's over. The hurricane's right above our heads now. In the borough of Queens, some way to the east of where we are, the first death has occurred: A tree crushed a house, along with the man inside. I actually gasp. "The first death"—as if they're sure there'll be more.

Then the lights flicker again.

For two seconds, it's dark. The TV screen goes black and the computer switches itself off.

My heart seems to stop along with them.

And then suddenly the lights are back on, nice and steady, with no flickering at all.

"This is kind of eerie," says Jim.

"But I don't understand how it's happening," Abby squeaks. "The way the power's going off, and then back on again. That means it must be okay. It can't actually be, like, really broken, can it? But then why were the lights flickering? I don't get it."

As Seth turns the computer and the TV back on, we listen to Sandy howling. She pulls on the walls and thumps at the windows. The rain beats hard against the glass as the TV shows us that more and more parts of the city are now underwater. I hear a crash outside and, moments later, the wail of a siren.

I move closer to Abby and look up at the lamp above the counter. Suddenly, I can't breathe. The lamp—it's one of those glass shades on a long cord—is slowly swinging back and forth.

That's impossible, I tell myself. The wind isn't blowing inside the building. The door's locked, and all the windows are closed. So how come the lamp's swaying? And then I realize.

It's not the lamp that's moving. It's the building.

The lamp is hanging perfectly still above the counter, but our building is gently moving.

I want to point and scream that bricks and concrete aren't allowed to sway in the wind, but I can't make a sound. All the noise in the world belongs to Sandy right now.

And then, without any warning, without a bang, without a flicker, everything goes dark.

And it stays dark.

24

For thirty seconds, we wait in silence.

We hear glass breaking somewhere in the distance. Sirens howl. And it stays dark. Darker than it's ever been this century. Not even a standby light on the TV. The letters of every digital display have gone out.

"It's not coming back on." Abby's voice is trembling. "What . . ."

Then she gasps because suddenly something *is* giving off light. Seth's turned on the screen of his cell phone. He walks over to the window to take a look outside.

"Jesus," he says. "The whole street's in darkness. I can't see anything at all—not even any buildings in the distance. There's a whole gigantic area without power!"

I feel my way toward him and look out. The stormy sky is just a shade less black than the buildings. Sandy doesn't care that we have no light. She roars on relentlessly, pushing and pulling at the windows. The glass bulges for a moment and then, with the next gust of wind, it hollows.

Seth and I let go of the blind at the same moment.

Think about it. If the window breaks while you're looking outside, shards of glass will go blasting into your face. And what do you do if you get seriously injured during a hurricane? Can ambulances keep driving in a storm like this? Is it dark in the hospitals now too?

"Fuck." Jim's cell is lighting up his face from below. "The Internet's down and I don't even have a signal. In the middle of Manhattan. Unbelievable."

"Seriously?" asks Abby. "I've never been without a signal, not in my entire life!" She looks at her phone. "And I've only got a little bit of battery left . . . That's what the mayor should have said: People of New York, charge your cell phones before it's too late!"

I stand still in the middle of the room. I can feel the darkness now. It's gently pushing against my skin from every direction. I breathe it in.

I feel like one of those really dumb farmer's sons in a fairy tale. The kind who's told he can make a wish, and then wishes something stupid that turns into a complete disaster.

There you go, the universe is saying to me. *This is what you wanted. A city without the Internet. Without Twitter threats and without obscene text messages.*

"This can't go on for long, can it?" I ask in a strange, unsteady voice. "We had a power failure at home in the Netherlands once. They fixed it within two hours. And this is New York!"

"Exactly," says Jim. "This is New York."

There's a moment of silence.

"What do you mean by that?" I ask him. Because his voice sounded a little strange too. "It's good that this is New York, isn't it? We're close to Wall Street, and all those banks really can't go without power. They'll just call in, like, a couple thousand people to repair things, won't they? So we'll have the lights back on as normal, right?"

"That sounds pretty optimistic to me," says Jim. "This could easily go on for days."

I almost choke in the darkness. "Days? Days without light and without a cell phone signal? Days just to solder a few wires together?"

"Look." Jim sounds calm. "America is . . ."

"Christ!" Seth explodes. "We don't need to hear some theory or other. Let's just hope they can repair it quickly. Whatever it is that's broken."

I want to yell: Why don't you just Google it to find out what's going on! But of course that's not possible.

This powerless, trapped feeling is something I've had only during exams. When you know all you have to rely on is your own brain. That there's no new information coming. That this is it.

And then I think of something else. I haven't answered my dad's messages for hours. I was going to email him one more time before going to bed. But now he's not going to hear anything from me at all.

I hate him with every cell in my body, but the thought of him sitting there in the Netherlands in the middle of the night, waiting for news from me, makes me dizzy. I haven't told him where I'm staying, so he has no idea what's happening to me. He doesn't know if I'm without electricity or if I've been swept away by a tidal wave and am lying on the bottom of the East River.

It's what he deserves, I say to myself. Let him worry. But the dizziness doesn't go away.

"I thought there were candles in here," Seth calls irritably from the other side of the room. "Abby, do you know where Mom put the things?"

She shakes her head and we look at each other by the light of two phones. We've been waiting for this all day. And all that time, we didn't get any candles ready. To be honest, I simply didn't believe it could happen. That here, at the center of the world, the power could fail.

Seth returns from the worst of the darkness and drops down into a chair.

"It's a good thing I just filled up the bathtub." He wipes his forehead. "At least that's something."

"It's the power that's out," I say impatiently. "That's not the same thing as the water."

He looks at me. "Do you really think so?"

I wave my arms around. "Duh! Look, no light! That's the problem."

"So why did you and Abby buy bottles of mineral water?"

"Just because. Because it was on the checklist. To be prepared for a hurricane."

I suddenly realize that I really did buy the water "just because." Because it was on the list. And that I didn't stop to think about why Americans think you might need water in your perfectly stocked kitchen cabinet during a power failure.

"The water here," says Seth, "is pumped up to the higher stories by electric pumps. So no power means no water."

"I don't believe it." I head straight to the kitchen. I just don't want to believe it.

"Wait!" calls Jim. "Put a pan under the faucet before you turn on the water. There's always some water left in the pipes. We can use it."

I look for a pan. My hands are shaking. No water—that doesn't only mean nothing to drink. It also means no shower. No water to flush the toilet. No water to wash your hands.

Abby stands beside me as I turn on the faucet. At first I think: See! Those dumb boys don't know anything! We still have water. But the flow thins. Soon it's just a drip. And then it stops.

By the light of my cell phone, I look at the empty faucet. I can feel the bacteria dancing over my hands. Cheering, because the universe has also made their dearest wish come true.

I bite my lip and I feel the world wobble. Why didn't I take another shower an hour ago, just to be on the safe side? Why didn't I wonder sooner why on earth I was buying bottles of water?

"Are you okay?" whispers Abby. She turns her cell on again. "Are you scared of the dark?"

"No," I say hoarsely, "the darkness isn't the problem."

I think of the nights when Dad and I climbed up onto our roof with our telescope. He told me about comets and taught me how to calculate in light-years—quietly, so we wouldn't disturb the neighbors. Up there on the roof, I discovered that you can actually see more in the dark, not less.

I stare at the faucet, which is gleaming by the dim light of Abby's cell phone, and attempt to breathe calmly. I try to come up with some kind of story to calm myself, a reason why it's not all so bad. But it doesn't work. Days without a shower—no story's good enough to cope with that.

"Oh," says Abby. "I get it!" She looks at me seriously. "Okay, so there's no water for now. But you still have your wipes, don't you?"

I don't reply.

"Emilia!" she says sternly. "How many packages of those things do you have in your suitcase?"

"Four," I whisper. "And I bought another three yesterday."

She nods. "So you can use an entire pack every day, for a whole week. Seriously, you're going to stay superclean."

I'm still looking at the empty faucet.

"Just think about it," whispers Abby. "This is an adventure. A real adventure. Normally, you have to try really hard to find some excitement, but now it's happening all by itself!"

There's a dull thud somewhere outside.

"Emilia?" she asks quickly. "Can I sleep in your bed tonight?"

I look at her and know that I can't refuse. If her mom had been here, then of course Abby would have been allowed to sleep in the big bed. But without power and without water, the washing machine won't work either. And you can't clean sheets with disinfectant wipes.

From now on everything's just going to get dirtier and dirtier.

"Yo!" Jim calls from the couch. "Are you guys holding a funeral service for that faucet? What are you doing over there?"

Abby skips back to the living room. "I get to sleep in the same bed as Emilia tonight!"

He laughs. "I already got to sleep next to Emilia on Friday."

"Does she snore?"

"No, but she does talk in her sleep. I couldn't understand what she was saying, though, because it was in that weird language of hers. Oh, and if you don't watch out, she snuggles up to you."

Seth gives something hard a kick. "I can't find any candles anywhere! And I don't want to drain my cell phone battery this evening. I'm going to bed. Then at least the dark will be normal."

"Wait," cries Abby. "Jim needs to take his antibiotics!"

He can take his pills without an audience, of course. But still Seth and I stand and watch. We watch Abby walk to the kitchen with her illuminated phone. We watch her take water from our supplies.

"The first bottle," she says solemnly. She unscrews the top and pours out half a glass.

"How many bottles did you actually buy?" asks Jim.

"Six," I say. I don't look at their faces. "Six times one and a half liters."

That's nine liters of water. For four people.

For days and days, if Jim's right.

I want to scream, but I hold it in. I dig my nails into my palms and listen to Sandy. Today, she does all of my gasping and wailing and screaming for me.

25

In the middle of the night, I awake with a start. Maybe another window broke somewhere. Maybe a tree fell. Abby's dark hair beside me is perfectly still. I pull my sleeping bag up over my nose and listen to Sandy. When there's a storm, you have to count the seconds between the thunder and lightning to work out how far away it is. But Sandy's raging on without stopping.

I have no idea how the rest of New York is doing right now. All over the world, people know more about it than we do. I wonder if my dad's still sitting at his computer. If he's read anything about the "first death." And then I wonder if he's been in touch with Juno since Tuesday, and suddenly I don't give a damn.

It's a strange thought that light isn't even an option right now. That I'm not lying here in the darkness because I want to, but because I have no choice. I hear sirens howling outside.

And then suddenly I sit up straight.

I don't know where my passport is. I thought it was too dangerous to leave it in my bag, but now I've forgotten where I hid it.

I crawl out of my sleeping bag, pick up my cell phone, and start looking. I know exactly which places I considered as hiding places. But I don't have the faintest idea which one I finally chose. Heart pounding, I drag my suitcase out of the closet and search every compartment. I pull drawers wide open and rummage around in the socks and underwear of a woman I don't know.

"Emilia?" Abby's voice sounds thin and reedy in the darkness. "What's wrong? Do you want me to get up?"

"It's okay," I whisper. "I'm just looking for my passport."

"But why?"

"I suddenly thought about all those candles out there." I'm out of breath. "Other people must have had candles to light. If a fire breaks out and we have to run, then I'll need my passport."

"Me too!" she says.

"But you're American. They know who you are here. If I collapse and lose consciousness, there's no one in this country who can tell anyone who I am."

"There's me."

"Do you know my last name?" I shine the light on her face. Her eyes are big and dark. Slowly, she shakes her head. And then she jumps out of bed.

"I'm going to get my school ID card."

I go on looking. The light of my cell phone screen keeps going off, and the light's actually way too weak anyway. I still don't have my passport, so I start taking the books off the shelves, one by one, and shaking them. Suddenly, I feel like the boy from that documentary—the one who thought for years that he wasn't real. I see myself as if I'm an actress in some impenetrable black-and-white movie, shaking books like a madwoman. Panting, sweating, sneezing from the dust. I could almost laugh at that girl in her checked pajamas—almost, but not quite. Because I know that girl is me.

Once upon a time, up on the roof with my dad, I learned that darkness isn't scary. But this darkness, now, feels too much like my own darkness. That breathless darkness where you can get lost and drop down dead. Without a passport. In a strange land.

Finally, I look at the back of the bottom drawer of the bed-side table and I can't imagine how I could ever have forgotten that my passport was there. I put it into my flowery bag, together with the folder full of printouts and my cell phone. And my charger and adapter. And painkillers, disinfectant wipes, antibacterial gel, toothpaste, and my toothbrush.

"Here," says Abby. She hands me a laminated ID card. "And can you put this in there too?" She's holding up a gray-ish bunny rabbit with ears that have been kissed and cuddled to death. I step back.

"Oh right," she says. She sighs.

I put the bag next to the door, and Abby places her rabbit on the other side of the doorway.

"I'll carry him if we have to make a run for it."

Shivering, we go back to bed. My dirty bare feet rub against the sides of my sleeping bag. Outside, something breaks again.

"Emilia?" whispers Abby. "Would you tell me a story? So I don't have to listen to Sandy?"

"I don't like made-up stories," I say quietly. "But I can tell you something that's true." I turn onto my side. "My last name is De Wit, by the way." I spell it for her. I tell her my date of birth too. And my mom's name, because that's easy enough to Google—in places that have the Internet, in any case. I know Abby will remember it.

And then I tell her about Benjamin Franklin, who flew a kite in a storm to catch the lightning.

When I wake, the other side of the bed is empty. I get up, open the curtains, and stare outside. *Light.*

I've never thought before how amazing it is that it actually gets light again every morning. Without us having to pay for it. Without two thousand Americans having to repair something—it simply gets light.

Sandy has passed. I can see that right away. The streets are gleaming. There are leaves and branches and garbage lying all around. No one is walking around outside yet, and the sky is still cloudy, but the heart trees have stopped whipping back and forth. And it's not raining.

In the cold living room, Seth, Abby, and Jim are huddled together on the couch. It's strange to see them sitting so closely together, but then I spot the gray radio in Abby's hands.

"We're listening to the news," she whispers when she sees me.

A radio. I don't believe I've ever seriously listened to a radio in my entire life. Why would you when there are cell phones and computers and TVs?

But just as I'm suddenly seeing daylight in a different way, I'm also seeing the radio with fresh eyes. This little one works with batteries, so there's no need for electricity. And while our dumb cell phones still aren't working, the radio is picking up a signal. Breathlessly, we listen to the crackling voices.

Since yesterday evening, a huge part of Manhattan has been without power. From where we are, all the way down to the southern tip of the island, where Seth and I stood on the waterfront, it's dark. And from us to the north it's black for another forty blocks.

But, as I listen, I realize that in fact we've been lucky. I take out my maps to get a better idea of the situation. I want to see where Breezy Point is, where more than a hundred houses burned to the ground. I need to know where Staten Island is, because that borough was hit really hard. Flooded. Washed away. Wrecked.

We greedily slurp up all the information, and at the same time I think: This is so inconvenient! All we can do is listen without any way to reply. And we can't just click a link if we want to find out more.

"We need to go north," I say when the news items start to repeat. "They have power and we'll be able to get a signal. I need to let my mom and dad know I'm still alive."

Abby jumps to her feet. "We have to call Mom."

And even Jim nods. "I've got to go to the hospital. My hand should have had a fresh bandage yesterday, but I'm not up for doing it myself. If I'm not careful, I could pull off my finger."

Abby shudders. "Does it still hurt?"

He nods, but doesn't say anything. That very first night, when I slept beside him on the woolly mammoth mattress, was the only time he'd actually said out loud that it hurt.

"You're so brave," whispers Abby.

"Seriously!" cries Seth. "There are loads of people who are having a worse time right now. Abby, did you even think about Aunt Leah?"

Her eyes widen. "She lives in Long Beach! That's . . ."

Without saying another word, she points out Long Beach on the map. It's a thin, stretched-out island with its length completely exposed to the ocean. Exactly where Sandy made landfall.

We get dressed in silence. I clean myself with my disinfectant wipes and shiver in the chilly bathroom. We eat everything that's left in the dark refrigerator for breakfast: chicken sausages, eggs, cheese, and chocolate milk. I'm amazed when Seth lights the stove, because I thought nothing at all was working. We don't have water, heating, or light, but we do have gas. And that's the only thing we have. Yippee. In our ice-cold, dark house in the desert, we can still cook.

We're hurrying, but no one says so.

"A coat," I whisper to Seth. "You said I could borrow one of your mom's coats."

I see him sigh and I know it's ridiculous to think about disguising myself when we've just been hit by a hurricane. But I'm still happy with the moss-green velvet coat. It comes down to my knees and has a belt that Abby makes me tie tightly around my waist. She also gives me an eggplant-colored hat and scarf, and then I'm ready to go.

We all take our ID cards and cell phones. And chargers, in the hope that we'll find a working power outlet. Seth slips his laptop into a backpack and Jim takes a bag of food, because we have no idea if any food stores will be open within walking distance.

Well, I say to myself, this is certainly an adventure.

26

The four of us set out on our journey toward the light. A few days ago we didn't even know one another. And now we belong together.

We walk along amazingly empty streets, and I know this must feel even stranger for the others than it does for me. I've only been in New York for three days, but they know exactly what this city should look like. The sky is dark gray. There are puddles everywhere, and piles of garbage. The wide street is absolutely silent and seems bigger than ever.

Abby stops. "Even the streetlights aren't working!"

And that's just the start of it. We keep discovering more and more things that don't work. It's so crazy to see all the neon signs without any illumination. All the stores and bars and restaurants are closed. All of them, except for one supermarket.

WE ARE OPEN—CASH ONLY, says a piece of cardboard by the door. The letters were written by hand, because of course printers aren't working either.

The door is open but it looks disturbingly dark inside the store. We see a customer with a shopping basket and a flashlight, searching for food, and someone calls out of the darkness that there's fresh hot coffee for sale.

"Let's keep on walking," says Jim impatiently.

Abby gives him a concerned look. "Are you okay?"

He nods. "I just want to get to a hospital as soon as possible. The ER is sure to be completely overrun."

We hurry onward. Sandy's over, but still there are hardly any cars on the street. There are just a few yellow cabs whizzing past, and they're all busy. Most pedestrians I see are lugging duffels and sleeping bags and pillows.

And suddenly it dawns on me.

"Seth!" I call. "Abby!"

They spin around.

"You must know people who have power! Why don't you go there?"

It's a moment before Seth answers.

"We do know people, but we can't just turn up with four of us. That won't work."

He looks at me with a serious expression, and I want to say something noble. I want to tell him that of course he should take his little sister and head for warmth—but I can't. I can't bear the thought of having to stay behind in the hurricane shelter without them. I wouldn't survive.

"If you want to go to the light," says Jim, "then of course you should. I'll manage."

High above our heads, a helicopter flies over.

"How about we wait and see?" Seth doesn't look at Jim. "I'm not going to let my little sister freeze to death, that's for sure. But maybe we'll have power again by tonight."

Abby takes hold of my hand. "No way am I going to stay somewhere without Emilia and Jim! Not even if they act tough and say they don't need us. That's what Dad always said too, and it's dumb."

"What are you talking about?" Seth stares at her.

"It's what Dad always said, isn't it? That we should do what we wanted. And he wouldn't try to stop us, and he could manage fine without us. Exactly what Jim's saying now!"

"You were tiny. You can't possibly remember that."

"I do so." Abby sticks her chin in the air. "He said it that time at Coney Island. We stuck our feet in the ocean with Mom and we ate corn dogs and went on the Wonder Wheel and ran to the end of the pier. And he didn't do anything at all. He just sat there. And that's when he said it. That we didn't have to stay with him and that we shouldn't worry about him. He could manage fine without us."

A stoplight has fallen off its post and is dangling by a cable. A taxi blows its horn.

Seth starts walking again, on his own. "You know nothing about it!" he yells. "Dad didn't know what he was saying. He didn't mean that . . ."

He's walking so fast that we don't even try to catch up with him.

"I really do remember," Abby whispers to me. "I'm good at remembering things."

I hold on to her sticky hand. Right through all those cuddly-bunny bacteria.

Block after deserted block, we walk northward. I time it on my phone. It takes us just over a minute to walk one block.

We finally stop when we reach Union Square. The island with the benches is sealed off with black-and-yellow tape.

Sandy has torn down trees and the park is a real mess. The rest of the square is packed with Con Ed trucks. I heard on the radio that Con Ed is the company that's supposed to restore the power.

A thin man with wild eyes tells us there was an explosion here yesterday evening.

"Didn't you see the flash of light?" he asks. "At first I thought aliens had landed." He rubs his hands. "The whole city's a disaster area. The subway's flooded, the bridges are closed, the tunnels are shut. It's going to take at least a week until everyone gets power again. And they say it's going to freeze on Friday. You know, it's going to get real cold here . . ."

I feel sick as we walk on.

We've only been going for half an hour and already I'm chilled through. I'm starting to worry now. Am I ever going to get warm again? Later, after hours of walking around a cold city, we'll go home to a cold house.

This happened to me once before, when I went camping with my dad on the island of Texel. After a walk in the rain, we got back to the campsite, half-frozen. Back inside the tent, I put on all the dry clothes I had with me and climbed into my sleeping bag. But I just couldn't get warm. I was so cold that I lay awake all night. It was scary.

Dad and I went home the next day, but that won't work this time. I can't leave now, because the airports are closed. Trains aren't going anywhere. The subway's not running. We're trapped in the cold.

All four of us are walking along with our cell phones in our hands now, so we'll notice as soon as there's a signal. Sometimes I spot someone else doing something on their cell phone and my heart starts beating faster, but it's always another false alarm.

Until, suddenly, we see a stoplight that's working. It's bright red, but Abby doesn't stop; she runs toward it with outstretched arms. Red no longer has any meaning for us—it's *light*, and that's what matters. Soon after that, our cell phones start beeping like crazy and we halt in our tracks. It's as if we're playing a game where you have to freeze when the music stops. Only today it's when the music starts.

Holding my breath, I read all my messages. My dad. And my mom too. I didn't know they could actually get that worried.

"Mom!" I hear Abby yell. "We're fine! We had sausages for breakfast and I have my ID card with me just in case I collapse . . ."

"Yeah," says Jim into his cell phone, "everything's okay here. No, I'm not on my own." He turns his back on me. "I've been living here two months. You really think I don't have any friends yet? There are four of us here. A great group of guys. Much better than Detroit."

"No, we don't want to go stay someplace," Abby shouts at her mom. "Seth and I have opened a hurricane shelter and everyone there really needs us." She frowns. "Well, you're not here, so you don't get to decide where we sleep!"

Seth has his phone up to his ear too, but he doesn't say anything.

"Aunt Leah?" I whisper.

He shakes his head. "I can't reach her."

I look again at the telephone in my hand. I was planning to send a text message. But suddenly I can't help myself. I have to speak to them. Not for my sake, but for theirs. Who knows what's happened to them? One of those lunatics from Twitter could have carried out his threats.

"Dad?" I yell when he answers. "Are you okay? And what about Mom?"

"Emilia!" he cries. "We hadn't heard anything from you and . . ."

"There was a power failure. But I survived the hurricane. I'm still here!"

It suddenly feels great to speak Dutch again. I can stand here, screaming in the middle of the street, and no one understands what I'm saying. I see Abby and Jim staring and I think: Yeah, just you look! This is who I am. This weird language is part of me.

"The lights started flickering at eight thirty yesterday evening. Twice, and then they went out altogether. And the water's not working and . . ."

I go on talking until I have to stop to take a breath. And of course my dumb dad uses that couple of seconds to start going on about the police. He says I really have to hand myself in, because he still hasn't been able to get a flight. And that I'm in danger and it's irresponsible and I have to do as he says.

"Just stop talking!" I scream furiously, because now that I know he's still alive, I'm allowed to think he's stupid again. "You still don't get it, do you? I don't want to go back to the Netherlands. Never! It's a hundred thousand times better here than over there with you. I have supercool friends, no one can send disgusting tweets when there's no signal, and, what's more important, you aren't here. Believe me. Even in the dark, this is fucking paradise!"

Before he can say anything else, I hang up.

Abby looks at me, openmouthed.

"Wow," says Jim. "Is that Dutchie language of yours one of those languages that makes it sound like you're always angry? Or were you actually mad?"

"I really was pretty mad," I say with satisfaction.

Six thousand kilometers, I think. There's an entire ocean between us. There's nothing you can do if you don't like me wandering around this city. I have my friends and my passport and a toothbrush. I'm free.

27

We are standing in the middle of gray, deserted New York and we're cold. It'll be light for five more hours before night sets in. What are we going to do with those precious hours of daylight?

"I really need to get to the hospital as soon as possible." Jim's face is pale.

Abby looks at her brother. "How about we go to Aunt Leah's? I want to find out how she's doing."

"Me too," says Seth. "But it's impossible to get to Long Beach. You heard what that guy said, didn't you? All the bridges and tunnels are closed. We're stuck in Manhattan."

I shiver. A hazy rain is falling, and my coat is getting wet.

"I know!" says Abby. "Let's go to Bridget's!" She looks at me. "Bridget is Mom's best friend and she lives uptown in a little box about the size of a rabbit hutch. But we should be able to squeeze in there with her for a few hours. She has the Internet and heating, and you can drink as much water as you want."

Seth has already started walking, but I shake my head.

"I'm going with Jim."

"Seriously?" asks Seth. "You'd rather go with him?" I nod. I haven't spoken to any adults at all for the past few days, and I want to keep it that way. I'm scared that this Bridget will start asking questions. That she'll cause problems and that I won't just be trapped in Manhattan but, to make matters worse, I'll be in a rabbit hutch.

"How are we going to do this?" says Jim. "Where are we going to meet up again later?"

My brain's never had to think this way before. I got a cell phone when I was eight, and I can't remember my parents ever not having a cell. In this part of town we can use our phones. But as soon as one of us heads south, there'll be no way to contact one another. We have only one key. And we don't know who'll get home first.

"This is ridiculous," says Jim after a while.

"Don't I know it!" says Seth. "Okay, Abby and I will get home before it's dark. So you can come any time after five."

"But the doorbell's not working!" I say. "And neither are our cell phones."

We rethink our plan. The apartment's too high up for us to throw something at the window. You wouldn't hear anyone shouting either.

Seth sighs. "After five, Abby and I will look out the window every fifteen minutes to see if you're there. And when it gets too dark to see anything, then we'll come downstairs every fifteen minutes to check if you're at the front door."

An ambulance goes by, sirens wailing.

"Seriously," says Abby. "How did people do this back in the Stone Age?"

We have no idea.

"Be sure to fill your water bottle at Bridget's," I say.

"And please," calls Jim. "Use the bathroom before you head back to the darkness!"

As Abby starts giggling, I remember my panic attack on the plane. Four days ago I was worried about a slurping toilet on a plane. Now I'm living in an apartment with a toilet that can't slurp at all and just gets the occasional bucket of bathwater thrown into it.

Jim pulls the zipper of his jacket up to his chin. "Emilia?"

I nod. Just for a moment, I glance at Seth. He's standing there all alone, locked up inside his time capsule. Ever since Abby told me about it, I can practically see the thing. Thick iron walls. A small, fogged-up porthole that he peers out through every now and then.

And then I follow Jim. I pull my hat down over my ears, put my hands in my pockets, and try to act like it's normal to be walking along next to a movie star.

It's just not fair. Whenever I look at Jim, I get a weak feeling in my knees. Not because I want to, but because—oh, how should I know? Because that's how *evolution* works.

How do the rest of us stand any chance at all when there are girls like Juno and boys like Jim? Girls with actual breasts and wavy hair, boys with muscly arms and sculpted faces. Boys who aren't trapped inside a capsule, but who want to conquer the world and still keep on smiling even after they've almost lost a finger.

It's so confusing. Why do I never get that weak feeling when someone's *nice* to me?

• • •

"Wow." Jim shakes his head. "These really are the weirdest months of my life. I moved to New York, chopped off my finger, survived a hurricane, and now I'm walking here next to you."

"You still have your finger," I say.

He sighs. "Hey, let me just pretend I have only nine fingers! I've been suffering for four days, and it's easier to bear if I'm allowed to play the part of an amputee."

"Okay," I say obediently, "you have nine fingers."

"Tragic, huh?"

I can't help laughing. "Absolutely megatragic."

His phone rings and he answers. "Mom?" He suddenly sounds younger. Kind of cute, in fact. "Hey, Mom. Calm down! Everything's fine. Like I just told Dad."

He listens for a while and then shakes his head. "He promised not to say anything about my finger! No, really. I'm doing fine. I can't even feel it now."

He listens again.

"No, I'm not alone. I'm out walking with Emilia, my girlfriend. She's from the Netherlands."

I feel evolution kick in again. He called me his "girlfriend"! Now there's someone out there in the world who thinks I'm Jim's girlfriend. Even if he did just mean that I'm a friend who's a girl . . .

"That's sweet of you," he says into his phone. "No, I didn't pray last night. I was asleep." He sighs. "But I don't want to come back! What am I supposed to do there? The city's half-empty and there's no work. Only losers want to live there."

He's silent for a moment.

"No, of course that's not what I meant! Mom, you know you . . ." He bites his lip. "I really do need to hang up now, or my battery's going to die. Talk to you later!"

The conversation's over. He sniffs and wipes his face with the back of his hand. I look down at the ground. He sniffs again, so I pass him a tissue from my bag.

"She's going to pray for you," he says. "That crazy mother of mine. She says she'll pray for Emilia. And for me, of course, but it hasn't helped much so far."

We go on walking. The streets are getting busier and I gaze at the people all around, who survived a hurricane last night, just like us. They look miserable and bedraggled.

"You know," I say, a little surprised, "this is the first time anyone's ever prayed for me. I don't think I know any people who believe in God."

"Really? I only know people who believe in God."

"Does it help?" I ask.

"What?"

"Believing."

He sighs. "Do you want a quick rundown of my family?"

I nod.

"Okay, hold on tight. My dad hasn't had a job for three years and he drinks too much. My mom's really smart but she works days in a supermarket and cleans offices at night. She's convinced that God is going to save her from this vale of tears, but the Old Guy's still keeping her waiting. I am the son who should have made everything right. But instead I just messed it all up." He sniffs again. "Now it's your turn. A quick rundown of your family of unbelievers."

I hesitate. And then I jump in.

"My mom's an artist and she's pretty famous. Nora Quinn—ever heard of her? My dad was the principal of my high school. Last week he had to resign because he'd been sending disgusting text messages to a student for months. And I was the perfect model daughter—until I sneaked onto a plane to New York."

Jim is silent for a moment. And then he starts to grin.

"Whoa! Those crazy atheists! Is it really bad of me to laugh about the text messages?" He sees my expression and quickly says, "Ah, yeah, I thought it probably was." He runs his fingers through his hair. "So . . . do you have any idea what he said in these text messages?"

"Seriously?" I cry. "You really want . . ."

"Never mind," he says. "Sorry, I'm just a filthy teenager and God will surely punish me. But no, let's just be serious for a moment. It makes quite a difference, what was in those messages. If it was hard-core porn or something more along the lines of, um, *your hair looked so beautiful and glossy when I saw you in class this morning . . .*"

I can tell he wants to laugh again, but he manages not to.

"It was more that kind of thing," I say.

A few of the text messages leaked and are now dancing around online. They're nothing like pornography. My dad sounds more like a thirteen-year-old nerd falling in love for the first time. He writes that he forgets all about vector spaces and diagonal matrices when he sees Juno. Tells her that every evening he calculates the chance of bumping into her in the hallway the next day. And that she shines like Sirius, the brightest star in the heavens.

He's clearly into recycling. Because my dad always used to say that thing about the brightest star to *me*.

"So there wasn't a single text message about her boobs?" Jim asks. "Or about his big wooden desk and how much he'd like to . . ."

"You complete sleaze!" I thump him on the same arm as the half-amputated finger and he winces. "When some horny president does that kind of thing, you're allowed to laugh. But this is my dad!"

He shakes his head. "I'm sorry, Emilia. I'll pray for him tonight."

We walk on and he starts talking about the financial crisis again. About houses that have to be sold and about ordinary people losing their jobs while big bankers are still getting bonuses of millions of dollars a year. I know now that he's not just talking about generalities and abstract figures. I understand that he's telling his own family's story over and over again. A true story about a dad who's been unemployed for three years. About a mom with two crappy little jobs. And about a son who left it all behind and escaped to New York.

28

As soon as we're through the sliding glass doors of the hospital, I stop. I can smell the blood and the sickness. I can see people with drips and slippers and wheelchairs.

"I'm sorry," I say. "This was pretty dumb of me. I can't go in there with you."

"But I bet I'm going to have to wait forever!" says Jim. "It's going to be mind-numbing. If you're there, then you can at least tell me some more fun stories about pervy text messages."

"Come on, Jim, how . . ."

"Sorry," he says. "I can't help it. Oversexed teen, yadda yadda." He sighs. "Seriously, I don't know what's wrong with me. Usually I'm pretty good with girls. If I do say so myself. But with you . . . Is that why you don't want to come with me? Because I'm a jerk?"

I don't look at him. "I just didn't think this through." I turn around and walk back through the doors. Away from the warmth, back to the cold.

Jim comes after me. "Can't stand the sight of blood? Is that it?"

"No. It's bacteria I can't stand, okay? I'm a freak."

"Hey, wait a moment!" He catches up with me. "At least take this." He pulls the giant package of Reduced Guilt Air-Popped Popcorn out of the shopping bag. "It's still closed, so there's guaranteed no bacteria." And then he smiles at me. "Yeah, you're a freak. A pretty cute freak, though. With cool hair."

When I've walked three whole blocks, when my knees are completely back to normal and I've forgotten his smile, I stop. I clean my hands with a disinfectant wipe, open the purple package, and start eating.

Half an hour later, I finally understand the hurricane checklist. Why they said we needed comfort food. It wasn't for during the hurricane. It was for now.

I am a popcorn machine. My hand dips into the bag over and over again. My jaws munch. My legs walk. And my brain stays calm. All around me, shivering tourists wander along the wet streets, but I have my own supply of food with me and I'm safe. For now.

No one looks at me. Last year in the Netherlands, after a heavy snowfall, people smiled at one another in the street. Because it was special and it made everyone think of Christmas. But today the street isn't glistening with a happy layer of snow. New York after Sandy is so unrecognizable that it's disturbing. The center of the world should not be *closed.* At the center of the world you shouldn't have to be scared of the moment when it gets dark.

I eat my popcorn and walk farther and farther to the north. I don't stop until I come to a giant glass cube on the corner in front of Central Park. An apple with a bite taken out of it hovers in the middle of the glass, and if you look down through the cube, you can see a bright white store full of iPads. There's another pathetic line of sandbags in front of the door, and lots of people are standing around the cube in silence, shivering in their wet coats.

For a moment I wonder if it's some kind of ritual. Are these people worshipping the latest iPhone? But then I understand. The store's closed, but the power here is still working—and that means there's Wi-Fi. If you hold your cell phone close to the cube, you're *online*!

As quickly as I can, I fold the bag of popcorn closed, clean my hands again, and start swiping my fingers across the screen of my cell phone. The people around me, on all four sides of the cube, are doing the same. I assume they've walked up here out of the darkness too. But I'll never know, because I don't speak to them.

Fuck solidarity, I think, WE HAVE WI-FI! I open Google and start searching. I want to find out how we're doing in New York. What we've been through these past hours. Where exactly everything went dark. What it all looked like. And what we're thinking now.

I finally tear myself away from my cell phone at three thirty. My fingers have changed into dead twigs—any longer and my touchscreen won't even recognize me as human. I must be about an hour and a half from home, and I really should get going. Or I won't be back before dark.

As I walk through the gray city, mechanically eating popcorn again, I think about the devastation I saw online. I think about the photos of water gushing into subway stations and the people who have lost everything.

Because Hurricane Sandy really was as bad as all that. She destroyed entire houses. Roads, electric cables, trees, cars, and bridges. And people.

While we were sitting safely inside our hurricane shelter, there were dozens of deaths. And people are still in danger. Old folks who live on the fifteenth story of an apartment building are imprisoned now that the elevator's stopped working. Thousands of people are without dry clothes, hot food, warm beds.

I wish I could help. On a website I saw that they need volunteers to distribute food and to visit old people and to clean away the mud. But I don't dare. I don't want to get any colder and dirtier than necessary. How can I spend a whole day scrubbing mud and then come home to an ice-cold apartment with no shower?

I can feel the blackness closing in.

Another three blocks and there won't be any power. I send a text message to my mom and dad to let them know it'll be at least eighteen hours before I have a signal again. At a diner that's actually open, I buy two large bottles of water and, shuddering, I visit the bathroom.

Just before the border, where the stoplights on the other side of the street are dead, I see a camping table covered with power strips. The table's on the sidewalk in front of a brightly lit supermarket, and handwritten signs say you can charge your phone here for free. Dozens of people stand waiting around the table, gazing at a tangle of chargers and cables and cell phones.

"Oh, it feels so good!" shouts a boy with spiky hair. "Power at last!"

My hands shaking, I take the charger from my bag. There's just one socket free in one of the power strips, and I go for it. I gaze, hypnotized, at the charging symbol on the screen of my cell phone.

"I was just at this hotel uptown," says a skinny girl in a crocheted hat. "I wanted to charge my cell in the lobby, but they threw me out. Can you believe it? They have no idea what it's like down here!"

"We are the People of Darkness," a man with a Mohawk and a scruffy dog on a rope says. "During the daytime we may enjoy the pleasures of a city with working traffic lights and heating. But then we must return to our City of Darkness."

As my phone sucks up power, I listen quietly to the conversations. The people around me haven't showered today, but I stay anyway. Because here, finally, I can feel it. We share something. I'm standing on a freezing sidewalk in New York, surrounded by people with Mohawks and hipster glasses, and I *understand* them.

It's getting dark, but I don't want to leave. It's crazy. I understand these people better than my own parents. We've been a family over there in the Netherlands for fifteen years now, but how many times have I ever felt that we were going through the same thing? How many times have we seen one another out walking in the snow and smiled?

I stand there looking at my phone as the sky slowly gets darker. The scruffy dog lies down and people talk about their day. About just one day, in fact—one day that we've all lived through today. And they share tips: There's an Indian restaurant on Second Avenue that's selling takeout from a dark doorway. The Korean deli on St. Mark's Place is partially flooded, but it's still open; the owners are proud that their store has never been closed for a day or a night during its entire existence. And that includes now.

I can no longer feel where my feet end and my boots begin, but still I stay. Because I want to.

Power at last.

29

I seriously underestimated those last few blocks home. Without lights, the streets are lethal. Cars can race across half of Manhattan and not encounter a single stoplight, and it's almost impossible to cross the street.

Am I really the only one who's out walking? My first few days in New York, when it was still light, I saw some homeless people out on the streets. Not many, but a few. Where are those people now? Are they happy that it's finally dark in their bedrooms? Are they waiting around the corner to leap out at me?

There's a vicious wind blowing but I can still feel sweat on my back. I open my eyes as wide as I can and do my best not to trip over curbs, basement doors, and cracks in the sidewalk.

I'm out of breath by the time I finally reach our street. As fast as I can, I head to the front door of our building, but just as I'm about to put my foot on the first step, I collide with something that's alive. I scream. Really loud.

"It's me," says Seth's voice.

"Jesus!" My heart is pounding away. My whole body is tingling. "You nearly gave me a heart attack . . ." For a moment

I think I'm going to cry, but then I start laughing. "I thought you were some homeless person, or a burglar, or . . ."

Seth clears his throat. "Do you know how long I've been waiting for you?"

I can't see his face, but he sounds pretty mad.

"We didn't agree on a time, did we?" I say. The adrenaline is still bouncing around inside my body. "We said Jim and I would be here sometime after five. That was all. Wasn't it?"

"But you didn't come back with Jim!" There's a catch in his voice. "Jim's been here an hour already, while you were out wandering around goodness knows where in a pitch-black city. Without anyone being able to contact you. I thought you'd gotten lost, or been murdered or kidnapped, or at least hacked into pieces."

"Well, I'm here now, aren't I?" I say. But at the same time I'm thinking: He was waiting for me. In the cold. In the dark. He was worried. Not about some girl who looks like a cheerleader, but about *me*.

"Emilia!" Abby beams as I come in. "Bridget gave us some candles and I've made the place supercozy."

I look around the room and hear the tune from that singing, jingling park in my head again: *It's beginning to look a lot like Christmas* . . . The apartment hasn't completely cooled down yet so, compared to outside, it's warm. It smells like oranges and there are tea lights everywhere: on the window ledge, on the counter, in front of the antique mirror.

"Hallelujah!" Jim calls from the couch. "The Dutch atheist is still alive. We had to send Seth outside, because the poor boy just couldn't stand it anymore."

I drop down next to him on the couch. My legs are exhausted from all that walking.

"So? Did the hospital pull off your finger?"

He nods. "According to my calculations, I only have eight fingers left now." He picks up a rectangular cardboard box from the floor. "I brought you a present."

By the flickering candlelight I read the label: "Single-use medical rubber examination gloves." One hundred pairs of disposable gloves.

"For the freak," he says quietly. "Handy, eh, now that we don't have any water? You can take a pee or pick your nose a hundred times without getting your hands dirty."

At first I think he's joking. That he's trying to make fun of me, like they do at school. But he's not laughing.

"Were they for sale at the hospital?"

"Let's just say they were lying around. And I thought: No one could put those things to better use than Emilia. Am I right?"

I give him a surprised nod. So the glamorous movie star can be a nice guy too.

Seth has remembered that there's a ton of food in the freezer in the basement. It's all thawing, of course, so tomorrow or the next day we'll have to throw it out. But right now it's still icy cold inside the big box. So our first actual hurricane meal is a five-course dinner.

At a table covered with tea lights, we eat tomato soup and hamburgers and corn on the cob and meat loaf and pancakes with lots and lots of syrup. And then Jim makes mulled wine so we can get extra warm before we have to go to our cold beds. He takes a big pan and mixes a bottle of red wine with fruit from the freezer, cinnamon sticks, star anise, cloves, and a few big spoonfuls of sugar.

"Mom says I'm not allowed to drink wine," says Abby. She's looking into the pan as Jim stirs.

"I'm heating it up," he says, "so the alcohol evaporates. Seriously, I know what I'm doing. My grandma makes the best mulled wine in all of Michigan."

I stand close to him, on the other side, because it's reassuringly warm next to the stove. I have no idea if I'm allowed to have alcohol. I talk to my dad about the universe and about prime numbers. I talk to my mom about art. But we don't talk about alcohol, condoms, cigarettes, or drugs.

Another subject we've never discussed is the fact that it's not appropriate to send text messages to underage students.

If only I'd given him better advice. He obviously needed a good daughter-to-father chat.

"Ready!" says Jim.

I wonder if he's heated the wine for long enough, but I don't say anything. I help him fill four mugs and take them to the couch. It's ominously quiet outside. There are no cars and no people out on the streets. It feels as if the polar night has begun.

Abby and I sit down next to Jim on the couch, and Seth takes a chair opposite. I can see that he thinks we're paying too much attention to the movie star. But can I help it that Jim got such a great recipe from his grandma? And that he's been so nice for the past couple hours that I actually feel brave enough to talk to him? My knees sometimes forget to go weak for a whole fifteen minutes.

I take a cautious sip of the wine. The spicy concoction is bitter and sweet at the same time. I can feel the warmth sliding down my throat and spreading through my body.

"Wow," I say, "this is good."

I take another sip and Abby does the same. Her eyes begin to sparkle.

"Wow, this really is fucking great!"

Shocked, Seth stares at his little sister.

"What?" Abby asks defiantly. She quickly takes another sip. "Jim says fuck all the time."

"People say a lot of things." Seth frowns. "But you don't have to parrot everything some high-school dropout says, do you? Surely you're smart enough to come up with a better word?"

Jim stays admirably calm.

"So do you have something against sex?" he asks Seth in a friendly voice.

"My sister's eleven years old!"

"And? She knows how people reproduce. There's nothing wrong with that, is there?" Jim tilts his head. "But perhaps you're the one who feels uncomfortable with that word? Because you're worried? Because you've never . . ."

"Eeww!" I yell. I put my hands over my ears and shake my head. "I don't want to listen to this. I flew across an entire ocean just to escape that kind of talk!"

To my surprise, they fall silent. I hadn't taken the eleven-year-old into account, though.

"Actually," says Abby seriously, "I don't really get it. *Reproduction*, I mean. How does it all, like, fit together?"

She looks at us expectantly. She's the toughest little girl I know and she can handle a hurricane, but still she's only eleven. I look at her little face and her shining eyes and I want to adopt her. I want to make sure she never sees any porn by accident and never has to read about icky erections in dumb magazines for girls and that no one ever tells her about girls who get undressed in front of webcams to show their boyfriends how much they love them.

I take three big swigs of wine, one after the other, and feel the warmth tingling inside.

"I have no idea," I say. "But maybe Jim or your brother could throw some light on the subject from their monkey cage . . ."

"Sorry," says Seth. "As Jim already pointed out, I know nothing about it."

We all look at Jim now.

"Well?" asks Abby. "How does it work? If you say 'fuck' all the time, you must know all about how to do it."

He looks down at the floor. I can see that he's finally realized what *eleven years old* actually means.

He sighs and shakes his head. "It's a great mystery to us all."

30

We made another pan of mulled wine and now we're playing crazy eights with Seth's old deck of cards. We keep inventing new rules and shouting louder and louder. Normally, I don't like playing cards, but in the dark, with cold pancakes and mulled wine, it's great.

In the middle of a game, as we're bent double with laughter, Abby suddenly looks at Seth.

"Now I remember! We always used to play this with Dad. I was really too young. But because I didn't understand the rules, you guys could let me win."

"Yeah. Mom didn't think that was good for you," says Seth. "She thought you needed to learn to cope with losing."

Abby nods. "And then Dad let me win again anyway."

"He said losing could always come later. When you were older."

The laughter dies away. The wine's now whirling through my veins. I've never felt like this before. Like fifteen years old really is a great age to be. Like everything's possible and it's only just beginning. And, suddenly, I feel brave enough to ask the question.

"So how did he actually die?"

Maybe they don't want to tell me. But I think not asking is worse.

"Car accident." Seth doesn't look at me. "His car went into the water and he couldn't get out in time."

It's very quiet. And then I feel Abby moving beside me.

"We don't know that for sure."

In the candlelight, Seth's face looks like a mask. "You don't know what you're talking about," he says quietly.

"I do so." Abby puts her chin in the air. "No one knows if it was an accident. And that includes you."

It takes Seth three steps to reach the couch. "If Mom ever hears you . . ." He's about to grab ahold of her, but I put my arm around her.

"This doesn't concern you!" he shouts at me. "She's my sister, not yours."

I hold on to her and Seth clenches his jaw. In the half-dark room he looks like a zombie that's been under the ground for two years and has just escaped.

"She's lying," he says. "Just as long as you guys remember that. Abby's a liar."

He turns on his heel and strides off. I hear his bedroom door slam. And then it's quiet.

Abby doesn't cry like a little girl. Her face barely changes, but tears are rolling down her cheeks. She stares at the tea lights in the window. I give her a tissue, but she doesn't notice. I dig my nails into the palms of my hands and wait.

"Was it suicide?" Jim asks.

I feel a shock go through my body. I wish he'd kept his mouth shut, but at the same time I hope Abby will answer.

She swallows, then wipes her cheeks and shrugs.

"We don't know. We really don't."

The crackle of a radio comes from Seth's room. That makes me even madder at him. He's not allowed to listen to the radio all on his own—and at full volume too. The batteries will run out way too quickly.

"I was nine," says Abby. "No one told me anything. Just that he wasn't there anymore. And that his car ended up in the water in the middle of the night. An accident, they said."

"Well, that's possible, isn't it?" I ask quietly.

She nods. "Yes, it's possible. But there are some strange things about it."

"What kind of things?" asks Jim.

"Dad was still wearing his seat belt. If your car goes into the water, you try to get out of it, don't you? You at least undo your seat belt."

"Maybe he was unconscious," I say. "From the impact of the car hitting the water."

She stands up and studies me from a distance.

"You're just like Mom and Seth." She wipes her top lip. "Now I'm not even allowed to mention it. But those first few months, whenever I asked about it, the answer was always: It was an accident. We have no idea how he went from driving along a perfectly quiet road to ending up in the water, but of course he didn't do it on purpose. We don't know why he was in that part of town either, or why he'd left his cell phone at home, but it was an accident. An accident. An accident."

She looks worn-out.

"But then isn't it better . . ." I pause. "I mean, wouldn't you rather it was an accident?"

"Duh," she cries, "of course! But that's not something you can *choose.* I want to know what really happened. Because there was something going on with Dad. Something wrong. Even before that, I mean. He never wanted to join in with stuff anymore. But yeah, Mom doesn't want to talk about that either." She's crying again. "I just want to be able to mention it. Without them getting mad . . ."

I stand up and put my arms around her. "I understand," I whisper. "I understand."

When Abby falls asleep, Jim and I carry her to the big bed. We stroke her cheek and then tiptoe out of the room. Jim ladles the last of the mulled wine into our mugs.

"Maybe next time you should let it boil for longer," I whisper.

"Good idea." He drops down onto the couch. "Fuck! Oh no, I wasn't going to use that word anymore." He sighs. "You know, I thought my family was messed up. But this . . ."

I empty my mug in one gulp. I leave the fruit at the bottom. "I have to go talk to Seth."

Jim looks at me by the light of the last candles. "Want me to come with you?"

I shake my head.

"Okay, then I'm gonna crash. Can you throw me that blanket?" I open the box of rubber gloves, put some on, and hand him the dusty old blanket.

"Freak," he says quietly.

"Sleep tight," I reply, just as quietly.

He closes his eyes and I stay there for a moment. The candles flicker and I realize that something's changed. Of course I can still see how good-looking he is. But it doesn't feel as if I'm looking at a billboard anymore. Now I can see him. Jim. A boy that I know.

31

When I go into Seth's room, I don't know if he's still awake. The crackling voices from the radio fill the pitch-dark box.

"Seth?" I say. "Wait, I'll get my cell phone . . ."

"No!" His voice sounds choked. "Leave me alone."

"Well, at least turn off the radio! The battery's going to die and then we'll be completely alone."

I wait in the doorway. And then the sound stops.

"What . . ." I begin, but I don't know how to continue. I take off the gloves and put them in my pocket. "Did you speak to your aunt?"

He sighs. "My uncle. They're alive but half the house is underwater and the car's drowned. My uncle got a ride to JFK in a pickup with a load of other people. There was a signal at the airport, so they all got to make just a couple of phone calls, and then the pickup turned around so that other people could go to the airport."

"Wow," I say quietly. "And to think that this is New York. Not Somalia or Honduras or India, but America."

Normally, as your eyes start to get used to the dark, you can make out a few things. But with no moon, no streetlights in the distance, and no devices on standby, you really can't see anything at all. No matter how long you stand there in the dark, you stay blind.

"So where are you exactly?"

"Sitting on my bed."

As I feel my way toward him, I think about his Picasso poster, which I can't see now. The woman with two faces.

"Whoa!" Seth suddenly exclaims. "Another step and you'll be sitting on my lap."

I giggle in spite of myself. "What about here? Can I sit here?"

Silence.

Then Seth says, "I nodded."

"Okay." I sit down with my back against the cold wall and suddenly, I feel calm. "Now I want to hear about it. Open up the door of your capsule."

"Seriously? Did Abby tell you about that?"

"That you and your mom are stuck inside a time capsule? Yes. And you know something? She's right. I can see you through the porthole. It's kind of like a submarine, but without the water. We—the rest of the world—are flying farther and farther away from you. And you're still stuck there. Inside your capsule."

"I work with computers, Emilia. With ones and zeros. I don't know anything about submarines flying around without water."

"Okay, then." I clench my fists. Not behind my back, but just on my lap. It's dark, after all. "Then tell me. One or zero? Accident or suicide?"

The mattress moves violently. I hear a siren in the distance and a thump on the wall close beside me.

"What do you want?" he growls. "I already told you it was an accident. I don't keep bothering you about your dad, do I? You told me your story. And I believe you."

I lean back, with my head against the wall. I breathe in the darkness, and his breath, and what must be years' worth of dust. How long ago did he build that model of the dinosaur? When did he get the Picasso poster?

"Christ," he yells, "you just don't get it! With computers it's always ones and zeros. But it doesn't work like that in real life. Sometimes you don't know if something is a one or a zero. And sometimes it's somewhere in between . . ."

I keep quiet, because I'd be sure to say the wrong thing. The wine is still whirling through my body. Or maybe it's something else. Maybe I'm sitting with Seth inside his capsule and we're floating through time. So we could easily zip back to a year ago, before my dad sent any of those text messages. Or back to two years ago, when Seth's dad was still alive . . .

"Okay," he says, "listen." It sounds like he's made up his mind. "We don't know if it was an accident. We just don't know. For months I hoped we'd find out. It was all I could think about. Every day I waited for the mail because I hoped my dad had sent a good-bye letter. A letter that had gotten lost, but would eventually be delivered. And at the same time I hoped someone would say: I saw what happened that night, he swerved to avoid a dog and the car went into the water."

It's a while before he continues.

"But there was nothing. No letter, no witness. No secret diary, no reason for him to be out driving there that night. And that's it. We'll never find out. We just don't know."

"But what about Abby?" My hands are trembling. I let them shake in the darkness. "Why isn't she allowed to talk about it?"

"We never said that. But her questions were driving us crazy. And if you can choose what it was . . . then you're going to say it was an accident, right? That's what Mom told everyone. And that's what everyone thinks at school."

My eyes are still open. I don't know why, because the room's pitch-black. But I keep them open anyway. I keep looking. I try to see.

"If you can choose," I say, "you're going to choose an accident. I get that. But what do you think? What do you think really happened?"

It takes eons before he answers. His words have to come from the other side of the universe.

"I think," he says quietly, "that it may have been something in between. Between a one and a zero. I can't believe he was really planning to leave us. Then at least he would have written a letter. Then he would have said good-bye. But I could imagine . . ." He clears his throat. "That it was a sudden impulse. He just did it. Turned the steering wheel. Left his seat belt on. And by the time he realized he was actually drowning, and he thought about never seeing us again—then it was too late."

32

On Wednesday morning I have tortilla chips for breakfast. Wearing rubber gloves, I take the chips out of the bag and Abby giggles as she copies me. I have a headache and I wonder out loud if this is my first-ever hangover.

"Yep," says Seth grimly. He looks gray and he doesn't want to eat anything.

"You have to tell Abby!" I whisper as soon as we're alone for a moment. "What you said to me yesterday—about the ones and the zeros. She'll want to hear it."

"That our dad may have committed suicide?" he asks. "You think my eleven-year-old sister wants to hear that?"

I nod. "She already knows. She just wants to hear from you that she's not crazy."

And then Abby comes back out of the bathroom.

"It's Halloween, so we have to wear costumes!" Her eyes are red, with big bags under them, but she smiles at us as if there's nothing she'd rather do than go out and party.

"I don't have any scary clothes," I say.

"But we have a dress-up box!"

An hour later we set off with two backpacks full of costumes. We've decided that we're going uptown to shower at

Bridget's and then we'll change our clothes. So at least we'll be clean zombies.

We begin our journey north in silence. We know what to expect now. The sky is still gray and our part of the city is dead silent. The stoplights aren't working, the stores are closed, everyone is gloomy. We trudge onward until our phones start beeping.

And then I have the shock of my life.

My dad has texted to say he got a flight and that he's landing in America tonight. The text message is too short for all the details, so I don't know exactly where he's flying to, or how long he'll have to be in a taxi, or how much it's all going to cost. But one thing is clear: He's not coming alone.

My mom is coming with him to New York.

She hasn't flown for twenty years, because she's convinced that airplanes are unnatural and lethal. No matter what fantastic offers she receives from museums in Asia and America and Australia, my mom always says no. And now, two days after Sandy, while the city's still a disaster area, she's getting on a plane to New York. The Museum of Modern Art and the Guggenheim couldn't persuade her. But I could.

I tilt back my head and start laughing.

"Bridget's not home." I hear Abby's worried voice. "She just texted that she won't be home from work until really late . . ."

My laughter dries up.

"Right." Seth shrugs. "So we can't shower at her place. Then we'll just go to a diner and change our clothes in the bathroom."

"But I need to shower first!" cries Abby.

I look at her in surprise.

Her fingers twitch anxiously. "There's no way I'm putting on a costume until I'm clean. Do you know how many bacteria you have living on your skin?" I bite my lip and say nothing.

"There are one hundred and fifty different kinds of bacteria on your hands," Abby squeaks. "Emilia knows all about it. That's why you should always wear gloves to eat! If I can't shower now, I'll get sick." She looks at me. Her bottom lip is trembling. "Emilia, tell them how dirty I am!"

It's like hearing nails scratching a blackboard.

Every cell in my body has goose bumps. I can see the boys looking at me.

Seth puts his arm around Abby's shoulders. "I think you . . ."

"Don't do that," she snaps. "You're dirty too!"

The nails go on scratching and I know I need to do something. This has to stop.

"Abby, listen." I'm a bit out of breath. "Everything I told you about bacteria . . . It's all true. But . . . *it doesn't matter*." I try to remember all the stuff that dumb psychologist told me last year. "People can deal with bacteria, no problem. You won't get sick from not showering for a couple of days. You might get a bit stinky, but that's not so bad—especially not now, after Sandy."

"That makes no sense," she says angrily. "So why do you keep washing your hands? Why wasn't my bunny rabbit allowed in your bag?"

I know Seth and Jim are looking at me. I can feel their eyes, but I have to forget about them. This is about Abby.

"Some people," I say, "are scared of mice. Some are frightened of heights. Others are scared of the dark. Well, it just so happens that I have a thing about bacteria. But if one of your friends tells you she's too scared to go up the Empire State Building, does that mean you'll never go up there again?"

Abby shakes her head. "I love tall buildings!"

"Exactly. Which means you're perfectly capable of turning into a zombie without taking a shower first."

"Really?"

I nod.

"What about you?" she asks. "Are you going to put on your costume without showering first too?"

Nails scratching open my belly from the inside. Slicing through my flesh, sharp as knives. Slowly ripping . . .

"Of course I am," I say cheerfully. "Why wouldn't I?"

33

Today uptown is gleaming like the hurricane never happened. For ten minutes we're happy that all the stores are open again, but the happiness soon fades. Because we really do feel like People of Darkness now. We eat chips for breakfast and have to drink wine to stay warm. We roam around, hunting for power sockets and Wi-Fi, and the rest of the world doesn't understand us.

"Dumb tourists," I snap. "All they ever do is eat and take photos and buy souvenirs. Don't they know people have died?"

"Of course they know," says Jim. "But that's what people do. They eat and take photos and buy things while people are dying all around." He looks at me. "Do you think every day about all the people who are dying?"

"No, but . . ."

"I do!" says Abby. "There's this website that keeps track of how many people are being born and how many are dying. You can see the counter rattling away. It's megaquick. In the time it takes me to eat a bagel, three hundred ninety-two people die."

Seth looks sternly at his sister. "Mom told you to stop looking at that website."

"But there aren't any naked people on it! I'm allowed to look at moving numbers, aren't I?"

"It gave you nightmares last time."

We're walking between gray skyscrapers with mirrored windows and I'm thinking about my dad. My brain's getting really messed up. Someone only has to mention a website with pictures of naked people on it and I think about my dad.

In a few hours, my mom and dad are arriving in this city. I texted them to say I don't want to meet up until tomorrow. I have better things to do on Halloween. They have no clue where I'm staying, and in the dark part of the city I'm completely unreachable, so for the next few hours I'm still in charge. And then tomorrow I'll transform back into their daughter, who's a minor.

The thought of it makes me sick.

In New York A.S.—"After Sandy"—I'm no longer interested in tourist attractions and famous places. When it turns out that the temple-like library on Fifth Avenue is still closed, though, I'm mad. Seth promised it'd have Wi-Fi. I glare at the stone lions in front of the building. Sure, they look great lying there. And yeah, I recognize them from at least fifteen different movies. But in all those movies, the actors had clean armpits and they could poop in their own bathroom.

At Grand Central, we finally find a few public power sockets. They're close to the ground in an ice-cold, drafty corridor beside the platforms, but we don't care. We eagerly descend on them.

"I want to write a travel guide," I call to Abby, who's at the next power socket five meters away. "*Out and About with a Plug: The Top One Hundred Power Outlets in New York.*"

"I'd snap that right up!" calls Seth from the other direction.

"And I'm going to make a movie," yells Jim from ten meters away, "about plugs slipping into power outlets. There's nothing that the people of the City of Darkness would rather watch right now than devices getting a good charge."

Abby giggles. "I bet Mom wouldn't let me watch that movie."

Jim enthusiastically waves his phone. "Sometimes two plugs at a time go into one socket! Sometimes five phones get charged at once, all in a line. And then another time the battery gets loaded so fast that—"

"That's enough!" Seth yells, but he's laughing.

We wander onward. Past stores with diamonds, chocolate fountains, and food carts selling roasted chestnuts—and then we finally find the place that will appear at position number one, inside a golden frame, in *Out and About with a Plug*.

Make a note for emergencies: the Barnes & Noble bookstore on Fifth Avenue between Forty-Fifth and Forty-Sixth Streets. Complete with a Starbucks, so they have muffins and mugs of coffee for sale. Good Wi-Fi. A free bathroom with a special faucet for drinking water. Enough books to last anyone for years. Warmth.

We drop down onto the hard carpet in an empty aisle. Then we take off our hats, pick up our phones, and decide to stay. The people from the bookstore leave us alone, and more and more People of Darkness gather around, people who, just like us, desperately want to know how the world around us is doing.

To my own surprise, I don't even check to see if everyone's still talking about my dad online. Today I just don't care. Why should I read what all those idiotic strangers have to say? I have better things to do. I need to know when the subway will start working again. And if it's true that the drinking water is polluted. And how many deaths the counter has recorded.

"I have a plan." Seth clears his throat. We've been silent for so long that I almost forgot there were people sitting around me. "The four of us together should be okay walking home in the dark. So tonight we're going to eat out in the light."

"That's a great plan," says Jim. "But I can't come. No money."

I shrug. "I don't mind paying."

"No," says Seth sternly, "you've already paid for enough. You bought all the hurricane supplies and you just paid for coffee and muffins. Now it's my turn. I'm paying this evening."

"But you never spend your savings on anything," Abby objects. "You won't be able to go to college!"

Finally, I understand why Seth takes his part-time job so seriously. It's very different here than in the Netherlands. American universities cost a fortune, and Seth and Abby have only one parent to rely on. Their mother can't earn very much as a kindergarten teacher.

Abby looks concerned. "Seth, you were going to save money for me too, weren't you? So that I can be a doctor even though it's mega-expensive. I know I was planning to learn to tell fortunes so that I could earn money in Washington Square, but I just can't do it. The things I predict never happen."

"I'm saving for you too," her brother says. "But we have plenty of time. We can afford to eat out now and then."

She laughs. "Okay, and later, when I'm a surgeon, I'll pay it all back. With interest. And lots and lots of presents!"

Jim and I act like we don't exist for a moment. All those big plans make us feel so small. I have no idea what I want to study when I'm older. Just something, anything. And Jim didn't even finish high school. He's having an operation on his finger next week and he won't be able to work for months. He'll be penniless, injured, and alone in the most expensive city in the world . . .

"Come on, Jim!" says Abby, as if she's calling her favorite dog. "We have to change for dinner. I'll help you with your costume."

As Jim walks off with the backpacks, Abby leans over to me.

"I'm going to marry him when I'm older," she whispers. "Then he can lie on the couch all day and talk about the financial crisis and I'll earn lots of money for both of us."

She skips after him through the bookstore and I watch her go. I wish I were still eleven years old too.

I sigh and fish the bottle of antibacterial gel out of my bag.

"Emilia," says Seth quietly, "you don't have to wear a costume if you don't feel like it."

He's looking at me again as if I'm that woman Picasso painted. As if he can see me from the front and the side at the same time. It makes me feel uneasy. Why would anyone want to study me that closely?

"Stop being so . . . understanding all the time!"

"What do you mean?" he says.

"You're always so nice. Like you *understand* me. But you're sixteen. And you're a boy. Just be a bit more . . . insensitive!"

His dark eyes look at me as if I'm an alien. Not even a normal everyday kind of alien either, but a deeply disturbed one. "So, let me get this straight, you think I'm being too nice? And you're telling me that I should be less nice?"

"Yes!" I can't even remember what I'm trying to tell him. But it seems like the best idea to agree.

"But I thought . . ."

"Well, stop. Just stop thinking! Stop paying for my food and stop being nice to me. You won't be able to keep it up. Believe me. I know how it goes. The better people know me, the dumber they think I am. Save yourself the trouble!"

Without waiting for his reply, I get up and walk to the bathroom.

"Abby!" I call at the closed doors. "Do you have my clothes in there?"

"Wait a moment . . ." She giggles. "I'm busy with Jim." That's another thing you have to be eleven for. Yelling in a public restroom that you're busy with a boy. And you have to be Jim to laugh out loud, so that all the waiting women can hear you.

A while later I'm standing in the little stall with the cat costume in my hands. Pantyhose, a short black dress with fur around the hem, a long velvety tail, and a headband with pointed ears.

I was wearing rubber gloves when I took the costume out of the dress-up box, and I'm convinced that dinosaurs once wore that tail. I clasp the headband and try to remember all the wise psychologist stuff I just told Abby when we were out on the street.

It doesn't work. I can feel the panic rising.

But then I think of Seth's serious face. I remember how worried he seemed when he looked at me just now. Jim makes jokes about my dad and steals gloves for me so that I can pick my nose. But Seth takes me seriously. More than that—he feels sorry for me. He doesn't say so, but I know it's true. Why else would he be so nice to me?

Really. A boy who is floating through space, disconnected from everything, feels *sorry* for me.

I pull my sweater and T-shirt over my head in one motion. Halloween, here I come.

34

We've all got grins on our faces when we leave the bookstore. Abby's a terrifying zombie in a ragged dress covered with splashes of blood, hair that's standing on end, and a creepy white face. Seth's wearing a black sweater with a skeleton on it and gloves printed with bones. And I actually make a pretty sexy cat, if I do say so myself.

But it's Jim who's making everyone stop in their tracks as if they've been struck by Benjamin Franklin's lightning.

He's wearing a floaty purple dress that's just a bit too small for him, with a black pointed hat. His face is painted bright green and he's wearing a tangled long black wig. The effect is stunning. Within two hundred meters, he makes five tourists collapse with laughter and three children cry.

When we pass a police officer, I look straight at him. With my new hair and my cat costume, I'm someone completely different. I don't think I've ever felt quite so un-Emilia in my whole life. We're all cold without our coats, but we want people to be able to see our costumes. We walk shoulder to shoulder down the broad sidewalk and everyone steps out of the way to let us pass. It feels like we're a boy band, or those four women from *Sex and the City*.

What I mean is: four people who are world famous. And who belong together.

Seth takes us to an ultramodern restaurant on a busy street, where he starts acting tough and not at all sensitive and understanding.

"Just give me the menu," he says. "I'll decide what we're going to eat."

I've never been to such a cool restaurant before. There are purple couches, and pink lights on the wall, and we're the only ones who are in costume. Within fifteen minutes, the table is covered with spring rolls and chicken skewers and Thai salad and steamed dumplings and duck pancakes.

"Right. So these are the appetizers," says Seth.

"Yummy!" Abby is holding her chopsticks at the ready, but then she looks at me with a worried expression. "Emilia won't want to eat from the same bowls as us . . ."

"Emilia needs to stop complaining," says Seth sternly.

And so I don't. The food is incredible: crispy and spicy and sweet, all at the same time. I go to the bathroom three times to wash my hands when I accidentally touch my black dress, but no one mentions it. We don't drink any wine, of course, because it's practically impossible to order alcohol in an American restaurant if you're under twenty-one. But somehow I can still feel something buzzing in my veins. That floating feeling is back again.

Maybe, I think, as I take a bite of the sweet-and-sour tofu that's now on the table, getting older isn't so bad after all. Maybe this is what it feels like to be an adult. To be able to decide for yourself: Tonight I'm going out for a fabulous meal. With my own friends. I'm going to stay here for as long as I want and I'll eat whatever I like. Because I'm not afraid anymore.

"What do you guys think?" I say. "Should we just abolish the Internet for good?"

Abby picks up her phone. "Smile!"

We put our heads together and smile for the photo.

"Abolish the Internet?" asks Seth.

"Yes! Who says we need to use everything that was invented by people who just happened to be alive before we were?"

"Exactly," says Jim. "We don't want their atom bombs and killer robots and pathetic schools."

Seth pops a piece of duck into his mouth. "I have to say, I'm rather attached to the wheel."

Abby puts down her phone. "I wish Obama would decide that we're only allowed to go online for three hours a day. No more than that. Then I could sometimes be offline after school. Now I'm always scared of missing out on something and that everyone will start gossiping about me if I'm not online . . ."

"I just don't get it," I say. "Why are some people so rude on the Internet? What makes them so much meaner and more aggressive than usual?"

"It's simple," says Jim. "If I bad-mouth someone to his face, then he'll beat me up. But online I can say whatever I want."

"That's exactly the problem!" I cry. "You end up saying more than you mean to. More than you really intend to."

Abby nods. "Bethany once wrote that she was going to scratch my eyes out because I didn't let her copy my homework.

But look! I've still got my eyes!" She looks happily around the table with wide eyes and a creepy white zombie face.

New dishes just keep on coming, and I eat more than I've ever eaten before. As I savor the sweet coconut milk and hot pepper and Thai basil, I watch the tropical fish swimming lazily around inside their illuminated aquarium. Glasses tinkle and the conversations around us sound reassuringly American. "I was, like . . . giiirl, that's sooo amazing, you know? And then she was, like . . . no way, he didn't! But then I'm, like, hello? He's a guy, what do you expect, you know?"

And then suddenly I hear a man's voice behind me.

"Emilia de Wit! Can I ask you something?"

He's speaking Dutch. And he knows my name.

I turn around. A tall, thin man with cropped hair is smiling at me. "Do you mind if I join you?"

35

I just stare at the man, because I have no idea who he is.

"Sorry," I say in English. "Do I know you?"

He smiles at me again and calmly sits down next to Abby.

"My name's Bastiaan Breedveld." He's still speaking Dutch. "I'm a journalist. I spotted on Twitter that you were eating here, and I happened to be in the area. I'm mainly writing about the hurricane this week, of course, but after that interview with Juno, I'm curious to hear what you might have to say."

I can't move. I thought I'd escaped, but it seems the hunt is still on. The journalist may not have a rifle, but he doesn't need one. A smartphone with a Twitter account is enough.

I want to yell that I'm not Emilia. But I have to know.

"What interview with Juno?" My voice is trembling. I can feel the cold barrel of the rifle on the back of my neck. "How does Twitter know where I am? No one here knows me!"

He takes a phone from his bag and shows me the screen. A tweet from Abby, proudly announcing that she's eating Thai food with #scarybrother, #moviestar, and #emiliadewit. And yep, with the photo of the three of us.

I hate all those dumb hashtags on Twitter. I hate #stupidlittlekidswhosecretlytweetduringdinner.

"You really mean to say you haven't read the interview with Juno yet?" asks Bastiaan. "It's been online for hours."

Dizzily, I stand up, because I need to get away from this man as quickly as possible. Away from his dumb accent, away from his flappy Dutch ears and his pale lips saying "Juno."

I look at the others. "Let's go."

"What about that guy?" asks Abby.

"Ignore him. He's a journalist."

"But what does he want?"

"Abby," says Jim. "Come on outside."

Seth is pale. "Will you two stay with Emilia? I'll go pay."

I walk to the door. When I look back, I see that Bastiaan is following me. Calm as anything, with his hands in his pockets. He could be strolling past a field of sprouts back home. Or through a meadow of cows.

It's dark outside, but nobody really cares about that in this part of the city. The streetlights here are shining as usual and the neon signs are dancing away as they should be.

"I understand that the past week has been difficult for you," says Bastiaan cheerfully. "And I really don't want to bother you. I just want to give you the opportunity to respond to Juno's version of events."

That name of hers, over and over again. I've never hated a word so much before. Juno, the goddess of light. Queen of the heavens. Goddess of marriage.

"People need to hear your side of the story too, don't they?" Bastiaan asks in a friendly voice.

"But I don't have a side," I cry. "What my dad decides to do has nothing to do with me and I don't even know . . . that girl. Just leave me alone!"

"Juno has plenty to say about you in the interview, though . . ." As he swipes the screen of his cell phone, I clench my fists. I can see Seth inside at the bar, waiting to pay.

"Here," says Bastiaan, "listen to what Juno said." He starts reading out loud in Dutch. " 'It's totally creepy, of course, a fifty-year-old guy being in love with you. If I'd met him in a chat room, I'd have instantly clicked away. But I was doing so badly in math . . .' "

He looks up from the screen and I dig my nails into my palms as hard as I can.

"Yeah. We already knew that, didn't we?" I say. I'm not even trying to play it cool—I really did know that already. My dad's a creep.

Bastiaan goes on reading. Abby and Jim listen in silence to the words they can't understand. Seth is still inside.

" 'People don't understand, though. We had something special. He told me things he couldn't talk to anyone else about. He has a wife and a daughter, but he said he often feels as if he's floating all alone among the stars. I didn't get it at first, but he meant he's lonely. Seriously. He said he feels like he's floating in cold, empty space. And that I'm the only one who sometimes flies past him within hearing distance.' "

I feel sick.

Could it be true? Has my dad really been locked up in his own capsule all that time without me noticing?

Bastiaan strokes his stubbly head. "Juno goes on like that for two pages. She pours out everything she can remember about your dad's confessions. As if she wants to prove that what they had was really special." He sighs. "But maybe she's just making half of it up. That's always possible." He looks up from the screen and frowns. "Is it true that your mom sometimes goes a bit wild? That she cuts her paintings to ribbons and that your dad has to give her a sedative?"

I can feel the cold barrel of the gun again.

And at the same time I can picture the ragged pieces of canvas. Sometimes she just cuts away wildly, until all that's left is scraps. But sometimes she slices the canvas into beautiful strips. I used to roll them up to make colorful bandages for my teddy bear. It's not true, by the way, that it's always my dad who has to give her sedatives. I've known for years where she keeps her pills.

Seth finally comes out of the restaurant. He's walking quickly.

"Let's go," he says, but I don't go anywhere. This journalist is talking about my life and I have to know what happens next.

"Is it true that you suffer from OCD?" asks Bastiaan. He's still speaking Dutch. "Juno says your dad is worried, but that the therapy hasn't worked. She says your hands . . ."

I see his eyes wander and I hide my hands behind my back.

He nods understandingly. "Your dad also told Juno how difficult it is to be tied down. To wake up every morning and to know you have a job and a mortgage and a wife and a daughter, and that you'll never be free. That you're a prisoner."

I know what this Bastiaan guy is doing, but suddenly I don't care. I've had enough.

"Seriously?" I say. "First that asshole says he's floating all alone among the stars and then he complains about being tied down? And he's supposed to be a math teacher? The man has a PhD in logic!" My voice is getting louder. "Does that loser really think he'll never be free of me and my mom? Well, I can put his mind at rest. If he wants, he can be as free as a bird!"

Seth takes hold of my arm.

"Come on," he whispers urgently. "I thought you didn't want to speak to this guy?"

I pull myself away.

"Why is everyone allowed to talk except me?" I shout in English. "Why do I have to run away and hide while the rest of the world is ranting away on Twitter? While Juno is giving an interview?" My cat tail is whipping furiously back and forth. The headband with the ears is digging viciously into my scalp. "What the hell was that moron thinking? Wasn't it enough to lust after some seventeen-year-old? Did he really have to *talk* to her as well?"

"Emilia . . ." says Jim.

"Just let me lose it! What difference does it make anyway? Everyone already knows all about my wretched life."

"Sure, you can lose it," says Jim quietly, "but wouldn't it be better to do it without a journalist around?"

"I don't understand," Abby says. "Who was lusting after a seventeen-year-old? Is lusting the same as fucking?"

"Be quiet, Abby," says Seth.

Cars race past. Passersby just glance at us and then walk on. Maybe they think we're doing some kind of performance piece, with all these costumes. I'm surrounded by a zombie, a witch, and a skeleton, but I know this isn't a movie. This is real life.

"So it's all true? All the things Juno said?" asks Bastiaan. "She also said something about . . ."

"Just go away, man!" I yell as loud as I can. "Haven't you heard enough already? I am really, really mad, just go write that in your newspaper. Emilia de Wit is yelling at the top of her lungs on a sidewalk in New York. She thinks the rest of the world needs to keep its mouth shut and that other people should mind their own business. If they have that much time on their hands, they can go help the hurricane victims!"

I have never been so mad in my entire life. Until this point I was always a black hole. When I got angry, I imploded and thought I was going to die. But it's different now. One day, I'm going to die. I know that. But not today. I have never felt so loudly, so luminously alive.

"Is there perhaps something you'd like to say to Juno?" asks Bastiaan.

"You still don't get it, do you? If I want to say something to Juno, then I'll do just that! I don't need your help. And those people on Twitter are all twisted and messed up. Let them go tell their wives that they want to set our house on fire and they want to castrate my dad. Why should I read all that stuff online if they're not going to do it anyway?"

"We're leaving," declares Seth. He pulls Abby along with him, but when he sees I'm not coming, he stops again.

I look at Bastiaan. "Now do you get it?"

"Well . . ."

"Fuck all those idiots in the Netherlands! I live in New York, and I just survived a hurricane. *That* is my story." I've been shouting so loud that I'm hoarse, but my voice isn't trembling anymore. "I've dyed my hair and I'm wearing a costume. You see? I'm celebrating Halloween! These clothes have been rotting away in a dress-up box for years, and I haven't showered since Monday morning, so it looks like I'm doing okay with my OCD. I just flew to New York all on my own. *That* is my story."

He rubs his stubbly head. "So when did you . . ."

I glare at the sprout farmer and decide the conversation is over.

"Just fuck off," I say, and I start walking.

36

We've split up. The zombie and the witch have taken a taxi home. Abby was so tired she could barely stand, and Jim's finger felt as if he'd just sawed through it.

Seth was already at the open taxi door when I shook my head.

"You guys just go! No way I could sleep now anyway. I need to walk."

He looked at me and gave his sister the house keys and a twenty-dollar bill. Then he closed the yellow door and stayed behind with me on the sidewalk.

And so now here we are, walking. It's half past ten at night, but that's not even bedtime for babies in New York. Cars stand in a line, honking their horns, cameras are flashing, the city is buzzing, and I feel like I could run a marathon. I could kick down fences, climb a building, or perform in one of those musicals where you have to sing and dance at the same time.

I remember when I first read about supernovas. That's what it's called when a star explodes. It doesn't quietly disintegrate; we're talking about an extreme explosion that shines with the light of a billion suns. When I read the words, I tried to imagine what that must feel like: *the light of a billion suns.*

And now I know.

"Which newspaper does that journalist write for?" Seth suddenly asks.

The sound of his voice makes me jump, because I've been acting as if he doesn't exist for the past fifteen minutes. As if there's not a skeleton walking along beside me, as if he can't see my two faces, as if I don't care what he thinks of me.

"No idea."

"But he did tell you his name, didn't he?" Seth stops. His face is the same color as the bones on his sweater. The muscles in his neck are taut. "If we can track down his boss, we can explain what happened. That the journalist was harassing you and that he didn't have any right to interview you without your parents there. If we're quick, we can make sure his article doesn't . . ."

"Seth!" I look at him without blinking. "I don't care. Let him write about me. I'm not scared anymore."

"Seriously?"

"You have no idea," I say slowly, "how wonderful it is *not* to keep my mouth shut for once."

He looks at me and I can see there are a thousand things he wants to say. But he doesn't.

The darkness is coming closer now. We walk past a brightly lit room of ATMs that's packed with people. They're lounging on the floor and perched on camping chairs, with laptops balanced on their knees, and are surrounded by power strips and telephones and empty coffee cups. Two tourists are staring in at them. All that's missing is a sign. "*Homo sapiens*, subspecies People of Darkness. Please do not knock on the glass."

"So we're not going to do anything?" asks Seth. "We're just going to let that guy do whatever he wants?"

"Yes."

"And you don't regret it?"

"No!"

The billion suns are still burning away inside my stomach. I point at the fairy-tale tower with the eagles' heads that I saw when I got off the bus on Friday. The tip of the tower is covered with golden scales of light now. "That's my favorite building."

He doesn't even look.

"What is it with New York?" I cry. "I only have to look around, and I feel like I'm in love." I stretch out my arms. "This is a hard, cold, unfair city—and still I'd give at least three fingers to live here."

He shoves his hands in his pockets and doesn't say anything.

"Stop being so difficult!" I yell at him. "As long as you hide away inside that capsule of yours, you'll be unhappy. You understand that, don't you? One thing's for sure: You'll never have any fun in there."

His eyes are dark. "Like you're having so much fun out there."

"Today I am!"

"Seriously? You thought today was *fun*?"

I think about it and realize that I'll never forget today. When I'm thirty and fifty and eighty, I'll still remember the details. Waiting next to a power outlet in an icy-cold, drafty corridor. Checking my emails, surrounded by People of Darkness. The four of us eating in extreme hipster cool. Yelling as loud as I could and having no regrets.

"So didn't you think it was fun?" I ask. "Would you rather have gone to school? Would you have preferred to stay at home alone in your bedroom?"

"That's lame. When you put it like that . . ."

"But that's how it is! You just don't see it, through that fogged-up porthole of yours."

We cross the street and head into the City of Darkness. The dark is a little less overwhelming than yesterday. Police officers with lights are standing at the intersections, and there's some kind of firework lying on the street that doesn't go bang but gives off a fountain of red sparks. I'm glad they've realized that the streets are lethal here without stoplights.

But then we pass Union Square and it's suddenly just as dark as it was yesterday. No police, no red fireworks, nothing. Does Mayor Bloomberg think it's good enough if just the residents to the north of Union Square survive? Are the people who live here more easily dispensable?

"It's totally dead down here." Seth looks around. "The only people still here are the ones with nowhere else to go."

"Well, it just so happens there's nowhere else I'd rather be," I say.

I hear him laugh quietly.

"How could I forget? You're having the time of your life." He clears his throat. "But you're right. I'm glad Abby and I aren't staying with Bridget. If this has to happen, I want to be here to see it."

We walk slowly. Sometimes we stop and look up. There's something magical about it, this metropolis in the dark. It's cold and absolutely silent, except for the occasional siren in the distance. Dark as pitch, the houses stand out against the sky. Up on the flat roofs are wooden water towers: colossal cylinders on legs, looking ominous in the night.

I breathe in so deeply that I feel the cold tingling in my belly and I can't help but think about the things my dad said to Juno. About him being so lonely. About waking up every morning with the feeling that he's tied down.

I can imagine loneliness very well, but not being *tied down forever.* I've known for years that I'm going to move out as soon as I've done my final school examinations. I don't have to live in the same house as them for the rest of my life. I try to imagine how I would feel if I knew that this would never stop. My life as it is now. That this was it. Exactly the same, until my death.

"Where are your mom and dad staying, by the way?" Seth suddenly asks.

I sigh. "With friends. They wanted to book a hotel, but everywhere's full of movie stars who have escaped the darkness. So they're staying with some famous sculptor. In the light, of course."

"And what about you?"

"I'm going to stay with you guys." He can't see that I'm looking at him. "At least if you'll let me . . ."

He kicks something.

"Fine by me," he says neutrally. "And I'm sure my mom won't mind. She should finally be able to get a flight tomorrow."

Their mom. I'd been so busy thinking about my own mom and dad that I'd forgotten all about her. Then it hits me. The adults are suddenly closing in from every direction.

My mom and dad are already in the city, and their mom will be here soon. In twenty-four hours everything will have changed.

I clench my fists, because I don't want this to stop. It's crazy, but I want to live in our hurricane shelter with Seth and Abby and Jim forever. I want to count the hours of daylight and wonder if we have enough drinking water. I'm disgustingly filthy and the bacteria are crawling all over me, but I'm walking here with Seth and, as long as it's dark, we belong together.

I'm not scared anymore, I'd said, but that's only true when Seth is looking out at me through his fogged-up porthole. When Jim is telling me about mortgage debt, and when I can sleep next to Abby at night. When the Netherlands is six thousand kilometers away. And when grown-ups keep their noses out of my life.

But tomorrow I'm going to see my dad again. And when I think about that, I'm actually scared to death.

37

When I open my eyes the next morning, Abby is looking at me.

"Are you still mad at me?" she whispers. "Because of that message on Twitter?"

I groan. In a few hours' time, I'll see my dad again. I wish I hadn't woken up.

"Remember, you told me to memorize your last name," Abby says miserably. "And I wanted everyone to know who you were!"

"It's okay." I sigh. "People are allowed to know who I am."

We eat chili con carne for breakfast. There's one clean pot left, and we use it to heat up the contents of two cans. The heat of the stove is welcome, as the apartment's getting colder by the day. The man with the wild eyes in Union Square was right: It's going to freeze.

I wear rubber gloves at breakfast. Abby doesn't. We both notice but don't say anything. We've become a machine with cogs that fit together perfectly. I give the others some wipes to clean off the rest of the face paint. After four pees, we throw a big bucket of water from the bathtub down the toilet.

We fill our bags with chips, chargers, and the last bottle of mineral water, and we head north.

We walk quickly to keep warm, puffing clouds of steam into the morning air. I don't tell the others how scared I am, but I don't have to. When one cog's stiff with nerves, the others feel it. I know I can't put it off any longer. I have to see my mom and dad today. They're here now, and anyway I've had enough. I don't want to hide anymore.

So, as soon as I have a signal, I arrange a meeting. By text message, of course. My mom and dad want to see me at the Frick Collection at one p.m. Nora Quinn clearly doesn't waste any time: By the end of the day she'll not only be able to check off her daughter, but also the most beautiful museum in the city.

"What now?" Abby asks me. "You don't need to be there until one . . ."

I don't have to think about it. "The bookstore. I need Wi-Fi."

The others nod.

Inside the warm bookstore, we plunk down in our own aisle. I start Googling right away, because I have to find out if there's anything online about a shrieking Emilia de Wit. When I look up, the others are staring at me. Abby knows all about my dad now too. After yesterday evening, I could hardly keep it a secret.

I find Bastiaan Breedveld's article straightaway. There's a link to Abby's photo on Twitter, and at first I can't look at anything else. A skeleton, a bright green witch, and a cat are all looking into the camera with great big confident grins.

And that superconfident cat is me.

The last time I saw an expression like that on my face was in my passport: I look like I'm *really excited* about the rest of my life. But the photo on Twitter isn't from four years ago—it's from yesterday evening. Fourteen hours ago, I looked like that.

"Is it a disaster?" asks Seth.

I finally stop staring at myself and start reading the article.

Okay, so I'm yelling on a sidewalk in New York. Bastiaan makes a big deal out of the passersby who stop to stare and the honking yellow cabs. There's plenty of cursing from me, and a few of the quotes aren't right. But for the first time in my life I'm not invisible anymore.

All my classmates and my teachers—and Juno—are going to read this. While they were at school, I was celebrating Halloween with my American friends. I have an opinion, I'm stamping my feet in the best city on Earth, and Bastiaan says my cat costume is "elegant."

"What did he write? What did he write?" Abby asks impatiently.

I hold up my cell phone and show them the photo. "That's how I want to be."

"Well, that's how you are," says Jim. "I'm sometimes a bit less green, but you always look like that, don't you?"

"Not all the time," says Seth. "But often enough."

I look down at my hand. All that's left of my nasty cut is a long, thin scab.

So my dad's going to have to read online what his daughter was yelling about him on the street yesterday. About him lusting after a seventeen-year-old. I have no idea what I'm going to say when I see him.

And then I sigh, because the solution is perfectly simple. I just have to yell at him, "Hello? What you did is way, way worse!" And I can scream that a hundred times, for a few years, until I'm eighteen and can leave home.

Thirty-six minutes later. Time is going way more slowly than usual. Abby and I are looking at a book of photographs of New York. She's doing her best to distract me, so I try to concentrate on the skyscrapers—but I can see my mom's and dad's faces floating in front of every picture. I can't think of anything else.

"Abby!" Seth comes back from the computer books with his cell phone in his hand. "Mom called. She finally managed to get a flight last night and she just landed. She's coming home."

"Really? Has she already picked up her luggage?"

He nods and Abby starts dancing wildly down the aisle, in and out and around the People of Darkness.

"Mom's coming home, Mom's coming home, Mom's coming home!"

Her dark braid swishes to and fro as if she's on a roller coaster; her pink boots make a massive din in the bookstore.

"Did you really miss her that much?" Seth asks.

"Duh!" she says. "Mom's never, ever been away for so long. And we had a hurricane! It was dark and cold and Emilia screamed and Jim's finger hurt and Mommy wasn't there."

Seth comes and sits next to me while Abby goes on dancing. We just watch her.

"We have to go," she cries excitedly, and tugs at Seth's sweater. "I want to be home when she gets there!"

"We can wait a bit longer, you know."

"But we have to walk all the way back!"

Seth sits there silently. I wonder if it's dawned on him as well. That our hurricane shelter is over now.

"I want to tell Mom . . ." Abby stops dancing. "No. I won't tell her Jim got us drunk or that Emilia wears gloves to eat and that she yelled at a journalist in the middle of the street."

Her brother still doesn't say anything.

"And I won't talk about Dad. I really won't. I know it's not allowed."

We look at Seth. For a long time, no one moves. And then I do, just a little bit. I'm sitting right beside him, so I can put half my index finger on top of half his index finger without anyone noticing. But he can feel it. I know he can.

It's a perfect bridge for bacteria, but that doesn't matter anymore. We're both as dirty as each other.

"You definitely don't need to tell her about Jim getting us drunk," Seth slowly says to Abby. "But you are allowed to talk about Dad. Not today—Mom's only just gotten home and there's been a hurricane and she needs to settle in. But after that, when it's light again, then it's allowed. Okay, Abby?"

She looks at him with a serious expression. "And what about him not being here anymore? Am I allowed to talk about that?"

Seth nods.

"And about me missing him? And that I'm really good at remembering things, but I've forgotten what kind of shoes he wore?"

I press his fingertip with mine. But I don't think Seth feels it, because he stands up.

"Come on, Abby," he says. "Let's go home."

38

Together with Jim, I walk along Fifth Avenue. I was too anxious to stay in the bookstore any longer, and Jim needs to go to the hospital again. I haven't looked at his hand too closely, but he says there's pus coming out of his finger. Or something that's making the bandage wet in any case. That can't be healthy.

My boots drag across the gray sidewalk. With every step, a little bit of Emilia remains behind in New York. If I just keep going, scraping away my soles and feet and legs and body and head, then I won't have to think anymore.

I keep trying to imagine what my mom and dad and I are going to say when we see one another. But I can't. It makes my head ache. I have a stomachache too, so perhaps I should just go with Jim to the hospital. If I have to choose between bacteria and parents, then right now I'll go for the bacteria.

The only thing that's not bothering me today is weak and wobbly knees. It's funny, but I can look at Jim now without getting that feeling. It's like I'm walking along with my fun, crazy cousin.

"This way," the crazy cousin suddenly says. He takes hold

of my sleeve and pulls me off to one side, up a wide flight of steps. "Maybe the Dutch atheist can still be saved."

It's a cathedral. An enormous neo-Gothic building that seems to have come straight from Disney World, but goes almost unnoticed among the skyscrapers. Jim wanders inside as if he's here to visit a good friend, but I stand there awkwardly. High above my head, arches reach up toward the heavens. The warm air smells of burning candles and dust.

Slowly, I start walking forward, still thinking about my mom and dad. My super-rational parents who never set foot inside a church—except on vacation, because then visiting a house of God is all part of the itinerary.

I look at the stained-glass windows and the organ, but then I forget the building and I can only look at people. The silhouettes I see sitting in the pews in the semidarkness are clearly not tourists. They're New Yorkers.

They're people who have just lived through a hurricane.

I slip quietly onto a smooth pew. I see people kneeling and praying. And I see people crying. Real, grown-up people who have come here to cry. God only knows what they've lost over the past few days.

I look at them, and for the first time in my atheist life I can imagine what a church can mean to people. Particularly in the past, when the whole world looked like our dark New York does now. In a world like that you'd need a place where the candles are lit. Where it's warm and where you can cry while the arches listen to you.

I get up and walk slowly to Jim, who's standing by the racks of candles. I take some money from my bag and light one. You're probably not supposed to light a candle for yourself, so

I look at the flame and decide that it's for my mom. And for the victims of the hurricane. For Obama, who's up for reelection next week. And of course for Seth and Jim and Abby. And then I take more money from my bag and light another two candles, because I can't imagine that God would want to help so many people for just one puny little flame.

Beside me I hear Jim sigh as if all is lost. "What am I doing here?"

"In church?" I whisper. "You know that better than I do."

"In New York! I can't work. I don't have any money to pay the rent, and I don't even want to think about the hospital bills."

"Do you really not have a plan?" I ask quietly.

He looks at the sea of flames. "No."

"Abby does. She's planning to marry you. She's going to make tons of money as a surgeon and then you can lie on the couch all day long, talking about the economic crisis."

He turns around and we leave the church together.

"Did she really say that?" he asks. He looks at the dark clouds. "Fucking hell."

"Don't you want to marry her?" I ask casually, but he's more serious than I've ever seen him before.

"That's exactly what my dad does all day long! He lies on the couch and talks about the crisis." He looks at me. "Seth and Abby are pretty annoying, huh? They're so well behaved and they work so hard and have all those big plans they're always coming up with . . ."

I think a moment. "I have no idea what I want to do when I'm older. I don't even know what I want to do next week . . ."

We walk past window displays full of diamonds, watches, and expensive candy.

"And do you know what's most annoying of all?" says Jim. "That it's actually pretty cool that Abby knows, even at the age of eleven, that she wants to be a surgeon when she grows up. And that Seth is going to be some head guy at Google or Apple."

"Really?" I say. "You think that's cool? You're way cooler. Neither of them has a leather jacket, their shoelaces are always perfectly tied, and their fingers are all intact. And you still think they're cool?"

He stops at the corner with the glass cube. On the other side of the street, a line of horse-drawn carriages is waiting. For tourists who want to pretend they're in a movie.

"Seriously?" he asks. "That's all there is to me? My leather jacket and my loose shoelaces?"

"That's not what I meant!"

"I know that," he says with a smile. And then he sighs. "It's true. I'm not capable of tying my shoes. I hope one day God will give me the strength to accept that . . ."

"The Lord giveth and the Lord taketh away, isn't that what they say?"

He nods. "God takes fingers and He gives pus." He looks at the bandage. "I really need to go to the hospital now, or they'll want to amputate my whole hand. Am I going to see you this evening, or are you staying with those supercool parents of yours?"

My stomachache instantly gets worse. "No idea. Maybe they've brought in five police officers and they're going to drag me off to the airport. But if they haven't, I'll come back to the hurricane shelter."

"Good. Well, say hi to your mom from me. And tell your dad he's a jerk. He should have kept his mouth shut to Juno and just screwed her."

"Jim!"

He grins. "I know. I'm a crass loser." As he starts walking, he holds up his hand to wave. "Good luck, Emilia! I'll pray for you."

39

What was I actually planning to do? I ask myself as I walk past Central Park to the museum. Last week, all I wanted to do was run away, that much is clear. I wanted to escape from the swamp, and it worked. And then Sandy came along and I could stop thinking.

But what had I intended to do, here in New York? Did I think I could go on renting an apartment here on my own forever? Had I really thought my parents would just forget about me? Of course not. But I don't know what I *was* thinking either.

I know what I'm thinking now, though.

It was crazy to come here. I should have just stayed in the Netherlands. Then I could have ignored my dad for months before starting—maybe, just maybe—to speak the occasional sentence to him. Beginning with "It's cold today," and moving on to "Is there any apple juice left?" and ending with "I passed my final school exams. Bye."

But now, because I ran away, there's going to be a Conversation. Which is an absolute disaster, because we never have Conversations. We just don't do it. When my dad becomes school principal or my mom sells a painting to the sheikha of

Qatar for a crazy price, then we nod at each other. And when my mom cuts a canvas to pieces or I start to hyperventilate, then we sigh briefly. But we never Talk.

Until today, that is.

I can see the museum already. It's not time yet, but I head inside. I'm more nervous than I was at Immigration. They had no idea who I was. But the people I'm going to see now, they *do* know me. The people I'm going to see now think they know me better than anyone else in the world. And I have to tell them they've got it wrong.

The Frick Collection isn't a big museum. It's an impressive building, but in 1915 it was simply a house that belonged to one pretty wealthy gentleman. And you can still see that it was once a home. You don't walk around bare galleries, but through the dining room and the sitting room and through Mr. Frick's study. And it just so happens that there are world-famous paintings on the walls.

I wander around the rooms without seeing anything. My feet sink into the thick carpet, but I hardly notice. I am Emilia. A scared little girl. A sexy cat. I sleep next to Jim, next to Abby, I am the daughter of a sleazy school principal, I am a girl who stands on the sidewalk, swearing at the top of her voice, and exploding with the light of a billion suns—I don't know who I am anymore.

And then I'm in the courtyard and I see my mom sitting on a marble bench by the pool.

She's alone. She's wearing the green dress I like so much, and her red hair is in a complicated bun. She looks up and sees me standing there.

"Darling!"

As I walk over to her, her gray-green eyes watch me. We don't hug. Suddenly, I feel again how incredibly filthy I am. Thanks to my seven packages of antibacterial wipes, I'm still way cleaner than Seth and Jim and Abby. But compared to Nora Quinn, I'm a prehistoric gunkmonster.

"You've dyed your hair!" she cries.

"It's greasy." I don't touch it with my hands. "I haven't washed it since Monday morning."

She looks at me as if she's studying a painting. For a long time, with a frown on her face. And then she nods. "That color suits you." She glances around. "Have you had a look at the museum already? I got here early, because I wanted to take my time. Did you see the Holbeins? And the miniatures from Limoges? Breathtaking!"

"Where's Dad?"

She sighs. "He's in bed with a migraine. He's hardly slept for the past week, and he finally collapsed a couple of hours ago. I closed the curtains and left him there."

I take a step back. "Hey, don't expect me to feel sorry for him."

"There's no need."

Light falls in through the glass ceiling. The fountain splashes.

"I don't get it," I say. "Why aren't you furious with him? Why don't you want to leave him?"

She frowns. "Have you really managed to acquire an American accent within a week?"

"Maybe." I put my chin in the air, Abby-style. "I have American friends here and we do everything together. The four of us are sharing an apartment and yesterday we celebrated

Halloween at a Thai restaurant. And we all wore costumes. Including me."

She studies me again for a while, and then she starts to laugh. "Do you know something? I think it was a good idea of yours to go to New York."

"So do I! But Dad . . ."

"Darling, we're in the most beautiful museum in the world! Shall we talk tomorrow about how terrible it all is and how badly your father has behaved? Right now I'd like to show you a Vermeer."

Her fingers are moving as if she's holding a paintbrush. Impatiently. With determination and longing. I'm no match for her.

No, I'm not feeling sorry for myself. I don't want to be a match for her. I just wish I were a little more like her. That I had a talent that everything else had to give way to. Then I wouldn't have any more doubts. Then I'd know who I was.

I don't say anything else, but let her lead me around the galleries.

For days I've thought about nothing but my most basic needs. My stomach and my phone had to be fed—that was my life. And now it's my soul's turn. I forget *Out and About with a Plug* and let the fiery colors, the wonderful pictures, and ancient stories wash over me. I remember that there's more to life than popcorn, disinfectant wipes, and power.

I listen to her in absolute silence, because it doesn't often happen that my mom gives me her undivided attention. Usually, there are at least two museum directors and three reviewers running around her. But this time she's telling her story just to me. And when Nora Quinn talks about a painting, you understand it. You *feel* it.

"Can you imagine?" she cries excitedly. "Frick had this particular gallery built specially for his paintings. In the evening, when he was finished with his work, he'd walk on his own around the masterpieces. As dusk fell outside, he'd quietly look at Rembrandt and Vermeer."

"Jim needs to hear about this," I say. "He thinks people nowadays are rich. But this Frick guy could just create his own museum."

My mom sighs. "Imagine what it must be like to live in New York. To be able to come here every week."

"To have a burrito at Dos Toros every week," I say. "To know the fairy-tale tower with its silver scales like the back of your own hand. To have a picnic with a view of the Statue of Liberty. To live in Seth and Jim and Abby's city."

"To be able to walk over to the Guggenheim before you start work . . ." She beams. Her silk dress swishes.

I look at her, and I know this is how I want things to be. If anyone should be furious about what my dad's done and someone should keep smiling, then this is the right way around. Me furious, and my mom smiling.

The other way around would be unbearable.

40

I am sitting on my own in a taxi on the way into the darkness. At the end of the afternoon, my mom wanted me to go with her to the place where they were staying, but I said I couldn't. I had to go back to the place where *I* was staying.

She looked at me for a long time. I tensed all my muscles to run away if she tried to grab me. But Nora Quinn doesn't grab ahold of people. And fortunately, she hadn't thought of bringing along five police officers to drag me off to the airport.

Finally, she nodded, like a queen who was not amused.

"Fine," she said in a chilly tone. "You can stay there one more night. And then you can stop acting up and come back to me and your father."

I didn't promise anything.

I pay the driver with money that the unamused queen gave me, and he leaves me behind in the night. For the first time, it's a bit less dark, because the sky is clear. The moon is shining. I can see stars in the middle of New York.

I put down the plastic bag with the mineral water in it and rub my hands. Now I have to wait. It was a risk returning to the hurricane shelter, because I don't know for certain that I'll get in. Seth and Abby were in such a hurry to get home this morning that we didn't agree what was going to happen this evening.

I hope they remember the arrangement we had on Tuesday: Open the front door every fifteen minutes after dark. But maybe they're not even home. Maybe they're eating out with their mom or staying somewhere else. I sit down on the sidewalk and put my hands in the pockets of the moss-green coat. Half an hour, I tell myself. I can wait for half an hour. If no one's come downstairs by then, I have to find a cab and go to my mom and dad. Then it really is all over.

I watch the time pass on my cell phone. And then, after thirteen minutes, the front door opens.

"Seth!"

He's standing in the doorway with a flashlight. I get up and take a step forward.

We don't fall into each other's arms, but it feels awkward all the same.

"We didn't arrange anything!" I cry. "I was sitting here in front of a closed door and I was wondering if I should give up and . . ." I'm a bit out of breath. "But of course your mom's home now and maybe she doesn't want me to . . ."

He shakes his head. "She went to stay with Bridget uptown. She wanted us all to go, but Abby had a fit. She insisted on staying with you and Jim, and she got so hysterical that Mom eventually gave in."

"So the hurricane shelter is still in business?"

He laughs. "Yeah. We're still open."

As I follow him up the stairs, almost stumbling when I hear something mousy dashing about, which might in fact be a mouse, I feel as if I'm someone who matters. As if people who hear about my life would be happy to swap with me. This afternoon, I was walking around the most beautiful museum in New York with Nora Quinn. Then we got a pastrami sandwich at a diner. And now I'm back home with my friends.

"Emilia!" Abby waves enthusiastically at me from the couch. "We've been waiting forever—I was so scared you'd never come back . . ."

Jim grins. "I gave up on you long ago, but Seth kept dashing downstairs in the dark to see if you were there. Without him you'd have been standing outside all night, that's for sure."

I glance at Seth and then down at the floor. Without Seth I'd have been standing outside all week.

Jim and Abby are sitting close together under a blanket. Seventeen tea lights are lit around them, and the radio is on. It looks nice and Christmassy, but it's desperately cold in the apartment, and it smells like baked-on chili con carne.

"Was your dad still being dumb?" asks Abby. "Was he sending text messages all the time you were trying to talk to him?"

"I only saw my mom. But that was okay." I remember us sitting together in the gleaming diner. As if we were just a couple of hungry people.

"If you wrap yourself in plastic from head to toe," says Jim, "you can come under the blanket with us."

"Plastic?"

"Duh," says Abby. "Bacteria!" I drop down onto the couch beside her. I don't need to keep my millions of bacteria inside the plastic with me. Let the little critters hop onto the others instead.

"And what about me?" asks Seth. "I was sitting there!"

I slide closer to Abby. "Go on, then. Sit down." I point at the corner. "There's enough space for you."

He hesitates.

"Who has hygiene issues now? You can come sit next to me, can't you?"

Abby sighs. "It's not bacteria he's scared of. It's girls!"

"Very wise," says Jim.

Without looking at me, Seth sits down beside me. He only just fits. We pull the blanket to our chins and Seth turns up the radio.

First we listen to the news. As the four of us sit there snugly on the couch, we hear about looting in neighborhoods without power, fights for gasoline, and people having to stand in line for hours to get food.

We listen in silence to the story about a mother who tried to run from the hurricane with her sons on Monday evening. When her car got stuck in the mud, she decided to continue on foot, carrying her younger son and holding the other by the hand. But an ice-cold tidal wave snatched both children from her arms, and the current swept the boys away. The mother spent all night looking for her children, but she never found them.

The police finally located their bodies this morning.

Abby holds my hand tight under the blanket. Her fingers are cold.

On the other side, I can feel Seth's shoulder against mine. His thigh against mine. Hey, just imagine, I think. If I'd sat down next to Jim, I'd be touching a movie star. All my friends would have been seriously jealous.

But then I realize something strange. Something that makes me a little short of breath.

I wouldn't rather be sitting beside Jim. Even if I'd been able to choose, I'd have sat here. Next to Seth.

We don't move. We just listen.

The guy on the radio asks what kind of music has gotten us through the past few days. He wants to hear which songs we'd like him to play on this cold, dark evening, and people start calling in. They tell their stories, and I feel the same thing I felt by that white camping table with the power strips. A sense of connection with people I've never met. We don't know one another, but we've been through the same experience.

As soon as the callers say which part of the city they're in, we know: He's in the dark too. She's cold as well. They've been busy wandering the city and surviving for the past few days, just like us.

A girl of fifteen calls from SoHo—that's our neighborhood. She says she's wrapped up in blankets with her parents and her bulldog on the big bed, and that she wants the DJ to play Bob Marley's "Three Little Birds." We listen to the song cheerfully telling us that *every little thing gonna be all right*. I want to believe it.

"I don't get it," whispers Abby. "How can those people be calling from the darkness?"

"On a landline," says Seth. "They're still working."

"That's strange, isn't it? When there's a hurricane, we need candles, a radio, and a landline. People from the Middle Ages were better at surviving than us!"

The next caller is from the West Village. We nod sympathetically. Yes, it's dark there too. A man with a quiet voice says that his wife is eight months pregnant and over the past few weeks she's been playing Tchaikovsky's "Autumn Song" to the baby, so the baby would recognize something when it came out of her tummy.

On Monday evening, as Sandy raged, they were playing "Autumn Song" to their unborn child when the power failed. The baby hasn't heard any music at all for three days now, so the man hopes the radio station will play the piece for them.

Of course the radio station will.

"It's so weird," I whisper, "that this is really happening now, right at this moment. A kilometer away, that man and his wife are listening in the dark. With candles and with blankets around their shoulders."

"I wish it was always like this," Abby says quietly. "That we all did the same thing at the same time."

"Try going shopping on a Saturday," says Jim.

Bright piano music fills the dark room. I feel the warmth of Seth's arm and let the notes wash over me. I've never listened so closely to classical music before. Sometimes my mom plays Mozart while she's painting, but I like words, and I miss them when they're not there.

This time, though, I make up the words myself. I listen to "Autumn Song" and hear the story of that man with the quiet voice and his wife with her big belly. I hear candles burning in the darkness, I hear people crying in the church, I hear the calm after the storm, I hear my mom looking at Vermeer, I hear my dad lying in a darkened room waiting for the pain to go. I hear the bacteria gently swaying to the music, and I imagine them holding tiny little cell phones in the air with their tiny little bacteria arms.

If only I had a tiny phone, I'd join in.

Or maybe not. Because then I'd have to move my arm and I wouldn't feel Seth's warmth anymore.

41

On Friday morning I wake up shivering. It's as cold inside the apartment as it is outside. The bathroom stinks, the water in the bathtub is almost gone, there are crumbs everywhere, and the stove is covered with splashes. It's a miracle we're still alive. We don't even have colds.

Seth searches through all the kitchen cabinets and discovers a baking dish that still seems fairly clean. We pour two cans of soup into it and put the dish on the stove. I hold my hands to the heat as Seth stirs the soup. Since yesterday evening, I haven't dared to look at him.

"I have a kind of . . . announcement to make," Jim says.

He stinks the worst of all of us, partly because he's been wearing the same clothes for four days. All his clothes were dirty when Sandy hit, and the Laundromat has obviously been closed ever since.

"It's pretty lame and sad, I know. But I've made up my mind." He takes a deep breath. "I'm going back to Detroit."

"For the weekend?" asks Abby.

"Forever."

We just stare at him.

"I mean . . ." He puts a spoonful of peanut butter into his mouth. "There's no way I'm staying there for the rest of my life. But it's going to be months before I can work again, with this hand, and I have ten dollars in my account." He shrugs. "So I'm going back to my mom and dad. And back to school. Because that's something I *can* do with eight fingers. It's extremely boring, I know. And embarrassing."

"Seriously?" asks Seth. "You're going back to school?"

"Ridiculous, huh?" Jim sighs. "But adults think a diploma means everything. And now I finally get how it works. You have to follow their rules for a while to start with. Live with their killer robots and atom bombs and the wheel. And then, when you've been good and gotten an education, when they think you've been deactivated, you strike. And then you can change the world."

"But we don't want the world to change!" Abby cries desperately. "Everything should stay just as it is." She takes hold of Jim's arm as if she's planning never to let him go.

I go sit at the counter and don't say anything.

Jim looks at me. "Aren't you proud of me? Don't you think I've become admirably wise and mature?"

"If you want to be all boring and good, then go ahead," I snap.

He raises his eyebrows. "You asked me yesterday if I had a plan."

"But that was so I could hear that you didn't have one! We were the people without plans—remember? But then you suddenly decided to be all sensible!" I can feel something trembling in my stomach. "In two hours, I'll be seeing my dad again. So what do you want? For me to be all grown-up too? For me to forgive him and for all of us to go back to the Netherlands as a happy little family?"

"That's different," he says calmly.

The soup comes to a boil. As Seth fills four mugs, everyone is quiet. The first spoonful burns my tongue.

"My dad," says Jim, "is a loser who drinks too much and my mom is a sweetheart who cheats on him with God. But they've never done anything to hurt me. Not like your dad with his text messages, I mean. You have every right to be mad. I don't." He sighs. "And I'm two years older than you. It's about time I tied my shoelaces."

"But they're cool!" says Abby. She kicks my chair. "And people who leave are dumb."

"Megadumb," I say.

She looks at me angrily. "What are you going to say to your dad? When you see the weirdo, what are you going to say? Do you know already?"

I shake my head.

"You don't have a plan?" asks Seth.

"Of course not! What do you think?" I put down my spoon and hold out my empty hands. "You guys can come up with one. You know what he did. Make a plan for me. What should I say to him?"

I would never ask my friends in the Netherlands anything like that. God, those girls seem so far away right now. Since Bastiaan's article was in the paper, they've known I'm in New York. They've sent me messages full of exclamation points and little yellow faces, but I haven't even answered.

Now that I'm on the other side of the ocean, I can see how dumb it really is. The way you end up in a class with thirty other kids and you have to put up with them. Those thirty kids are your life. If you're lucky, some of them will be your best friends. But if you're unlucky, you'll be in a classroom full of vague acquaintances for years. Acquaintances you really don't want to ask for advice about how to live your life.

Jim takes another spoonful of peanut butter. Seth wrinkles his forehead, and Abby licks her mug empty as far as her tongue will reach.

"I know," she says. "You have to pay attention to what kind of shoes he's wearing. So that you remember forever. And even if you have a good memory, you need to write it down. To be on the safe side."

"Okay," I say. "I'll pay attention." I mean it.

"Tell him he's an asshole," says Jim. "Tell him he had no right to do something like that to you and your mom. Tell him to keep his paws off his students and yell at him like you did with that journalist. Show him you're not a scared little girl anymore."

I clear my throat and nod. And then I look at Seth.

"Just ask him," he says. "Why he did it. Ask him if it was a zero or a one. Or something in between."

42

For the first time since Sandy, the sun's shining. It's icy cold and bright, and New York looks stunning. Even the streets without power are boldly gleaming away.

I don't know if it's the sun, but suddenly there are more people out and about. In front of a dark soup shop there's a wooden table with big pans and happy people. "Free chili!" they call. "Take a croissant or a doughnut too—all free!"

On the next block, a café has put out all the stock that was in the freezer. They're giving away fruit and chocolate cakes and sandwiches. I don't take anything, of course, because I understand perfectly well what's going on. These restaurants held on to their food for as long as they possibly could. Even if the lights and the refrigeration come back on now, they can't sell those cakes to customers. And so they're letting us have it for free.

The others grin and gobble down chocolate cake as I study the cast-iron facades. I feast my eyes on the pillars and the rusty fire escapes, and suddenly I think: What if I became an architect? You have to be good at math and physics, but you're secretly an artist too. You don't just provide someone with a roof over their head, you also create something for their soul.

Well, at least for the souls that need that kind of thing. Some souls aren't interested in buildings and would rather stuff three stale cakes into their mouths, one after another.

When we start walking again, Jim is still looking anxiously at his phone to see if there's a signal yet. Now that he's decided to go back to Detroit, he wants to tell his parents as soon as possible. So that he can't change his mind.

I look at the boy with the bandaged hand and the model's face that he doesn't want to use for modeling. I think his plan is brave, but also dangerous. What if you take off your leather jacket and tie your laces and suddenly you're just like everyone else? What if you discover that you can make lots of money by working with killer robots and iffy mortgages? And so you just go on doing that, without changing the world?

Isn't that basically what happened to all adults? They just surrendered and joined in.

"You guys go ahead," says Jim when our cell phones start beeping. "I'm going to call my mom and dad." He sighs. "Hey, how about we abolish parents too, when we're older?"

"No," says Abby fiercely. "Parents will definitely not be abolished."

Jim grins. "Maybe Obama can at least order that they're only allowed to be on for three hours a day. Even that would make a big difference." He looks at me. "Don't just fly back home to the Netherlands, okay? I want to know how it all turns out. You have to tell me before you go home. Promise?"

I nod, clear my throat, and then just nod again.

As I walk on with Seth and Abby, I look back only once. Jim raises his bandaged hand in a wave. "Good luck, Emilia. If you can survive a hurricane, you can face anything!"

We have another twelve streets to go before we reach the happy park I saw from the bus on my first day. I told my mom yesterday that's where I want to meet my dad.

It was ridiculous. It felt like I was meeting up with some kind of criminal. I instinctively wanted to meet outside. Somewhere with a lot of people, somewhere I can escape if I have to.

"Do you want to walk the last bit on your own?" asks Seth.

I shake my head. I don't want any more time to think.

We cross Thirty-Eighth Street. Walk the entire length of the block without saying anything. Then across Thirty-Ninth Street. Shouting people, crowded souvenir stores, steamy kebab carts.

And then we reach Fortieth Street. The park's on the other side of the street. Yellow trees, glass stalls for the Christmas market.

Seth hesitates, and suddenly I don't care anymore. He's probably thinking about the websites he's going to build as soon as the power outage is over, and I'm sure he'd lose interest in me if he knew me for any longer than a week, but it still hasn't been a week yet. And I need him. I take hold of his hand.

"You guys have to come all the way to the park with me." I don't look at him. "Please?"

The three of us cross the street together, in a line. Seth's hand isn't sticky. It's warm and dry, and I don't know if I've ever been so aware of feeling a hand. Until now I've only ever felt the bacteria.

The ice rink isn't working, almost certainly because of Sandy. But the glass houses selling Christmas stuff are open. We walk past herbal soaps and dancing Santas and socks with dogs on them. The paths are busy, but I hold on to Seth's and Abby's hands. One member of our boy band happens to be missing right now, but people can still see we belong together. They step aside for us.

In the middle of the park there are green tables and folding chairs beside an empty fountain. And that's where they're sitting.

My mom looks completely at ease, as if she's on some desert island. Her red hair is blowing in the wind and she's wearing a beautiful black coat with a collar that's a work of art in its own right.

My dad's sitting next to her. I hardly recognize him because he looks exactly the same as all those times we cycled along the river and gazed at the stars from our roof. In my mind I'd made him look much more like a criminal, some sleazy porn producer with claws and drool.

There are lots of things you can say about my dad, but not that he looks like a porn producer.

He's wearing one of his seven pairs of corduroy pants. His hair is thinning on top, and he looks like a guy who goes birdwatching on the weekend. He's nervous. I can see that even from a distance.

They've spotted me now too. They're looking at me as if I'm not only their daughter, but also someone else. Someone they don't know, but someone who matters. Their boss's boss. A doctor who's going to tell them if there's any chance of recovery. I squeeze two hands. Two hands squeeze back.

We walk to the fountain and stand there in front of the green table. I watch my dad looking at my dark hair and then at my hands. He hasn't seen me touch anyone for the past three years. All around us, the tourists are laughing and yelling. Four of us have no idea what to do next, but luckily Abby's there.

"I'm Abby Greenberg," she says solemnly. She looks at my mom. "And you're Nora Quinn. I memorized your name in case Emilia collapsed and was unconscious." And then she looks at my dad. "Emilia told me what you did. I'm glad to see you're wearing nice shoes. But I'm still really mad at you."

"Let's leave," whispers Seth.

Abby goes on looking at my dad. "Your daughter has plans for you. But first I have one thing to say: Emilia is awesome. And she's my friend."

I have no idea why she feels the need to say that, but it sounds fantastic. Like she's a mafia don threatening that if anything at all happens to Emilia, he'll chop whoever's responsible into tiny little pieces and throw them in the East River.

"Emilia is almost my sister. On Wednesday night we ate from the same bowls, even though there are more bacteria living in your mouth than there are people on this planet. Are you going to remember that?"

My dad nods.

"Okay," says Abby. "Good luck."

I feel the two hands disappear. Seth nods at me, almost imperceptibly, and then brother and sister walk away between the Christmas stalls. I can see them for another eight seconds and then New York swallows them up.

I'm alone with my parents.

43

Now we're free to give one another long, meaningful looks and experience all our emotions. But I'm not in the mood.

"Did you see the article?" I ask my dad. I speak to him in Dutch, because that's our language. My mom leans back. She understands what I'm saying, but she doesn't feel that I'm talking to her now.

"That article by Bastiaan Breedveld," I say. "About me being dressed as a cat and yelling on the sidewalk."

"I read it yesterday evening."

Even his voice is still the same. He sounds like a bird-watcher, not like a porn producer. An old, tired bird-watcher who hasn't spotted any new birds for a long time. The only new one he saw cost him almost everything.

"Okay," I say. "Then think about that article. Remember all the things I yelled when I was standing there on the sidewalk, and imagine I just said them to you now. That'll save me half an hour of screaming. But everything I said is true. That really is what I think."

I can see he's doing exactly as I say. With mathematical precision, he's running through everything I said in that piece.

"You saw the photo too?" I ask. "From Abby's Twitter account? There was a link." He nods.

"That's what I look like when you two aren't around." The billion suns are smoldering away in my chest. The three of us are sitting together on that desert island. I don't see the Christmas market anymore.

My dad clears his throat. "In that article, you suggest some terrible things." He leans over to me. "Surely you don't think that I . . ."

"I have no idea! I don't know what you got up to with . . ." I can't even say her name. ". . . what you got up to with her."

He looks at me with an expression that I don't recognize.

"Do you really think I touched her?" he asks. "My student? A girl of seventeen? I never laid a finger on her!"

"But on the Internet . . ."

"On the Internet, people rant and rave without knowing what they're talking about! I wanted to tell you my side of the story, but you wouldn't listen. And then you just left . . ."

"Fine!" I snap. "So you didn't touch her. But you did send her sixty-seven extremely embarrassing text messages. And you told her all about Mom and me. It's like someone read my diary to the whole world. Suddenly, everyone knows all about us. No, not everything—only the bad stuff. Everything that's wrong. And it's going to be on the Internet forever now."

His hands are shaking. "I made some terrible mistakes," he whispers. "I know I can't make it up to you. It's unforgivable. I really don't know how I ever . . ."

I look at him and I think: So this is my dad.

"Stop feeling sorry for yourself," I say. "I have one question for you. Why did you do it?"

He sweeps his thin hair to one side. I know the brain beneath that hair better than any other brain in the world. For me, my dad was what a mother is for most other children. My mom's changed maybe five diapers in her life. He did everything else. He put me to bed, took me to school, to art lessons.

"But you're only fifteen . . ." He shakes his head. "I can't. I really can't. These aren't things you can talk to your daughter about."

"Grow up," I say. "I just survived a hurricane without the two of you. People have died, and I haven't showered since Monday morning. I'm old enough to hear it. So why don't you explain?"

"What I did to the two of you . . . It's terrible . . ."

"We're well aware of that!"

My mom doesn't say anything. She just sits watching her husband and her daughter.

"Let's say it's a mathematical problem," I say. "And I don't get it. So help me understand. What kind of equation was it? What was the value of *x*? What was *y*?"

He looks at the skyscrapers around us. The park is a small green rectangle surrounded by huge, magnificent buildings. An enormous tower of reflective glass, a dark brown building with golden trim, the angular Empire State Building in the distance.

"I had . . . a kind of crush on her," he says. "Like with a movie star. For no good reason, but it was overwhelming. I thought she was stunning. I couldn't take my eyes off her."

I think about Jim. How perfectly his blond hair falls over his sculpted forehead. How handsome I thought he was before I knew him—when he was still a movie star and not just Jim.

"I knew I had to get a grip on myself," says my dad, "that I simply had to wait for the feeling to subside. Irrational notions like that soon pass. But then she needed extra help in math, and suddenly we were spending time together. We had conversations. She listened to me. I thought she was genuinely interested. And for the first time in a long while I felt a little less lonely . . ."

My mom still hasn't moved. She's looking at the tops of the trees.

"So what are you trying to say?" I ask my dad. "That this was our fault?"

"No! Of course not. Absolutely not." He hesitates. "But sometimes it wasn't easy, you know that. Our family is . . ." He looks at my mom, and then at the ground.

"What do you mean?" I ask angrily. "You know how our life works. I wasn't even there when the agreement was made and I know. I keep to it, don't I? It's not that difficult, is it?"

"What agreement?" he asks in confusion.

"The one about our life! For Mom, it's her paintings that take first place. And for us, Mom comes in first place. If you make an agreement like that, you can't start complaining later that you're lonely!"

My mom's gray-green eyes suddenly refocus on the scene around her. She looks at me. "Darling! What on earth are you talking about?"

"I don't mind," I say. "I get it. Your paintings come first. Not many people have your kind of talent. I want you to paint, and so does Dad. We're proud of you. I just think it's stupid of Dad to start complaining about being so lonely. And to say that he's fucking floating on his own among the stars."

She sighs. "We're all floating on our own among the stars. You have to accept that. And if, during the course of your life, you find a few people who float alongside you, somewhere within hearing distance, then you should be happy." She smiles at me. "For me, that's the two of you, Emilia. Without you two, I could never paint. You come first and then the paintings."

I look at her and I love her. I know it's not true. Without us, she'd slowly get back on her feet and make fantastic art. Without painting, she'd just stay in bed.

I look at my dad. "Idiot."

"You're right. He is an idiot," says my mom. "No doubt about it. But everyone makes mistakes. Sometimes big ones. And of all the people I know, he's still the one who's made the fewest." She stands up. "Now, shall we just enjoy New York? I'm finally on the other side of the ocean again after twenty years. I want to see the city!"

I'm not surprised. Sometimes she plays dirty—she always has, ever since I was born. She takes advantage of being a temperamental artist. Her talent is her get-out-of-jail-free card, and she plays it whenever it suits her.

"Sit down," I say. "We're not done yet."

I wait until she sulkily sits back down.

"What do the two of you think? That we can just shrug our shoulders and say, 'Oh, it is what it is. People make mistakes, let that be the lesson for today.' Jesus, this isn't school! This isn't a 'learning experience.' "

My mom shrugs and the work-of-art collar goes up and down. "If you don't want to learn this time, there'll be other opportunities."

"But this isn't just a little mistake!" I shout. "This is our entire life that's been destroyed. People on the Internet wish we were dead. Dad's lost his job and no one's ever going to give him another one. And I'll be damned if I'm going back to that school!"

"I know I've done an incredible amount of damage," says my dad. "But what do you want from me, Emilia?"

"I want to stay here."

"You know that's not realistic." He sounds almost fawningly polite. "Sweetheart, you're fifteen. You can't live here on your own, and you know how attached your mom is to our house and her studio and . . ."

"There's nothing I'd like more," says Nora Quinn calmly.

"What?" he says.

"I'd love to live in New York. If Emilia's happy here and . . . And just imagine! Then I could go to the Frick every week."

44

We let my mom play her get-out-of-jail-free card. We gave her some time off. She doesn't have to take part in the Conversation anymore and she can explore the city.

I walk with my dad to Grand Central, because he asked for a tour. Seriously, he wants to see the route I'm going to describe in *Out and About with a Plug*. He wants to hear all about the hurricane and about how I've spent the past week.

If I didn't know better, I'd think he was playing dirty too. That he's hoping I'll start to like him again if he acts interested enough. But I know him too well for that. He's not faking it. He really does want to know everything. He wants to hear all about Seth and Jim and Abby, and he wants to see the power outlets.

So I walk with him along the cold and drafty corridor beside the platforms. Together we stand looking at that one power outlet low down on the wall. I stare at it until everything turns hazy.

You can't compare people's misery. But if you look down at the earth from space, then Hurricane Sandy made more of an impact than my dad's sixty-seven text messages. I know that. And while I'm telling him about the wrecked houses and the mom with the sons who drowned, I can even feel it a bit. While I was in the dark, the swamp has gotten a little smaller. It's still there, but there are new parts to it now. Hard rocks. Grassy earth that doesn't stink, where the ground feels firm beneath your feet.

I know that'll change if we go back to the Netherlands. The Netherlands is still one big swamp. They'll look at me, whisper about me, point at me. Even if we move to another town. Even if I go to another school.

What the truth is, what really happened, if he really touched Juno, none of that matters to them. Only the stories count. And they'll be on the Internet forever.

"Do you see that building?" I point at the tower with its silver scales and eagles. "Imagine living in the same city as that skyscraper . . ."

My dad shakes his head. He doesn't want to hear anything about living in New York. He refuses to talk about it. But he has to.

"If we move here," I say, "it'll solve all our problems."

"It's not possible," he says immediately.

"Yes, it is! This is one of those mathematical models that solves everything in one elegant swoop. If one part isn't right, the whole model is invalid. And you have to discard it. But this is completely right. It's watertight."

"Real life doesn't work like that."

I stop by the stone lions in front of the library. They look very regal in the sun.

"If you want to leave us," I say, "then you should do that. Mom and I will move to New York, just the two of us. We're not holding you prisoner. You shouldn't think that you're tied down. In fact, you're absolutely free."

I manage to stay calm only by yelling "Loser!" inside my head as I'm looking at him. *Loser who feels that he's trapped. Big baby who's crying because he's floating through the universe all alone.*

He looks very serious. "I've thought through all the possibilities over the past few days. I don't want to leave you. Not at all. Not in the slightest. If I was convinced it'd be better for you if I went—after everything that's happened, I mean—then I'd do it. But I don't actually think you and Nora could . . ." He clears his throat. "Is that what you want? Just you and your mom?"

I remember the colorful toy bandages I used to make from strips of sliced-up paintings, and I shake my head.

My dad takes a deep breath. He looks at the white lion beside him and pats its stone fur.

"In the Netherlands," I say, "they'll never forget who we are. And New York is the greatest city on Earth. You could look for a job here, I could go to a school where no one knows me, and Mom could visit a different museum every day."

A bride and groom are having their photograph taken on the sweeping steps in front of the library. They look happy in the sunshine.

"You have no idea how complicated it would be," says my dad. "America isn't a country you can just decide to move to. You need a green card, and it's really expensive to live in New York, and . . ."

“You’re ruining everything! Again!” I yell. I go and stand in front of him. “Imagine there’s something you could do to put things right between us—after what you did with Juno. All those dumb text messages and calling her the brightest star in the heavens when you always said that was me.”

He winces. “Emilia . . .”

I don’t give him a chance to act all sorry for himself again. “Imagine there was something you could do. Would you be prepared to do it?”

The lines running across his forehead like a graph are deeper than I’ve ever seen them before. He’s an exhausted bird-watcher. One who might be happiest to lie down forever in a silent dip in the dunes.

“You know I’d do anything within my power,” he says wearily.

“Promise me this, then,” I say. “Promise that we’ll find out if it’s possible. Promise me we’ll try.”

He nods.

I look at him and hope I never fall in love with the wrong person. I hope I’ll never, ever make a mistake that destroys other people’s lives. Because when you destroy other people’s lives, you want to go lie in a dip in the dunes and become invisible. And that’s something I really, really don’t want to do.

I want to be in New York. I want to live.

45

For the last time, I walk on my own back to the darkness. I don't know how long I can continue to play the my-dad-behaved-really-badly-so-now-I-can-do-whatever-I-like card, but it worked today at least.

I ate a burger for lunch, with the pitiful bird-watcher. Then we went to a movie because the Conversation had gone on for long enough, and then we met my mom for high tea at the Plaza Hotel. And now I'm going back to the night, all on my own.

My mom and dad wanted to come with me to meet Seth and Abby and thank them for taking good care of me. My answer was, courtesy of Jim: No fucking way. As soon as I said it, I started to wave the my-dad-behaved-really-badly-so-now-I-can-do-whatever-I-like card around, because until a week ago I'd been a model daughter who had never cursed out loud in her entire life.

But yeah. This is something I have to do on my own.

I didn't take a cab, because I need some cold evening air. I have to be able to breathe before I say good-bye to our hurricane shelter. And to Abby. And Seth.

I told my dad that all our problems would be solved if we moved, but I have no idea if that's really true. Imagine having to go to school here. Are American schools really like the ones in the movies? With a rigid pecking order of cheerleaders and emo kids and honors nerds? I know Seth's been beaten up three times, and Abby was always delighted when the radio said the schools would remain shut for one more day.

Would I survive the American teen battlefield? And would Mom really want to live here, or would she get desperately homesick after three months?

Suddenly, I think about the Statue of Liberty. The gray-green woman standing on her island to the south of the southernmost point of Manhattan. In the darkness. I think about the immigrants of the past, who left behind everything in Europe to start over again. They were at sea for two weeks before finally sailing into the harbor. The first thing they saw from the deck was Lady Liberty's burning torch. I don't know if I could ever be that brave. But I do know something has changed. A month ago, whenever I was in doubt, then I thought: Okay. I just won't do it.

And now I think: Yeah, let's do this. Let's give it a try.

I look around in surprise. Have I mixed up the street numbers? Shouldn't it already be dark here? I walk to Twenty-Fifth Street. To Twenty-Fourth—and then I know for sure. It was dark here yesterday. And now the lights are on again. The streetlights are on, the stoplights are working—the power is back!

It's incredible. Everything looks as if it was never dark. Illuminated window displays, neon letters, stoplights going on and off—exactly how things should be at the center of the world.

I almost start running. Over the past few days I kept checking online to see if there was any news about the blackout. I know more about the New York power grid than I could ever hope to understand about the Dutch one. I know they were going to restore the power neighborhood by neighborhood. Block by block.

Has everything really been repaired now? Or are Seth and Abby still in the dark?

I quickly walk onward. At every street I cross, I'm scared the black will begin again. Everything is light, all the way to Union Square. But after that the difference between zero and one becomes clearer than ever:. The blocks to the left of Broadway are sparkling in the light, but the houses on the right-hand side of the street are still as dark as ever.

I'm walking along the border. None of the houses is somewhere between a zero and a one. But I am.

I go deeper and deeper into downtown Manhattan. And when I come to Seth and Abby's street, I laugh out loud. For the first time in a hundred hours, I can see their apartment by the bright glow of a streetlight. I can simply ring the doorbell. It feels strange. And suddenly I'm really nervous. Is their mom back home? What should I say to them? And how am I going to say good-bye?

Seth opens the front door. His hair's wet and he's wearing a blue sweater I don't recognize.

"The power's back!" I scream.

He nods. "Everything suddenly went back on at four thirty. Faucets started running, devices flashed, my cell phone beeped . . ."

"And what about your mom?" I ask. "She must be home by now, right?"

"She just went out shopping with Abby. And Jim's gone back across the street."

So there's no one home. No one but Seth.

I look at his dark eyes and his short tousled hair and his shoes with tied laces—and I feel my knees go weak.

"You must be disappointed," he says.

"Why?"

"That Jim's not here. You and Abby both . . . like him, don't you?"

"Not me," I say. I'm a little out of breath. "Well, I like Jim, but not like that."

Seth frowns. "But he's so handsome! And so 'megacool'!"

"Well, he is handsome! And cool. And funny." I look at the ground. "I actually thought that maybe I was going to like him that way. I kept expecting to. But that's not what happened . . ."

I look up again, but just as I'm about to say something else, Seth turns around and starts heading upstairs. I hurry after him, because he's walking quickly. He's almost running.

It's warm again inside the apartment. The used tea lights have been cleared away, the crumbs have been swept up, and half the dishes have been washed.

So there we are. Facing each other in the light.

Suddenly, I don't understand why anyone ever invented lightbulbs. What was wrong with candles? Electric lights are way too bright. We can see each other so clearly that we don't dare to look.

"I'll get my things," I say quickly. "I'm staying with my mom and dad tonight, so I'll be out of here in five minutes. You can finish doing the dishes."

In the bedroom I throw everything into my suitcase without folding it and without thinking about whether socks and underpants are allowed to touch one another. It's all dirty anyway. I hear plates and glasses clinking in the kitchen. But then the noise stops.

"You can't leave yet," says Seth. He's standing in the doorway.

I try to say something, but he goes on.

"Abby will kill me if I just let you go. And Mom wants to meet you too." He makes a hesitant gesture with his hand. "Come and sit down. Would you like some tea?" And then he sighs. "Okay, I don't know what's going on. It's so dumb, now that we don't have a hurricane shelter anymore. I just don't know what to say."

I laugh nervously. "Did you ever know what to say?"

Fortunately, he acts like he didn't hear me. "So tell me all about it," he says. "How did it go with your dad?"

I walk with him to the kitchen and sit down. My knees are still weak.

"What did he say?" he asks.

I look at the clean white counter. "My dad is a loser who had a crush on a seventeen-year-old girl. I have no idea if I'll ever be able to look at him in the same way again. But it's his problem now. Well, yeah, sure it's my problem too . . . But it's not as bad as it was."

I think Seth's forgotten he was going to make tea.

"So you don't mind going home?" he asks.

"Well, actually . . . There's kind of a plan. Nothing's certain. But there's kind of a plan for us to move to New York."

I've never seen him look so shocked.

"What?" I ask. "I'm not allowed to live here?"

"Of course you are . . ." I can see him hesitating. "But you're Dutch. I kept telling myself that you weren't going to stay. That I shouldn't . . ."

Now I can really feel that the electricity's back. There are sparks in the air.

"Nothing's for sure," I say. "First we have to figure out green cards. My mom has to sell some paintings, so we'll have enough money. And my dad has to stop hiding away in a corner like a timid little bird."

Without saying anything, Seth starts filling the kettle. He stands there forever with his back to me.

I get up and walk over to the window. The streetlights are working again, so I can see if Abby and her mom are coming back from the supermarket. But the brightly lit street is completely empty.

"You want to hear something dumb?" I clear my throat. "I'd been looking forward to that radio show, the one with all the songs that got us through the hurricane. But now that the lights are back, of course it won't be on anymore."

"You want to listen to some music?" Seth turns around. "My laptop's working now . . ."

I shrug. "Okay."

I follow him into his room. There's the woman with the two faces above his bed. There's the spot on the wall that he thumped when I asked him about his dad.

"What do you want to listen to?"

I don't need to think about it. " 'Autumn Song.' But first that other one, about every little thing being all right."

He looks at the floor. "You do know it's just a song, don't you? Doesn't mean everything's going to be all right, not in real life."

"Yeah, I know," I say. "But I happen to like real life. However it works out."

"But what if . . ." He pauses and brushes a couple of socks underneath the bed with his foot. "What if you could *choose* what happens." He looks up. "Would you choose for Abby to get home right now? Or would you choose for her to get back a little later?"

I feel the electricity crackling. This isn't a movie. This is real life—with all the associated risks.

"I'd choose for her to get home later," I say.

He turns to his laptop. I sit down on the bed, which is a lot more crumpled and dusty than I could have suspected in the darkness. But hey. I've sat on it before. And I'm still alive.

Seth clicks his laptop and the song begins.

Don't worry 'bout a thing, 'cause every little thing gonna be all right . . .

He sits down on the bed beside me, leaving at least half a meter between us. We both sit stiffly, with our backs against the wall, just listening to the music. My heart is pounding.

"This is ridiculous," he says after a while.

"I know," I reply.

He's still looking straight ahead. "You know I'm not going to kiss you, right?"

"Eeww," I say. "Of course you're not."

It's silent for a moment. And then, as I hear the opening notes of "Autumn Song," I imagine what it would be like. Him moving to sit closer to me. Taking my hand. And me—feeling his dry, warm skin and not thinking about bacteria. I imagine his face coming very close to mine, and I picture myself not starting to shiver. Seeing his eyes from up close without a misty porthole between us.

I imagine us flying together through the stars. Not alone and not just within hearing distance, but very close to each other.

"I know why it feels so weird," I say. "The light should be off."

He nods. "That's exactly what I was thinking."

ANNA WOLTZ was living in New York when Hurricane Sandy hit the city in 2012. She spent the days afterward wandering through Lower Manhattan, searching for warmth, food, and electrical outlets. When the lights came back on, she began writing *A Hundred Hours of Night*. Born in London in 1981, Anna grew up in the Netherlands, where she now lives in Utrecht. She has written twenty books for young readers, and her work has been translated into nine languages.

LAURA WATKINSON studied medieval and modern languages at Oxford University and taught English around the world before returning to England to get a master's in English and Applied Linguistics and a postgraduate certificate in literary translation. She is now a full-time translator from Dutch, Italian, and German. Her translations have twice received the American Library Association's Mildred L. Batchelder Award for the year's most outstanding children's book in translation. Laura lives in Amsterdam.

This book was edited by Emily Clement and designed by Yaffa Jaskoll. The text was set in Galliard, a typeface based on the design of Robert Granjon, with display text set in Eurostile. The book was printed and bound at R. R. Donnelley in Crawfordsville, Indiana. Production was supervised by Elizabeth Krych, and manufacturing was supervised by Angelique Browne.

Fables of a Jewish Aesop

FK

FABLES

OF A JEWISH AESOP

Translated from the Fox Fables

of Berechiah ha-Nakdan

by MOSES HADAS

Illustrated with Woodcuts by Fritz Kredel

1967

Columbia University Press

New York & London

Moses Hadas, late Jay Professor of Greek at Columbia University, wrote among many other works *A History of Latin Literature*, *A History of Greek Literature*, and *Hellenistic Culture*.

Library of Congress Catalog Card Number: 66–27477
Printed in the United States of America

Introduction

Fables in the Western European Tradition

ALTHOUGH the exact dates of the life of the author of the *Fox Fables*, Berechiah ben Natronai ha-Nakdan, are much disputed, it can be stated with certainty that the fables were written at the end of the twelfth century or the beginning of the thirteenth and that the author must therefore have been dependent on the collections of fables then available in western Europe. The Greek texts of Aesop were available in Constantinople, but there is no evidence of their being known in the West at that time. There the Aesopic tradition was represented by a number of Latin fable collections. The best-known of these was the so-called *Romulus* collection, of which several manuscripts are extant. The earliest dates from the tenth century. The number of fables in this collection differs according to the manuscript: The manuscript in Corpus Christi College, Oxford, has forty-five fables; that of Munich, thirty-nine; that of Bern, forty-seven. The total from all sources is eighty. The order of the fables is closely related, although by no means identical, in all the manuscripts.

The chief source of the *Romulus* collection was the work of the Roman poet Phaedrus (fl. c. A.D. 14–60). Some thirty-seven of the *Romulus* fables are derived from his poems, and it is generally believed that most of the others are adapted from fables of his which are no longer extant. It is hardly necessary to add that the *Romulus* collection does not contain all the fables which appear in the Greek collections attributed to Aesop. The different *Romulus* manuscripts have various prefaces in which the origin of the selection of fables is "explained." The commonest explanation is that an emperor named Romulus chose them for his son, sometimes called Tiberius. It is impossible to make even an informed guess about the true origin of the collection.

The fables in the *Romulus* collection are in prose—often no more than prose adaptations of the verse fables of Phaedrus. There is, however, another collection of fables which is clearly based on the prose *Romulus* but is written in elegiac verse. It is often referred to as the *Anonymus Neveleti*, because it was published, without an author's name, by Nevelet in Frankfurt in 1610. Many scholars now accept its attribution (proposed by Hervieux) to Galterus Anglicus, who wrote about 1177. There are sixty fables in the collection, all of which can be found in the prose *Romulus*. The collection was very popular, and numerous translations and adaptations were made into the vernacular languages.

Although there is no lack of such fable material which can be dated before the thirteenth century, it is highly probable that there was a great deal more which has since been lost. The story (Fable 85 in this collection) of the sick lion who was cured by being wrapped, on the advice of the fox, in the skin torn from a wolf, is to be found in the Greek Aesop but not in any of the early medieval Latin fable collections. Yet there is an adaptation of it in a poem by Paulus Diaconus in the early ninth century, and it appears at greater length in the *Ecbasis captivi* (*Escape of a Certain Captive*), probably written about 940, and in numerous beast epics of the twelfth century. Whether it appeared in a fable collection now lost or was transmitted orally can no longer be determined.

The tradition of Aesop was also represented in the Middle Ages by the fables of Avianus, an author whose dates are very uncertain—conjectures vary between the second and the sixth centuries A.D. These fables were to a large degree different from those in the *Romulus* collection and they also were adapted into both prose and verse by such authors as Alexander Neckham, in his *Novus Avianus*, and the "Astensis poeta" (c.1100).

There was one other source of medieval fable material, which had no direct connection with Aesop, the *Panchatantra*. This consists of Indian fables which entered Persia in the sixth century, some of which were incorporated into the *Kalila and Dimna*, originally written in Persian, and translated into Arabic in the eighth century. The work was essentially a frame story into which various animal fables were fitted. The form remained constant in the numerous adaptations into other languages, of which the most important for western Europe was the *Novus Aesopus* of Baldo (c.1190). This work, probably based on a Latin prose version of *Kalila and Dimna*, consisted of 1242 leonine hexameters and contained thirty-five fables. Twenty of these are the same as those found in another adaptation of *Kalila and Dimna*, the *Directorium humanae vitae* of John of Capua, but it is unlikely that there was any direct influence. Few of Baldo's fables have any direct counterparts in the *Romulus* collections or the Hebrew *Fox Fables* but it is possible that his work was known to Berechiah.

We have named only a few of the extant fable collections of the Middle Ages. Since there were undoubtedly many more which have not survived, it is pointless to try to discover the precise source of each of the Hebrew fox tales. One possible connection, however, should be described in a little more detail: the fables of Marie de France. These are very close in time to the fables of Berechiah, since they were written in the latter part of the twelfth century, probably between 1170 and 1180. All scholars agree that Marie used a source written in English, but that it was not the fable collection of King Alfred mentioned in her prologue. There are in her work a large number of fables from the standard *Romulus* collections; a few demonstrably from Eastern sources; some from the beast epic *Roman de Renart*, which was rapidly becoming popular in the twelfth century; and a few about human beings, which may have derived from contemporary anecdotes or orally transmitted tales. There remain, however, a number of fables from sources completely unknown, and it is thus the more remarkable that many of these appear not only in Marie's collection but also in the *Fox Fables* of Berechiah. Of the thirteen such fables found in both authors, seven have precisely the same plot, and six show a basic resemblance. Another thirty-seven of the Hebrew *Fox Fables* are to be found both in Marie's work and in the standard *Romulus* collections, and it is clear from correspondences of detail that Berechiah was using the work of Marie rather than the Latin versions. This does not mean that the Latin collections were unknown to him. Fable 48 in Berechiah's work, for example, is found in *Romulus* but not in Marie's collection, and there are others in which the *Romulus* versions obviously have been used. Twenty-seven of Berechiah's fables seem to have been taken from those of Avianus, and others from the *Kalila and Dimna.* For twenty-seven of his fables, no source can be found.

The uncertainties about the exact dates of both Marie de France and Berechiah preclude any final decision about which of them was the source for the other, but all the evidence we have indicates that Berechiah drew on the collection of Marie de France. It is very likely that she wrote her collection while he was still very young, or perhaps even before his birth. There is also internal evidence that he used her work. Fable 41 of Marie's collection tells of two *serfs* who did not wish to discuss something in their master's hearing. In several manuscripts the critical word was transcribed as *cerfs* [stags], and it was a manuscript containing this error that Berechiah used for his fable of the two deer (Fable 19). The story surely has more point when the speakers are serfs. We may therefore say that Berechiah almost certainly used the collection of Marie de France as his main source.

He did not observe the order in which her fables are collected, however, and to the fables he derived from her work he added numerous others from the main sources of fables available to him, chiefly the *Romulus* and Avianus collections. The few fables he derived from Arabic sources are very probably taken from Latin adaptations of *Kalila and Dimna*. Although it is possible that he invented some or all of those stories for which no source is known, it is much more probable that they were based upon sources now lost or on Hebrew oral tradition.

The Author

THERE is very little definite information about the life of Rabbi Berechiah ben Natronai ha-Nakdan. It is known, however, that he was French, born perhaps in Burgundy, and that he spent much time in Provence. There is also evidence that he was the same person as the Benedictus le Puncteur mentioned in an Oxford document of the late twelfth century, for Berechiah means "blessed" (*benedictus*) and ha-Nakdan means "the punctuator" (*le puncteur*). It must be admitted, however, that the term was frequently applied to Jewish scribes and grammarians; so the identification is not completely certain.

There is considerable disagreement among scholars about the exact dates of Berechiah's life. The consensus is that he wrote his works at the end of the twelfth century, but some critics would place them rather in the first half of the thirteenth. The point is of some significance, since so many fable collections and beast epics were appearing at the time that a difference of even ten or twenty years could markedly affect the number of possible sources. Fortunately, there can be no chronological objection to assuming that he knew the work of Marie de France. And if he was in England, as the Oxford document may indicate, it would be even more likely that he had firsthand knowledge of the work of Marie de France, which was written there toward the end of the twelfth century. The *Fox Fables* (*Mishle Shualim*) are Berechiah's best-known work, but he produced several others, among them a lapidary, *Koah ha-Abanim* [the power of stones], and an imitation of the *Natural Questions* of Adelhard of Bath, *Dodi we Nechdi* [uncle and nephew].

The Work

BY NO means all the "fox fables" of Berechiah are about the relation of the fox with other animals. The title can probably be explained by the contemporary popularity of the *Roman de Renart*—the involved account, appearing in many branches, of the struggle between the cunning and unscrupulous fox Renart and the greedy and stupid wolf Isengrim. Several of Berechiah's fables are in fact taken from some version of the *Roman de Renart*. We have mentioned that the sources of many of the *Fox Fables* are known, but this does not mean that Berechiah merely translated or adapted them. Not only are details frequently changed, but sometimes even the kinds of animals taking part are different, either because the author felt that those substituted were more suitable for his setting, or because there was no word for the animals in his source, in the Old Testament Hebrew which he used. The fables are in rhymed prose, with a large amount of Biblical references and quotation. Indeed, it may be said that some of the stories are centos of Old Testament quotation. The didactic element is stressed, as it always is in fables, and it may well be that here, as so often in the beast epic, there are numerous references to contemporary personages and events which we can no longer identify but which would have amused the relatively restricted audience for which the fables were intended. Berechiah's purpose was social and moral instruction, combined perhaps with gentle satire. The language he used was inevitably that of the Old

Testament but there is no evidence in his work of any stress on religion.

The Translation

THE translation is based on the critical text of the original edited by A. M. Haberman, *Mishle Shualim l'Rabbi Berekhyah ha-Naqdan* (Jerusalem, Schocken Publishing House, Ltd., 1945–1946). No attempt has been made to reproduce the rhymed prose of the original, but the translator has taken great care to indicate the very numerous Old Testament reminiscences and quotations by incorporating the wording of the corresponding passages of the King James Version of the Bible. The result is a translation which not only reflects the style of the original but which also has a Biblical flavor highly appropriate to the gentle and at times ironic advice which the fables convey. Thus readers of the English translation can be aware of what is perhaps the most interesting feature of Berechiah's work —the change which Aesop's fables underwent when viewed in the mirror of medieval Hebrew culture.

While this book was in press, the news came of the death of Moses Hadas. This is thus the last work of a man who contributed as much as anyone to the understanding and perpetuation of the humanistic tradition. It is perhaps fitting that this work, whose translation gave him great pleasure in the making, reflects that union of the Hebrew, Greek, and Latin traditions of which he himself was so fine a representative.

W. T. H. JACKSON

Contents

Fables of a Jewish Aesop

Author's Proem

SAITH Rabbi Berechiah ben Natronai ha-Nakdan:
To impart prudence to the simple, to the young knowledge and astuteness, my heart inditeth goodly matter, wherewith to satisfy hearts like a garden well-watered, with parables of foxes and beasts. Verily these parables are current upon the lips of all earth's progeny, and men of diverse tongues have set them forth in a book. But my practices are different from their practices, for I have enlarged and augmented them with like and similar matter, in verses and poems, like sapphires veiled. Whoso reads them will attain many things choicer than fine gold and precious rubies, as the eyes of them that look forthright will perceive.

Blessed be our Rock, who hath given man mouth to speak, and hand to write words and compose them, and eye to behold them that ascend and them that descend, and ear to hear instruction.

The saying of Berechiah ben Natronai ha-Nakdan, who caused these parables to sprout and gave them birth:
How could I look on at their perishing? If I wrote them not down for a memorial, what profit in my labor? If I be accounted a fool or hasty, yet is my tongue the pen of a ready scribe. Would that my words be inscribed! The fortune of the pen which writeth my parables is upon the world's revolving wheel, which is obscure to the eyes of my understanding—a vagabond upon an island of the sea am I. These it slayeth and these it letteth live. It spreadeth abroad over the wide places of the earth to wreak breach

upon breach, and with its chariot wheel confounds the righteous until they are consumed. By its devices the course of its chariot is perverse; it charges upon the good and humbles them, upon the evil and delivers them. When it sees Truth standing in the plain and laying her hand to the spindle, it smites her in the fifth rib and lifts the sickle against her feet and hews them off and crushes them, the flesh along with the bone. It degrades her from being mistress, as though she had conceived in harlotry and had become blemished and walked bowed down. Instead it loves Falsehood, and to him extends the golden scepter, and summons him to its presence, and he finds grace and favor in its eyes; it sets him up upon his feet and adorns him with comely shoes and brings all his friends and kinsmen near and keeps his enemies and them that scorn him afar, until the workers of iniquity have ascended as on stairs. They have framed slanders to cut off sucklings and sprigs and twigs from the poor and needy and all who do not as they do. Weapons of war are in their mouths: Their lips are swords, their teeth spears and darts, to reduce the humble to be trampled like the mire of the streets. Few, therefore, are they who mend the breaches, for the wicked are supported while the knowing ones are without favor. The righteous groan, but the bitter are sweet; the sons of evil ascend but the lofty are abased. Prayer is folly, praise slander, sacrifice iniquity, prudence scorn. Their root is open to falsehood; they walk forth with a high hand; by their own name they call upon lands, which are thus likened to cattle. But men of righteousness are like a hedge of thorns, like untempered mortar. They that dwell upon the heights, the lofty among men, are abased in darkness and thick mist; their heads are bowed down like a reed, and they are fearful of the voice of the multitude, men whom their fathers despised. They abide in their towns and castles; they are compassed about with pride and haughtiness as with a chain. They covet silver and love gold, but are reluctant to put their hands forth to their wealth. They lie with their tongues, and yield not their necks to the service of their Creator. They titivate themselves with pride, but bestow no gifts. They are waxed fat and shine; in all their craft and guile, in spoliation and overreaching, in smooth flattery, they succeed and prosper, even as the days that they encamp. But he that walketh in righteousness and speaketh uprightly is in thick and disordered darkness. From the noise of the scornful archers my twigs have burgeoned and I make bold to direct my pen to a parable against falsehood, which holds sway, enthroned above the exalted ones of the city, whereas truth is bereft, and he that turns aside from evil is confounded, and the wicked gloats over his desire, and the face of the world is filled with vain folk who wreak abomination. They that honor God are lightly esteemed, but their pursuers are fleet of foot. Alas! Truth, which stood fast, hath been snared in a gin, and the vile have mounted upward while the gentle have descended to the pit. Every head has been rendered a tail, and every rogue and thief has attained dominion. The ways of truth are curtailed and hidden, but deception is augmented and conspicuous. In the eyes of the rich the poor are like bears, but they that love the rich are many. The foolish take root, but the wise is sated with penury. They multiply and grow strong, they wink their eyes and make them hard. Brotherly kisses are hooks in their jaws; they that hope for sweet counsel of fellowship will find them evil, slanderers in secret. He will say, "Eat thy fill"; with his lips he praises but inwardly he curses. He bows down and kneels, but his thoughts are only to work injury.

The wheel which weldeth these diversities passes over us incessantly. Wrathfully it smites and afflicts all whose palate studies truth; but whoso boasts himself of a false gift, his honor is measureless, though it be clouds and wind without rain. The vile and nameless, with burning lips and a wicked heart, will lengthen his days and see seed. He is clothed in a robe of fine linen and swathed with an ample garment about his neck. But peace hath nought, it hath no garment. All they that deal treacherously are very happy. With flattering lips he destroys his neighbor; he embraces and kisses him, and he flatters him with his mouth, but in his heart lurks iniquity, his ambush is within him. He is drenched in wickedness, and he supplants every brother by the heel. When I behold such a conjuncture as this I curse.

And I plied my poesy and said:

Lament, my pen, over the chariot wheel,
Which revolves and rolls, overturns and destroys.
Fallen is the tongue of truth, falsehood is risen high.
Pure prayer is folly; the innocent head is covered with shame.
Praise is slander; wickedness is exalted.
The right hand of wrong is in the ascendant;
The guiltless, vanished and scorned.
In the island of the sea is a congregation bereft of wit,
A base breed, crowned with shame.
The ear of its many rich is uncircumcised
For them that ask, but for them that give, circumcised.
The treacherous frame false charges
To plunder the upright of cloak and tunic.
The congregation of flatterers rejoices and is jubilant,
But in the camp of the upright wailing is heard.
They bless lips that utter abomination,
And curse the speakers of verity.
Evil is like good, hag like virgin,
Like sweet, bitter, light like darkness.
Berechiah curses and abjures the times
And their fortunes, small or great.
Better a dry crust with toil, apart from them,
Than to share a heritage with them.

When I reflected upon this, my thoughts confounded me and sleep fled from my eyes that I might commit to secret discourse the words with which I am filled. I say to him under whose eye my writing shall come, "Eat this scroll, for out of the eater shall come forth meat, and sense shall issue from the sensible." Let him who reflects on my parables not say, "As a thorn goeth up into the hand of a drunkard, so is a parable in the mouth of fools," a mass of dreams and vanity; for only from the wicked does wickedness come forth, but from deliverers, deliverance. And if a man make his palate rebel against me—"the wisdom of the prudent is to understand his way."

Lo, I draw parables of beasts and birds to strengthen hands that are weak, and of creeping things that crawl upon the ground; these are for a similitude for them that walk on earth. I shall begin with the lion who rules over them all, great and small, for they changed his honor for shame. So when a rich man grows poor, his comrades make themselves strangers to him.

I

Lion, Beasts, Cattle

MANY ARE THE LOVERS OF THE RICH
MAN WHEN HIS SPLENDOR SHINES;
BUT WHEN HE IS HUMBLED AND HIS
POWER CURTAILED, THEY CHANGE.

ONCE there was a lion, old and sick, whose loins were diseased, so that his spirit panted in travail; his fate was uncertain, whether he would live or die. To behold the lion's discomfiture there came all cattle and beasts, even from the desolate ends of the earth: some for love to visit the sick, some to see his anguish, some to succeed to his rule, some to know who would reign after him. So grievous was his malady that none could discern whether he were yet alive or already dead. The ox came and gored him, to try whether his strength were ended and empty;

the heifer trampled him with her hoofs; the fox nipped the lappets of his ears with his teeth; the ewe brushed his moustaches with her tail, and said: "When will he die and his name perish?" And the cock pecked at his eyes, and broke his teeth with gravel. Then the lion's spirit returned, and he perceived that his enemies were gloating over him, and he lamented: "Alas for the day when my trusted counselors despise me, when my power and glory have turned to my bane, when my erstwhile slaves lord it over me and they who loved me aforetime are become my enemies."

The parable is of a man filled with riches and honor whose neighbors serve him all. But when the day of calamity comes upon him, when he is bowed down and his power humbled, then they stand afar from his plague and separate from him and strip him of his righteousness, and despise him they had chosen.

And I, Berechiah, when I beheld this rebelliousness frowardly visited upon a noble, I plied my poesy and said in my song:

Woe to the lions prostrate before a calf,
To the chieftains who kiss a foot!
The feet of the faithful are trodden in mire,
And the sons of falsehood have raised their banner high.
Debased are the rulers, and the wicked exalted.
The unrighteous exult;
Truth is reduced to slavery,
A queen become a handmaiden.
Now hath truth no feet;
Falsehood's flattering tongue hath ravished them.

2

Mouse, Frog, Eagle

HE THAT DIGGETH A PIT WILL BE REQUITED ACCORDING TO THE FRUIT OF HIS DEEDS.

A MOUSE sat at the threshold of the gristmill, his lips and jowls covered with meal. As the sun shone upon him and upon the palms of his hands and feet, he luxuriated and fondled his whiskers, as was the manner of his father and all his folk. And as he abode there without fear or qualm a frog happened to pass and paused to investigate the state of the mouse: "Is the master of the house present?" Answered the mouse: "Mine is the house and mine the grain, and mine the seed in the granary, whether for food or trade. This is my house and refuge, and I fill my hole with provision. When the upper and nether millstones are at rest, I too rest at their side, and they provide me abundant food, for both are filled with flour. Such is my wont all my days. And when I hear a multitude of folk I hide in my crannies, and emerge again when no man is nigh, and gather my provisions." The frog observed that all the mouse's members, his hands and the smooth of his neck were white, and she said: "Why is your habit hoar; has age sprinkled your hair?" And he replied: "With whiteness is my dwelling, and of fine wheaten flour have I tasted, and the meal has flowed over me and spread broadcast, for the doors of meal and of flour are not shut in my face." Then said the frog in her cunning: "All your life is fear and trembling. Why do you glory in fine flour and dainties, when your life hangs suspended before you? All that approach your lodging confound and affright you; every gathering of people, every sound, terrifies you, for all seek to entrap you. Your food is hard and dry, your clothing always dusty. But my dress is clean and shiny, and in my abode no enemy lurks; and my food is fat and sweet. You are beset with snares, but my dwelling place is secure. Hearken to my words and my discourse: I shall supply all your wants. Come willingly with me to my shelter of reeds and clay." The frog overwhelmed him with the smoothness of her lips, and strutted before him and flexed her thighs. The mouse took no heed until they came to the river's bank, when he said to the frog: "Where is the house where you dwell?" She answered: "Across the river. There you will see all that is in my tent, the good things your heart desires. Turn your face to the river and cross its calm waters, spreading your limbs as if to do obeisance." But the mouse was apprehensive for his life and hesitated to go forward, for he had never made trial of water. And he said: "Where is the abode you spoke of? Who will cross the sea for us? In traversing waters I am untried; better for me to sojourn at home and there abide all the days of my life, for the way before me is perverse." Said the frog: "Hear me, good sir. In your crossing the water I shall be with you, and the streams shall not drown you. The enemies who pursue you, you shall leave far behind. This cord bind to my foot and yours. Your feet shall stand on the surface; and I shall go with you to guide your path, by this thread which you tie to my thigh, by deed and by word. No harm shall befall you; you shall flourish amidst brethren. Now shall you see whether my words come to pass." Said the mouse: "If it is as you say I shall make a covenant with you. Show your thigh and cross the river." The frog's eloquence deceived him, and they compacted together. Frog and mouse proceeded apace, joined by the cord attached to their legs. When they reached the depths of the abyss the frog thought to submerge the mouse and bring him down to the pit. And as the mouse mustered his strength on the surface of the water an eagle traversing the sky noticed that the two were entangled with one another, and flew to the prey. Fierce was the eagle, and pitiless. He spread his pinions and seized them; they were ensnared by the strong cord which bound them together, and could not separate. The eagle was ravenous, but when he saw he could not reach the mouse because of the thick hide drawn tight over his back and the black hairs that sprouted from it, he turned his attention to the frog, which he found goodly to behold and pleasant to eat, and swallowed her down at a single gulp. The mouse turned this way and that, and when he perceived that his fetters were broken, he set his feet for rapid flight, and escaped, himself alone. The frog, which was fastened at his side, fell into the snare she herself had spread; her deed was returned upon her head.

This parable I apply to a man who digs a foul pit to ensnare his neighbor—who flatters him to mislead him. But his guile is his own punishment; his deeds return upon his own head, all that he devised against his neighbor. The innocent escapes to his tent unharmed. And so hath Solomon said in his wisdom [Proverbs 11.19]: "He that pursueth evil pursueth it to his own death."

I plied my poesy and said:

Folly was the cunning the frog devised.
Freed was the mouse, and safe returned
To his granary filled with grain. Neither devoured
Nor buried was he, nor imprisoned, nor crushed.
She that spake honeyed words perished, nor returned
To her forest home. Such is the requital
For the beguilement of smooth lips; of no avail,
The deceptions of the false heart; ill devised,
For the neighbor finds the deviser and destroys him.
But the righteous shall dwell in the land,
And they that seek goodness and cherish purity.

3

Wolf & Sheep at the River

EACH TURNETH TO HIS OWN PROFIT, AND IF HE BE POOR HE WILL OPPRESS HIS BROTHER.

A WOLF walked solitary to the river to quench his thirst, and there espied a sheep standing opposite him at a distance. The wolf called out: "Wherefore hast thou troubled me? Mine is this river, I made it." The sheep replied in innocence, with words goodly and sweet: "My lord king, I have not troubled you. Master over my head have I held you all my days. I went forth from my tent to drink the river's waters; if this displeases you I shall return. Your words brook no challenge." The wolf spoke harshly to the sheep, saying: "Who are you not to dread me? Do wolf and sheep feed together? Has anyone beheld them together quenching their thirst at water courses? You have troubled my water and I cannot drink, but must return thirsty because of my shame. Your primal ancestor sinned against me in word and deed; for four years he rebelled and transgressed." The sheep replied: "Wherefore doth my lord so cruelly mock me? I am only a little sheep, not yet a year old. Why do you devise quarrels against your neighbor? Sons should not die for their fathers' failings." Answered the wolf: "It is because of you that I am thirsty and dishonored therefore shall you never more behold me." Thereupon he smote the sheep and stripped his fleece and tore his flesh and devoured him.

The parable applies to everyone who pursues his own profit. He that is stronger than his neighbor swallows him down. So do the judges and the bailiffs who pervert the justice of men and ransack their purses for silver and strip them of their fine garments in their very presence. The sage's saying is current [Proverbs 13.23]: "For want of judgment is a man destroyed."

And I plied my poesy and said:

Fools love folly, scorners scorn;
Harshly speaks the rich man to him whose words
  are complaisant.

4

Cock & Gem

THE FOOL DEPRIVE HIS EYES
OF WISDOM; HE DESPISES GOOD
AND CHOOSES EVIL.

A COCK mounted a midden heap and with his claws scattered and uncovered the dung to find worms for his food, as it was his habit to search for food there. He found the gem called jasper, and would scratch in the midden no more. Said he: "I thought to find some profit in my toil, some worm or fly to nourish me. But it is you that I see, jasper, and of what advantage is my finding you? True, you are handsome to look at, and if some rich man found you he would be proud. He would grasp you in his hand, set you in fine gold, and your glow would be multiplied sevenfold. But now you are trampled and trodden underfoot; my soul has no pity upon you, for you do not satisfy my desire. Better for me a worm, or even half of one, to restore my famished soul, than the finding of a precious stone."

This parable I find abundantly applicable to a man who scorns the honorable and withholds his eye from the righteous, who spurns the good and prefers the evil. Such is his rule and statute, but it touches him not until the hour of his need. And so said Solomon in his proverb [Proverbs 13.13]: "Whoso despiseth a thing shall be constricted by it."

Against him I raised my voice to revile him in my poesy:

The man whose heart turns from desiring wise counsel
Is like the cock who forsakes the jasper in muck and
mire.
In his heart sprouts an ulcer; the loathsome
Is his desire, the honorable he esteems lightly
As a thing scorned and despised. Contemptuousness
He likens to discernment; filth, to cleanliness,
To choice gems set in gold.

5

Dog, Cheese, Water

WHAT DOES NOT SUPPLY A NEED GIVES NO PLEASURE; EYES ARE NOT SATISFIED WITH MERELY LOOKING.

A DOG seized a cheese in the house and carried it hither and yon in his mouth and turned this way and that, until his path took him to a bridge, from which he looked down into the water. When he saw the reflection of the cheese held in his teeth he said to himself: "If I had the cheese in the water together with that in my mouth, the two would be better than one." His plan was to incline his head like a reed and so swallow the gobbet in the water. But when he opened his mouth and parted his teeth to grasp what was not his, the morsel he had seized in the beginning fell from his mouth, and he found himself plucked on this side and on that. He emerged from the water with nothing to show for all his effort.

I have observed this trait in the man whose heart is full of desire. Though he is laden with silver and gold, he covets all—and loses all. I am pleased with Solomon's proverb [Proverbs 13.7]: "Be thou content with what thou hast in thy hand and thy possession; and envy not that which is another's."

And I plied my poesy and said:

Heaven vouchsafed sustenance to all living creatures,
But oft they covet twice their need.
He that covets and ravins more than his portion
Will fare as did the dog with the cheese in the water;
He thought to add to what was enough,
And lost provision for two days.

6

Fox & Fishes

MANY GIVE COUNSEL IN THEIR OWN BEHOOF, TO DRAW OTHERS UP BY THEIR HOOK.

A FOX walking by a river bank saw one fish hastening to escape while another fish pursued him. Overtaking him, the second fish attacked him with animosity, and the two fought, with none to deliver between them, each charging angrily against the other. The fox said not a word, but approached the water in the hope that he could sink his teeth into them or trap them by the snare of his cunning. But the waters proved a barrier to his lust, so he turned thence to another spot, where he addressed them with no hesitation. When he saw the fish fighting, the great oppressing the small, the gentry snapping at the lowly, and the war between them growing heated, he called out to them: "Are all of you such fools that quiet is impossible? Is this the covenant among you and the sole statute of your congregation: that each destroy his neighbor, that the larger swallow his companion which is smaller and hew him asunder on the slightest provocation? If all the fish of the sea would assemble and say to me 'Rule over us,' I would not forsake my resolve, for all the day they are in terror and confusion; each fights his brother, every man his neighbor. Perverse is the path before them with their bowstrings drawn and weapons whetted, and on this path they wander astray, knowing naught of the path of peace. Hear now the logic of my discourse; incline your ears and come unto me. Depart from thence and come hither. In joy shall you go forth and in peace, if you hearken to my counsel, and ye shall bless me also. Depart from the sea to dry land, and together we shall inherit the earth. Then shall your tranquillity be increased, and nation shall not lift sword against nation, for none shall cause a breach. Serene and untroubled shall all the world abide, and the joy of wild asses shall be ours. Hearts that are troubled shall be refreshed, and all the inhabitants of earth shall shout for gladness upon their couches of ease, by day and by night without surcease. None shall do evil, none destroy." But one of the fish replied: "If thou wilt verily rule over us, wilt thou indeed ordain peace for us? Even when we abide in quiet waters, surrounded by our kin and in peace, the robber assails us, the destroyer rises against us, and we live in terror of men's snares. Many fishermen fish for us, many hunters hunt us; we all roar like bears. If you had experience of our plight, your anguish would equal ours. If now by thy cunning thou devourest spoil, when thou hast done spoiling thou shalt thyself be spoiled, for suddenly thy creditors shall rise up against thee and thy ways will not prosper. How dost thou spread a web of deceit against us and count thyself secure in a land of peace? Surely the fowl of the heavens and the fish of the sea and the beasts of the field all are ambushed and hunted, and even humans quarrel for the envy that is between them. But there be higher than they, and he that is higher than the highest regardeth."

This proverb counsels vigilance against those who advise for their own advantage. Beware of their seduction, for by earth's transgression flatterers have multiplied, and the face of this generation is as the face of a dog. Every man must be aware of him that would destroy; but the wise man hath his eyes in his head.

And I plied my poesy:

The face of this generation is the face of a dog;

They speak with two hearts.
Their words are like butter, their thoughts tallow.
They press the breasts for pleasure,
As a nursling drawing milk.
Spies are they, but there is no Joshua nor Caleb among them.

7

Dog, Sheep, Lion, Wolf, Bear

INFINITE IS THE EVIL WHEN A RULER GIVES EAR TO FALSEHOOD.

A DOG cried loudly against a sheep before the lion and his assessors, saying: "My lord, have mercy on thy servant. Yesterday this sheep stole from me a loaf of bread which I had laid up for my provision." The sheep answered: "This is not true; if aught of it be found with your servant, it shall be death." Said the judge to the dog: "Have you witnesses to corroborate your tale?" The dog replied: "Aye, my words are right and true, and I call upon credible witnesses to testify. The wolf and the eagle saw this sheep in my house, which she had entered without my permission, and she carried the bread out between her legs. Take no pity upon her." The witnesses were instructed to render their testimony on an appointed day, which suited their honor and dignity, and they took counsel together to make their accounts match. One falsehood they fitted to its fellow to make their lies uniform. The day came and they entered the court; the judges, who had been bribed, examined the case and studied it, but came to a single conclusion. Even the judges corroborated the dog's charge and supported him. The ear is accustomed to falsehood, and man transgresses for a crust of bread; therefore was the judgment perverted. They enjoined the sheep to pay according to the weight of the bread which she had purloined. She returned sighing and groaning, for she had nothing at home. So she sold her fleece, and the shearers foregathered. Before her shearers the sheep was mute. With the fleece shorn from her back she bought bread, and she returned that which she had not ravished. But her anguish was sore, for the heat afflicted her and the sun dealt obdurately with her. And when the chill of winter came her flesh was harried with cold, for there was no fleece to protect her skin. She would not be comforted for the sake of the bread, and her sorrows for her little ones increased; Rachel [sheep] was weeping for her children. Winter came on and snow reached to the knees, and there Rachel died by the way. For this the wolf and the eagle had waited, and upon the news of the sheep they came to the field where her body had been cast, and said: "For our reward and for our testimony this flesh shall come between our teeth; let each serve his soul with this flesh before it be cut off."

The parable is for a generation whose teeth are as swords when they conspire to devour the meek. Each hardens his face. Not to have committed violence or deceit is for them an abomination. Each seeks his own blemish in his fellow; and the ruler hearkens to falsehood. The one slanders, and the other presses the charge; the one pursues the victim, the other strikes it down; the one sells its hide, the other devours the flesh.

And I plied my poesy and said:

Ah, the jackal is turned into a lion,
The righteous kisseth the shoe of the vain.
The workers of deception are robed in dignity,
The evil have attained the upper hand.

He that abominates wickedness must drink the cup
of poison;
They that wreak evil lord it over him.
His efforts win him no profit;
Though armed with helmet and corselet, they avail
him not.
They that measure wealth by handfuls
See him descend never to rise.

8

Wolf & Crane

WHOSO SERVES WICKED SINNERS,
HIS REWARD IS ENOUGH IF HE
IS DELIVERED FROM BLOWS.

A WOLF in affliction besought the lion to assemble the multitude of his subjects; a large bone had turned and become lodged in his throat, so that he could not raise his head. His soul chose strangling, for the bone wounded him as it pressed upon him in its strait lodgment. All the cattle and the beasts and the fowl assembled, from the least to the greatest, and approached the wolf, whom they found prostrated in his anguish. He sought their counsel to extract the bone, but they would not respond; "For," said they, "this is his cunning; he seeks but a pretext to destroy us and swallow us alive like the pit. Let us deal shrewdly and remain unattainted." But when the wolf continued his pleas, not once or twice but many times, their hearts melted and turned to water. They all took counsel together and said with a single voice: "Blessed be he that did take cognizance of thee! Lo, the crane hath a long neck and a beak that is strong and sharp and narrow; he will withdraw the bone from its lodgment—who but he can do so? Call him, there is none his equal." So the wolf called the crane and awakened his sympathy (yet the gall of asps was within him), and persuaded him by his speech and vowed to requite him if he would extract the bone and to make him ruler over all that was his. The crane spoke: "Open thy mouth, and I shall see whether I may remove this death from upon thee." So the wolf spread his maw open without measure, and all stood from afar and shrunk back, for they feared to come nigh. The crane grasped the bone between his teeth—for his beak reached down into the throat—and withdrew it; then he asked for his reward. Answered the wolf with harshness: "Who hath heard such a thing, who hath seen it? Am I not the mightiest of the beasts and cattle, and are my fangs not surrounded with dread, and is not the rule of my mouth to rend and destroy? Who hath ever come into my mouth and remained whole? This once hast thou escaped from between my teeth, and I have not strangled thee; twice thy hire have I rendered thee. Depart from me lest I slay thee, lest thy life be for a prey."

The parable is of a rich man whose neighbor does him honor and inclines to his every desire and serves him with all his might. But the master hardens his heart and makes his spirit stern, and if he ask the payment for his service and his toil, he gives it not but works iniquity and scourges his body with rods, and says: "Depart from me! How oft hast thou wearied me! Frowardness hath multiplied among slaves, for they are grown lax and are not disciplined. Make haste, march, do not stand, if thou valuest thy life." So do the shameful ones, men that are harsh and workers of iniquity. But the humble trembles and is afraid; the needy separates from his fellow.

And I plied my poesy and said:

He that relieth upon his wealth and his flocks,
And dealeth with his neighbor as with a slave in his
tent,
And wickedly works iniquity: when he asketh,
"Give me my hire; I shall gather it and have done,"
He answers, "Quickly begone, depart from my
boundaries
Ere I thrust thee out"—in the pit shall his lodging be,
Never shall he sojourn in shining light.

9

A Pregnant Bitch & Another

HE WHO MAKES ANOTHER RULE
OVER HIM CARRIES HIM UNTIL
HE BECOME HIS MASTER.

A BITCH yearned to lodge in a house, for her time was near to whelp and winter was coming on apace. One evening she approached her fellow whose house and chamber were in her vicinity and wept and implored her to hearken to her cry and receive her into her house until she be released from her travail and her full womb be disburdened. The other had pity and said: "Lo, my house is before thee: do as is good in thy sight. Remain while thy offspring are small until thou hast weaned them." So the bitch rested there in peace until she whelped puppies in her own form and image. But the mistress of the house was displeased, for their yelps rose to heaven, and they abated not their desires. The puppies grew large and strong, ate flesh and waxed robust; and as they grew fat their heart was lifted up and they made of their entrails an ambush and left no livelihood in the house. Said the mistress to the stranger: "My friend, go forth from my house; depart from me and dwell in thine own abode. Though I love thy nighness we cannot abide together, for thy children give me no peace. The dogs are truculent and vex me sore. Their cry robs me of slumber; woe is me that they sojourn with me so long! They drink my water and eat my bread; my soul is weary of their trouble, and I have no peace at all." The stranger replied with smooth lips: "My honored and upright lady, let my life be given me for my request and my people for my petition. If thou abhor my nighness with thee, do thou send the mother afar but the young shalt thou take for thyself. Then if my offspring and my people say, 'Return to thy mistress and be humbled,' no dog shall raise a cry in thy hearing, and the latter loving-kindness shall be more acceptable than the first. Let me abide until the winter's chill be overpast, and at the time of singing of birds we shall seek another house. Do not bring my old age down to the grave in blood; if my sons be left without shelter at such a season, drought would consume us by day and frost by night. The mercies of the bitch of the house were warmed, and she said: "What is mine is thine, my house is thy house, according to thy request and thy petition." But when the time of the singing of birds came round the stranger and her brood made their hearts adamant. The mistress said in her hearing: "To the right or to the left, go thou and thy sons from my tent. Twice shall affliction not arise. Wherefore wilt thou resolve to repay evil for good?" Then spake the stranger like a robber, and cunningly devised to remove the mistress far from her boundaries. She said to her: "The house is mine. Get thee gone from my place and my demesne. Depart, thou and thy dependents, make haste, begone from my folk." And they hastened to thrust her out. So she departed from her home sorrowing, and the sons of the stranger inherited it. But the shepherds came and drove them forth.

The parable is of a pleasant and complaisant man that is approached by a subverter who works deceit in his house. Cunningly he deludes him with his snares, and in his coming and going ponders deception. He sighs, to lead his patron astray, as if all peace had forsaken his soul, and his eyes pour forth water. The patron's mercies are warmed, so that he fulfills his desires and makes him ruler in his house. He that came as a sojourner betrays him: "Mine is the house and its chambers, and thou art but a guest in my dwelling place." The patron cries out bitterly; if the stranger's society pleased him for a day, he will grieve twice as much on the morrow. And so hath the sage said in his wisdom [Ecclesiastes 7.15]: "There is a just man that perisheth in his righteousness."

And I plied my poesy and said:

The houses of the faithful and their foundations are desolate;
In none is there a speaker of truth and uprightness.
The times have silenced and destroyed them; flattery and falsehood they have let live.
Righteousness is ended and hidden away and forgotten,
And the righteous have descended to the pit.
But the crooked mount upon a ladder.
Sweet is bitter; light, darkness; stinking water, dew.
The light are esteemed as the weighty; their sin illumines their shadow.
If a man approach his friend, he will be paid evil for good.
But whoso resists flattery, whoso abides steadfast, receives his reward.
He that rendereth evil for good will be blinded;
He shall never behold the light in its splendor.

10

City Mouse & Country Mouse

HE THAT SEEKS GREAT THINGS
WILL BE PLUCKED ON THIS SIDE
AND ON THAT AND WILL CRY OUT
IN BITTERNESS.

A TOWN mouse journeyed from his native place to visit his kin in another city. All the day he walked, until evening came on, when he saw a forest nearby in which country mice were disporting themselves in their soul's paradise. In this place he lodged with a country mouse in whom he took pleasure, and each uncovered all his heart to the other. He observed his food and his drink and how his hand apportioned them by measure. Their food was herbs and the like, and the root of the broom. Said he to the forest mouse: "Thy foot shall follow in my steps; tomorrow shalt thou journey with me and I will make thee drink of my beverages and thou shalt eat of my viands. Better for thee will be a day in my courts than a thousand in the forest midst straitness and oppression, in the blast of the storm wind, and in lack of food. In winter how wilt thou find livelihood when the grass is withered? Them that dwell amongst it it fails, so that they are affrighted and ashamed. Thou wilt look forth at the windows, but the grass withereth and the flower fadeth. Come with me and lift thy head high; I will bestow dainty sweetmeats upon thy soul." So he enticed him to come from the forest to the city, a place of wheat and barley, of granaries and grain. When they came to Bethlehem ["house of bread"] the city mouse said: "I have compassion upon thee; lo, all my house is before thee—eat as is thy pleasure." And as they were eating and making merry, with flour and bread and flesh and fish, the man came there as was his wont to fetch bread and supply his board. The city mouse fled and hid in his shelter, and the country mouse hastened after him; so nimble had he not been since his youth. When the man departed thence, the city mouse descended from his cranny and each emerged from the holes where they had lain hidden. The town mouse set his teeth to the corn and the meal and ate and was satisfied and waxed fat; the country mouse kept his distance to see what would befall him that had made himself his companion. He quivered with dread of the man he had seen; his flesh trembled and his spirit was crushed for the path which he had taken, and he repented him of his imaginings. And as the country mouse reflected thus in his heart the city mouse fled from the battlefield and hid him in his place of concealment. Said the country mouse to the town mouse: "Happy he who departs hence in peace and is no longer in fear and dread. From the moment I forsook my lodging the iniquity of my steps has encompassed me. See to thy house and thy place, for I will no longer tarry with thee. Terror has breached our covenant. Come to the rock, hide thee in the dust from before the man, lest he gather thee in his drag, lest the lurker stir from his ambush. All thy life is vexation and wrath; but bread in secret is sweet. Why hast thou slandered the forest? Better a dry crust and tranquillity therewith than a house filled with the sacrifices of contention. From every man that approaches thou fleest in panic and in breathlessness takest refuge in one tent and another. In my place I shall find song and joyful shouting, the beauty of Carmel and Sharon."

The parable is for him who seeks great and wonderful things, who forsakes the good and pleasant and is not content with his lot and his wonted food, but strives to ascend on mounting stairs. Generally he comes to shame; he attains this but loses that, and even the second he contemns. Then he says with lips and tongue: "I shall go and return to my first way, for better for me was it then than now." At times he descends lower and lower, and his cry is bitter, for he is plucked on this side and on that.

And I plied my poesy and said:

Better a dry crust and tranquillity therewith
Than a fatted swan with contention;
Better a handful of meal with love
Than twenty with hatred;
Better a mess of herbs with security
Than venison with contention and greed.
Abide in thy house in peace, and spy not
Another's house with passion flaming and panting.

II

Fox & Eagle

WHOSO INCREASETH HIS GREATNESS AND WEALTH BY VIOLENCE WILL IN THE END LOSE WHAT HE HOLDS MOST PRECIOUS.

A FOX went forth to inspect a garden, his progeny of kits accompanying him. The eagle swooped down and carried one off. The fox perceived that one was missing but knew not whether he had been stolen or was hid, whether he was dead or maimed or captive. He lifted his eyes and saw that the eagle was bearing the kit on his pinions, and he raised his voice and wept and cried out to the eagle: "Deal gently for my sake with my son and return him; thy days will be long if thou preserve him. Wherefore shouldst thou cut off from his kin him thou hast not toiled for nor raised up? Hearken to prudence and knowledge. Wherefore shouldst thou incite evil?" The eagle replied: "Who art thou to spring after me, and what ails thee that thou criest out?" The eagle would not hearken to the fox's voice, and the fox followed along his course. When they came to a tall tree of the forest the fox was filled with fury, for the eagle had cast the kit to the eaglets in his eyrie. When the fox saw that he could not ascend to him he called out: "To cause thee sorrow I shall burn thy tall cedars and thy choice cypresses." So the fox went and set fire to the beams, wool and flax together upon the oaks and the dry timber, and flaxen straw and brittle briars, and piled heaps of logs for a pyre. The fire burned and would not be quenched. As the flame shot out from the wool and flax the fox said: "Let my soul die with the Philistines and my son be consumed with the eagle and his young; before he become food for their fangs let him be destroyed along with them: lo, he is given to the flames to devour." When the eagle saw the great fire he cried a loud and bitter cry and called to the fox: "Take thy son, whose life is precious to thee, and extinguish the fire which thou hast kindled in thy wrath. Wherefore should we die in thy sight?"

The parable is for one who, persisting in his sinfulness, puts his hand forth against his peaceful fellows. He covets and ravins, he robs and plunders. He maketh perfumer's oil to seethe with stench. For that he is strong and rich and powerful he plunders and robs the humble and needy. Even if the poor man address him with words of supplication he stops his ears like an unhearing asp. In the end his secrets break forth, and he too is rendered small in his sight.

And I plied my poesy and said:

The haughty despiseth the humble; the wicked the righteous.
But when the humble waxes strong he maketh his utterance smooth:
"Account it not unto me for a fault, for I have repented;
I shall be to thee as a father, and thou to me as a son."

12

Lion, Goat, Sheep, Cow

HE THAT MAKETH FELLOWSHIP
WITH ONE STRONGER THAN HIMSELF,
IN THE END WILL HIS GLORY BE HUMBLED.

A LION went forth to seek prey, to hamstring it and crush the neck, to take game and fetch it home. Accompanying the lordly beast were a goat, a sheep, and a cow. When they came to the forest they said: "All that we shall encounter we shall lay low; we shall find prey and divide it." They saw a hind and took it in their snares, and they asked the lion to show what portion he desired to satisfy his need and what each should take for his share. Now the imaginings of the lion's heart were lofty, and his right hand was a hammer against the weary; and he said to them: "Hear my rede: Take not of the flesh; the hind has fallen to my lot. I found it, and it is wholly mine—the first portion, because I am king; the second, because I pursued after her and overtook her; the third, because I apportioned the prey, being the mightiest of all my generation; the fourth—but who will stand forth to separate it from the three? Who will answer me with boldness and take the prey without my leave? Who is so fierce as to dare stir me, who will stand before me and breach the law my lips have framed?" When they heard his reply they trembled and quaked before him. At each who asked a portion the lion laughed, and rebuked him so that he fled afar. And when they had all dispersed at the sound of his voice, the whole prey was left to him.

The parable is for a man who associates with one stronger than he. If they conclude partnership the richer will roar like a lion and reply in wrath that he hath no portion and inheritance with him. And he shall lose his wealth and his love, either upon that day or its morrow. But the righteousness of the virtuous shall be revealed, even as the sun that goeth forth in his strength.

And I plied my poesy and said:

If a poor man seek the company of the rich,
Portionless will he be driven off, like the lion's companions
When, their lots in their bosoms, they asked their share.
Quickly, he dispatched them empty-handed, in furious rage,
Bearing chaff, not grain. Such his lot who companies with one stronger.
Instead of myrrh, rebellion. He sits in folly and walks aimless
Who desires to share in power.

13

Crow & Fox

GREAT IS THE POWER OF PRIDE,
EVEN SURPASSING GREED.

A CROW mounted a fig tree, carrying a cheese in his mouth. Under the tree stood a fox, devising and scheming how he might bring the cheese down to earth. He called to the crow: "Stately, handsome, and sweet bird, good and agreeable and lovely, happy is he who is paired with thee. If all the beauties were at thy side their comeliness would not equal thine. If thou shouldst essay to sing songs thou wouldst surpass all birds in music and wouldst be sole perfection, for no flaw is to be found in thee. See whether thy voice matches thy stature and the majesty of thy plumage, for thou art free of fault." The crow said to himself: "I shall let him hear my voice, and he shall heap praise upon praise." So he opened his mouth to raise his voice, whereupon the cheese immediately fell and landed near the head of the fox, who said: "Of the precious things of heaven above this hath come to me from him that raiseth his voice; no longer will I listen to the sound of song." So he went to his own place after he had obtained his desire of the crow.

This parable is for the proud and haughty and for the flatterers and falsifiers who deceive them with their lies and honeyed words, and extract their wealth which they had secreted in vain and in utter futility. Beware, therefore, of the seducer, and be not swayed by the aspect of his figure and the loftiness of his stature; let him not trap thee with his eyeballs, with his false lips, with his violent hands.

And I plied my poesy and said:

A friend hath fooled me; 't is easy to befool a fool;
Easier still it is when one makes himself a fool.

14

Ass, Dog, Man

ENVY BREEDS COVETOUSNESS,
A THING OF VANITY.

IN THE house of a municipal official there lived a small dog who ate of his bread and slept in his lap, walked with him and rode with him. In the house an ass lowered, for that the man was friends with the dog and often played with him like a pair of gossips. Said the ass to himself: "I am not inferior to the dog. I too shall approach the master; perhaps he will be friends with me, as with the dog. I will embrace and kiss him and lick him with my tongue, I will put my eyes to his, and my face over against his. And I will be his companion when his friends are by. All his clothing will I slobber and trample, every shred and shoe latchet. To win his favor I shall bray at him, just as the dog frisks and barks. And thus shall I prove whether I find favor even as the dog." When the master returned home the ass put his plan into execution. He ran quickly toward him and licked him about the ears and embraced him with his forelegs and raised his voice to him and applied his head to his, just as he had learned of the dog. But the master was stricken with fear, for the ass went up and down upon him, and hemmed him in with his mouth until he thrust him from his seat, and he clung to his neck

like a necklace until his weight was heavy upon him. Cried the master: "Hither, all who are with me! Remove the ass from upon me, for his terror is grown great." All the folk assembled, one with a dagger and another with a stick; one pelted the ass with stones and another smote him with a rod; one cried: "Strike, but spare his life." So they chased the ass to his crib, bruised on back and belly.

The parable is for a fickle man whose eyes are broad and whose heart is high; he is lordly in his haughtiness. For such as he there can be no success. In his desire to hold sway he suddenly stumbles and falls and is thrust from his station, and no man heeds his speech. Solomon's proverb remains valid [Proverbs 24.20]: "There shall be no reward to the evil."

And I plied my poesy and said:

Before destruction comes crookedness of ways;
Sloth is a stumbling block on the path to honor.

Recall the man who found a kingdom, and uttered prophecy
As he returned from seeking asses.
[I Samuel, Chapters 9–10]

15

Lion, Mouse, Snare

BETTER TO BE GOOD AND
KINDLY TO ALL, FOR THERE
IS A TIME AND OCCASION
WHEN EVERY CREATURE AVAILS.

A LION was slumbering in a desert place when a mouse trod upon him and awakened him from his sleep. He turned to see whose feet had trampled so great a king as himself, and perceived that the mouse was standing alone at his side, no creature else. Said the lion, "His time is come," and called to him: "Vile mouse, thy sentence is death, for thou hast awakened me and contemned me. Wherefore hast thou troubled me? It is the frowardness of thy heart that persuaded thee to tread upon me. But I understand justice: Thou canst not evade me but must pay the penalty." The mouse replied with heart exceeding bitter and contrite: "Surely I am innocent and pure. I beseech thee with all my might, let my words find entry into the ears of my lord, and let not thy wrath kindle against thy servant. Forget thine anger in thy lovingkindness. Thou canst perform what thou hast never essayed, but what thou performest thou canst never turn back. If the heart within thee beats warm, he that confesseth and repenteth will be pardoned. I know that I have behaved foolishly; I have erred, but have not been froward. Who that hath stretched his hand against my lord hath remained guiltless and not come to grief? Far be it from a great and mighty king to put forth his hand to crush a vile mouse." As the mouse spoke thus, the lion's mercies grew warm and he struck a covenant of peace with the mouse. He called to him with kindly lips: "Keep thee, and abide tranquil; fear not."

And it came to pass at midnight, in the midst of thick darkness, at the season of roaring of lions, that the lion was roaring for his prey in a forest and fell into a spread snare. He cried a loud and bitter cry, but when he gathered his strength to rise the snare held him fast. His heart was confounded as his struggles constricted him. At his voice the mouse shook off sleep and went to him and found him entangled from head to foot. He said to the lion: "Who art thou that hath awakened me?" And the lion answered, "Here am I." Said the mouse: "The folk thou hast despised—go now and fight in its midst. But the time has come and the season is at hand for my faithful requital of thy good deed. It is in my power to deliver thee from the spread snare even according to the kindness thou didst show me. I shall convoke my fellows to cut the cords of the net and sunder your bonds, so that you may go upon your way prosperous." The lion said to him: "Make haste, good sir; wisdom is better than strength. Thou wilt be more righteous than I if thou wilt bring me forth out of this snare." The mouse assembled his fellows and did as he had said. With their teeth they cut the nets, so that they were severed in an instant. The lion said to him: "Now am I beholden to you, for you have set my feet at large." The mouse turned his shoulder to go upon his way. And the lion returned to his lair unharmed.

The parable is for the poor and humble who are innocent of transgression and rebellion in relation with their rich neighbors. If they sin through error and unwittingly, and the rich forgive their error, then when the day of calamity comes upon the rich, the poor strengthen their hands and cleave close to give support, like a girdle to the flesh. There is a friend that cleaves closer than a brother. And there is a man who deals with his brother as on a brazier; he will not deliver his life from the burning. Tried and tested is the sage's saying: "At times a man of giant's stature may be strangled by a fly." A highly esteemed sage was asked: "Whose love is greater, a brother's or a friend's?" And he answered: "Hearken to my words: I do not love my brother until he is also my friend."

And I plied my poesy and said:

Return the kindness of him who deals kindly with
thee;
If he err and do ill, take pity, for it may be on the
morrow
He will afford succor in straits, though yesterday he
were despised.
Make thy heart humble; circumcise it for the innocent.
But wither the head of the wicked.

16

Dove & Flax

WHOSO HEEDS NOT COUNSEL,
IN THE END HIS EYE WILL
MINISH AND DROP TEARS.

A DOVE who saw flaxseed strewn upon the ground by the hand of the sower was filled with wrath and said to all the fowl: "Strengthen your weak hands; let none of you be wanting. Let us go forth and eat the seed that wicked man has sown lest it prove our destruction. They that work in fine flax, weave nets to snare winged creatures, whether on the ground or upon branches. My heart is stirred when I behold this sowing, as a reed is stirred in water." For this counsel they said to her: "Not persuasive is the heart of the dove; or her thought is too wonderful for us. Deep it is; who shall plumb it?" And they slandered her, for so was it ordained of heaven. When the dove saw that the birds scorned her words she recounted to her kin and her helpers what the man would do to them and declared that the day of their doom was nigh. Said they: "To understand the report is a vexation." All the kindred foregathered to discover deliverance and enlargement, and each lamented in his heart for the violence which the oppressor prepared. They pleaded with the sower with their tongues, with eloquent discourse; and he said to them: "In the clefts of my house shall ye lie; repose where it seems best to you. If I go to the left or the right, go ye not hither and thither." The doves remained confident in their abodes all the days they tarried there. But of the seed which the man sowed he fashioned gins and every species of snare, and there fell into his snares every manner of bird. But upon that day the doves who heeded the counsel were not for a shame amongst their enemies. They sat in their cotes, and no voice of the pursuer reached them. But those who scorned and mocked the dove were farther astray than she. At the brink of the gaping pit they lamented, and found no resting place for the soles of their feet. Only the doves in the cotes escaped and survived the calamity.

The parable is for one who heeds no counsel; in the end his eye drops tears. In time he perceives that his hand is grown slack; his doom extinguishes the candle of his glory. He will say: "My heart and my eyes have vexed me, for I heeded not the voice of my teachers." And the sages, whose heart within them is wise, have said [Proverbs 12.15]: "The way of the fool is right in his own eyes, but he that hearkeneth unto counsel is wise."

And I plied my poesy and said:

Uncircumcised are the ears of the fool;
His heart is empty of understanding.
He is not warned by the admonishing voice;
Hence will it come about that he fall and rise not.
But the wary perceives the evil, and hides
When the many are suddenly overtaken.
Woe worth the day Gedaliah son of Ahikam
Refused to heed Johanan son of Kareah!

17

Cicada & Ant

REMOVE THE HEDGE OF SLOTH,
AND THINE EYES SHALL NOT
LOOK AND LANGUISH.

A CICADA approached an ant to ask food of her, for she was in sore need of provision for the winter. But the ant turned her back and scorned her speech and mocked her. Said she: "Thine end is sorrow. Whom dost thou pass in beauty? In the summer thou didst slumber and hast prepared no food for the winter. How foolish of heart he that would give thee what he hath stored up! Know that my hand is too short for thee. What didst thou in harvest time? The hay appeareth and the tender grass showeth itself; all the folk go forth to glean, each diligent to prepare for the winter. The sluggard sayeth, 'There is a lion in the streets.' He that wishes to store up grain must collect ears, even as I, who bore them upon my shoulder and prepared my bread in summer." The cicada replied: "All the season of birdsong, when the wagon was loaded with sheaves, I learned to sing pleasant songs and enlarged my fellowship and chased sorrows from my heart, for the songs were true in my sight, and they said my voice was sweet. But now drought hath consumed me, and the chill of winter's ice is vexatious to me." Said the ant: "Now will granary and winepress give you no help, because you have taught your voice song and have taken no thought for food. If thou makest thy nest in the cedars and thy neck comely with chains, go to the house of a rich man; make your music fine and multiply your songs, to fill your soul when you are hungry. To me your words are an abomination. Depart from me, begone! All the men of my counsel abhor thee. Because I am of lowly stature and have no strength or power I have filled my tent with good things. But if I have been wise, I have been wise for myself. But you will not be sustained by song when the northerly blasts blow, for slumber is clothed in tatters, and sluggishness begets deep sleep."

The parable is for a man too slothful to find provision for his house; will others then heed his cry? In the summer he slumbers and sleeps. Such a man is accounted guilty.

And I plied my poesy and said:

Be diligent, my son; cross road and city in the heat of day;
Gather for the winter, garment and steed, ox and sheep,
But all in innocence. Pierce the fool's right eye,
Muzzle his mouth, break his teeth.

18

Raven & Sheep

CHANGE NOT WHAT IS THINE UNTIL
SOME OTHER FALL TO THY LOT.

A RAVEN perched upon a sheep's back. Now hear what she did: She pulled and plucked the fleece from his back. Said the sheep: "Raven, depart from me. Hear my words and my discourse; so will you do if you possess understanding. Go and perch upon the back of the dog, and pluck his wool from his back, leaving him only bare skin." Said the raven: "Not so. Thou counselest me for thine own behoof. Thy wool have I found first, and here shall I sit, for I delight in it. My counsel is better than thy counsel. I shall not change nor substitute the dog for thee."

This parable is nigh unto my palate. The cat knoweth whose beard he licks. He that offers counsel unasked is reckoned a tedious fool, for to give counsel to one who loathes it, is wrong.

And I plied my poesy:

Give counsel to him that asks, but let secrets remain hidden.
Be strong and of good courage in thy lot, and thou shalt not encounter the froward.

19

Two Deer

A FOOL THAT IS SILENT IS RECKONED WISE, AND SITS AMONG THE UNDERSTANDING.

TWO DEER stood in the fields conversing in a hushed whisper though there was none to overhear. Each put his ear to his fellow's lips to catch his words. A passer-by came upon them and proceeded to inquire why they spoke their counsel in a whisper, since there was none to interpret, and even if they should shout with all their strength none could understand their conversation, for they were remote from man. They answered: "We are constrained to make our sweet counsel together, and neither of us reveals his secret. This is our usage for that we are weak."

The parable is for fools that are silent or whisper to one another; then people say, "They are exceeding wise." But when their counsel is revealed, then is their wisdom shown brutish. And so hath the Preacher declared in his proverbs [Proverbs 14.18]: "The simple inherit folly." And the sage hath said: "Better to endure a fool in all his concerns than to endure a fool who is wise in his own sight."

And I plied my poesy and said:

Be wise, my son; and discern and know;
Acquire truth and cultivate innocence.
Reckon a fool as the shadow of an idol,
And turn aside from the counsel of the simple.
If he bids build, then destroy;
Turn to him who understands the matter.

20

Eagle, Snail, Raven

THEY THAT ARE SHREWD
IN CUNNING COUNSEL
ARE WISER THAN HUMANKIND.

A SNAIL went his innocent way, his house with him wherever he went, for he carried it upon his back. His head and torso emerged; and his horns, which grew from it, stood upright as he came forth. When an eagle soared before the snail he became aware of it and lowered his horns, and his heart was vigilant for fear—the prudent hides when he sees evil. The snail quickly hid himself in his tent, in the upper chamber which was his. The eagle saw that the snail was hidden and gone, but the path to his privates could not be seen. He neared the tent and overturned it and perceived that what he had first observed was there hidden in its resting place. He raised the house upon his pinions and declared that the snail would not escape from within before he worked his will upon it. And as he bore it between heaven and earth he essayed to breach its shell and crush it with beak and talons, but saw that he could not penetrate it. Before him stood a raven, who drew ever nearer and called to the eagle: "Sense hath betrayed thee. Lo, thou seest with thine eyes but thou shalt not eat of it. Why rouse thy wrath for this? The battle is not to the strong. Who shall open the doors of his face? He is proud in his scaly armor, which is molten like stone upon his back. He that made him can reach him with His sword. Not thine is the science of piercing him; it is hidden from the fowl of heaven except only me, who am now come, and am wise and expert. The prey attached to thee is exceedingly desirable; if thou give me a share and portion thou wilt break it like the crushing of a crock and see what is cunningly concealed within; then wilt thou know the paths of his house." Answered the eagle: "After that thou hast bruised the enigma's head just are the terms thou hast stipulated. Teach me to remove the covering, and receive a share alike with mine." Said the raven: "Go up to the strong cliff; its descent thence will crush it. Cast it to the ground as with a sling, and thou shalt shatter it upon the rock. The shell will be powdered to dust, and then canst thou eat the flesh." The eagle heeded this counsel, and cast the snail from the cliff down to earth. But before it left his hand the raven went to the foot of the cliff, and there he found the snail shattered and scattered. He devoured it, leaving not a morsel. The eagle grieved sore for having heeded the raven's counsel, for his own prey he had made ready for the raven; his cunning had made him release his booty; and he had cast food away from his teeth.

The parable is very pleasing: Better is wisdom than warrior gear, and the shrewd and clever can by their counsel destroy what the sons of men have builded. Though a man be confident in the strongholds he has made and in his towers, his enemies may devise cunning schemes against him. Wisdom must have a smooth path in his heart, lest their cunning overreach him, as did the raven's the eagle.

And I plied my poesy and said:

A man wars upon his neighbor for wealth, and defeats
  him;
But a passing stranger gathers it up in his skirts—
Like a bone over which two dogs fight,
But a third comes and seizes.

21

Wolf & Goats

THEY THAT MULTIPLY WORDS HARDEN THEIR HEARTS, AND IN THEIR MIDST LURKERS SET SNARES.

A GOAT raised her kids in the flock, surrounded by a house with wall and hedge. When the man rose early to his ploughing the goat would seek all manner of herbage and spy out pasturage in the hills. Said she to her buck: "Know that my grazing is far hence; I shall not return until I have filled my belly and my bare bowels to provide milk in plenty for my kids. Shut the door upon thee, and hide; depart not until I return. Put not thy hand forth to open the door until thou see me before thee; then will I show thee all my good things." The buck replied, saying: "We shall go together and feed and watch." So the twain went together. A small kid they left behind they bade fasten the door, and she locked it after them, and the house was barred to entry. Now the wolf was lurking in his lair, crouched for destruction, his reins yearning to attack the flock and ravage it, to seize prey and devour it. He knew that the goat and buck were not there, nor yet their master the man. So he disguised himself and his voice simulated that of the kid's mother, and he said: "Open for me, for the milk I bring thee in my udders is abundant. I am weary of grazing, and they cannot carry more food." The kid answered: "The voice is the voice of my mother, but I fear that it is not my kin that stands behind our wall. In the forest are they that lurk for us; I shall not open until eventide because of the lurking wolf, lest my mother be transformed into a stranger and the wolf destroy me in my vale of peace. Let not the men of my counsel declare that with me is fulfilled the prophecy: 'The wolf shall dwell with the lamb, and the leopard shall lie down with the kid.' " The wolf perceived that his words would not avail, so he said: "If thou open not I will bring thee down in sorrow to the grave. For that thy heart is filled with violence I will break thy walls and thou shalt be trampled down. With my blade I shall make an opening in thy door." Said the kid: "Let not him that girds on the sword boast as one who has opened. Neither by suasion nor by anger nor by deception wilt thou enter here with me."

The parable is for men whose hearts and words are harsh, the rebellious and lying folk who wrap themselves in fringed mantles in order to deceive at the gate. Each neglects his own labor, for deception, and in time of trouble they dissemble. They speak with two hearts; though they display love in their dealings, there is falsehood in their right hand. If he that dwells amongst them is not their like, if his heart be not false midst their false hearts and deceive not with their deception, if he prepare not his refuge within him and devise not shifts against cunning shifts and guile against guile, he will not survive amongst them save through a miracle; for the evil are at peace and the good, humbled; the false, upstanding and the faithful, tottering.

And I plied my poesy and said:

Berechiah's house departs from the men of falsehood
    and is not taken,
Even as seven stars disperse at the cock's crowing.

22

Serpent & Rich Man

HE THAT REPAYETH EVIL FOR GOOD, HIS SOUL INCURRETH DEBT.

A SERPENT moved freely in a rich man's domain; regular commons were provided for him by the rich man when he came, and milk to quench his thirst. One day the rich man was stirred so that his lips were filled with fury; he raged, and cursed his people and his house and his comrades. The serpent came as was his wont to obtain his supply in the house, and his foot fingered the rich man's face. He smote the serpent in anger, for he escaped not his wrath; and the serpent returned to his house bruised and smitten and downcast. Calamity twofold had befallen him, and he was no more seen in the rich man's domain or its approaches.

And it came to pass in the course of time that the rich man was wonderfully debased. His wealth vanished, and poverty overtook him; his cattle and all his wealth perished, and his cares grew ever heavier. Instead of barley there was noisomeness; the path of his destruction was paved smooth, and his hand availed not to deliver. Said he: "It is for my transgression that I am stricken. Yesterday the serpent was in my house, and in my anger I bruised him though he committed no violence or deception. I shall go and seek his face in his tent; perhaps he will be appeased and I may prevail upon him with persuasion and smoothness of tongue to return to his former habit." So he came to the serpent and lamented and wept before him and implored him to banish his hatred against him and not kindle all his wrath. So said the man, weeping: "Serpent, hear my rede: Though thou art angry with me, return, and I shall supply all thy requirements. Thou knowest that I love thee and that I befriended thee in my house and that my affection protected thee so that thou hast lacked nothing. If in my anger I smote thee, lo, in my benevolence I had compassion upon thee. Bear now the transgression of the bruise, and I shall be your willing servant." In reply the serpent said: "I will not requite a man according to his former deeds, for the blows I received afflicted me so sore I had near killed a man for my bruise. Let not my hearers be astonished; all thy household know that dread of me did not affright thee. Wherefore persist in thy pleading? I shall no more return to thy house; I do not long for thy dainties. Thou hast wounded my head and breached the palisade of peace to raise thy sword against me; if today thou laugh, tomorrow I will make thee sad. Thou shalt not rejoice at the sight of the death thou hast brought upon me. I shall not visit thy sin upon thee nor be vigilant for thy evil; yet whenever I recall and behold, my bruise is sore and my heart, anguished, and a fire smolders in my nostrils. Depart, lest I slay thee in my wrath, for the pain is strong upon me and my wound is exceeding heavy. If not, I will remember thy sin in fury and thy heart will study dread of my elder son, the viper. For out of the serpent's root shall come forth a cockatrice, and his fruit shall be a fiery flying serpent which shall encompass thee to avenge me. At his sudden rebuke thou shalt be astonied and unstrung."

The parable is of a man who deals frowardly with his friend to do him ill in his hatred, though he be not an enemy or one that wished him ill, but dwelt with him secure and did him and his house no harm. But by reason of the evil he inflicted upon him he sowed the seed of enmity in his heart, to be harvested when occasion offered, for the friend sees that his day must come. His requital is twofold: If the culprit do not pay the penalty, the kindred of his flesh who know his nature will do so. He never despairs of wreaking his vengeance, with furious rage and flaming fire. Therefore should the worker of evil not be astonished if one that received evil at his hands is filled with wrath against him. His hands bring his doom near, and he is harassed in all his ways. He will rejoice in his misfortune and instigate it. Blind is he who puts trust in a man he has injured. And the sage hath said: "He that governeth not his anger, how shall he govern another?" My heart inclineth to the saying: "He that soweth hatred reapeth regret."

And I plied my poesy and said of them that make light darkness and sweet bitter:

Berechiah has inscribed with his pen:
Who soweth hatred will reap regret;
He inflicts a gash upon himself,
Fashions it with a graving tool.
Who bruises his fellow or plucks his hair
Whets a sword against himself.
If the way of his enemy is perverse
He will gather the gleanings of his hatred.

23

Lion & Fox

HE THAT HIDES IN AN EVIL
TIME WILL NOT FEAR TIDINGS.

IN THE dead of night and deep darkness a lion pondered and reflected, and a wicked plan took form. The lion said in his heart: "Every king sits in his house at ease, and why do I toil, my soul in want, a wanderer and a vagabond in search of food? Nothing comes into my mouth except by chance encounter. Why do I labor in vain and exhaust my body in struggle and find no peace? Who of all my servants takes pity upon me? Better is a handful of quiet than heaping handfuls of toil." Guilefully he published abroad that he was sore ill, and with smooth and lying lips he summoned the cattle and the beasts: "Make haste and come to see me, for I know not the day of my death. There is none to plead my cause that I may be bound up and healed. I shall scatter among you riches and spoil; your wants I shall satisfy, and I shall give even as you bid me. I will render to each according to his righteousness; for the greater, I shall increase his heritage. If not now, when? Lo, I shall sleep with my fathers." They journeyed all to visit him, great and small. And it came to pass, when there was yet a league to go, that they were told of the king's injunction and its reason: Visitors must come singly and not two at once to visit such an invalid as he, lest their voices disturb him. So they went each one alone, and found the lion lying upon his side in his lair as one dead. Said the visitor: "Truly, my lord, to behold thy welfare have I hurried my steps." Answered the lion: "What hast thou to do with my welfare? Turn thou behind me. Full oft hast thou wearied me; now shalt thou be shamed for seven days. Thy flesh will I eat and thy bones crush; the fleet shall not escape, nor the strong deliver himself." And the lion did according to his words; he rent him in pieces and devoured his flesh. While he was yet eating another came and said: "My lord king, of thy sickness is my flesh wracked." The lion enticed him into his lair by the smoothness of his tongue and did unto him as he had done unto the first. So fared also the third, and also all that followed after the flocks. The lion stirred not thence until they were dismembered; and so fared all until they were ended. There remained only the fox, who pondered in his heart to know and understand what the king sought in his heart, and what would be done to him, for it was not explained. His heart fainted, for he trusted not what was said among the peoples, that the king would give fields and vineyards to all. And if the truth were with them, why had he enjoined his servants not to come to him, two together? "I shall not go," said the fox, "lest I fall into a gin and a snare." And he went and sate him afar off, two bowshots' distance, and he hid him alone in a secret place to hear the bleatings of the flocks, and he said: "I observe the adder goeth as a wind goeth and returneth not; lo, they all go with no fear, but not one returns. I know not what it means; it is the manner of Jehu [who came unto them and came not again]. Their path is like a slippery way in the darkness; surely the king cheateth them, and they will never return to their homes. Calamity will befall those who expected to see his calamity; they will not eulogize him, 'Alas for our lord, alas for his majesty!' " And because the fox's heart was fearful and vigilant, shrewdly he hid him when he perceived evil. And it came to pass when the lion had finished rending all comers, that he understood that the fox had cleverly hidden himself, and he called out: "Why and wherefore do thy footsteps tarry? Surely thou hast put forth thy hand against thy comrades." Answered the fox: "The way of those going I saw, but I found no footsteps of those returning."

The parable—so say they that speak in parables: The pressure of the times is fortune's wheel. When a wondrous thing comes about, each man seeks his own welfare. Remain each man where he is; let none go forth from his place. The news is not good; the evil report multiplies. But there is one who hides, in the day of wrath, and fears no evil tidings. Enough the trouble, in its own time, when it reaches thee, and there is destruction in thy tent.

24

Frogs, Oak, Serpent

WHO DWELLETH SECURE IN HIS OWN WORLD ACQUIRES NO MASTER OVER HIMSELF.

FROGS consulted amongst themselves to set a king over them. On the question—Who should be king?—they disagreed; one said so, and another so, until they all agreed that the king over them should be a tree planted upon streams of water, whose height reached heaven. They said unto the tree: "Rule over us; thou hast a garment; be thou our chief." The tree was silent and uttered not a word, but the voice of their multitude prevailed and they said all with a single breath: "Our lord the king live forever!" They reached their desired haven, and joy beat strong in their hearts. From the first day of his reign the oak began to look upon the fruits of the valley. One came to the king and another returned, but there was neither hatred nor love. From the day they made him king they made pilgrimage to him, to sit beneath his shadow. They knelt and bowed down to him and said: "Our lord the king, we have come to thee. Who is like thee in stature? Our souls long for thy words. Look down from thy holy mansion for the benefit of thy servants, lead them and teach them the good way, for love covereth all transgression." They called to him in a loud voice but there was neither sound nor response. Then said they all: "Lo, if thou wilt not tell us thy name all we frogs will turn aside from thee."

And when they saw that he told not his secret they exchanged his glory for shame and plotted to separate from him. And they said: "Not good is his timber and not good, his leaves. If evil come upon the land the fixed spike shall not budge; from him issueth neither tears nor laughter." Therefore did they transgress the law and change the statute. But he was plagued by God and smitten with blindness. All the flocks assembled there to call him The Oak of Weeping, for the majesty of royalty beseemed him not, for that his heart was like flint and stirred not from its place. Verified was the proverb on the lips of the multitude: "All that are tall are fools." "From the day this one reigned over us," said they, "our people have become a lowly folk; their aspect is diseased, as in the beginning." They trampled him with their feet and wearied of his being king over them, and they spewed upon him and made of him a jakes. One said: "Lo, I have seen a chieftain for us; we will forsake the bramble and choose the cypress." And they said: "No bruised reed shall rule over us, neither bramble nor cypress. We shall not regard his tall stature nor his appearance. There is no breath in his nostrils; what is his worth? We shall choose a king terrible and awful, one that is alive as we are this day, who will fight our battles and speak with us mouth unto mouth." So they chose for their king the serpent, who heeds no enchantment. He joined their band as a comrade, and his society was approved by them. Frog and snake walked in company, shoulder to shoulder, so that no breeze came between them. But one day when he was with them and the waters were calm the serpent grew famished and became angry, and he said to them: "Be ye humble at my hand; do ye come to search me out?" And he smote them a great smiting, and maligned them, and hated them yet more, and devoured their flesh and their bones, until all that were in the rivers perished. He gathered them in great heaps and devoured ten portions, from the houses and the fields. Better for them it were to be without overseer and ruler than to multiply destruction in their camps.

The parable is for the sons of man in whose power it lies to abide peaceful in their houses, but they conspire in their schemes and their inward plottings and an evil thing sprouts among them, so that their peace is banished, as befell the frogs. And the sage hath said: "The king is likened to a fire, in which thou hast no hope; in storm thou hast need of it, but if thou draw nigh it will burn thee."

25

Sheep, Ram, Lion

BE NOT FOR A MOCKERY AND A JEST WHEN THOU SEEST THY WORDS FIND NO FAVOR.

SHEEP were left in the fold when the shepherds went forth where they listed and shut not the door behind them. They were far from man, and all went forth from their fold to spy out their food in the fields. The sheep grazed as is their wont, scattered here and there, and their sweet counsel was to eat grass. They had not gone far from the fold when a lion journeying toward the forest gathered his strength to pursue them. When they became aware of him one called to another: "The lion hath roared; who shall not be afraid?" When they saw that the lion would charge them and their escape was lost they said to the ram who marched at their head: "Go toward the lion on the course he is taking and appease him with smooth speech. Mayhap he will be appeased and depart from against us." So the ram journeyed forth from his host and set his face toward the wilderness. Before he neared the lion he cajoled the beast with blandishments, saying to him: "My lord the king, blessed art thou in thy coming; thou shalt find festival in the eyes of all that behold thee." Answered the lion: "The festival which I shall find will proceed from thee and thy fellows. What greeting can there be between me and thee? Forbear thy pleasant discourse. Shall a king like me be informed by the words of thy mouth? There is no joy but in thy flesh, which I shall eat; for the words of thy mouth I shall not praise thee."

The parable is for one who sees a day of trouble, but his purse and its contents are precious in his eyes, so that he gives no ransom for his soul but thinks to escape with goodly words and soft and smooth speech. But all his words kindle fire and compass sparks; he shall not escape in the day of wrath. But pleasant shall it be for another, who shall say: "Take this host and plunder its gold." He has heaped on silver, but they shall not slander him, for in time of trouble his head is high. All that a man hath, he shall give for his life.

26

Ass, Bees, Wasp

SCORN NOT ANYTHING, FOR THERE
IS A TIME FOR EVERYTHING,
AND OCCASIONS ARE EXIGENT.

AN ASS was grazing upon a hill, surrounded by a swarm of bees. Before him hovered a wasp, until it hid in one of his ears. It shook and trembled and roused him with its buzz as it stormed about hither and thither. The ass was wearied of his life and startled, for he was bitten and stung. He was sore vexed and greatly pained by the noise of the great tumult, and he said: "Today my torments are increased; what is the sound in my ears? Surely it is an ill wind. If thou art within my boundary, wasp, wherefore hidest thee in my cranny? Come forth and do battle with me, that we may look upon one another face to face. Hast thou strength and power to go forth and muster a swarm of bees to battle with a company of asses?" Answered the wasp: "Would that it were so, that we might fight together in the valley, battle line against battle line, wasp against ass and ass against wasp, with the vanquished banished from the congregation." Answered the ass: "Let us appoint a day on which we shall go forth to battle." So the day was there appointed. The ass went to take counsel of the lion who ruled over them all, and told him all that had befallen—of the wasp in his ear that had stung him, of the battle day appointed, and how his heart abode in terror lest the wasp again invade his ear. Said the lion: "Give ear, I will counsel thee. Hearken to my voice, and no plague or pain shall befall thee. With leathern strips stop up and seal all thy perforations; then will not thine enemies prevail over thee. When they see this they will be confounded before thee, and thou shalt hold sway over them but they shall not hold sway over thee. Set thy face toward the battle, and gird thy loins." All the asses did so, and on the day appointed they came, archers and marshals, and the wasps fought against them. But when they saw that every opening was blocked, front and rear, they hid under the belly and there displayed their prowess and inflicted twofold affliction upon the asses. The asses countered by scratching against trees and brush and sought to slay the wasps, until their bonds broke and their holes and crevices were revealed. These did the wasps then enter with vigor, and bit and stung and harassed. The asses were breached from end to end, their ambush within them, and their hearts were overwhelmed with weariness. Said they to the wasps: "We shall no longer be headstrong and rebellious. Lo, we are thy slaves; only depart from us."

The parable is for one who boasts of his stature and his large limbs; the little man rules over him by clever devices. Therefore make not thy flesh to sin with thy tongue, saying to the little man, "My little finger is thicker than thy loins," for many have stumbled and been crushed by excess of pride. No battle is good save the battle against lust.

27

A Planted Tree & Reeds

THE SIN OF PRIDE IS HARD AS CEDAR; THE QUALITY OF HUMILITY SOFT AS A REED.

A TREE stood planted in courses of water, but the stormwind blasted it once and again and uprooted it and overturned it and cast it upon the river, so that it wandered and was tossed hither and yon, even as the reed is bent, and the waves and the breakers passed over it; but the reed and the sedge that were there, were strangers to it. It said to them: "How have I fallen while ye withstand the wind that hath laid me low? Tell me if ye know." They answered: "If thou hadst yielded to him as do we and hadst bowed down, thou hadst not been thrust from thy post. Of all the host of reeds the wind hath felled not one, for he hath found them with heads bowed, as in the swamp."

The parable is for the haughty with neck outstretched. Double destruction is their lot. When the feet of the humble stand fast, sorrow afflicts the proud. Therefore, where there is no man, endeavor thou to be a man. Be thou lowly without vileness and stately without haughtiness.

And I plied my poesy and said:

The words of the proud man are without substance;
Who would stand in his lot?
The dust of his feet is of equal worth with himself;
Why then be slave to his shadow?

28

Mouse, Sun, Cloud, Wind, Wall

IF A MAN PURSUES AFTER HONOR AND DOMINION, QUICKLY WILL THEY FLEE FROM HIM.

A MOUSE said in his heart: "Of what sort is a male without a wife? I have seen all living things and all flesh, but among all these I have not found a woman." His soul was eager to search and seek out a beautiful woman, one of goodly favor—white tinged with red—who tasted no food, and who, when he turned his shoulder to go forth, would not go forth with him. But in all his speculation he found no woman without fault, but only the sun perfect in beauty. And he said: "If the heavens are darkened for all the dwellers of earth, the sun abides righteous and bears healing on its wings." And when the sun shone before him she won favor and grace in his eyes, and he said to her: "With an everlasting love have I loved thee; therefore have I drawn thee after me and will betroth thee unto me for a wife. Mine is the right of redemption and inheritance." The sun answered with guile: "Dost thou reckon this wisdom, to take thee a light which darkened yestereve? The sun rises and the sun sets; thine eyes look darkling upon it, and it is gone. Ever doth the cloud conceal it, for lo, I am a bounden handmaiden to the cloud, for by its will I am clothed with portions of darkness. But take thee a wife from thy mother's kindred and her birthplace." But he stood fast and said: "I do not wish to take such." The sun said: "Then lift your eyes to the cloud. I know that she will not turn her face from thee." The mouse's loins yearned to go to the cloud straightway, and he said to her: "This day have I labored and found my beloved, my beauteous one, my perfect one; by the sun's counsel I take thee, and I will never forsake thee." The cloud answered and said: "He that watches upon the height of heights placed me in the power of the wind, who shifts me according to her will, north and south, east and west, with outstretched arm and mighty strength. If thou desirest a wife like me, thou wilt be a wanderer and a vagabond upon the earth. Forsake the handmaiden and take the mistress, for I am delivered over to the power of the wind. Go to the wind and prosper with her; you will persuade her and win her over. Go thou and so do." So the mouse went to the wind, whom he found in a desert land, and said to her: "Be not ashamed; with me, my bride, thou shalt come forth from Lebanon, for of all the women I have beheld for myself, thee have I seen before me in this generation. No other wife shall I take beside thee; thou shalt be mine and I thine." She answered him: "Now hast thou come to take me, but thou knowest not my lowliness. In me there is no strength or force to raze a wall—whether of stone or of sand—by my shout. Thy covenant with me shall be voided, for the wall is stronger than I. If she is suitable in thy sight and thou availest to persuade her, she shall be thy fortress in time of stress." So he went to the wall and said: "Know that I have come to thee by the counsel of Sun and Cloud and Wind to visit thee for happiness, and I shall betroth thee unto me with loving-kindness and mercy." The wall answered in anger: "To demonstrate my shame and disgrace have they sent thee unto me, to make me a mockery. Thou hast come to me to rehearse my shortcomings, for they ascend and descend, whereas my stones and sand never budge and no power or strength is in me. Every mouse and creeping thing mines at my source and uncovers my foundation and makes paths upon me. I am a wall and my breasts are as towers, but the mice according to their families chip me with mouth and foot and sojourn in me, mother and sons, in more than two hundred warrens, and I cannot withstand them. Wilt thou desire such a wife as I?" When the mouse saw that his enterprise was betrayed he took him a wife of his own kindred, who was born in his own neighborhood and vicinity, and he found her a proper helpmeet.

The parable is for one who pursues honor to attain it, but dominion and glory flee from him. Whoso exalts himself beyond his proportions is destined to return to his vile origins, for each returns to his own station, the honorable to honor and the lightly esteemed to his own sort. The Arab sage hath said: "Whoso dyes his hoariness will be betrayed by the growing of his hair." And of one who goeth up without permission Solomon hath said [Proverbs 25.7]: "Better it is that it be said to thee, Come up hither."

And I plied my poesy and said:

With head bowed and heart contrite and eye lowly,
  feet stand fast.
Behold, the fire which rises sinks, and waters minish
  and stand still.

29

Crow & Other Birds

HE THAT BOASTETH OF WHAT IS NOT HIS,
THE SPIRIT OF FOLLY STIRS IN HIM.

THE CROW thought his nature ill, for his appearance was darker than black and his feathers were like pitch, whereas all other birds have beautiful feathers, red and white and golden and green. Hence it was that all birds whistled at him in scorn, for he was blacker than them all. So he sighed and turned his back, and in his reins conceived a plan: He would take a single feather, no more, from every bird, and go into a secret place there to cast his plumage and in its place assume another which should be compounded of all colors and make him more beautiful than all his peers. This plan he carried out to the full. To the highroad he then ran, up the path, quickly in the joy of his heart, and his feathers were of mottled colors. There he preened himself on his colorful plumage. His fellows gathered about him, and a mixed multitude attended them, and they all sat about him and wondered who and what he might be, for among the agreeable sorts there was none like him. But his stature was the stature of a crow, and when they examined his form each recognized his own feather. This one said, This is my feather, and that one said, This is my feather; this one said, Thou hast vexed me, and this one plucked out his feather, and this one scratched his body, so that he remained naked and plucked, for he had made his way perverse.

The parable is for a man who adorns himself with what is not his. If he hears a wise saying he says he thought it in his own heart; but when he is asked counsel he is silent as a stone. Some there are who give chaff in the place of grain. As a result of his wisdom a man will go bowed down, for instead of wheat he puts forth briars. Better to be a silent fool than to be wise in one's own esteem. If he open his mouth he will reveal his folly, and all will laugh at his counsel. Many have extinguished the light of their glory and paved the path of their doom.

30

Ox, Lion, Ram

WHO HATH A LURKING ENEMY SHALL TREMBLE MORNING AND EVENING.

AN OX saw a lion and ran away, for the lion roared and bellowed and trumpeted after him, and he hid him in a certain pit beneath thick flaxen cordage, where a ram was hidden. His heart's terror made him tremble in fear of the ram. Said the ram to him: "Why art afraid? Surely thou and I belonged to the same herd." The ox answered: "Every animal I see alive is in my eyes a mighty lion. If I had found thee alone I had not feared thee, but now because of the lion I am confounded and atremble."

The parable is for a man that has an enemy whom he fears always, morning and evening, walking and sitting, rising and lying down. Every man he imagines is his enemy, and says, Now shall I be pursued; but it is the sound of a driven leaf that pursues him.

31

Young Dog & Old Dog

WHOSO BOASTS OF HIS ELOQUENCE IS UNWITTING OF HIS EVIL.

A MAN had a little dog that snapped at every creature. He hung a bell upon the dog's neck to make a loud sound which was heard when the dog ran, so that he might no longer bite without warning. From the day he wore the bell, the dog's heart was uplifted; he arose as a young lion, and as a lion comported himself. He imagined he was king over the dogs, and walked proudly with neck outstretched. An old dog looked upon him and raised his voice against him, saying: "Why art thou proud of the bell thou showest? It is not for thy benefit or thy delight but to warn against thy wickedness folk thy teeth bite and rend. Therefore let thy words be few."

The parable is for a man who treads his bow for false speech. He searches out the faults of his neighbors, but his own ambush is strong within him. He goes forth in the street to speak, and the ruler of the city shares his counsel and makes him govern his domain, though he know him a slanderer and a sycophant. Proudly he lords it over the humble in his vicinity, but he knows that it is not for his own merits.

32

Cock & Hen

WISDOM MEET FOR A TIME
OF RECKONING IS BETTER
THAN ANY CHOICE VESSEL.

A COCK said to his hen: "There is no more wheat or ears; wherefore are we laggard? There is famine in the city and we shall die. Let us go and lodge in the villages. My brother hath a granary of barley, and there shall we dwell for a whole year, about the granary and its plenty." The two went forth together and walked a day's journey until they came to the city in a land of wheat and barley. There the hen built her nest, and before the year's end there were chicks in her form and image, seven robust cockerels and a puny, ailing pullet. When she clucked to her brood, they scratched for grain with their feet as did she. They ate share and share alike; there was abundance, and the mother rejoiced in her offspring. When the time of harvest came, they spoke of returning to the place of their own dwelling, and the cock said: "Give ear. We shall not return to our folk empty-handed, lest we be for a mockery in their eyes, as if we had come from a place of famine. Rejoice and be glad at my saying. Look upon me and do ye likewise. Each one—cock, chick, and hen—shall carry an ear of corn in his mouth, until ye come to the land of wheat; and ye shall bring forth the old before the new." Said the hen: "Thy counsel is good and sound. Give a portion unto seven, yea unto eight, and each shall carry an ear in his mouth." The eighth was unequal to the burden, for he was sickly; this is what befell him: As they walked by the way of the wilderness, their band in confusion, a fox lay hidden in the forest thickets and watched the band as it came on. The cock was aware that it was upon him and all his host that the fox cast his eye, and he said: "Trembling hath seized me, and my heart is confounded. She that hath borne seven is waxed feeble. The apprehensions of this ambush terrify me, lest he come and smite me, mother upon children. But let us plot cunningly how we may escape, lest he be master over us as he was master over our fathers, for ever is he guileful toward us." As the cock was yet speaking the lurker emerged from the covert where he had lurked, and approached the sickly one and said: "Whose are these and what do they carry in their mouths?" He answered: "The tails of foxes are they carrying, which they wrested from the foxes by their strength, and then flayed the skin from upon them." The fox said: "If such are their deeds, why then is your mouth not laden as is theirs?" And he answered: "It is for this that thou hast come toward me, for it is *thy* tail that I await. Thou shalt no more return to thy tent; my lot I shall make fall upon thee." When the fox heard this he ran away, as the strong man runs a course.

The parable is for a man whose garments are tattered and whose words are not heard. In the assembly of the rich he is for a mockery, and his timely wisdom is despised. But at the day of reckoning the wisdom that issues from his mouth is better than any precious vessel.

33

Brazen Pot & Clay Pot

WHOSO WISHES TO SWALLOW
ONE THAT IS RICHER THAN HE
WILL DISCOVER THAT HE CANNOT
VIE WITH HIS SUPERIOR.

TWO POTS, one of copper and one of earthenware, looked upon one another as they floated on the water. The clay pot envied the copper, for it was clothed in scarlet, and said to her: "How canst thou be proud in thy much praise, for that thou art styled polished brass? Though thou glisten like gold, mine is twice thy strength to fare speedily over the face of the water. I can run two miles twice ere thou run a mile. Because of thy ponderous weight thou lovest repose. It is seemly for me to hold dominion over thee, for I am clever and shifty." The copper pot replied: "Well known is thy shiftiness. If thy claim is just, let us essay to proceed together, battle line facing battle line." And they journeyed as if bound together, joined at their two shoulders. The copper pot went a straight course because of its weight, but the clay pot overturned from its face to its belly because of its lightness, and showed a back side instead of a face, and it went a crooked way. The wind cast it upon the pot of copper, and the waves abetted the wind, and they cracked and shattered the clay pot on the copper.

The parable is for a poor man who strives to overreach the rich. He cannot vie with one stronger than he, and when he vaunts himself over him he is humbled and outstripped, for the race is not to the swift.

34

Frog & Oxen

WHO BOASTS OF HIS DEEDS
MUST BEWARE LEST HIS SHAME
BE REVEALED.

A FROG saw oxen in their ploughing approach the reeds and marsh of her tent and hastened forward to meet them. She inquired their name and the name of their father, for she desired their acquaintance. Said she: "Mine is wisdom and counsel to diagnose every wound or ailment and to apply bandages and potent remedies. By the aspects of the urine and the pulse of the arm I discern improvement or the reverse, and I have restored health to many; as I interpreted, so it came to pass." An elderly ox looked upon her that was boasting for her manifold wisdom and said to her: "If thy words are true, why is thy appearance as of one dead? Thou art the meagerest of all creeping things, as if tomorrow thou wouldst descend t the grave. But wisdom is recognized by its effects; wisdom quickeneth its owner's life. In thee there is no ruddiness, but thou art all green; before thee I cannot forbear spitting." The frog was overwhelmed with shame and sunk her head between her two thighs. She went speedily to hide in her covert of reeds and fens.

The parable is for one who boasts of his wisdom and achievements. Let him beware lest his shame be proven upon him, for it is better to remain silent until others speak of one's splendor than to exchange honor for disgrace. There are some whom others praise and introduce into the presence of the great. And the sage hath said [Proverbs 27.2]: "Let another praise thee, and not thine own mouth."

35

Mouse & Hole

WHOSO LORDS IT OVER THE WEALTH
OF STRANGERS WILL RID HIMSELF
OF IT EVEN AS HE SWALLOWED IT.

A MOUSE lean and black entered a granary through a hole and put his tooth to the grain. He ate and was satisfied and grew fat; he covered his face with fatness, and his little finger was thicker than the loins he had brought thither in the beginning. When he wished to return upon his path he could not pass through the hole by which he had come. The cat looked at him and said: "The hole is not of a size with thee. Mouse, what is this thou hast done?

Thou art waxen fat, thou art grown thick, thou art covered with fatness. Before thou return by this path the fat of thy flesh must grow lean. Never shalt thou see the fathers thou didst know if thou vomit not forth that which thou hast swallowed." The keepers of the granary heard him, and they chased him and smote him and bruised him.

The parable is for a man whose heart made him lord it over the wealth of strangers. Even as he swallowed so did he rid himself of it. A host he swallowed, but he spewed it forth; in the half of his days it forsook him.

36

Wolf & Cattle

WHOSE FEET ARE ACCUSTOMED TO ROBBERY'S PATH, HIS EYE WILL NOT SPARE ANOTHER'S WEALTH.

A WOLF who was the king's vizier and a chief made it his goal to destroy all flesh. He robbed and ravaged, plundered and uprooted; all that he found he pierced. And the beasts and the fowl and the cattle upon whose families confusion had been visited went to the lion to complain of him. Said the lion: "Evil it is and rebellious if, as ye say, he hath bared his teeth. Hath he indeed destroyed according as the cry that hath come unto me? I shall judge him, so that he will turn his back from destroying, and I shall cast the prey from his teeth." And he sent word to the wolf: "Come unto me on the morrow. Hearken and obey, delay not." So he came, and the lion addressed him with sternness and said to him: "Wherefore hast thou done so? No more crush the neck of the cattle, nor rend the beasts for prey. Thine own food are such carcasses and mangled bodies of fowl or cattle as thou wilt find dead in the field. But the living thou shalt not lurk after nor hunt down. If thou canst not keep my words, swear to me that thou wilt not eat meat for two full years, to atone for thy sins, which are inscribed and sealed. This is the sentence that I determine for thee." So the wolf swore this matter: that he would not eat flesh for two years from the day he preyed upon any that dwelt among the beasts. The wolf departed thence and went upon his way, and the lion was left king in his lair. The wolf ate not of any four-legged creature, in keeping with the oath which he sware, unless he found some mangled body or carcass cast out into the field or upon the road. One day when he was famished he turned this way and that and saw a fat kid, desirable to look upon and good to eat; and he said: "Who can keep the commandment?" Within him his thoughts were at war whether to set his face against the kid, and he said in his heart: "If my lust vanquish me and I again smite a living creature as I have done aforetime, from that day I must count two full years during which I must not eat flesh. This is the thing I sware to the king; but my heart hath devised a way to fulfill mine oath: The days of the year number three hundred and sixty-five; let the opening of my eyes be reckoned a day, and their closing a new night." And he opened his eyes after that he had shut them tight, and the evening and the morning were the first day. So doing he counted two years, and his iniquity was removed and his sin atoned. Then his eyes turned to the kid of their choice and looked upon him and pierced him; and he said: "Lo, I have made atonement before my food." So he seized the kid by the neck and cut it up and ate it, as was his wont in the beginning. Still is his arm stretched out against living things, as in days of old and years gone by.

The parable is for a man wont ever to steal and rob, whose eye spares not the wealth of others. Their wealth and their toil he spoils and plunders; and if he swear in the presence of all, his heart will cunningly circumvent his oath and he will account himself innocent of his curse.

37

Eagle, Fowl, Lion, Beasts, Bat

HE WHO SPEAKS SMOOTH WORDS
WILL BE FELLOW TO THE STRONG
IN OPPRESSION.

THE EAGLE ruled over all winged creatures, whether on land or bough, and the lion over all cattle and beasts from all remote ends of the earth. The eagle and the birds made war with the lion and all the beasts and cattle. Said the bat in his heart, for wickedness engulfed him: "Verily, I have wings like the birds and feet like the cattle and beasts. I know not which host will prevail over the other, or who will die or be taken captive or be crushed. I shall stand spectator and see whether he be strong or weak, and my hand shall be with the folk whose hand prospers and prevails." So he withdrew from the host and stood over against it to see what would befall. He took his stand upon a tall tree in the distance and said: "It is a time of battle for the birds and not a time of play. I shall lift mine eyes to the victors to help them. I shall abide quiet and look forth from my mansion." When he saw that the beasts had the upper hand and that confusion had fallen upon the host of the birds, he descended from the tree and went on all fours, and swore to all the beasts and the cattle to help with all his might. And he said: "Be strong and do battle. Let not the winged creatures escape; let every man be zealous against them." But as the day waned toward evening the battle waxed strong; the birds gathered might, and confusion fell upon the lion's host. Said the bat in his heart: "I will return to mine own people; I will no longer continue in sorrow with the lion's host. I will fly up and perch, and I will hide my feet under my wings." So he gathered his feet between his shoulders to make himself wings and quickly flew among the birds and said: "Strengthen your weak hands and inflict bruises and wounds and festering sores upon the beasts and the cattle that walk on all fours." But the birds recognized the bat and said: "Why art thou so transformed to walk among us so willfully? In the morning we saw thee with the lion's host, walking on all fours like them, when their hand was strong; and thou didst put thy hand forth against our position, when thou wert a bird like ourselves. But when we prevailed, then didst thou spread thy wings toward us. Blood hast thou hated, and blood will pursue thee. Wherefore hast thou mocked thy skin and worked deception and unrighteousness? Thy ambush is within thee, for now that thou art returned to those of whom thou wert ashamed, the iniquity in thee is found out. This shall be thy penalty: Thou shalt be accounted among the species of creeping things. A wanderer and a vagabond shalt thou be in the land. For that thou hast played the stranger with thy fellows so shall thy seed be, black and plucked and bald and blind, and strangers in our midst. Thou shalt no more walk with neck outstretched. The light of the sun will be for thee blindness. Leprous and a vermin shalt thou be called. Of every encounter shalt thou be afraid." So they conspired against him, and they brought him to the eagle, who said: "Is this he who simulated the cattle and the beasts? For that his spirit is lying he shall be plucked and bald and shall flee from the light of the sun. In the evening he shall flit about as one confused. Not even in the tenth generation shall he enter into the congregation. He shall not avail to stand upon his feet if the sun shine upon him." And so they plucked him and scraped him and blinded his eyes, and they drove him confounded from the dwelling places which they inhabited, and all the birds of heaven became strangers unto him. Now he is like neither bird nor beast; they call him vermin upon the earth.

The parable is for one who sees his friend or relative fall under the power of his enemy, and addresses the enemy with blandishing words. With the strong he pretends strength, for crooked gain; but if the lowly acquire firmness and strength, with his false heart he returns to become his comrade, for he knows no shame or remorse. And with this comradeship he acts deceitfully, saying: "Lo, I have strengthened and helped thee and with the right hand of my righteousness I supported thee when the hand of thine enemy was strong upon thee. I did not slacken in the day of tribulation." What befell the bat will befall him in the end, and he will leave no name or remnant. His fate is fitted to the pattern carved: The wicked shall not be unpunished.

38

Hare & Hounds

HE WHOM FORTUNE GOVERNS

SHALL NOT SPEEDILY FIND ESCAPE.

A HARE and her children resolved to leave the place where they dwelt, for they found no respite there. The dogs were harsh of soul and always pursued after them; they ran and never tired, they walked and grew not weary. Said the hares: "Lo, we are left few out of many, and the fire that rages against us is never quenched. Even in our chambers there is dread, and our spirit can no longer stand erect. Let us journey forth and go to a field where there is none to track and chase us." One of the family, upon whom rested the spirit of wisdom, made answer: "If ye will accede to my counsel and hearken to the instruction of my lips, ye will not remove hence.

Many have I seen journey from their place and their native land, but they have returned to the spot of their shame; where they had hoped to find a land peaceful and serene, they found twofold perturbation. For living creatures have no governance over their lot to escape the machinations of fate. He that acknowledges his own abiding place will not change or seek a substitute for it; for wherever the soles of your feet tread, the voice of terror will be in your ears." But they hearkened not to what he had said to them and forsook their place and their tents. They walked until the sun set and there was no light; and all, great and small, encamped by the bank of a river. But when they thought to find a resting place for the soles of their feet, lo, frogs' voices roared from the river, and dread and terror fell upon all the hares; one lamented bitterly with his voice, and one scurried from his place, one went a crooked way. There was no refuge for the swift of foot. When dawn broke, lo, there were men passing and returning upon the road, riding upon horses, with dogs before them. Their yelping was loud as they sniffed from the road the tracks of the hares scattered over the field, and the riders tarred them on to spread confusion among them, and they smote them and desolated them. The remnant said: "We will return to our people and our native place. Alas for the day that our souls were impatient of hearing the counsel of the sage and our hearts were enticed to folly! Better for us was it then than now." So with souls grieving and sorrowing the remnant that survived turned back until they came to the land of their dwelling.

The parable is for a man whom fortune governs. He says: "I will make my wandering far, I will seek me a refuge"; and he forsakes his place and his native land. But his glory shall not abide upon the path which he takes. If one say to him: "Cast thy desires upon thy creator and endure his destiny; who can straighten that which he hath made crooked? Abide until the storm shall pass from thy tent and the spirit of the ruler favor thee"—he will not hearken nor consent. The many who heed not counsel are as fickle as coracles; they journey forth from the tents which they had fixed fast. Better than fine gold and than jasper set and enclosed in a ring, is when the wise admonishes an ear that hearkens.

39

Starling, Eagle, Birds

THE SMALL MAY HOPE
FOR LORDSHIP, FOR WISDOM
IS BETTER THAN STRENGTH.

A STARLING came to rule by reason of his wisdom and not his great strength; though he was smaller than all winged creatures, he was raised and exalted over them. When the birds foregathered in the beginning and took counsel to set as king over them what bird would soar highest in their camp, the eagle said: "Who among those that fly is as I am, and who but me is swift?" When the starling heard this, he plotted in his thoughts to make his perch firm on the eagle's wing; wherever the eagle would fly, there would his own encampment be; the eagle would bear him upon his pinions. So he hid on the eagle's wing, as he had planned; and when all the winged creatures soared, the eagle rose twice as high into heaven as any bird that flew, and he said: "I am king over all the birds, for I have enlarged and exalted myself." While he was yet speaking, the starling came; he had hidden under his wing and until then had rested on his back, so that his reason stood firm within him. When he saw that the eagle was weary and his hands were lax, he gathered his strength and girded himself to fly higher, above the eagle. So they gave him the majesty of kingship and royalty.

The parable is for a man filled with silver and gold, beneath whom the supporters of pride are humble, while he boasts of his painted chambers. But the strong must not glory in his strength to despise the humble and the small; for time will turn to be his pursuer and will cast him down from his ambitions, and a humble man with understanding will search him out. Right is the saying of the sage to make wise: "Better is wisdom than strength."

40

Bear & Doe

LET A MAN'S SOUL NOT BE PRECIOUS IN HIS EYES, TO ESCAPE IN PLACE OF HIS SONS.

A BEAR saw a pregnant doe whose labors had seized her so that she travailed sore. The bear perceived that her time was come to give birth and that her bearing was difficult, and in his cunning said to her: "Hasten, dispatch thy throes, for I shall put mine eye upon thee for kindness and upon the fawns thou wilt bear, if I know where they are. Leave thy sons; I will give them life and find their sufficiency of food. There shall be a covenant of peace between me and thee forever." It was in slyness that the bear spoke, to devour her young; but she made her reply with wisdom: "I know thine eyeballs look fairly upon me in the innocence of thy heart and the purity of thy hands, and I rejoice in thy saying. Thou hast spread thy wings over thy handmaiden. But I beseech you, my lord, fulfill my request: Remove thee two bowshots from upon me, for in the article of birth it brings us shame if males look upon us. Pass over from me, and thou shalt be the diligent one who profiteth. Look not behind thee and stand not in all the plain. This day it is not proper for males to be with females in their environs. I can do nothing until thou go hence. Already had I given birth, hadst thou not restrained me for my great shame." So the bear went and sat afar, the distance of two bowshots; and when she saw that he was far off, the doe's feet carried her away. By her wariness she delivered her own life and the life of her sons.

The parable is that a man should not hold his own soul precious, to escape from the snares of death, and give his son in his place. A woman big of belly should not make her life precious in her eyes, saying: "Would I might empty my full belly, for until now have I labored for vanity." Like the doe she should take her life in her hands to deliver her offspring by flattery and deception.

41

Peacock, Wheat, Crane

A MAN'S PRIDE WILL BRING HIM LOW, AND HE SHALL NOT AVAIL TO ENTER INTO JUDGMENT WITH ONE STOUTER THAN HE.

THE COLORFUL bird called peacock found a heap of wheat, and the crane also came and set his mouth to the grain. Said the peacock to the crane: "Why hast thou no awe of me? Who art thou to associate with me? What hath chaff to do with corn? Who is so beautiful as I among all the fowl, and to whom wilt thou liken me to be mine equal? Who can find any taint in me? My plumage is as a coat of many colors, and princes and princesses make headdresses of my tail to wear as tiaras. Have I peers? Who can recount my splendor? Happy the fowl to whom I communicate my secrets. Gold exceeding fine is the crown of my head. Mine is glory and dominion. No bird is like me for beauty. Mine is the plumage and mine the broidery. My tail is beyond calculation; two cubits and a half is its length. But thou art like a thief, curtailed for his crime. Why art not in fear and dread to enter into the same camp with me? Depart, and let us be two camps. Thy meagerness cannot be described." Answered the crane: "If my twigs are silent, yet thy lies make men hold their peace. Why dost thou vaunt thy tail and feathers? Let another praise thee, and not thine own mouth; a stranger, and not thine own lips. If thou art comely in thine own eyes, thou art lowly and feeble for thy size, lowly in voice and lowly in stature. Thou walkest not forth with a high hand and art undone by the rebuke of any fowl. Thou canst not fly like them, and therefore thou dwellest on dry land. But lo, my sheaf arose and also stood upright; my neck is long, my throat outstretched. I make my shout heard among the stars. My legs are straight; of me was it said, Thy stature is like to a palm tree. It is not out of weakness but out of strength that my tail is short; to cast dread upon mine enemies I gird my loins for battle. But thine ornateness is only a flaw. Favor is deceitful and beauty is vain." When the peacock heard this stern speech he fell mute, for it was time to be silent.

The parable is for one who boasts of his beauty. If his heart is empty of wisdom, this is his flaw; for a man's pride will bring him low, and he cannot enter into judgment with one stouter than he. Pleasant indeed is the saying of the Arab sage: "A man can bequeath his son nothing better than wisdom." He that boasts of beauty and wealth is smitten with blindness, for what avails an open eye if the heart is unseeing?

42

Smith & Bramblebush

AMONG ALL MEN ON THE FACE
OF THE DRY LAND THERE ARE MANY
WHO REPAY EVIL FOR GOOD.

AN IRONSMITH labored and toiled and with his strong arm fashioned a peerless axe of steel. Its edge he whetted to remove its bluntness. Then he inquired of his neighbors whence he might procure suitable wood, for he desired to make a strong helve and sought timber that would not rot. His advisers responded as follows: "Take thee of the branch of the bramblebush; it is tougher than all other wood and will last forever." So he went to the bramblebush according to this counsel and cut a branch. Laboriously he fitted the wood he prepared to the steel, and fashioned the axe and finished it, saying of the joint, "It is good." To make trial of its goodness and beauty he seized the axe and cut the bramblebush down entirely, root and branch, for its day was come.

The parable is for a man who loved his neighbor and cosseted him and made much of him, and fed him and gave him drink when he was hungry and naked and needy. But when he saw him waxed fat and grown great he turned wicked and betrayed the kindness he had done him, and requited him evil instead of good and enmity instead of love. And he hated him with bitter hatred, more than any man on earth. Their nobles shall be of themselves, and their governor shall proceed from the midst of them. Shall the axe boast itself against him that heweth therewith? What this man finds is bitterer than death; his destroyers and they that make him waste shall go forth out of himself.

43

Wolf, Dog, Flock

A MAN MUST NOT BETRAY HIS FAITH NOR VIOLATE HIS COMMANDMENT.

A WOLF who was in fear of a dog carried a loaf of bread to the sheep which were enclosed within a hedge. The dog awoke from his sleep, and the wolf in his cunning said to him: "Know that what is mine is thine. Take my blessing which I have brought thee; but not by bread alone will I be thy helpmeet. Take all I have that is desirable, but for the present, eat bread." The dog answered: "In vain hast thou wearied thy footsteps; though thou urge me I shall not eat thy bread, for it is the bread of falsehood. In my sight thy words are not good; not for my benefit hast thou brought me bread from thy house, but to stop my mouth lest I raise my voice against thee when thou spoilest the sheep. Thou didst think to find a favorable opportunity; but far be it from me to quench the candle of my honor. My master has entrusted the sheep to my hand; how shall I betray my faith? I love my master and my house; from my youth he has brought me up, as a father. But for thy cajoling words thou shalt grieve." The dog whetted his tongue against him, and the shepherd arose in anger and ran with the dog to chase away the wolf, who hated him in his heart.

The parable is for a man who guards his spirit lest he prove faithless and make his way crooked. In his mouth and in his heart the law is one. For no reward or bribe will he betray his faith nor will he cheat his comrade to raise his heel against him. Not from granary or winepress but from the dog he draweth his example, for he is not corrupted by bribery. And the sage hath said: "Cleave unto faith and keep the commandment, for no wealth is greater than forsaking lust."

44

Kite & Doves

HE THAT BESTOWETH HONOR UPON HIS DESTROYER ACQUIRETH A MASTER OVER HIMSELF.

A KITE dwelt and watched among the doves, and if one was alone he flew with him and would suddenly strike and devour him; in the flicker of an eye he disappeared. The doves consulted amongst themselves, for the kite deceived them, and resolved to seek his peace and to conclude a covenant with him if he would walk in innocence and uprightness with them. They said to him: "Thou shalt be our lord; come thou and rule over us, and our weak hands shall be strengthened, for the birds will fear thee." So they gave him dominion and the majesty of royalty, and he was received into their company. But each day the kingship afflicted them with wrath outpoured, for he robbed them and their company, and tore and plucked their plumage. He said to them: "How can ye stand in the place of my coming? If I am lord where is my terror?" And he preyed upon them and devoured them in every corner, and none stirred his wing nor opened his mouth to chirp, and they that remained fled to the hills. They were wearied and sickened of their lives, and confusion fell upon their families. The doves of the valleys all murmured and said: "What is this we have done to put over us a brazen-faced king? What he hath formerly done in secret he now doth in the open. Who shall be left? Better our life without him, when we could take pleasant counsel with him."

The parable is for a man who gives honor to one who

is his destroyer; he acquires a master over himself. Better that his eyes should avoid him than that he should speak with him, good or evil. For he nurseth rebellion in his heart, and ever is his ambush within him. The man who serves and honors him will rejoice and be glad at his doom. And the sage hath said: "Honor him thou lovest and he will love thee; beware of him thy heart hateth."

45

Cormorant & Birds

A MAN FILLED WITH VIOLENCE SHALL BE FOR A SPOIL IN THE LAND OF HIS HABITATION.

AMONG the birds the cormorant was for a scorn and a reproach, for his was the shame of the backside. Through the aperture he ejected his excrements a thousand times in an instant; his stench was noisome at all times and he made their camp unclean. They hated him sore and banished him from their world, saying: "Without the camp shall be thy resting place, and thou shalt turn and cover thine excrements. The plague of emerods is in thee, and it seals thy passages; our doom for thee is death." He stood rooted in shame, for he was a mockery and a laughing stock. And he saw a place afar off, atop a lofty hill, and there he sat with soul downcast. But even there he found no rest, for the winged creatures sent a messenger to bid him depart. And he said: "I stand in awe of every bird in the land of my habitation. I will fly away and settle at the end of the sea; I will wander far off to a distant country. No longer will I hear the voice of oppressors and persecutors, and there shall I be honored instead of being despised and lightly esteemed. There is none that holdeth with me in this matter." So he flew toward the sea. At eventide the raven encountered him and said: "Whither goest, cormorant? Surely thou seekest a resting place which shall please thee?" And he answered: "I shall find me a resting place beyond the sea, for thy fellows have driven me from my heritage and cried 'Unclean, unclean!' against me." Said the raven: "Carriest thou with thee thy rear, which hath driven thee far from thy resting place?" The cormorant answered: "My rear I cannot leave behind me, for I have carried that shame from my youth." Said the raven: "That will be a scorn and a mockery to thee wheresoever thy foot treads. Just as thy friends have turned into enemies because of it here, so there all that go and come will keep far from thee. Abundant plumage and mighty limbs will not avail thee, for thou wilt be helpless and crushed."

The parable is of a violent man who is for a spoil in the land of his habitation for that he treads the bow of his tongue for falsehood, is a talebearer, a betrayer of secrets, and a searcher for gossip to which he may add falsehood. When he sees that his fellows hate him he journeys far from his dwelling place, where he has wrought no good among his people but put forth his hand against men who wished him well; but there they hate him as men had done in his former place. Death and life are in the power of the tongue. Of the bearers of slander our sages have said: "This shall be the law of the leprous." And the Arab hath said: "Ere thou utterest thy word consider what its end will be." For as a man undergoes cautery to remedy his body, so should he labor to heal his soul of the incidence of flattery and cruelty and to remove his destroyer from his tongue.

46

Cat & Mouse

THERE IS DELIVERY AND RECOURSE
FOR AN OATH TAKEN UNDER DURESS.

A CAT went forth one morning to hunt his food, and he saw over against him a mouse in a vessel full of strong drink; this had befallen him because he could not make his way out. The cat, hungry and eager, went toward him joyfully. There he would display the inveterate hatred which was his guilt, for he hated the mouse from yesterday and the day before. He sprang to the lip of the vessel and crouched and rose against him and lifted his voice against the mouse and framed false charges against him, saying: "My righteousness and thy guilt have driven thee thither. Woe to them that rise early in the morning to pursue strong drink! Hasten, come forth, stand not; I shall work my will upon thee. Thy sorrow shall be turned to my delight, for thy flesh is dainty." The mouse made answer: "I am oppressed and tormented, I am plucked and bald, without taste or flavor. I have fallen and cannot rise, I am broken down and cut off. The fat of my flesh hath grown lean from the day I fell into this pit, and my countenance testifieth to my sore grief and affliction. Now for a month nor bread nor pottage hath passed my lips. If gladness hath burgeoned within thee, rejoice not when thine enemy is fallen. Work no ill against me now, deliver me that I sink not, and I will make thee my beneficiary. At the appointed time I shall return to thee, and I shall be plump and my hair sprouted; when I return thou shalt rejoice in my flesh. Only bring my soul forth from its straits, for the waters have risen over my head." He raised his hand to the cat that he would return to him at the appointed time and show himself in a month. And he swore an oath: If the cat would deliver him from captivity, he would keep his covenant and stand fast by it. So the cat who was his troubler turned to be his helper; he remembered not his hatred but drew the mouse out of the strong drink. But when the mouse was departed from the cat he turned his back and rebelled against him. He feasted his heart with all good things and tarried beyond the appointed term. The cat sent him word, saying: "Thy covenant thou must keep; thou must return to my domain, plump and fat as thou hast sworn. Let not thy footsteps tarry, for thou hast added to thy term. If thou deceive me and abide, then give thy son in thy stead." The mouse acknowledged his oath, but declared that it was given under duress, for he was confronted with ruin when he swore. Furthermore, it was in drunkenness that he had recklessly sworn, when he was not master of himself. The oath was given both in drunkenness and under coercion; law is for life, not death. With such a claim he escaped, and the cat had no power over him.

The parable is for a dispute between two men, where each studies and seeks to transform the complaint to a plot or accident, to be acquitted of offense, for what is done under duress or in drunkenness has no validity but is accounted youthful folly. And the sage hath said to his son [Ecclesiastes 10.2]: "A wise man's heart is at his right side." If thou art wise thou wilt be enlarged and exalted. Be not wise in words if thou art not so in deed, for when a man's words do not resemble his deeds, it is folly on his part and shame.

47

Ass in Lion's Skin

IF THE SPIRIT OF PRIDE HATH BREATHED IN A MAN, THE SPIRIT OF WISDOM IS NOT IN HIM.

AN ASS went from his master's house to graze in the hills and high places, and there he found the flayed skin of a lion. In this he resolved to clothe himself, and he put his hands forth to throw it over him before and behind and over the smooth of his neck and his hands. His heart was uplifted and he walked in pride, exalting himself and saying: "I shall be king." And he went to terrorize the beasts in the hills and the valleys, and like a lion he hunted and tracked man and beast in the fields. For fear of him the shepherds abandoned the keeping of their sheep, for they thought he was a lion, when he was only an ass; and the tillers of soil fled before him nor pastured their sheep and kine. Each cried to his brother: "Hear thou me; cast away the sheep which is thy wealth, for he that shall be found in the field shall not live." To them the ass was a lion; and out of his heart's delight at being thought a lion he dealt frowardly with his master and said: "He shall no longer lay burdens upon me." The ass knew not his master's crib and returned not to his house; but he cast his terror over all that walked on fours, for so had he vehemently sworn in his pride. A report was heard: "A lion hath gone up from his lair. Gird ye every man his sword upon his thigh and we shall surround him with spears and snares; mayhap we shall avail to smite him. If we trap him in forest or plain we shall send him to the king for a gift." The master of the ass said to his neighbors: "I have lost my ass, but how shall I seek him?—The lion may make me his prey." One day the master went and wrapped his face in his mantle, and came to one of the hills. There he saw his ass disguised as a lion to terrify all that caught sight of him. By his stature and tail and ears the master recognized his ass, and when he saw his master the ass cast his eyes down. Said the master: "Because thy heart was high and thine ambush within thee, because thou hast made bold to shed innocent blood and cast thy terror in the land of the living, hast walked with neck outstretched, hast dreamed and thyself interpreted, hast been enticed by the rebelliousness of thy heart to become stranger to thy master and thy tasks, thy toil and thy yoke shall be made heavy and thou shalt be cast down to the dust. Thou shalt not pursue the sheep as if they were thy booty. Now remove thine adornment, and I will make thee stand naked as on the day of thy birth; thy glory will turn to thy doom. Thou shalt know who thou art and whence thou comest, and whether thou hast seen thy father king over the beasts." The ass was stripped of his adornment, and received twofold punishment from his master for his rebelliousness.

The parable is for a vile and nameless man over whom a breeze wafts so that he sins and the spirit of pride stirs in him; there is no spirit of wisdom within him. A people who knew him not serve him, and they honor him in his walking and his sitting down, for in his walking abroad he is recognized only by his garb and his fine raiment. He deals haughtily with them, saying, "I have found them slaves." His crest was among thick boughs, and he walked with neck outstretched, forgetting who his fathers were. He vaunted his height and the length of his branches, but when they recognized his taint and the taint of his fathers they exchanged his glory for shame.

And I plied my poesy and said:

An ass clothed himself in lion's skin he found,

And his approach frightened bear and leopard.
So the vile one who clothes him in fine linen and is
  proud,
But knows not decently to lift head or feet.

48

Fox & Crane

TO MAKE THE PATH OF HIS DEEDS
STRAIGHT A MAN SHOULD
COMPANY WITH HIS EQUAL.

THE FOX said to the crane: "Why art thou ever shut in? Come and dine with me, and see my house and my people." And he enticed him to come with him, to be merry with him and eat his bread. The fox dashed forward for flesh; he made a sudden attack upon the poultry and smote a hen who had closed her eyeballs in the face of the sun and had sighed and spread her wings. While the fox prepared his repast he devised cunning plots and said in his heart: "Lo, simple am I if I do not eat of what I have prepared and only lick the food which is so sweet, while the crane swallows the whole at once." With his wonted slyness he ground his food fine and spread it upon the table and invited the crane to eat. But the crane could take none into his mouth, for it was not his manner to eat food fine and scattered and spread. But the eye of the fox took no pity upon him, and he left the table empty, even as the ox licketh up the grass of the field. But the crane returned to his house fordone and weary, hungry and heavy and depressed. He spoke not to the fox, neither showing his impatience nor concealing it, but in his reins he was perplexed and sought to exact vengeance. While he was devising a plan, a tree taught him his invention: All its limbs were full of apertures, and these holes he filled with provision. Any food he prepared he thrust into the hole, so deep that none could find it, and it would be his with no stranger to share. The crane bored a hole in his door whereby he entered his domain, and there deposited his food. Then he invited the fox and urged him to come

with him; and he showed him the food and said: "What is before thee is thine; eat as is good in thy sight." But the fox could not lick it free with his tongue to subject it to his tooth; neither with tongue nor paw could he move it. At this the crane rejoiced, for he could bring the food out and eat it heartily in the presence of the fox. He requited the fox for his deed; as he did, so was it done to him.

The parable is for one who seeks plots and accidents and contrivances to befool his neighbor that is a perfect and upright man and dwells with him in security. The other will become infected by his composition and his malefactions, in the way that he has taught. The stouthearted are spoiled and their heart is as fat as grease. He thinks to find good when he doeth ill. How can he harvest wheat who sows thorns? He that fashions calamity for his neighbor, the instrument of his wounding is in his own hand.

49

Sow, Doe, Beasts

IF A MAN'S SOUL IS POLLUTED AND DEFILED HE CANNOT EASILY BE HEALED.

A SOW of the forest wallowed in the mire and found delight in trampling the muck. In the forest there was the sound of banqueting and gaiety, of a board laden with dainties, for the stag was marrying his kinswoman, and all that walked on fours had assembled at his wedding canopy. Each feasted and was filled with bread and meal, flesh and fish, all eating and making merry in their gladness; great and small participated in the festivities for seven days. The sow heard the sound of rejoicing but laid it not upon her heart. A deer looked upon the sow, her gaping mouth befouled with filth for she had rooted in the dung heap, had eaten to her full, and showed the remains, and the deer said to the sow: "Come to the house of the bride, where is the sound of a happy throng. Thou shalt lack nothing; all that thine eyes ask, thou shalt there take; not by measure shalt thou there eat thy bread. Present there is every bird after its kind. His ornament maketh the stag master, and the spirit of joy prevails mightily in his heart. The winged creatures utter song. There are viands of all manner in abundance, and vessels of diverse sorts. The amiable doe hath made herself beautiful for the stag, and over all the canopy is a glorious shelter." Answered the sow: "If indeed food of all sorts was there, did ye eat bran steeped in hot water and mire trampled in the streets? There is no dainty like them in all the land, and if these two are withheld then all the rest is nothing worth in my sight, for from the day of my birth I have tasted no viands as delightful as these."

The parable is for one whose comportment is repulsive and whose lust never abandons the glitter of his sins, until his soul is defiled and polluted. The healing of his transgressions is negligible, for his errors flourish within him and he does deeds which are not done. His heart hath played the harlot by the path of his eyes; and even when he grows old, he will never depart from his ways. In the eyes of his neighbors he is abominable and filthy, for he hath troubled the waters with his feet. When his comrades say: "Lo, how goodly and how pleasant it is to cleave to the way of the upright and innocent, whose portion is for life and for whom much good is stored up; be thou strong and do as they do."—Then will he say: "That which I have tried I love, for I have made lying my shelter and by falsehood am I hidden. I will fulfill my desire and satisfy my lust to add drunkenness to thirst. Better for me is the pleasure of my eyes and the enjoyment of my inclinations than to await royalty in another world. I shall have peace, for I shall walk in the imagination of my heart."

50

Lion, Beasts, Ape

MASTER AND CONSTRAIN THY HEART TO BRING ALL THINGS NEAR AND KEEP THEM NOT AFAR.

THE LION published a notice throughout his realm that all that walked on fours should attend him on an appointed day. He wished to know which was superior in favor and comeliness, beautiful of form and beautiful of aspect, for he intended to make that one who won favor in the eyes of his beholders second to himself in authority. When they were all gathered together, the ape said: "None bears such favor as my son or is so handsome and so adorned. How great is his goodness, and how great his beauty! The majesty of my lord the king will be increased and augmented by my son, he will find thine own pleasure and speak thy words."

They that speak in parables say: To him that loveth toad and mouse they appear as two great lights. Therefore should every man compel and constrain his heart to bring his neighbor near and not keep him afar. Even if the fire of hatred burns in him like a flame, his left hand should repel but his right hand bring near.

51

Four Oxen & a Lion

A COMPANY FREE OF TERROR IS
THE DWELLING OF BRETHREN TOGETHER.

FOUR OXEN agreed to unite into a fellowship, bound close together and not separated. They concluded a covenant and were moved by a single spirit. Many days they continued in this fellowship; when they stood they stood together and when they walked they walked together. A lion circled about the four of them but saw that their time was not come, for they stood as one in the battlefield, and because they were four, they were stout in their going forth. The lion brooded in his soul, month by month, how he could bring destruction upon them if their bond were loosed. One day he stood from afar and gaped his maw wide for he was hungry and weary; hope long deferred had made him heavy and displeased. He called to the ox whose feet stood in the plain and cajoled him by the smoothness of his lips until he separated him from his band; and when he was separated from his fellows, the lion dedicated him to evil, for he spoiled him in his anger and devoured him. The voice of the three that were left in the camp terrified him not, nor did he make answer to their bellowing.

The parable: How goodly and how pleasant it is when the counsel of comrades is gathered together in sweetness. When brethren dwell together, their fellowship is free of fear. Their enticers are as waters that fail. They consult only to cast down and their goal is guile, to separate their victims from their fellowship and alienate them from their delight. With him who has strayed from the band the treacherous dealer dealeth treacherously and the spoiler spoileth. The wise take it not to heart if their associate is slandered; they have ears but hear not, for their soul is pure and innocent and they abhor the false tongue of them that work deception. The bond between two wise men will not be loosed, and the threefold cord is not quickly broken.

52

Lion, Wolf, Fox, Ox, Calf

THERE IS ONE WHO IS DESTROYED WITHOUT JUDGMENT, BUT THE TONGUE OF THE WISE IS FOR A HEALING.

A LION who ruled by his strength summoned a wolf and a fox to his presence and said to them: "A month past my lioness bore me a cub; let us go together and bring provision for her." So the two went with him. Their king passed before them, and their hearts were fortified with gladness at his fellowship. The three strode boldly on. In the field they looked about them like spoilers, and upon that day they broke the necks of an ox, a cow, and a calf. Said the lion to the fox: "Thou hast been set on high; is thy heart within thee uncircumcised that thou knowest not how to divide booty without lots?" The fox answered and said: "I am young in years, whereas the wolf is reckoned amongst the exceeding wise, and the passage of years implants knowledge. His apportionment will be perfect." The lion said to the wolf: "Why is the wise loath to choose portions? All that issueth from his mouth shall stand fast." The wolf answered: "The ox is for my lord the lion, and the cow shall be brought to his mate, the lioness; the calf shall be divided between me and the fox." Said the lion: "In rebelliousness and treachery and guilt and frowardness and intransigence thou hast not remembered a portion for my firstborn son. Therefore thy blood is upon thy head, and I shall make thy soul grieve." He drew his hand upon him and smote him and flayed him of his skin head to foot until his skull and hide wallowed in blood. He said to the fox: "At thy word shall the booty be divided." And the fox answered: "I shall divide it with justice and equity. To my lord the king, the ox; to the lioness, the cow. For the cub in whom thy heart rejoiceth I adjudge the calf as a portion." Said the lion: "There is none so wise and understanding as thou in all my realm. From this day forward I shall make thee my confidant, for in mine eyes thou art very desirable. From whom hast thou learnt to divide booty?" The fox answered: "When I saw the miter upon the wolf's head wrapped in blood when he stumbled in the utterance of his lips, and that a deceived heart led him astray—therefore did I not allow my tongue to sin."

The parable: A man must not hasten to speak before one that is stronger than he. He shall fashion a bridle for his spirit and acquire counsel, that he make not his path crooked, for some are destroyed without judgment. But the tongue of the wise is for a healing; for he reflects and ponders, but delays the words of his mouth. The wise man is instructed by the example of another. And the sage hath said in his book of instruction [Proverbs 19.25]: "Smite a scorner, and the simple will beware." And the Arab in his wisdom hath said: "The portion of one man is from his ear to his soul, and the portion of one man from his tongue to another."

53

Sun, Wind, Man

THE WISE MAN ACHIEVES MORE
BY HIS WISDOM THAN THE STRONG
BY HIS STRENGTH.

SUN AND WIND compared their qualities. Said the sun to the wind: "I am upright and innocent, and for my great beauty they have made me ruler over the day. If thou boast against me, it will be accounted folly in thee, for mine is the strength and the favor and the splendor, like unto heaven's self for purity." Answered the wind: "If thy merits were twice thy praise, the prevailing wind would be thy superior. At night thou art no longer seen; the sun knoweth his setting. But my dominion is by day and by night; therefore it beseems me to rule. My deeds are known in the land: I rend the mountains and break in pieces the rocks." Said the sun: "Let us try our strength. Here is a man coming forth toward us, clothed in tunic and mantle. Go thou now and fight with him and wage cunning war against him until thou strip mantle from tunic. If he leave his garment by thy side I shall bestow the majesty of kingship upon thee. Thy work will prosper and thou wilt strip him: thou hast a garment: be thou lord over us." The wind said in his heart: "I will sway him by my cunning or strip him by my strength." So the wind went forth in the sight of the sun and blew strong before him. The man walked straight upon his way; when the cold wind came out of the north, he wrapped his mantle and tunic together and swathed himself in them so that the wind should not come between. When the wind put forth all the strength of his might, the man tied the loops of his mantle around his forehead and with his right hand grasped his skirts and made them a turban about his head; the wind did not lay bare the face of his raiment. When it appeared that the wind was wearied, for all his boasting and did not avail to wrest the mantle away and his hopes were disappointed, the sun said: "Now shalt thou see what I shall do to him." He rent his robe of darkness and his shade and dispersed all the shadows. The sun went forth over the land and confronted the man in his might; as the sun issued forth in his strength he looked upon the man from on high. When the south wind quieted the earth and the steady eye of the sun gazed upon him it wrested the weight of his garments from upon him and stripped him of his mantle. Naked did he flee that day, and availed not to carry his gear with him. When the sun shone upon him it stripped him in quietness when it reached him; not so the wind, which stormed mightily and raged.

The parable is that a wise man can achieve by his wisdom what the strong cannot by his strength. The words of the wise are as arrows in the hands of warriors and as flames of fire in a blaze. The auxiliaries of pride stoop when the gates of wisdom are opened in the wall of understanding. Though they be like gins and snares to captivate hearts, they are heard in calm; but no man has awe of a boastful fool.

54

Cedar & Bush

LET NO MAN BOAST OF HIS WEALTH, FOR NOT FOREVER WILL HIS LIGHT SHINE BRIGHT.

THE CEDAR of Lebanon, whose name shall be continued as long as the sun, was proud of his limbs and his stateliness, of his height and his many branches. There was none like him in the forest; the cedars would not hide him. He looked about him in the camp and lo! near him was a bush, and he said: "What hast thou to do here that thou hast come into my boundary? How wert thou not afraid to dwell in my shadow? Can timber be taken from thee to do any work? Me kingship beseemeth, for I bring forth fruit and bear branches and in me dwell winged creatures. My little finger is thicker than thy loins. With whom hast thou left thy briars and brambles? Thou art only a shoot of pine, but of me they make oars and masts, which stand as an ensign for the nations. Thy root is the root of the broom." Answered the bush: "With the words of thy mouth thou hast stumbled, in that thou hast sought to boast of thy beauty. Remember that thy place will be ploughed as a field, and they will destroy thy stock to the root. Thine adornment of lush branches they will cut for planks and pillars and bars. I shall look upon thy place, and it is gone; but against us none that hews down shall arise. Thy stateliness is turned upon thee for destruction, to hew thy wood and cast down thy leafage. Thy fruits every passerby will pluck and gather, while I shall rest secure and tranquil."

The parable forbids a man to boast of beauty or riches

over his neighbor or brother or stranger. For the young lions who lack and suffer hunger will seek him day by day and he will not avail to hide; all of his days he will eat in darkness. But for the humble, over whom he has spoken strong and proud words, there may be a hope.

And I plied my poesy:

With head bowed and heart crushed and eye lowly
Thy steps will stand steadfast.
See how the fire that rises is quenched in the end,
While water that descends abides.

55

Small Fish in Net

CAST NOT AWAY WHAT IS IN THY HAND, TO TAKE IN THY NET WHAT IS NOT THINE.

A SMALL FISH caught in a net said to the fisherman: "I am too little to be game, that thou put me on thy hook. Spare me, that I comfort myself; thy heart will easily abandon me. Neither boiled nor roasted on the fire can I restore thy soul. Let me go and refresh myself, and I will serve thee two full years. Then wilt thou find me in my river as aforetime, large of stature and seven times as fat. If then I be boiled in water, it shall be as a festival in thy house, and then can thy heart be sustained with me." Answered the fisherman: "Better is a little fish which is now within my grasp than a great leviathan which my neighbors will rule a year hence."

The parable is known in every city, and its interpretation is familiar upon the lips of every creature: Better is a handful of satisfaction in thine own palms than heaping handfuls of hope in the hands of another. Better is a bird enclosed in a cage than two hopping on the hedge. Take what is good, even if it be little; lay your hand upon it and grasp it and let it not go. Do not choose hope deferred for doubtful increase of advantage and blessing.

56

Lion & Hunter

MANY ARE THE WORKERS OF INIQUITY
AND THE SPEAKERS OF DESTRUCTION,
FOR HEARTS ARE NOT EQUABLE.

A LION roared from within the wilderness, for he knew that a hunter of the fields was gathering his strength against him and would come thither with bow and arrows to stand stalwart against him in battle. The heart of the lion was apprehensive with fear lest the children of the man's quiver should reach his vital parts; but the hunter was twice as fearful of the lion. At length they entered sweet counsel together. With yearning eye the lion called to the man: "Keep thee, be secure, fear not, let not dread of me confound thee, for my heart longeth for thy fellowship." In purity of heart the hunter answered: "Neither shall I put my hand forth against thee." So the two walked together, with the sweetness of fellowship between them. Said the man: "I have seen all the beasts of every flesh, and I find the majesty of kingship only in one created in my form and image. In an image handsome and desirable and pleasant walketh man; therefore is his greatness increased over all the earth and he rules over all creation, even over the majestic and mighty lion in his prime." Answered the lion: "Nay, to me beseemeth kingship over all the inhabitants of earth and its isles, for I have cast my dread over all the land of the living. There is none to compare with me on earth's sands; who can stand before the roar of my voice? If I look upon him with the eye of hatred, his hopes are frustrated. Upon my neck lodges strength, and grief is rampant in the expression of my face." So they walked through all the desert, speaking their rivalry as they walked, each exalting himself over the other and saying: "I shall be king." At length they saw a heap of stones with a carved monument at their side. Graven upon the stone were a lion and a man; the man was seated on a royal throne like a king, and the lion was pictured crouching upon the soles of his feet. Said the man: "Where is thy mouth now? Shall the saw magnify itself against him that shaketh it? Now shalt thou see whether my words find their mark in thee; thou wilt find that man hath ruled over the lion from the day beasts and cattle were created, in days of old, in former years. This heap be witness and this pillar be witness; lo, my sheaf arose and also stood upright." Answered the lion: "Lo, the witness is false; if I had essayed to draw the likeness at the time appointed, I would have done to man as he devised to do to the lion; if I had desired mine own dignity the lion would be transformed to be king, with the man kneeling prostrate at his feet."

The parable: There is a man who eagerly desires to fill his soul; he looks upon all that he has done and finds it very good, for he has given sway to his wishes and inclinations. But his neighbor comes and searches him out, to tear down what he has built up and sell what he has bought, and his reins ponder and his heart grows sour to debase the assurance which the other has increased. Because not all hearts are equable, many are the workers of iniquity and the speakers of evil.

57

He-Goat & Lion

BEWARE OF HIM THAT GIVETH COUNSEL FOR HIS OWN ADVANTAGE, AND OF THINE ENEMY WHEN HE MAKETH HIS PALATE SWEET.

A HE-GOAT was wandering astray on the tooth of a sheer cliff where no shoots or grass was to be found, for brimstone and salt had scorched all the land. A lion at the foot of the mountain over against him perceived the goat and said to him: "What ails thee that thou hast gone up to a place of withered herbage? Thy folly thou hast set on high; when the herbage of thy plain is sere thou hast made thy dwelling on the heights, in a waterless land, thirsty and weary. Come down with me into large pastures and the fruit thereof shall be for meat. It is a place where lie rams and goats and fat kine, a joy of wild asses, a pasture of flocks. My young and theirs find delight in deep peace; they make their children lie down together. Say not that there is grass and seed in thy place: Woe to them who say of the evil that it is good and of the good that it is evil." Said the goat: "I know, verily I know, that with me there is no grass or seed and in thy place is the beauty of Sharon and Carmel to heal the weary and brokenhearted; before thy words reached me I had contemplated descending thither to graze. But now that I have heard thy counsel I have repented, for thou art he who hath wounded many a head in the land. Better is a dry crust and tranquillity therewith than the shaking of the environs at the sound of thy voice, when thou comest to shed blood and destroy souls."

The parable teaches understanding and admonishes if the imaginations of your heart are barren of understanding. If your enemy makes his palate sweet to entice you, beware of him who advises you for his own advantage. See and understand the tale of the goat, whose heart was not persuaded by the counsel of the lion who thought in his cunning to make him a prey, but understood that the advice was a deception. And the sage hath said: "Do wholly as he that loves thee advises; hear what thine enemy advises, but do it not." The words of thy friend, bring near like sapphires and emeralds; the words of thine enemy, hear, but do the reverse. If thy neighbors are without counsel and mute as a tree and thou findest none to consult, turn away from that counsel which is nearest thy desires and thou shalt be secure, for there is hope.

58

Boy & Man

A PERVERSE GENERATION ARE THEY
THAT PAY THE PRICE OF PEACE WITH WAR.

A LAD was walking innocently in the forest when the east wind began to storm and rage. His hands snuggled in his bosom, for he was chilled with the blast. Ice was cast forth like morsels, and there was snow and hail. He longed for the warmth of fire, for who could withstand the frost? A man of the forest who dwelt among the bushes saw him and took pity on him, and said: "There is sufficient for the burning, and the blaze is large." He urged the lad until he came to his house, and spoke upon his heart as though he were his kinsman and redeemer. And he covered him with garments, but he was not warmed. Before he came thither he had blown the breath of his mouth and nostrils upon his nails to dispel the chill of his hands. The man apportioned him food, for that his eye took pity upon him, and brought of his drink to strengthen his spirit. And the lad accepted of them and grew warm. He gave the lad liquor to share with him, but when he put it to his lips he could not drink it because of its great heat, so he breathed upon his wine goblet with his breath to cool it. Said the man in anger: "Quickly depart hence; a man such as thou I do not desire in my midst. This morning didst thou blow upon thy hands to dispel the chill, and this evening thou blowest upon thy warm wine to cool it. Far be it from me to make a friend and comrade of so perverse a mouth as thine. Verily I will cut thee off from the company of the upright in heart."

The parable is for flatterers who are not honest but have two hearts and many faces. They pay the price of peace with war, for they are a perverse generation. Out of each proceedeth flattery, and their chief desire and hope is to speak to their neighbor with cajolery and enticement. Iniquity and injustice are under their tongue. After they have spoken the pleasure of their soul and the desire of their heart, they mock and overturn the words they have spoken. Their hearts within them are not steadfast; therefore their reasoning standeth not fast, for the sense in their mouth is not firm. If they prevail in the earth there is no faith. The swallowing of words is as a plague in the chambers of the belly, as a sledgehammer that crusheth rock. A man shall desire in his midst only one formed in his own image.

59

Lion & Toad

THOU SHALT SURELY SAY TO MEN OF MIGHT THAT THE GREAT MUST BEWARE OF THE SMALL.

THE LION, whose strength surpassed all, was sleeping in the shade of a rock in the wilderness, and behind him in a cleft of the rock there stood a toad. Said the toad: "Who is this before my hole?" He knelt and crouched like a lion, and was moved with choler, and dashed up to him in the fury of his spirit; he bit the lion upon the forehead like an adder, and the lion awoke from his sleep. His eyes were like coals, and like flames they roved abroad to see who and where he was whose heart emboldened him to do such a thing. The toad had already returned by the way he had come; he looked at the lion, and behold, he was raging and furious, as if he would lop his biter down with terror. The toad called to him: "Art thou seeking him who hurt thee? It is I, the toad who stands before thee, that bit thee in my furious anger. I am greatly vexed that I did not kill thee. Alas for thee that thou hast sinned; thy sins will find thee out. Suddenly they shall rise up that shall bite thee, and they that shall vex thee shall awake. Wilt thou be my persecutor in thy strength and stature because I am accounted puny and contemptible in thy sight? Thou hast neared my rock to stop the entry to my house, and in my anger I have come forth to be thy persecutor."

The parable is to admonish the great with respect to the small, lest by reason of their strength and might and power and pride they sin against those smaller than they.

For the pursued are tenacious of life, and though they be small, the might of their heart is great. Within themselves they set their ambush to take vengeance in spite. The vain should be wise, for a giant is sometimes strangled by a fly, and there are times when towering giants stumble into pitfalls, and lions fear sheep.

60

Bullock & Ox

SWEETER IS THE SLEEP OF THE TOILER THAN OF THE IDLER.

A BULLOCK saw an ox at his ploughing, and the hand of the husbandman was heavy upon him and placed fetters and rods upon him so that he could not move his neck. When the ox turned from the road, the bullock said to him: "Thy covenant with peace shall be disannulled by reason of excess of toil and labor. I am like a wild ass that runneth upon the way of the forest, in the path of the vineyards, and I have not been worked nor borne a yoke; I walk in the olive orchard amidst its foliage like a swift dromedary traversing her ways." The ox answered and said, with words of knowledge and in level speech: "All the while that labor presses heavy upon me and I am in bondage to the field and draw the yoke with all my strength, I rest secure and my soul liveth. But do thou not trust thy life, for that they have set thee free to be well-fed and fat, that thy neck hath not been subjected to much toil, that thou dost rest both at ploughing time and harvest, suddenly the chief of the butchers will take thee. Thou art indeed surrounded by snares." And it came to pass at the end of a month that a numerous folk came after the bullock and dragged him by ropes upon his neck, and they beat him to make him go and terrified him. While the ox ploughed his furrow with a song, the bullock was thrashed and tormented without mercy. The ox called to him: "Better for thee to have worked the earth than to go to the court of death, for from thy fall there is no rising."

The parable is for a man who labors heavily at the yoke to supply his need. Sweet is the sleep of the toiler, and his righteousness will be revealed in the congregation, for there is hope for his latter day. Not so the way of the sluggard. He prophesies that he will be saved without labor or toil, but he knows not his time, like the fish that are caught in a net.

61

Lion & Dog

BETTER TO LACK FOOD AND RAIMENT THAN TO BE BOUND TO THE TABLE OF ANOTHER.

A LION that had grown lean of the fat of his flesh, so that only bones and skin were left upon him, went upon his way slowly and without strength. There met him a fat dog, who mocked him and said: "Whither goest? Why art thou so meager, prince? Easy it were for thee to be among men and keep guard for them, to carry their burdens and serve them as a slave. Then wouldst thou not eat bread with scarceness and not suffer want, but eat flesh to thy heart's content, even as I who am become their servant and am waxed fat and thick and cov-

ered with flesh, instead of thy being meager of flesh and a wanderer by the way, pursued by the east wind and swept on by the blast. Even when they bind me with ropes and fetters, flesh and wheaten bread are given me for my repast; never has my expectation of my wonted fare been disappointed. My yoke is dissolved because of my fatness, and the bondage of my chains is love." Answered the lion: "Thy pride is the pride of one sated with bread, therefore dost thou not discern between thine honor and thy disgrace. Such a dog as thou are proud of speech; in thy hand is the custom of thy fathers who were bound to flocks of sheep to keep them, and fixed by a nail to the crib of an ass. Shall I be like you, bound with chains? Far be it from me to hear the crying of the driver! Better for me to be without a ruler and meager of fatness than to be a willing slave for the sake of abundant food, for if now my hand falls short of salvation, it is better for me to endure my affliction and my misery and to be free as my father was than to be a slave and dine on loaves of bread.

The parable: Thus shall it be done to the man whom the king delighteth to honor—to take prudent instruction and his admonition from the lion. Let his flesh be poor in fat, but let his honor not be poor, lest he acquire a master over himself and quench the light of his glory. Let him not boast of the fatness of his belly and the stoutness of his back and of the fatness wherewith he hath covered his face when he hath been crammed by the food of others. Better to be among those of small power, without abundant food and clothing, than to be bound to the table of others. Can a prudent man esteem himself lightly? Can he who doeth such things prosper and be delivered? He is trampled upon like a slave with ear bored; upon his garb is violence and beneath him a bed of shame. And the sage hath said: "A sufficiency which keepeth a man from vileness is better than money which bringeth him to shame and humiliation."

62

Wolves, Goats, Dog

HE THAT GIVETH THE SWORD FROM HIS HAND TO HIS ENEMY GIVETH HIM HIS DAY OF DOOM.

THE WOLVES, each proud and lofty in his heart, fought with the goats and their keeper the dog. The strength of the dog and the goats prevailed, and the lowly vanquished the stalwart; their hand smote the wolves, and the strong were as tow. The wolves sighed and groaned, and the goats whistled and gnashed their teeth at them. Then said the wolves to the goats with cunning guile: "We shall not go forth against you to war any more. With this only shall we be contented: that ye will hearken and be like ourselves and we shall no more rouse up battle against you if ye will give us a hostage and inform us when ye disperse and when ye wish to assemble. Then will wolf dwell with sheep or goat, and your righteousness shall be recompensed in the earth, and there shall be a covenant of peace between us and between you forever." The goats consented and said: "Whom of us will ye choose for yourselves to be a hostage in your hands? We are eager for your fellowship." Answered the wolves with guileful heart: "We ask of you only the dog." So the goats summoned the dog and gave him for a hostage; but for them this was for a sorrow, as if they had given up the ghost. For the dog had fought at their side, and all followed him as a marshal. He would say: "Stand steadfast, and deliverance shall spring up; I will heap evils upon them. Stand and fight after my example; let no neighbor say, I have waxed faint." Always he had strengthened their spirit, but now hope and victory were lost, for the wolves made battle upon them and smote them and crushed them to desolation.

The parable: Let not a man minish what is in his hand, to augment his enemy who wishes his downfall. His heart's sorrow takes root when he puts a sword in his enemy's hand wherewith to slay him. He that doeth these things is smitten with blindness; he debases the one and exalts the other. He that giveth foolishly is captured or crushed, and he that receiveth is mighty in his course and prevails.

63

Cock & Hen

THEY THAT PURSUE REWARDS AND BRIBERY SOMETIMES QUARREL TOGETHER.

A COCK borrowed a bushel of wheat from a hen and brought it from her house in scarves and wimples. But the appointed day upon which the cock had agreed to repay the loan passed, and he neither came nor asked an extension of the term. Said she to him: "Surely thou wilt faithfully repay the bushel as of yesterday, though it is passed; buy the truth, and sell it not." Said he to her: "Far be it from me to falsify my faith. The wheat is stored up in heaps in my house; come with me to my house and I shall pay it out by measure; for no precious gain would I defraud thee." Said she to him: "Lo, guile sprouteth in thy spirit. I call upon thee in the presence of my brethren and thine: Return the wheat in the place thou hast received it, so that my chicks can gather the grains that fall from thy measuring. Starvation hath well-nigh slain them, and they say to their mother, Where is corn? For their hand is waxed feeble and they are in want. Now they can gather what hath been scattered; therefore I bid thee bring the grain to my boundary, so that those dependent upon my food may find the corn that falls." Said the cock: "Nay, with what is scattered and spread abroad thou shalt not sustain thy soul and the soul of thy children. Rather shall I measure the grain in my tent: Rise, hearken to my voice. There my host shall eat that which shall fall before your eyes, even as thou hast thought to do for thy children."

The parable is drawn from advocates and judges who

debase justice and righteousness. Some that pursue rewards and accept bribes quarrel together when a suit comes before them, and they murmur in their tents, saying: "This suit shall be in my house and court, and no whit of my honor and dignity shall fall to the ground." And the other saith: "Nay, but in my boundary and threshold; and it shall be heard only at my word." This they do only to receive bribes and to subvert justice by deception and trickery. None cries out for justice and none judges in good faith, and not one rouses himself to make justice strong but only to grind it fine. He that wishes fills his hand and makes his words crooked. Woe to him that coveteth evil gain for his house!

64

A Bird Buildeth Her Nest in the Grain

BE DEAF OF HEARING, BLIND OF SEEING, MUTE OF SPEAKING; THEN WILT THOU ASCEND ON STAIRS AND MAKE THEE STRONG.

A BIRD had made her nest in the standing grain, and when harvest time appeared she continued living there as was her wont, the mother brooding over her chicks. They said to her: "We have heard them saying to the messenger: 'Put ye in the sickle, for the harvest is ripe.' " Dread entered the heart of the bird; she was afflicted, tossed with tempest, and not comforted, and she said to them: "Before the sun sets I shall know whether they will raise the scythe against the standing grain." She went in the footsteps of the master of the field, going and returning, and seemed like a bird gone astray from its nest. Before he returned to his house she hovered before him, and she heard him beseech his neighbors: "Be ye prepared to come to my assistance upon the third day in the portion of field which is mine to reap my harvest." But they would not hearken unto him, and the man returned to his tent heavy and displeased. She sighed no more as she returned to her house; the mother of sons rejoiced. Said she: "The soles of our feet shall not trouble alien and brackish waters like birds astray from a castaway nest. I have heard their secret; the foot of man shall not pass over it. Lodge ye here, depart not; before the time comes when they reap, when the sickle masters the standing grain, the Lord will defend and deliver, pass over and preserve." Daily she went to hear what their counsel might be, and when the day came when his neighbors consented to aid him, she said: "Go forth from here, tarry not; fear and shun sickle and scythe."

The parable: When thou seest that respite hath come, for that thou dwellest in tranquillity and security; if then the ruler desire to raise his hand against thee, make thy spirit lowly, for it is better to yield to a man who hath helpers. And Solomon hath said: "Let the ways of instruction not depart from thine eyes." Be understanding and wise amongst thy neighbors, a deaf man that hears, a blind man that sees, a mute man that speaks; then shalt thou ascend by the steps of prudence and increase thy strength daily.

65

Lion & Ass

THE MAN THAT KNOWETH NOT HIS OWN PLACE WILL REVEAL HIS SHAME; HIS HEART IS NOT WITH HIM.

A LION invited an ass to show him the choice splendors of his greatness, and the ass was proud in his heart, saying: "Who is as I am? To whom doth the king desire to show greater honor than to me, now that I go to join his company? Now they will call me the king's second, for he hath made me his suite; me hath he chosen, and no stranger, with him." And he said to the lion: "I shall cast my dread over the cattle; they shall tremble at my voice and flee at my rebuke." Answered the lion: "Make thy work lofty, let thy voice be heard on high. We shall go forth to spoil much prey, and thy face shall advance to the battle. Thou shalt roar and I shall rend; thou shalt seize the prey and I shall break its neck." So they went forth into the field and found sheep and steers and fat cattle, and set their goal to spoil and lay waste. Said the lion: "Make them hear the roar of thy voice; thunder upon them with my sound." The ass raised his voice, and the sound reverberated in their camp. At the sound all the ewes were scattered; at its lifting the rams were terrified. Panic fell upon the camp of those that walked on fours, and when they turned to flee, the lion spoiled and devoured and was sated with them. As they fled hither and thither with the noise of a great host, the lion said: "Make not thy voice heard longer; enough of thy thunder." When he had finished his spoiling, and the ass and the lion were standing beside a carcass, the ass said: "Surely thou hast heard the majesty of my braying and hast seen that my neck is decked with a mane. In thy wisdom thou wilt choose me, and at this time tomorrow I will frighten the cattle and cast their victory down to earth, for it is not to the king's profit to suffer them, neither them nor their bellowing. Now these are the judgments which thou shalt set before them. They shall flee at my rebuke and be terrified by it. We shall make our lips strong; who is lord over us? Hear me, my lord the king; surely my words shall find favor with one that walketh aright." The lion answered him: "Whoso knoweth thy generation from above and below will not be afraid of thy voice nor abase himself for its noise. Despised and lowly and stubborn creature, wilt thou spoil prey for the lion? Those that will become estranged from me will say in my ear, 'How hast thou spoiled the goats and not crushed the ass?' "

The parable is for an honored man who makes a despised and contemptible man his associate. The spirit of pride will sprout and be revealed in the latter when he boasts of his fellowship and recognizes not his lowliness. As the obstinacy of his heart is revealed, his tongue will utter large boasts: "Such and such have I done by my wisdom and understanding." And the sage hath said in his wisdom: "The fool's silence is his remedy."

66

Mule & Fox

WHEN A MAN IS ASKED HIS NAME AND BIRTH IT DOTH NOT ALWAYS SUIT HIS GLORY TO TELL OF HIS FATHER AND MOTHER.

A MULE walking by the way was met by a fox who had never before seen him. The fox observed the majesty of his face and that his eyes were bright and his ears long, and said in his heart: "Who is this I now behold? What is the nature of this creature? I have never seen a picture like him, nor himself, until this moment. With his long ears stretching aloft he must be filled with wisdom and knowledge and shrewdness." The fox approached to hear his sayings and add cleverness to his own cleverness; perhaps he would obtain his confidence. He asked the mule who had given him birth, and the mule answered: "My uncle walked in pride; he was the horse upon whom the king rode. On the day of battle and destruction he leapt and pranced, and he pawed the earth with stormy passion. His neck was clothed with a mane, and his lordly neighing was terrible. His hoofs were like flint; they thirsted for hot battle and hungered for destruction. They never broke ranks but sped like sparks of fire, each shattering the rock like a sledgehammer. His eyes were like flame, like flashing lightning. He was a tower of strength for his rider and strode with neck outstretched. From afar he sniffed war and shouted for the enemy's destruction. He pursued and overtook all that rebelled against his rider. Such is the genealogy of the mule."

The parable is for a man magnificently attired from head to foot; there is no blemish in him, and he preens himself on his grandeur. But when they ask him his name and birth, because it suits not his splendor to tell of his father and mother, he mentions his relative who ennobles him, and makes no mention of him that begot him. Either his uncle or his cousin shall redeem him; it is their honor and glory that rise to his lips, their great deeds and their prowess. I have searched but never found a true man among those who say of father and mother, "I have never seen them," and who claim kinship with the great of the family, for that the family's glory has fallen away from his father and himself. And I, Berechiah, have said in my haste: "Woe to a man who is called 'of the family of Buzzi'; whoso has fallen from his fathers' merits, an untimely birth is better than he."

67

Two Apes & a Lion

WHEN DECEITFUL MEN ARE FILLED WITH ENVY, EACH AROUSES HATRED OF THE OTHER.

TWO APES came before their king, the lion, each seeking a gift. The lion perceived that the one would make objection to what the other would say, for the one was covetous and the other envious, so he said to them: "If ye look to me to ask something of mine, I shall give you as ye ask me, but my consent is on condition that ye heed my voice; one of you shall reveal his request to my ear, and after he hath spoken, I shall not recant but grant his petition. The second, if his mouth and tongue remain silent until the first have done with his request, I shall esteem so highly as to give him twofold my gift to his fellow, for I shall desire his honor and dignity." The covetous one spoke cunning guile in his heart: "I shall surely remain silent; to do so will be wisdom on my part. I shall hear what my fellow will ask and what speech he will utter, and I shall obtain twice what accrues to him." And it came to pass when he fell silent and hearkened, that the envious one said in his heart: "My fellow who is silent shall not be accounted wise; I am as clever as he and no less prudent. Though he be wise he shall procure evil." So the envious one called to the king, saying: "The utterance of thy lips thou shalt keep, and thou shalt do as thou hast spoken in my ears. I ask of thee to pierce one of my eyes. Lo, I have revealed my desire to thine ears; would that my request be fulfilled." Said the lion: "I shall heed thy voice and fulfill thy petition, nor shall I forsake thee until I have done that which I have spoken unto thee." And to the covetous one he said: "Lo, I will take from thee thy two eyes; thou must surely understand what is before thee." And he rendered them requital for their guile and gave them their request.

The parable is for contentious men who are filled with envy. One arouses hatred against the other; one says in his heart: "How hath my neighbor been uplifted and exalted? I shall smite him with my tongue and not leave him root or branch, for to me he is briars and thorns. Rather than that any of my intention fall to the ground I shall give fields and vineyards and houses; let my soul die with the Philistines." He is stranger to himself in order to harm his neighbor; his profit is as a purse of holes. In their hearts they search out deceits and pitfalls and trickery and plots. Even if the king should say to them: "Make your counsel sweet together; wherefore should I be bereft of you both in a single day?"—they have ears that hear not, for they have strayed far from the path of prudence. Until that one hath broken and destroyed the wealth of his neighbor, the child shall behave himself proudly against the ancient and the base against the honorable. And the sage hath said: "Shun the envious man when he sees thee; he will mourn for thy joy and prosperity."

68

Lion, Man, Pit, Snake

THE TIME IS SHORT AND THE WORK MUCH AND THE MASTER OF THE HOUSE IS PRESSING.

A LION went up from his lair to the crossroads of the highway, awaiting and lurking for his prey from morning till evening, to take it in his drag. An innocent passerby saw the lion roar, and trembled with fear and anxiety, for the lion charged upon him furiously, resolved to spoil him. Finding death bitter, the man ran toward a pit amidst clay cisterns; the pit was empty, there was no water in it. In the midst of the wall of the pit he found spikes extending from this side and that and was glad of them, for his feet stood upon the spikes; he thought he had found a refuge and escape from the lion who had lorded it over him and that he had escaped forever from slaughter, so that his footsteps would never be moved. But at the extremity of the pit he saw lurking a fiery poisonous serpent awaiting to swallow him alive, like the abyss, and his terror was redoubled. In the midst of noonday his shadow was as the night; tribulations poured over him without surcease. He had escaped the lion but encountered the serpent, who opened his mouth wide to swallow him. If he eluded the lion, the asp's tongue would slay him, for after the lion he was faced by the serpent. Said he: "Alas, who shall live? If I ascend, the lion will smite me; if I descend, the serpent's tongue will be my grave. Whence cometh my help between the two camps of lion and serpent? Furthermore, lack of bread and all sustenance hath afflicted me with cleanness of teeth, and I can find no water. But this is my comfort: I have found a faithful footing and rods of strength to support my feet until the lion depart from upon me. I shall take my stand upon them like a mighty man and shall not descend to the edges of the pit." As he spoke thus in his heart a rat emerged from over him, and he looked upon it and perceived that there was no black hair in it but only white. From the other side, opposite the hole, there emerged a rat wholly black. They put their teeth to the spikes upon which the man's feet were standing and gradually gnawed them away; day by day they destroyed his support. When the man saw that the spikes were weakened and shaking, three were the afflictions that beset him, and he lamented for his misfortunes: "Woe for the lion, woe for the serpent before whom my foot is apprehensive; woe for the two rats who gnaw away my standing place; woe for thirst, woe for hunger. Speedily I shall be for a mockery, and my soul will be humbled by the pit and by my torments. There is but a step between death and me, and I shall never return to see my comrade. In the darkness have I spread my couch, and it is thou, thou pit of gloom, in whose boundary I stand. If I am famished I shall not say unto thee: 'Shall I bring forth my bread and the manna of my sustenance from the rock?' " When he had so spoken twice and had not forgotten his plaint, as if he were in the pouch of a sling, the Rock whose power is over all gave him honey to suck from the flint, and said: "Open thy mouth and eat, and thou shalt not lack all thy days. Honey hast thou found; eat thy fill and take pleasure in its goodness and richness." With honey and milk beneath his tongue he stripped off the terror wherewith he had clothed himself and said: "What is sweeter than honey?" He forgot what was above him and what below, and that he was sitting in darkness, what was before him and what behind, the white rat and the black who were thrusting him from his perch and banishing him from the world; he did not remember the lion above him nor the serpent under his feet, but found delight in the honey which he ate as it were wheat of Minnith and Pannag. Wafers made with honey did he taste. But Jeshurun waxed fat and kicked; and when he had grown fat and portly, the rats who had daily gnawed his standing place removed his goodness from him. Suddenly the spikes were broken and cut off from the hole of the pit and from the wall, in deed, not in word. As either spike was severed and fell, the man who had stood upon them reached the edge of the pit and the mouth of the serpent that heeded no enchantment. Never again did he see his house and his people, and his place knew him no more.

The parable is goodly instruction for the soul, to clothe oneself in the raiment of freedom. The lion that approaches is death, which, as it were, lurks for a man and never turns its back nor lies down until it has devoured its prey. The pit is the world in which he stands. He flies to the pit that he be not seized, and every stranger there is a permanent sojourner in his own sight. He regards himself firmly fixed as a spike, to live long and see seed. The evil inclination in the heart of man is the serpent below him with its mouth open toward him, which always cries, "Give, give! Now shalt thou despise what thou hast loved." The rat wholly white is the day which gives him light, and the black rat, the night; together they combine to consume man utterly. As man proceeds toward the cemetery, they circle round and about him, for they are pledged to destroy his standing place and thrust him away. But he does not perceive his end; the honey which makes him oblivious to all this is the pleasure of the world, which suffuses his soul, and the delightful pastimes which spread a net for his feet. It causes his joy to flourish and his calamity to crumble, and its taste is as of a wafer made with honey. But while he is intent upon his dainties the roots of this joy wither in an instant, and the height of his harvest is broken; he lies with his fathers, whose dwelling place is the grave. The wise man who has indited sage sayings and linked them together into a chain has said: "The pleasure of this world is honey smeared over poison." I render my creator thanksgiving and praise for sustenance and livelihood. For one who does not as I do, his day is trouble and perplexity. In the midst of their food is a stone, for they have filled their teats with milk and have murmured in their tents, and have not taken thought to praise their creator and shepherd.

And I plied my poesy and said:

Lion is death, the pit a serpent which heedeth no enchantment;
The white rat the day; the black, the night. My heart perceiveth
They are pledged to end the life they symbolize,
As the pit symbolizes the world. His foot rests on delusion.
His world is as a wafer of honey, but its fruit is deceptive.
The spike of the pit breaks, and he dies.
Not with fleeces is he then covered.

69

Wolf, Fox, Dove

THE FELLOWSHIP OF FLATTERERS AND THE PERVERSE IS ALWAYS FOR EVIL.

THE WOLF, the fox, and the dove entered into a faithful covenant to spoil prey for their food and to divide their booty equally. Together they came to a covert, for the shadows of evening were falling, but found only a bat, which they brought forth from the holes in the dust and the reeds; and so they returned hungry and weary. Said the fox: "How can our booty be divided? If it be slaughtered will it suffice us? We walked in the desert, the mountain, and the lowland; but the dove found no resting place for the sole of her foot. But it is fitting that we give her her portion, that she be not robbed amongst us and that we deal not deceitfully with her. Come, let us cast lots. He that first telleth his age and prove elder than his comrade, we will hearken to his voice and give him the bat." Now the other two were not so old as he and would be deprived of the booty. Said the two: "Thy counsel is good and just." So they cast lots, and the lot fell upon the dove; said she: "Though I have toiled with you and not found a resting place, I am the dove that came forth from Noah's ark. Amidst the strong I divide prey and cleave it asunder; the wings of the dove are silvery with age." Said the fox: "I am old, and none can tell the number of my years. But from my fathers of ancient days I have received by tradition a sign for ascertaining the number of years that have passed from the day of my birth: The white hairs upon me are my witness; each hair represents a year. If the truth be sought, the number of my years is beyond calculation."

The wolf answered in anger and said: "Fox and dove, hearken to my words. There is none beside me older than I, for I am hoary and full of years. The sign of my age is neither whiteness nor redness. If I count my years they are more numerous than the sands. I have labored to ascertain and have discovered that when I passed two years I reached the third, but I know not the last nor the first. Who will instruct me and bid me leave the bat to one smaller than I?" So he ate it before their eyes and left them not a morsel.

The parable is for flatterers and deceivers, froward men who work iniquity, who bring people near with their lips but keep them far from their reins. If a man have business with them, they reply with soft humility and shamefacedness, but the paths of uprightness depart from their eyes. Widows are their prey and they rob orphans, but with their lips they say: "My will is bound by His will, to do what is good and upright." If one is involved in a suit and is judged and the judge says, "Pay," then he is deaf to words he desires not to hear. He gnashes his teeth and speaks angrily and arouses all his wrath, for he is confident, like a strong man in his strength, in provoking robbery and destruction and in walking ways that are crooked. So did the wolf to the dove and the fox: He made his counsel sweet with them and in the end dealt treacherously and took their portion against their will and smote them as if they were wicked. But they that sow the truth will reap sevenfold their portion and will shine over against the light. Before me it is inscribed and before me sealed that the guilty must pay and innocent win merit.

70

Lion & Cattle

IT IS GOOD TO APPEASE BY SWEETNESS OF LIPS IN ORDER TO PREVENT COALS OF HATRED FROM WORKING DESTRUCTION.

THE LION was strong among the cattle, and his teeth were encompassed with awe. Among the sheep he caused widowers and mourners, and turned not back before anyone. To the north and to the right he fought; he was cruel and showed no mercy. Even when they fled before him, he confounded them with the terror of his roar. The archers hated him and shot at him and wounded him, once in the belly and once in the back; his hand was against every man, and every man's hand, against him. He pitied none that walked on fours except the deer and the camel. All the cattle in their fright cursed him with mighty curses when they hid themselves from before him and took shelter in the crevices of the rock. But the deer and the camel were his comrades and departed not from the land of his dwelling; each made his heart kindly and restrained those that cursed him. But the persecuted cursed and wept, and while all cursed the lion, the deer and the camel blessed him. They called to the cattle and the beasts: "Ye that graze in the fields and in desert reaches, it is because ye curse him that he arouses all his wrath against you. If ye turn the curse to a blessing, great advantage will accrue to you. Do as we do and it will be proven that ye will find favor in his eyes and he will no longer smite you, but give you his covenant of peace. Behold, and do as we do; our peace he hath not disturbed." They hearkened to the counsel, and the lion rested his hand and was appeased.

The parable is to prevent coals of hatred from working destruction, and to appease an enemy by sweetness of counsel. Foolish indeed is he who storms, and kindles wrath against wrath. Who thinks to murder is murdered; who vanquishes wickedly is vanquished. If thou abominate and curse thine enemy, thou wilt ever desecrate thine own honor. Consider the ways of the Rock, whose works are always perfect; never are his loving-kindnesses ended or exhausted. He cursed the serpent and made his bread the dust; but wherever the serpent goes, his bread is with him—whether he ascends or descends he is in no fear for his provision. He cursed the woman in her youth, but all men run after her. He cursed the earth which he established, but all are sustained by it. He cursed the slave because he was shameless, but he eats and drinks as does the master. Hear instruction; let it be firmly established and builded, and thou wilt walk and rest secure. And the sage hath said: "Though thy excellency mount up to the heavens and thine enemy is bowed down before thee, he will make thee sin with evil thoughts."

And I plied my poesy and said:

Wherefore should man of tongue rage when the
  Rock hath not raged,
Wherefore should the generation be in terror of thy
  mouth?
His she-ass the swordless Balaam availed not to slay
  with his tongue,
What time he went forth to curse the people.

71

Starling & Princess

A MAN FILLED WITH WISDOM AND KNOWLEDGE HATH AN OBSERVANT EYE AND AN ATTENTIVE EAR.

A PRINCESS raised a starling and taught him to speak plainly and brought him to her chamber in her father's house, in her youth. In clear speech and pretty wit the starling was cleverer than all the birds, and he understood, when he heard news, that there is a time for speaking and a time for remaining silent. But he could not go and come, and his heart grieved. She had made him a cage of iron reeds, and amongst the reeds his voice was heard. One day a knight who intended to cross the sea came to the court of the king and queen and commended his house and sons and land to the queen. Her palate was smoother than oil, and she said: "I will surely hearken to thy voice and keep mine eye over all that is thine." The starling understood that the knight sought to cross the sea and as he passed his cage called him by name and said to him: "Lo, thou wilt cross the sea; I shall speak glorious things of thee. If thou see a bird in my form and likeness, be mindful of me and give him greeting in my name, and graciously and mercifully ask him counsel how I may go forth from my barred prison. My soul is wearied of it, for I am surrounded by hedge and wall. Neither have I offended here, but I was stolen from my family and shut up amongst men. Deal with me in kindness and truth. He that is pent in prison is considered as one dead; I am pent and cannot go forth, and my food will have no savor until I am free. Then will I lift up my head. Therefore I adjure thee to recall me to thine acquaintance and upon thy return to tell me the words of his responses." The knight departed thence and went down to the sea. Flying toward him was a bird of the form of him that had spoken to him, and before he approached, he raised his voice and said to him: "A bird of your form and likeness who dwells amongst men and is pent up in their barred gaol sends you his greeting. He hath adjured me to ask counsel of thee how he may redeem his soul and go forth from his prison cell. Deliverance will not fail him if he can again appear in the forest and change his prison garb." When he had finished speaking, the bird folded his wings and fell upon the knight in a swoon, as if death had swept him away. The knight took him up and put his eyes to his own, to restore his breath, and sprinkled fresh water upon his face, and then put him in his bosom; mayhap he would grow warm. When he saw there was no hope he threw him away; his heart grieved, and he knew not what had ailed him. Then he departed quickly, to proceed to his desired destination, and returned to his family in the city of his dwelling. The king received him joyfully on his return and embraced and kissed him. As the starling paced back and forth he perceived that the knight was returned from his journey and asked him whether he had remembered his life of sorrow, whether he had found a bird of his likeness, what he had done and what he had said to him. The knight recounted all that had befallen: that it had been a day of wrath for the bird when he heard his words—how his plans were cut short, for with no hunter or fowler he had fallen dead on the field; that he had sprinkled him with water, to return his breath, and covered him with garments, without his growing warm; that before his stink and ill savor should come up, he had cast him away in revulsion. The starling listened attentively. When the princess came to her chamber and did not hear the bird chirping, her wrath burned in her. She opened the cage and saw him, and sent her handmaiden to take him up. He was lying as one dead, and she was vexed when she saw that he stirred no wing, as if paralysis had seized him; where he crouched, there he lay. She threw water upon his head: perchance she could restore his soul; and she took him and put him in her lap. But he neither rose nor moved, and she abode in silence. Then she cast him from her hands to the ground, wet her face with the tears of her eyes, bewailed and lamented him, and departed from his side weeping. When the bird heard that she had gone, all his wishes were attained; he spread his wings and flew, and his pinions wearied not of flight.

The parable: A man filled with wisdom and knowledge hath a seeing eye and an attentive ear. He hears what men say abroad, and his eyeballs look straight before him. Before others perceive his plans he is quick to begin and complete them, in give and take, in purchase and sale. Like the starling he will be diligent and prosper. He who reflects in his wisdom and proceeds accordingly, cometh forth from prison to reign.

And I plied my poesy and said:

A man of sense is praised for his sense; and a fool, reviled for his folly.
There are wise men who are so openly, not in riddles,
And there are simpletons wrapped in a cloak of folly.
Folly fits close, and moves not, though continually reviled;
But a hint suffices for the course of the perceptive,
And his understanding is proven by his acts.
So the starling fell as one slain and won his life for his prize.

72

Ram & Ten Ewes

THERE IS NO FAITH ON THE LIPS OF THE ENVIOUS, FOR HIS STOCK IS FALSEHOOD.

A RAM had ten ewes, who took delight in his company. He loved the two who were without peer in the flock, and neither was barren; but if he approached one he aroused envy and sorrow in the heart of the other. One saw that he loved her fellow more than herself, and Rachel [ewe] was envious of her sister. Her tongue was as an arrow shot out, she uttered slander against her, she trod her bow for falsehood—for the dagger of envy pierced her heart. Said she to the ram: "Thy spouse taketh newcomers each morning; she receiveth strangers instead of her husband; a ram other than her husband has lain with her, to seduce her from thee and make her obedient to him; willingly she revels in his shadow; in the evening she goeth and in the morning returneth, and how canst thou show her compassion? Her filthiness is in her skirts; her sentence is beheading. In the lust of her soul she hath snuffed up the wind, to separate from thee in her harlotry. Her uncleanness is within her; let the scum be cleansed away." Such words of falsehood and treachery did she speak, and added many similar words to their number. Answered the ram: "I do not believe thy saying, for I know that boldness and shamelessness are under thy tongue. Thou hast imagined evil things in thy heart and hast spoken lies against her in thy hatred and envy of her, which pervert ways of uprightness. If thy soul were bound to her soul with an eternal love ready and watchful in all things, then had I attended to thy saying. But as long as life is in me I will keep afar the slanderous woman moved by hatred and envy; I will not reward hypocritical mockers at the feast with a cake.

The parable: If a man speak against his fellow according to his wickedness, thou shalt be wise if thou fairly investigate whether the words are sound; for if his fellow be turned to his enemy, thou wilt understand that in willfulness hath he spoken. But if he loves him as his life and has never caused him hurt, consider that the thing is true and the heart of the second, purer and more innocent than the first. The arrows of slander are sharpened with coals of broom. The words of a talebearer are as wounds, and turn love to its opposite; and a whisperer separateth chief friends.

And I plied my poesy and said:

Keep afar the talebearer that separates loving friends
And hurls the arrow of slander like lightning;
His heart is bitter though his palate is sweet,
And his lips compound hypocrisy. Scorn the willful
Who kiss thee with their mouth, while within them
Rivers of hatred flow deep. They cleave close
On the day of your joy, but speedily distant
On the day of calamity shalt thou find them.

73

Flea & Camel

HATRED IS INSCRIBED FOR THE POOR MAN; THE RICH MAN LOOKS UPON HIM WITH THE EYE OF ENMITY.

A FLEA mounted a camel. The camel went upon his way to traverse a large stretch of land, and the flea was hidden in the wool of his neck; the camel bore him upon his shoulder and knew not of his lying down or rising up. When he came to the end of his boundary, the flea fell at his feet and wept and besought him not to grow angry for his trouble, for his goodness and kindness overwhelmed him and he would be his slave in all places. The camel answered: "How have I benefited thee, and where have I seen thee?" Said he to him: "On thy shoulder hast thou borne me, and I have reached my desired destination, thanks to thee, who hast been willing to carry me. The sole of my foot hath not essayed to touch the ground. For that thou hast brought me hither, peace and long life be thine." Answered the camel: "Woe is me that thou hast laid the burden of thy yoke upon me! Abhorred and abominated art thou, though thou raise thy nest high as the eagle. How wert thou not afraid to rest upon me? Prepare thy steps for flight. Is it seemly for me to bring near me one of thy form and image? On the day thou seest my face again thou shalt die. Woe for the day I was so heavy-laden and burdened; from carrying thee my back is become chafed." So was the flea dismissed by the camel, whom it cost no effort to carry him.

The parable is for a poor man who consults the rich

man's peace and honor. He expresses his gratitude for a service which is no deprivation to the rich but benefits the poor. Into the rich man's heart it pours bitterness; and in return for love he hates the poor man and turns his face from him and looks upon him with the eye of enmity. For hatred of the poor is inscribed in the heart of the rich.

74

Stag & Dogs

HE WHO BOASTS OF HIS GREAT MIGHT WILL FALL, AND NONE WILL HELP HIM.

WHEN the stag, desiring to slake his thirst, came to a running stream, he cast his eye upon the water and from his reflection observed that he possessed antlers. Said he: "I am rich. I have discovered my might. Who can compare with me to win praise like my praise? My horns are not like the horns of an ox but are planted in the plain of my forehead and arranged like ascending stairs. Both are perfect in grace and beauty. He who stands over against me, for him sentence of death is digged and hewn. Any with whom I quarrel, I can gore with them, to the west and to the north." As his feet strayed in the water, lo, a brace of dogs were tarred against him by their master. The stag bethought him to flee in haste; he ran not to the highroad and level ground but into the dense forest, amid thickets of thorns. His counsel tripped him and he stumbled in his pride, for when he set his face toward the branches, lo, he was caught by his horns in the thicket, and there the dogs and the hunters butchered him. So he was destroyed through his antlers, which were his pride;

pride goeth before a fall. Like them all his limbs were delivered to be carved up, though in his sight they were the fairest of all.

The parable: Let thine eyes see and thine ears hear; and fear not to approach the tree of knowledge, lest thou be hasty in thy thoughts and embrace all that is right in thine eyes. For ofttimes that which thou dost approach and choose by thine imagination is like the fury of sea serpents and the heads of asps; if by reason of love and pride thou stumble by them, that which thou hast considered solid footing for thy shoe will prove a gin and a snare. Let strength and glory be supreme in thy heart.

75

Wolf & Shepherd

COUNT NOT THE KINDNESS YOU CONFER UPON A MAN AS A DEBT.

A WOLF was pursued on his way, through desert, mountain, and lowland, and in his great terror went astray. He accosted a shepherd and said: "The tumult of the chase is pursuing after me; I flee the sound of horseman and archer. They have spread a net to catch me, and have gone to the right and to the left; they have risen to the clouds and ascended the cliffs. Because a desert wolf ravaged them, they said: 'Come, let us cut them off, that no trace be left of them.' Would that thine eye take compassion upon me and not deliver me to the soul of mine enemies! They rage to scatter me and have chased me from the forest; they are gathered together under the nettles. Do thou, who gatherest in the strayed, be my shelter from before the ravager; let my soul be precious in thy sight. Make not thy mouth large in the day of tribulation, and let me hide until my pursuers turn back; they pant after me to their heart's content. If I come now with thee I will multiply their sorrow and send the tooth of beasts upon them." Said the shepherd: "Go and hide in the cleft of the mountains of Bether. I shall confuse the enemy's counsel and deliver thee from the edge of the sword." So the wolf ran to hide in the cleft of the rock, where he crouched and bent low and was saved. The pursuers who wandered astray after him came to the shepherd and said to him: "Hast thou seen the wolf which has lain awake against our cities and torn away an arm and even a head?" He answered them: "See his path; this is the way ye shall go. Surround him, chase him, drive him from his covert;

hurry after him and catch him. Cursed be the man who withholds his sword from killing him." Every man that ran after him went astray, for their course was mistaken. When these grew weary, fresh hunters came from nearby, and each drew his sword. But the people labored in vain, for the shepherd had misled them with mouth and hand to point a road which led them astray. But his eye he had turned to the wolf, and his face toward the wolf's. When the pursuers turned back, wet with the showers of the mountains, the shepherd went to the wolf and said to him: "Arise and go thy way; I have fulfilled thy words and have not permitted my mouth to sin against thy flesh. I have given thee surcease of all thy sighing and have not suffered my palate to sin. I have delivered thee from descent to the pit. Be strong and of good courage; fear not and be not afraid." The wolf answered: "Thou hast done me great kindness with the word of thy mouth and the gesture of thy hand, in that thou didst teach my pursuers to go on crooked ways. My complaint is of thine eyes, for they looked at me steadily, without rest or respite. Thine eyes that looked straight were my troublers that would deliver me to my foes; with them wouldst thou have breached the wall, for thou didst look upon the land before thee, where I lay hidden. But for a little, I had been destroyed by thy gaze."

The parable: Let not your eyes be talebearers. If you speak of your comrade's deeds to a man and your words are judicious, take care not to turn toward your comrade, toward his aspect and stature, his form and image, for your eyes will communicate the words of your heart to his intelligence. With my ears I have heard the saying of the sage: "I made a covenant with mine eyes not to look upon a man when I speak of him." For from the look of my eyes he will understand in his heart. If I speak long of his shame or his grace while my eyeballs gaze straight at him, if he perceives it, the shame will be turned to abuse and the grace to flattery. And Solomon in his lofty wisdom hath said [Proverbs 10.10]: "He that winketh with the eye causeth sorrow."

And I plied my poesy and said:

Wise is he, except that when he deliberates concerning a man
Thither his eye turns. Who speaks of pressed curds
Must not look to the cheese.

76

Sun & Moon

A MAN HEAVY WITH HONOR AND POSSESSIONS IS NEVER SATISFIED WITH THEIR EXTENT.

THE SUN, whose rule is by day, besought all living substance, requesting that the moon be given him for a companion. They answered him: "Thy hand is exceedingly strong and powerful; we shall not give thee a helpmeet. Lo, when thou art alone thou wreakest violence upon the snow: The sun waxeth warm and it melteth. When thou goest forth in thy strength, the king and his host are confounded: If the sun shine upon him he incurreth guilt. Thou goest forth from thy canopy like a bridegroom: Lo, thou hast dried up mighty rivers. Then how shall we join the moon to thee? Thou shalt not go with her, here nor there."

The parable is for a man who possesses wealth and riches and honor and cattle, and he desires to heap up as much again, to multiply what he hath and make him strong, for the might of his hand he finds insufficient. Do not consent to him, do not hearken to his voice to add forces to his force. Fitting is the instruction of wise Solomon [Proverbs 22.16]: "He that giveth to the rich surely cometh to want."

77

Viper & Man

KEEP AFAR HIM THAT COMES NEAR THEE FOR THE SAKE OF THY SILVER AND THY GOLD.

A MAN saw a viper and by the smoothness of his lips persuaded him to come into his boundaries. With great eloquence he besought him, until the viper hearkened to his voice and came round about his dwelling. When the man saw that he trusted him, he rejoiced and his heart was glad. He honored him greatly in his dwelling, and watched over him as the apple of his eye; he fed him to his satisfaction, with butter of kine and milk of goats. The viper too turned his desire to the man, until he told him he would show him his treasures. Thus for many days were they joined together and did not part from their love. The viper contrived a plan to test the man, to see whether his heart were just toward him; he called to the man and said: "My beloved, man after mine own heart, hearken unto me and I will reveal all my way, for thou art a man of mine own esteem. I shall return to my native land, to the sons of my people and my family, and I am resolved, good sir, to bring to you the most precious of my treasures, but thou must not lay thy hands upon it." He answered him: "I shall heed thy voice; thou shalt decree a thing and it shall be established unto thee." The viper went forth and brought the man an egg. Said he to him: "This egg is white and pure; no man knoweth its worth nor hath understanding of these matters, for it cannot be valued with the purest gold. If my soul be removed from thee, guard this egg from being cracked, for if so be that it is cracked, then is my hope perished. In thy hand I commit my spirit, for my welfare is bound up with it, so long as it is cared for and guarded." Then the viper departed, and the man rejoiced at his going. Quickly his heart fermented and he pondered iniquity upon his couch. He said to his wife, who shared his counsel: "This egg which has been entrusted unto us let us crack for ourselves, and there we shall find a treasure. Nor will our hand fall short, for the viper will lie smitten, and we shall fill our houses with booty." Even as they plotted so they committed evil. They cracked the viper's egg, and the liquid issued forth and spilt on the ground. Then were they ashamed of their counsel and found no profit in their deed. The viper returned from his travel to the inhabited city, the goal of his desire, and saw that the egg was cracked. Said he to the man: "Thy heart hath gone astray. For thy friendship I say, 'Woe is me that I have brought thee near to me and that I dwelt in thy midst until iniquity was discovered in thee.' Thou hast not desired my nighness but hast breached the wall of peace." The man declared that it was not by his will that the egg was cracked. He had not uncovered its fountain and had not laid hand upon it to break it; the blow that had struck it was by accident. With suchlike words did the man answer, seeking to atone for himself and his house; but the viper said: "Thou hast walked rebelliously with me; therefore will I hide my treasure from thee. I shall go and return to my nest, to the cockatrice's den, and thou wilt abide shamed and humbled, and wilt see me nevermore."

The parable: A man should keep afar from one who draws him near for the sake of his silver and his gold. When his welfare is entrusted to the hand of such, he will deal guilefully with him and deprive him of his soul for the sake of his silver and his wealth.

And I plied my poesy and said:

Him I thought a comrade, I discovered evil.
In goodly days and in bad season I tested him;
In days of joy and gladness I encountered him,
But on a day of stress in an evil season I lost him.

78

Ape & King

WHOSO JOINS COMPANY WITH ONE OF FALSE LIPS, HIS SOUL IS NOT PRECIOUS IN HIS SIGHT.

AN APE was exalted by a king. Many days he stood at his side, until he knew all his works, the food of his table, and the posture of his servants, how he exercised rule over them and maintained his strength. Nothing was concealed from him. The ape was eager to depart thence and rule over his brethren abroad. Came the day when he had prepared his flight, and he went forth into the field to his brethren, in the mountains of the wilderness and the forests in the clefts of the rocks. He said to the apes of the forest: "Woe to the land whose ruler is a child! Therefore are the good sunken low; every head is plucked bald and every shoulder sore chafed, and not one of you walls up the breach. Would that I were judge in the land, to render to the righteous according to his righteousness. No man would cheat his fellow; to each I would do according as he plotted, for I would ensnare the clever in their guile. Me it beseemeth to rule over my fellows and to govern them, for I am the son of sages, the son of the kings of the east." The apes hearkened to his words and said: "Thou shalt be lord over us." He chose the strongest and handsomest of the apes to be his guards, others to prepare his food, and the contemptible and weak-loined he made hewers of wood and drawers of water. The elders he established as judges. And it came to pass in the wheat harvest that two men went astray in the wilderness and came to the place where the apes had pitched their tents. They saw that there was a king within the camp and that everyone cried, "Long live our lord the king!" Before the king stood a small ape who found grace and favor in his eyes, wherefore the men thought him the king's son. At his right stood a concubine. By the thorny bushes they ate and drank and made merry. One was the chief of bakers, one chief of butlers, and one guarded the empty vessels. One was lightly esteemed and one, honored; one served and another was served, as is the law and statute among men, where the poor serve the powerful. The ape perceived the men and his reins were astonied. When he saw them he called them to himself with willing lips, and said to the greater: "I adjure thee, tell me what is in thy thoughts, whether the majesty of kingship rests upon me, whether my guardsmen are mighty heroes, whether my son be not exceedingly handsome, be he strong or weak, whether my wife who is joined to me is not comely to look upon, whether my attendants and they that keep my house and treasures are not exceedingly well favored." The man of good faith who had sworn to speak according to the sight of his eyes said: "I shall not belie my faith in all that I have seen. Like father, like son; like mother, like daughter; like manservant, like master; like maidservant, like mistress. Apes are ye and apes were your fathers;

blessed be he who made you despised. Thy wife is an ape, thy son an ape. The concubine who stands at thy right hand is of an aspect deformed and blear; all are vile and contemptible before all people. Ye are the most fractious and distorted of beasts, ejected from every communion of the living. Instead of honor ye have shame, instead of a girdle a rent, with plaguing thorns and prickling briar. After you no path is illumined, but ye make every lodging to stink. Your heritage is shame and disgrace." The king-ape watched the matter, and inquired of the second man, who said: "Would that I might live in thy environs! Happy are thy servants, and happy thy folk, who hear thy words and behold the beauty of thy suite, whose hand is exceedingly powerful. Thou art the handsomest of the sons of men; if all that are handsome were assembled at thy side they would not cause the light of thy countenance to dim. Thy wife is exceedingly well favored, the perfection of beauty and wisdom; at beholding her the heart of any king would exult. Beautiful of form is she, and beautiful of appearance. The majesty of thy son is beyond calculation; from the sole of his foot to the crown of his head he is without fault or blemish. There is no living thing his like for beauty." The apes applauded the liar and honored him without end. But the honest man's garments they tore, and they beat and bruised him. Then the king commanded that he be returned to his ways, to make his prowess known to the sons of men.

The parable is for a man in whose calculations there is no falsehood and upon whose lips no iniquity is to be found. If he join a company together with one of false lips his soul is not precious in his eyes, for the one distorts truth to utter flattery, while the other changes not nor alters. But if they are bound together by fetters of truth, in the end they will be honored. Woe worth the day when a man makes his soul filthy with his tongue, when he sweeps unrighteousness together to produce flattery. And because the lovers of flattery are many, the earth is defiled under its inhabitants.

79

Ape & Fox

ALAS FOR HIM THAT SAYS TO HIS COMRADE, "THE BED IS SHORTER THAN ONE CAN STRETCH HIMSELF ON."

AN APE saw a fox upon his way. The fox's tail was long and broad, so that it reached to the dust and he trod upon it with his feet. The ape followed his desires and implored the fox, saying: "Lo, I the ape love thee; give me a small fragment of thy tail. Tailless I issued from the womb, and my privy members are exposed. Thou hast more than enough for a covering, and the excess will make a portion. Or give it to my elder son, and he will pray for you and you will live long." Answered the fox in furious anger: "Enough of vexation and anger and deception! Thou askest of my tail, for the which thou hast not labored neither madest it grow. If I had double so much twice over, I would not give thee so much as to cover thy skirts, nor shall thy son exalt his glory with it. You shall be brought down to the ground, so that your foundation shall be uncovered."

The parable is for the doughty of heart who are far from righteousness. When they hear the cry of the needy not one says, "Here!" They respond not to the cry; and if they answer, their wrath is kindled, for their silver is precious in their sight. Their purse is broad but their heart narrow to show the needy compassion in their straits, and they look on when the righteous is forsaken. The hail shall sweep away the refuge of lies. Woe to him that says to his fellow: "The bed is shorter than that a man can stretch himself on it."

80

Woman, Husband, Knight, Vizier

LITTLE RECK THE LIVING
OF LOVERS NOW DECEASED.

A WOMAN smote her palms, and her eyeballs dropped tears; in bitterness of soul she sat forlorn, grieving in her heart for her husband who was dead and buried. In the wilderness beyond, a knight was hanged upon a tree, and the king's vizier and counselor went from city to city and cried out the king's decree that the body of any who took the hanged man down would be roasted in fire. Another knight, who strayed from the road, saw his brother hanging, and the matter vexed him sore, for he was his brother of the same father and mother. He made a way to his anger and at night took his own life in his hands and cut his brother's cords and buried him with his fathers. He feared mightily for his soul, lest they remove his head from upon him for that he had not kept the king's commandment. His flesh trembled for fear, and he ran to hide in the house of the woman who bewailed her husband in bitterness of soul. He spoke upon her heart with pleasant words, uttering goodly and comforting speech, and said: "To me shalt thou be for a portion, and I will betroth thee unto me in good faith. Forget thy sorrow and be comforted for thy husband, and come and lie with me."

And she, even she, said: "Thy fortune hath led thee true. The woman that hath now fallen to thy lot will answer thee in peace and open to thee." She pressed him to know all his affairs, and he told her what had befallen him: His soul was bowed down to earth, for upon that night he had violated the commandment of the king, wherefore he would die before his time and no more return to his kin. The woman said to him: "Be not afraid. My husband that is buried we shall hang in place of him that is hanged upon yonder tree, before a man can see to recognize his neighbor. Who shall know what we do in secret? There shall be neither speech nor words. Now heed my counsel; therefore hast thou come under the shadow of my roof." Quickly she led him to the grave, love making her line crooked, and they removed the buried man from his sepulture and did as they had said; she went and wandered in the wilderness to hang her husband that had been buried.

The parable: Few among the living take thought for those beloved and dear in their life. They pound their love to fine dust. He that dies can have no trust in those who embraced and kissed him. They put him from their hearts as one dead, and take no thought to remember his righteousness and keep his commandment—"Remember, pray, my loving-kindness, and deal not falsely with me nor my son nor my son's son." The man dies and they cover him with dust, and the living violate his commandment.

81

A Sick Man, His Daughter, a Physician

THEY THAT THINK TO ENSNARE
BY THEIR GUILE WILL FALL
IN THEIR OWN DEVICES.

A PHYSICIAN let blood for a patient and said to him: "This blood thou shalt watch over strictly until the third day, and upon the third day I shall see whether thou wilt go free of the disease that troubles thee and how thou mayest be relieved of it. By the blood I shall recognize every stumbling block, every plague and source of ill. All that plagues a patient is made manifest by the blood, whether it be green, black, white, or ruddy, for blood is the soul of all flesh." The patient bade his daughter to take the blood from him and guard it as the apple of her eye from being spilt hither or yon; for any that overturned the vessel, by man would his blood be shed. She took the blood and carried it away and put it underneath her chest. A cat walking by in innocence spilt the blood, whereupon her hands waxed weak and her spirit was darkened, and she said: "Alas, hope is perished! How can I say to my father, 'It is no more?' If he demand it, what answer can I give? May a lion rend him that spilt it; whether beast or man he shall not live." As her thoughts oppressed her, her reins counseled her to empty into the vessel so much of her own blood as the measure of what had been there. She bethought her of a leech and summoned him to her chamber and bade him drain her blood into the vessel. The physician came in his season to ascertain the source of the ailment, and the patient described his state. The physician asked for the blood which he had bidden him keep, and the patient replied that it had not been moved. The blood was sought, and the daughter brought it. When the physician saw the ruddiness of the blood and its aspect, it was accounted unto that man as an offense of blood. His wrath was kindled and he said in passion: "Thou art pregnant! Never has there been such a thing and never shall be, that an embryo be found in the body of a male. I do not wonder thou art sick; thy sins have caused these things. Thy guilt becometh such a man as thou; thou shalt put a knife to thy throat." The physician returned upon his way, and the patient sorrowed in his heart, for his heart misgave him. He summoned his daughter and again and again adjured her to know whether it was his blood she had brought without diminution just as she had received it, or whether she had spilt it on the ground and substituted other blood in its place; for that cause was his reason unsteady. The girl answered: "I did not spill the blood, nor do I know who spilt it. I found the vessel overturned and all the blood spilt out of it; and lest thou fall angry with me, I substituted my blood for thine." Said he: "I thought thee a wall but thou art a door. From bran I hoped for fine flour. I thought thee shut-in, but thou art pregnant of a man, and of men hast thou sown seed. I had hoped for good and there came evil. Repeatedly I adjured thee in thy chambers not to go after young men. By the cords of thy guile hast thou stumbled; thou hast not clothed thee with beauty and majesty."

The parable is for those who think to trip others by their wiles so that they might suddenly smite them, but in the ambush in which they lurk they are caught by the guile they themselves contrived. Their evil and deception is revealed when their foot is caught in the snare they have hidden. He who plots to capture his fellow with false lines, false will be his return. So it befell the girl in her deception; her father thought her a virgin but learned that a man had uncovered her source, and he despised the soul that had been precious in his sight.

82

Ewe, Goat, Shepherd

GIVE EAR AND HEED: HE THAT DRAWS THEE NIGH IS ACCOUNTED THY KIN.

A EWE was within the farmyard, and a goat, far from its hedge. The shepherd waited for the ewe to yean, and when she had yeaned he took the lamb and brought it to the goat, who suckled it until it grew big and was weaned; with much labor had she swaddled it. Then she said: "Look to thy ways. Return to the land of thy fathers and thy birthplace and do mightily. Thy mother is a ewe, thy father a ram; if I have brought thee up until now and swaddled thee and raised thee, thy father and thy mother will rejoice when thou returnest unto thy people." The sheep answered: "Nay, but thou art my mother, for that thou hast heaped thy loving-kindness upon me. I shall not call the ewe my mother, for she thrust me far from her boundary and would see me no more; not to her is my desire."

Give ear to the parable and hearken: He that brings thee nigh is accounted thy kin; whereas he that keeps thee afar, though he be thy kin, account him negligible in the crowd. He is estranged from his brethren and an alien; he troubleth his kin and is cruel. He troubleth himself who says: "None may love me except he be of my mother's and my father's kin, who gave me honor amongst the dwellers of the world; 'tis a brother who is born for time of trouble."

83

Thief & Witch

HEED NOT THE EVIL, WHO STRENGTHEN THE HANDS OF THE WICKED.

A THIEF brayed among the bushes, and thence plucked mallows. In the evening, when the sun set, he could go no further, desolate for need and hunger. Destruction had wasted him at noonday; he was weary and toil-worn and weak of hands, and he panted for thirst. A witch came by upon that way and heard his cries for water. She filled the waterskin with heaven's rain, and he was humbled and confessed his transgressions. In his passion he cursed his moments, for that he had ended his days in shame and his sin had spread a snare for his footsteps: "Woe is me for my mother that bare me; all that live curse me for my transgressions and my sins. Mine iniquities have overtaken me." The witch gave him to drink from the bottle, and rebuked him for that he had repented of his evil. She hastened to approach him and hardened her face and said to him: "Lo, I have found thee when thou wert forlorn and heard thee when thou wert astray. For thy manifold transgression thou didst curse thy days and thy moments; therefore did I approach thee that thou mightest not withold thy foot from evil. Nay, let thy thoughts goad thee on, let thy feet run to do evil. Murder, steal, commit adultery, pant after every work of deception; then will thy ways prosper, and I will bless them that bless thee. Fear not of descending to the pit, be strong and of good courage, be not afraid nor dismayed. Even when thou art found tunneling through a wall, my hand shall give thee aid and my arm shall prevail over thee to afford thee escape from the snare with fire and magic and enchantment. Let thy foot hasten to deceit, and leave not thy former doings behind. At oppression and at famine thou shalt laugh, and I will walk in thy company. Give ear to the voice of thy handmaiden; add not nor diminish." The wicked thief yearned for evil, to resume his original practices; and he returned to his ancient uncleanness. His fury was ever vigilant to open its mouth for murder, but he did not remember to benefit his soul. He stole and slaughtered and sold. The helper he chose helped not, but counseled him to do evil. She taught him witchcraft and enchantments. Divination by arrows and consultation of teraphim were no mystery to him, and he spoke with her that was old in adulteries. Came a day when he went out into the field to lie in wait for merchants and plunder them. The nations heard of him, and he was taken in their pitfall. They searched out all that was closely hidden; one recognized his coat upon him and another said that he had killed his uncle. They overwhelmed his eyes and beat him with sticks, and they led him to a tree to hang him. He called to the witch: "Hasten to save me ere the evil cleave unto me. My enemy holds dominion over me, and I cannot escape. Spread thy wing over me; stand now with thine enchantments and with the multitude of thy sorceries." She answered him: "Until now I have helped thee and with my charms supported thee. I have compassed thee with pride as with a chain, in order to add drunkenness. So have I dealt with thee many times, but when I see that there are no bands to thy death, wherefore should I labor in vain? In an instant of time thou shalt be a ruin, and for this my counsel is vain and my right hand falls short. There shall come upon thee an evil whose dawning thou shalt not know."

The parable: Do not listen to the wicked, who strengthen the hands of evildoers, to wizards and sorcerers and magicians and dreamers, who say that evil shall not come nigh unto them and that they who work wickedness shall be built up. The hook of time is in their nose and its bridle upon their lips. Bloody and deceitful men shall not live out half their days, for with a single fall they are destroyed, whereas the righteous shall arise though they fall seven times.

84

Horse, Merchant, Man

HE WHO TRUSTS IN A MAN SHALL NOT QUESTION OR TEST HIM.

A MERCHANT had a handsome horse. His neighbor visited him early, saying: "Sell me thy horse; take his value and put it in thy purse." The merchant answered him: "What matter the horse between me and thee? Mention his price no more; lo, he is thine without silver." The man answered: "Not so shall it be; he that hateth gifts shall live. Reveal his price to my ear and accept the money from me." Answered the merchant: "I would prefer to give him to you. But in truth I did not find this horse but bought him for twenty pieces of gold, and he is worth twice so much, not less than forty pieces of gold. If thou dost not wish him gratis, his sale shall be according to the evaluation of an arbiter. Let us both arise early to the vineyards, and the first man who encounters us shall judge between good and evil; thou shalt not add to his valuation nor diminish it." So they arose early in the morning, and a man came toward them on their path;

he had only one eye for his right eye was blinded. They said to him: "Let not thy palate sin. This horse hath been sold according to thy estimation; thou art the judge to determine its value, and the money of thy estimation shall be assured to him." Said he: "Far be it from me to belie my faith. The value of this horse I have examined in my heart, and I perceive that he is worth five pieces of gold. Yesterday I saw a horse like him sold for five pieces of gold; the shepherd and the farmer are witnesses." The merchant was angry and led his horse thence; his neighbor dropped five gold pieces from his purse, but the owner of the horse would not accept them. The man with goodwill brought the gold to his tent; mayhap he would persuade him and prevail upon him. Said he: "Give me the horse; here is his price." But the merchant made his palate rebellious. The purchaser complained to the judges, and the wise of heart were inclined in his favor. They bade him render the horse since the price had been fixed. The merchant took wily counsel, with deceit and guile and falsehood, and he told the judges such a story as this: If the man who had made the estimate had had two eyes, he would have made his evaluation twofold. But inasmuch as his right eye had been gouged out, when he inspected the horse he saw him with half vision and hence estimated him at half his value. Then said the judges: "Be thine that which is thine; discernment and understanding have fallen to thy lot, and thou art more righteous than we. With one eye he could not evaluate him."

The parable: Thus it befalls a man who puts his trust in humankind. Wherefore question and wherefore test him? When thou leanest upon him, he is broken; he speaketh with two hearts. So the merchant said to his neighbor: "Here is my horse, gratis"—and then wished to sell him at twice his value. Such a man taketh no delight in his honor. Thou mayest perceive here yet another proverb and parable: Enter not into judgment without a plan, but take counsel with thy thoughts ere thy lips speak. So did the merchant in his suit, when he brought his case into the light.

And I plied my poesy and said:

If thou bringest kindness out of my vessels,
Then canst thou draw kindness out of a rock.
A fool is he who thinks to fashion a nail of bad iron.

85

Lion, Wolf, Bear, Fox

WHO FORGES EVIL AGAINST HIS NEIGHBOR, UPON HIM A VAIN CURSE DESCENDS.

THE LION fell sick of the malady whereby he would die, and the wolf and the bear came to speak upon his heart, as did all the beasts of the earth after their kind. Only the fox hid himself, his heart panting to know the end of the matter, and what would follow the storm, and whether he would be missed by the king. He watched in secret to overhear what they would say, and he heard the wolf say to the lion: "My lord, hear my words. Send the fox to fetch balm of Gilead and spices and perfumes which will satisfy thy heart, for his is an ear that trieth words and his hand will grind the ointment. He is most expert of us all in paths and he knoweth the merchants of Gilead; there is none like him for wisdom and understanding." Said the king: "Summon him." But the wolf had acted with guile, to malign the fox, to bring him trouble and sorrow and keep him far from his ways. He spread evil reports against him for not coming to visit the sick king and made false rumors flourish. The fox heard his voice when he opened his lips to spread destruction and said to the king: "The fox is not here; may the whirlwind sweep him away, both living and in his wrath." When he heard the words of the wolf, the fox drew cunning from the depths of his heart to inflict grief upon the wolf. Upon his lips a fire smoldered to do unto him as he had plotted; he brooded in his reins and sat silent until he saw the king's countenance furious. Runners issued forth posthaste to seek the fox hither and yon, and the fox feared lest he stumble. Slowly he came, leg touching leg and sole, sole as if he were weary and fordone, and he said: "My lord the king live forever! Hidden from him and unknown is the toil and weariness I have undergone in seeking a healing remedy for thee. From the day upon which my lord fell ill and lay him down, my rest ceased and my wandering began; until I reached Gilead and returned, I took no rest or respite. These forty days have I been sated with vagabondage, and the bread of my provision was dry and moldy. I have passed over hills and valleys, mountains and lowlands; in dusk and deep darkness I knew not where I was. I have cut my life off like a weaver. But the physicians gave me to eat of all the powders of the merchant, and all with one mouth said they had chosen a remedy for thy malady: Strip the skin of the living wolf from off his flesh, and let the warm skin be taken for a turban for the king's head, and it shall be for a sign and a wonder. All thy loved ones shall come and sprinkle of his blood round about thee. Say not, 'My hope is perished'; let them lay it for a plaster upon the boil and thou shalt recover." The king hesitated not to do according to these words. They seized the wolf and flayed off his hide; only by the skin of his teeth did he escape. He was a reproach to his neighbors, for they left him naked and his bones burned like a hearth. The fox had caught him in his snare and had removed his hope like a tree. He stood opposite him, mocking him and gnashing his teeth, and he said: "Art thou he whom the king delighteth to honor? Can the Ethiopian change his skin? Nay, but by the sayings of thy mouth hast thou stumbled, and by the wickedness thou hast forged against me. Upon thyself shall thy wickedness be poured, for I did dwell secure with thee."

The parable: He seeketh not peace for his soul who forgeth evil against his neighbor and speaketh against him in frowardness. When one letteth out water, it is the beginning of strife; his one verdict is death. Who slandereth his neighbor in secret, him will I cut off.

86

Hen & Mistress

YEARN NOT FOR THE DAINTIES
OF HIM THAT PERSUADES THEE
BY THE SMOOTHNESS OF HIS LIPS.

A HEN scattered her food and gathered it between her feet; she separated ears and cut them off; she opened her feet out to uncover the dust with her claw and the chaff blown out of the granary. Often she labored in vain, for she did not find enough to satisfy her. Her mistress looked upon her and saw that her heart was persuaded to give her soul livelihood by her toil; her mercies were warmed and she said to her: "Lo, I have swaddled thee and brought thee up, and therefore do I take pity upon thee for that thy corn is scattered and dispersed—the leavings of the hail—and thy soul falls short in seeking it. The seeds are rotten under their clods; therefore art thou meager and wonderfully reduced—as one that gathereth ears in the valley of Rephaim—and thou crouchest in a troubled vale. Better for thee half a homer, aye, a homer of wheat, as thou sittest at the gate of hope, than that thou

shouldst grieve all the day. Lo, I put before thee all my grain, my threshing and the corn of my floor, worth a hundred pieces of silver, current money with the merchant. Go not to glean in another field. Lo, thou hast uncovered the dust and covered it again; what hast thou gathered this day, where is thy labor? Thou art wearied but hast not found that for which thou hast toiled; before thy bread cometh sighing." As the mistress spoke thus in her ears, she was despised in her eyes, and she said to her: "If thou wouldst give me each month thy granary full of wheat threshed and ground, I would regard it as bread of idleness. Better for me to endure poverty, to defile my horn in the dust than that some cruel one drive me from the granary. Whoso rests his hope upon another, the increase of his house shall depart. Better for me to go forth free and seek whom my soul loveth and eat what I shall find; better for me to go forth and stray like a lost sheep. Sweet is the sleep of the toiler, and the ear which is innocent of man; but thou settest a print upon the heels of my feet. Let thine be thine and mine, mine, for that is my portion of all my toil. I shall go softly all my years in my toil, for I am no better than my fathers."

Hear and understand the parable: If a man say to thee, "Accept grain in place of straw," despise not what thine own hand findeth, for thou knowest not the weariness thou shalt find if thou hearkenest to his voice. Whoso despiseth the word shall be destroyed by it. Reckon the words of the enticers as nought; eat not the bread of him whose eye is evil. He that persuadeth thee by the smoothness of his lips, eat not of his dainties, for before thou are sated he will be sated with thee and on the morrow will thrust thee from his company. A violent man cajoles his neighbor and smites him with the rod of his lips. Even if he conclude a covenant with him he will cast brimstone upon his abode. The way of the scorners is to love scorn, and he that searcheth for good will seek favor.

87

Camel & Caravan

STRENGTHEN WEAK HANDS IF THOSE HANDS ARE WEAKENED BY TOIL.

A CAMEL proceeding with a caravan knelt and lay down under his burden, and when he had no strength to rise all disdained him and hid their faces from him and made their eyes unseeing. He cried to them: "Hear me, my people! Surely I am your bone and your flesh, and your name is as my name; wherefore should riders and they that pass upon the road on foot say, 'This specimen shows their nature? When he is fallen and strayed from the path, the others go on.' See, there is no fault in all my toil. Be merciful unto me, be merciful, for ye are my brethren; until ye have raised me up, journey not forth. Do not, my brethren, do evil; lo, my heart is whole with you—how can ye ignore me?" They answered him: "If thy hands and feet put their strength forth to raise thee, then we shall surely help along with thee; but if thou cravenly follow idleness and lie inert as one fordone and weak of hands, then in vain wilt thou hope for our help, for that thou art sluggish in helping thyself."

The parable teaches and gives us to understand that weak hands incapable of help must be strengthened, if thou see a poor man whose hand falls short and he seeks thy face with a bitter and sorrowing soul, when his force is spent in vain and his hope and expectation have perished. But if thou see that poverty has prevailed over him by reason of idleness of hands and sluggishness, and his household are famished and impoverished by reason of idleness, then are all his comrades who hear his cry ashamed and his evil is revealed in the congregation, for he hath not made his hands firm, to gather as they did, and he begs of them with the brazenness of a harlot. This is the lesson of the vile and the nameless. And the sage who hath mounted the steps of good sense hath said: "I have tasted every bitterness, and there is no bitterness like the taste of begging."

88

Osprey & Pot

IF GOOD SENSE AND KNOWLEDGE
ARE IN THY REINS, THOU WILT
BRING THEM AND PLANT THEM
IN THE MOUNT OF THY HERITAGE.

THE OSPREY'S throat was dry with thirst and his tongue failed for dryness, and he was wearied for seeking rivers and broad marshes. For three days he went in the wilderness and found no water, but on the fourth he found a pot wherein was water. He knew not whether it was half full or more, for the pot was deep and narrow. The osprey would fain drink, but could not lower his head to the water. His labor was vanquished, and the eagerness of his soul redoubled. He descended to thrust the vessel from its position and overturn it and spill its water. He walked about it and pushed it, seeking to cast it down with flank or shoulder, with beak or feet. When he saw that he could not succeed, he gathered stones, mostly pebbles—for he that removeth stones shall be hurt therewith—and his cunning devices taught him to cast them into the pot. The waters rose up and reached all the brim of the pot. And so he broke his thirst, and the cold water was for a healing for his weary spirit.

The parable: Acquire wisdom and shrewdness and clever schemes and cunning, for a man may be weak of loins if shrewdness is bound fast to his heart. Better is wisdom than strength; therefore let knowledge and good sense take root in thy thoughts. Thou shalt bring them and plant them in the mountain of thy heritage, and sow it with the seed of understanding, and water it from the fountain of sense. Turn not after folly lest thy soul be affrighted and polluted by it. And the sage hath said: "He that engages in wisdom shall not be put to shame if his neck be not stout and his body stalwart." He that takes my words to heart, the fortresses of the rocks are his stronghold. The wise shall see my parables and increase their wisdom; they will heed my sayings, for they are pleasant.

89

A Fearsome & Awesome Knight

BOAST NOT OF THY PRIDE, FOR THOU KNOWEST NOT THY LATTER END.

THERE was a fearsome and awesome knight whose name was known in every city; a multitude of people trembled at his voice. To him princes were a jest. From afar he scented battle, and they feared to come nigh him, for the belt which was upon his loins and the shoe which was upon his foot. The thunder of the warlords and their horn blasts were for him a deliverance; when he heard the sound of their tramping, he put his hand forth to the top of the mulberry trees to shed the blood of the proud upon dry land. No archer put him to flight, for a brazen helmet was upon his head, and he dragged mighty heroes by his strength. At destruction and famine he laughed, at the lash of the whip and the rumble of wheels. His right hand was mighty to rend armor and crush it, as a thread is snapped on the weaver's beam. His hands fought for him, and the hooves of his horses were as flint. His name was bruited afar, for his rule was to pursue and overtake. When they that fought against him saw that the fir trees were shaken, they ascended the clouds and mounted the treetops. To a man they fled from before him, some in chariots and some on horseback. Dominion over the knights was placed upon his shoulder; they conferred upon him the glory of strength. If he encountered a merchant heavy with silver and gold, he made him the pottage which he loved. Against armed highwaymen too he put forth his hand, and overturned their glory to the earth. But while his honors were still fresh upon him, time put forth its hand against his peace and spread a snare for his footsteps. The days of the hero did not prosper. Whenever he entered battle he was either crushed or taken captive, and if he ran he stumbled in his going. There was no healing for his bruise, and his wound was grievous; his loins were filled with pain, his heart melted and his knees smote together. By a new name was he called: the weakling, not the hero. A bruised reed shall he not break. Every lowly man teased him with his hook; he had fallen from the height of his power. And it came to pass when he fell and rose not again, that his thighs were bound with chains, for one that dasheth in pieces came up against his face, and shut his eyes, and his hands were fettered from the bow, and those it had pierced gazed upon him. The merchant and the highwayman joined together; each was vigilant, and he retired from the place of their abode. Always he was in flight, and after him was a hue and cry, "Go up, thou bald one." If a price had been offered for his soul they would have removed his head from upon him. From that day forward he went backward, from before the flaming sword and the burnished spear. Instead of being stronger than his brethren and dominating them as heretofore, he went no more to battle nor took thought of it for any matter. Those who were his servants aforetime, he honored and served, and he was sated with disgrace instead of honor. Before the eyes of all his kindred he swore to burn all his gear of war and no more go forth to battle; and he kindled a great blaze wherein to cast his weapons. For he said: "I will burn and blot out prancing steed and leaping chariot, and with them corselet and helmet shall be erased; no shield or spear shall be seen." He thrust his sword into the belly of the horse he loved, and the haft also went in after the blade. Thereafter he broke the sword and did as he had said to his weapons. If hosts had feared them aforetime, there was not left of them any that survived or escaped. On the morrow he remembered his horn, upon which he was wont to blow in his woodlands and forests, and as he carried it to cast it into the fire, weeping as he went, his wife said to him: "Wherefore didst thou bethink thee of this to burn it? It is not a weapon of war; wherefore burn it in fire? Let thy heart forbear to destroy it; let it be a brand saved from the burning. Lo, I am ashamed of thy doing; be not as one dead." And it came to pass when his rib spake to him not once or twice, that he smote the rib with his staff two times and said to her in anger: "Thou art a daughter of rebelliousness; as speak one of the shameful women, speakest thou. The horn too was among my troublers, to rouse me to the sports of my youth. For when I heard the blast of the horn I ceased all my sighing and among the trumpets I said, Ha, ha! Therefore shall I cast it into the brazier. When I heard the horn's alarums I set my course thereby and roused me to war against mine enemies, and my sword came into play and seized them. And when I returned from battle I sounded my horn to hunt game and fetch it, and my dogs whetted their tongues, for it was the horn that mustered all the hosts."

The parable is to bear in mind this excellent law: He that scatters is like him that disperses; he that seizes a foot, like him that strips it. Even the horn, which was not a weapon of war, the knight verily sought to burn along with his weapons of war. If he that sees through his lattice turns a blind eye, his guilt is as the guilt of the thief.

90

Fly & Ox

A WEAK COMRADE LIKENS HIMSELF TO HIS COMPANIONS THOUGH THEY BE STRONG.

A FLY walking in the field saw an ox upon whose neck the farmer bound ropes and oxbows and bands and ceased not to ply his flanks with the goad. The ox set his face to plough, and the fly went and perched between his horns; as the ox traced the furrows, going and returning, the fly continued to sit upon his horn. His kinswoman the bee observed him and stood from afar to see what he sought between the horns of the ox and whether the ploughing would continue all the day. Said the bee: "Are the horns of the ox thine encampment? Why abidest thou among the sheepfolds?" The fly answered: "Know that all this field which is before us, I and the ox have ploughed by our strength. Do thou as we have done if thou hast the strength. Awake, awake, Deborah [bee]."

The parable is for the lowly who walks amongst the mighty or for the iniquitous who is mustered in the camp of the upright. In their counsel and in their strength he cannot stand, but by the utterance of his mouth he is joined with them to make his might equal to theirs and his wisdom to their wisdom. He says: "Thus have *we* done in *our* strength, and thus have *we* done in *our* wisdom."

91

Wolf & Fox

BETTER TO SOJOURN WITH THE RICH THAN WITH ONE WHOSE HANDS FALL SHORT.

THE WOLF said to the fox: "Hearken and I shall inform thee what thou shouldst do. Come with me, and the king shall not know. I will teach thee what way thou shouldst go, for the days of thy sojourn with the lion have been long, and he hath oppressed thee and made thee hunger, in order to prove thee. Lo, beyond the hedge I have seen chicks, strayed from their mother and lost; thou shalt come upon them suddenly and smite them. Seek not their peace nor welfare. Breach the wall to the measure of thy head; hasten and thou shalt find dainties for thy soul. By the length of the hole and its breadth foxes may go through it." Answered the fox: "If the lord of the house and court is rich, nothing of all thou hast said shall be wanting; but if he is poor and needy, my heart will eschew heeding thy counsel, lest he pursue after me and overtake me and in the bitterness of his soul smite me to death."

The parable: Understand what I teach thee, and be thy heart not froward or rebellious; for if thou wax wise from the parables of instruction thou wilt not be an example in the assembly of the understanding. Better for thee to challenge the wealth of the rich than to challenge one whose hands fall short, for the hand of the rich is abundant and superfluous, and a sated soul despiseth honeycomb; if in the morning they grieve at their loss, come evening they sorrow no more, for their right hand is clothed in the strength of the remnant that is escaped. But the poor are bitter of soul to purchase peace through war, for they have no escape or reserve. For their abundant passion and grief no violence can terrify or affright them; a lion's heart sprouts within them and gives them no respite, and they spoil the soul of those that spoiled them.

92

A Goring Ox & His Master

THE WICKEDNESS OF A PERVERSE AND CROOKED MAN SHALL BE HIS STUMBLING BLOCK.

AN OX sinned against his master. He was a gorer from yesterday and the day before; whensoever he took him out to plough he proved himself a goring ox. The master's hot anger rose against the ox, and he polled his horns with a knife and told his neighbor his demeanor was bad but that his long horns were cut off. And it came to pass in the morning, when he ploughed at his back, that the ox attacked him with his teeth. The master desired to debase all his pride and knocked most of his teeth from his mouth. And it came to pass when the grinders were gone from his mouth with only a paltry few remaining, the ox chased after every man, striking with flank and shoulder, nor was he humbled by his mishaps. Upon the third day he smote the master a great blow with his foot, and his neighbors said to him: "This outcome of his mutinous heart and deeds thou shalt not avail to remove from him by cutting off member after member but only by breaking him wholly."

The parable: Do not challenge a perverse man, for if thou ensnare him and bray him in a mortar, his perversity will not depart from him. Nay, keep him afar in every direction; he is an abomination that is not acceptable, for his heart is bitterroot and rank wormwood, the shoots of an alien vine.

93

The Man of the Field Knoweth Hunting

THEIR HEARTS ARE IN DARKNESS
WHO BELIEVE IDLE TALK.

THE MAN of the field knoweth hunting. He lurks for beasts and takes them, and they recognize him as he walks, by his bow and quiver. His spirit is watchful to hunt by night, wherein all the beasts of the forests stir; but ere he come they move away and their tracks are not known. Hart, roebuck, and hare, wild goat, pygarg, wild ox, and chamois, when they behold him face to face, all the hairs of their flesh bristle for fear of the oppressor they recognize. All these banded together for flight. A leopard under one of the bushes saw them all running with terror in their hearts and posted himself at the crossroads to learn what this might be and wherefore—whether for some dream or vision they had all fled as one. With one mouth they said to him: "Lo, we have seen the man lurking for us in the wilderness. His weapons of war are with him; his bow is firmly planted and always drawn for shooting, and his quiver is an open sepulchre. The arrows therein are his battalions, which his mighty arms scatter." Answered the leopard: "Move not from the camp; stand firm without turning." And when they turned their shoulder to go, the leopard did not stir from the battle line, and said: "I am not afraid of the man; if I meet him I will rend him in an instant and cut him off. His sure doom is death. Abide with me and fear not wrath nor cruelty; I will lead you as ye walk erect." The lurking man approached nearer for his shot; he trod his bow and shot his arrows to reach their target. Like lightning his dart issued forth and wounded the leopard in the second rib, so that his heart grieved and trembled. He gathered his strength for speedy flight and overtook the beasts for the soles of whose feet there was no rest. Before he neared them, they called to him: "Is it possible that the king should flee, with heart melted betake him to hasty flight? If thou hast not rent and slain the hunter, what price the assurance wherewith thou hast assured us?" Humbled by his anguish he answered them, and his voice was like a ghost's out of the earth: "Lo, my calculations were confounded. The man mine eyes did not behold, but at his bidding the fleas of death have bitten me; it is they that are called the sons of his quiver. Alas for the day that I trusted in my strength, alas for my breach and my aching wound! Such a hero as I am cannot prevail by great strength and prowess when he dispatches one of his tiny servants with me as its target, and the evil cleaves unto me and I die."

The parable: When thou seest men fleeing in terror, moaning and sighing with bitterness and breaking of loins, with every heart melted and every hand waxed weak before the whetted sword and the sound of the cries of the fordone, stand not in the place of evil if thou covetest thy life. Be not overpersuaded by thy strength or thy cunning, lest thy feet be plagued by thy devices.

94

Fox & Cat

WHO HATH IN HIM ONLY THE PRAISE OF HIS OWN LIPS WILL SWATHE HIM IN HIS SHAME AND CLOTHE HIM IN HIS DISGRACE.

UNDER a tree planted upon waters the fox called to the cat, saying: "Hear me; henceforward let us conclude a covenant, thou and I. My feet are swift as a hart's, but thou art tried in mounting places where a fox may not ascend. Lo, up above I have observed the flesh of a sheep, moist and fat. If thou do not believe my words, come and I will show thee that place. Under this tree shall we eat it." The cat returned his answer: "At thy word shall I march or halt." So they concluded a covenant between them, and both walked together. Said the fox to the cat: "Open thine eyes and behold the place which is before thee; see whether thou canst fetch the flesh. Ascend thou on high and take thy captive, and I shall await thee here until thou return to me in peace." The cat ascended upward to the hanging flesh which he longed to eat; when he reached the sheep he turned back carrying the flesh between his teeth. The fox, who awaited his coming, went forward to meet him, rejoicing for that he had kept his commandment, and uttered this counsel to the ear of the cat: "Let us go under the tree and there make division by lot, without guile or deception." As they walked together along the road the fox pondered guile, plotting to seize the flesh. As he approached nigh the cat, she scampered hastily up a tree, before the fox, who was hungry and impatient for food, could prevent her. The fox could not climb the tree, and said: "Treacherous cat! Wilt thou eat whilst I stand in thy presence? Wilt thou not keep thy covenant and the utterance of thy lips? Give me wherewith to restore my famished soul, so that I grieve no more." The cat answered: "In the delight of my soul shall I eat flesh, and the belly of the wicked shall lack. I shall eat and thou shalt go hungry; the mocker shall be the mocked. Mine is this flesh, sound and fat, and the teeth of the wicked shall be set on edge." Said the fox: "Is this my requital from thee, is it thus thou dealest with me? For thine iniquity thou wilt be sore straitened, for I will besiege thee, to pay thee out measure for measure. What wilt thou do for the day of reckoning? Thy doom is graven and hewn. I will lay siege against thee with a mound and not stir hence until thou descend. Instead of the flesh I will take thy soul and remove thy head from upon thee." The cat answered: "This shall not be. I shall not die but live, for from the mountains are descending horsemen riding in pairs with spirited dogs before them. They are coming thy way; flee and find thee refuge, for wherefore should they smite thee to the life? Set thy footsteps upon the way before thou art delivered into their hand; attend to thy way, shake off futile dallying." The fox answered: "I am not afraid, nor am I terrified of the dogs. Who can reach me to harm me? My heart will not fail of its cunning and its hundred shifts and turns. Many such have I, wherewith to deliver my soul and elude their hands to go free. Nay, I shall not depart until I see thee caught in my snare. Between my teeth wilt thou be crushed; no more shalt thou chase after the rat." And it came to pass as he spake to him thus that the dogs came on in battle array and the riders tarred them on against him. One bit him in the back, one in the tail, one in the ears; one set his teeth in his neck, and one bit him in the sinews of his stones and testicles. When this mischief had befallen him the cat called out: "Do but work one of thy hundred shifts, and escape, so that thou wilt be master of thine own body; of what avail thy cunning if it save thee not in time of evil?"

The parable: This is the habit of boasters, the practice of sinful men who say, "Our hand is too lofty to put sickle to standing grain." They vaunt themselves much upon their cunning, and boast of their professions: "I am a weigher, I am a scribe; I am a smith, I am a tailor; I am a goldsmith, I am a merchant; I am a sage, and what other is there like me to equal me? I am a physician for every malady." But he delivers not his soul from his own trouble, nor does he sustain his household, for wisdom is not with him and there is no spirit in him. Who hath in him only the praise of his own lips will swathe himself in his shame and clothe himself in his disgrace.

95

Image & Man

A SOFT ANSWER TURNETH AWAY WRATH AND LEADETH NOT TO HATRED.

A GRAVER fashioned an image and finished it; by a craftsman was it made, and it was no god. A rich man sought eagerly to purchase it of the craftsman, for he wished to make it his god. Its beauty, its stature, its height, were correct in his eyes, and it was painted and portrayed with vermilion. Another man in the vicinity wished to purchase it to make of it a monument for the dead. He would set it up on good hewn stone, and therewith cover the grave of his kinsman whom he loved as his own life.

The image wept, and implored him that carved it to give him his body for his petition and his honor for his request; said he: "Lo, I am thine, and thou art my keeper; I am the clay and thou the potter, and in thy hand is all my spirit and glory, to exchange my honor for shame. Thy hands have made me and fashioned me; with compasses and a line hast thou drawn me, and wood that would not rot was chosen for me. For that I was precious in thy sight I have been honored. Thine was the workmanship of my pipes and tabrets, of my arms and my hands. Consider the end of such a beginning; have thou a desire to the work of thy hands. Deliver me not to the soul of mine enemies, who would vex me and purchase me of thee to cover the dead—a stinking and lifeless carcass—and so desecrate my manifest beauty. Would that my request come about, that thou sell me to one who will fear me and call upon my name! In my honor is thy honor, and the man who worships me will honor thee as he prays to me. My honor he shall not desecrate, and all they in the islands will show that they bow down to the work of thy hands. If thou take no delight in thy handiwork and its esteem, what profiteth the image which its fashioner hath carved?" Its fashioner heeded the image's petition, and sold it to the man who would serve and honor it.

The parable: Flatter any whose hand is strong upon thee; make thy counsel with him sweet, to draw his heart to thee; cajole the heart of the perverse, to gain peace, so that it may be good with thee and thy days may be lengthened. And one of the sages who saw visions of the Almighty hath said: "It is permissible to flatter the wicked in this world." And another sage hath revealed to mine ear: "Bow down to the fox in his day of power."

96

Conies & Hare

BETTER TO BE AT THE FEET OF NOBLES THAN TO BE A KING OVER FOOLS.

THE CONIES are not a strong people, neither fierce nor deep of speech. They made their home in the rocks, and the lion wrought havoc amongst them. Said they: "Let us choose lords of our families; the rocks are a shelter for the conies. If we place a king over us, what will the lion do to us? Will he pursue after us in holes and in caves, in rocks, in high places, and in pits?" They sent messengers in all their boundaries to summon them all for an appointed day. And they chose them a hare of tall stature, old and strong and full of wisdom, and they said to him: "We have chosen the king to rule and protect; naught that issueth from thy lips shall be withheld. This lion of whose voice thou art in dread, we know not what hath befallen him. Ere he confound thee and become thine enemy thou shalt shake his yoke off from thy neck." He answered them: "Far be it from me to become your king; I shall not rule over you, for there is no majesty of kingship nor glory nor dominion for one who ruleth over a humble nation and a younger family. Very foolish is he who seeks to hold sway over them; their judges are overthrown in stony places. Wherefore have ye angered me to come up and walk in crooked paths? The kingdom and the rule which ye would give me shall be the lowliest of kingdoms. Better for me to be one of the least servants of the lion than to rule over a people without strength or power or might. My burden shall not rest upon you, but we shall be fully equal." So he stayed them with his words and frustrated their plan.

The parable: It is better for thee to be at the feet of the nobles of the people than to be king and shepherd among vain folk. For amongst the great thou wilt acquire a name for thyself and in their company wilt thou be established and built up, whereas amongst the vile over whom thou wilt hold sway thou wilt become as one of them. Of old, great sages have said: "Be thou a tail to lions, but be not a head to foxes." And a sage summoned his son and said to him: "My son, my firstborn, thou art my might and the beginning of my strength. Know that the Rock hath ordained to exalt the humble and debase them that rise in pride, and dominion flees from any that seeks greatness. Therefore humble thyself, and thou wilt be raised on high."

And I plied my poesy and said:

If thy heart labors to pursue dominion,
Wonder not if what is pursued, flies.
Beloved, humble thy soul, and therein be exalted,
For grace and strength bloom for the meek.
The high of heart will not find honor; but know
It shineth upon the broken in spirit.
If thou choose greatness it will flee from thee
And liken thee to a budding boil.
If thou imitate the fox thou'lt be a lion;
Think thyself a lion and thou art bald.
If thou lovest to abide upright and perfect,
Thou shalt be a welcome guest in thy world.
In the measure that thou art humble and bowed down,
The majesty of honor will abound for thee.
Pride and haughtiness, keep afar; for its taste is evil,
Upon its path, a noisome stench.
Pride over all rulers beseemeth Him
Who ruleth over sun and moon.

97

Lion, Goats, Fox

FORGIVE HIM THAT HATH HARMED THEE, AND GIVE TO HIM THAT HATH DENIED THY REQUEST.

A LION sent his kindled wrath against goats, and hid the prey he had spoiled. The fox knew the paths of his house, and in his cunning silently stole in and ate of his flesh and gnawed of his bones, and was sated with them nor paid their price, as if he had found a windfall in the field and carried it off piece by piece. The lion perceived that the fox did not keep his faith but dealt treacherously, and he accosted him with soft words, not in anger: "This time it is bone of my bones and flesh of my flesh, which I have spoiled by my labor and the toil of my hands. My reins counsel me and my thoughts impel me to say, Go, leave my provision and eat thine own. If thy hand continue thus a second time I will teach thee 'Thou shalt not steal, thou shalt not covet.' The third time thou wilt sink as low as thou hast stood high in thy rebelliousness, and I will sweep thee out with the besom of destruction, nor will I forbear to break thy bones and rend thy sinews, as the weaver's cord is severed when he smelleth the fire. Shall the fox eat while the lion aches, and shall the lion's whelps not tread him down? If one that had spread his net for thee had fallen into thy hands, then only the slothful man roasteth not that which he took in hunting. But how did it enter thy spirit to search in my hidden store, and wherefore hast thou thus cheated me? Attend to my instruction, and return no more to folly." Answered the fox, sweetening his palate with persuasion: "Was I ever wont to do so unto thee? I have heard thine instruction and the sweetness of thine utterance; lo, I am insignificant; how shall I answer thee? Nay, I am ashamed and sorry for my deeds, and shall no more add unrighteousness to such as I have committed."

The parable is to deliver thee from the snare of the seducers. Have I not written thee excellent things—saws and proverbs and parables—that thou be hard to make angry and easy to appease? Nay, make thee paths in the heart of understanding, for yielding pacifieth great offenses. If thou see thy neighbor walking in the way of the violent and drawing his hand with the scorners, ceasing not to add to his sinfulness and kneading the dough until it be leavened, poured over with wicked things, then do thou rend the lock of his heart with pleasant speech and repeat thine instruction and repeat it again to turn him back—I know his pain—and say to him: "He that repeateth his folly and doeth a very horrible thing, his doom is one, mourning and lamentation. Who hath woe, who hath sorrow, who hath contentions?—Those who repeat their folly like you." If after the second admonition he transgresses, twice and yet again, then there is no hope for his latter end. Even the ox that gores is a proclaimed offender after three gorings. So is it graven upon the tablets: If he return neither knowledge nor understanding to his heart, thy hand shall be upon him first. And the sage hath said: "Forgive him that harmed thee, and give unto him that denied thy request."

98

Raven & Carcass

SILENCE ADDS, AND DIMINISHES NOT, FOR A MAN OF KNOWLEDGE.

A RAVEN was over a river known to no vulture and sailed by no galley. He flew hither and thither in his hunger and was wearied of seeking his provision, until evening. He came upon a place where he found a carcass, and thereat rejoiced exceedingly. Out of the abundance of his joy he gazed upon it and fluttered his wing and peeped. His mouth he opened beyond measure and his voice was heard afar. The ears of the eagle tingled, and he said: "I will hasten to see whether it is the voice of them that shout for battle or the voice of them that shout for being overcome." He came to the raven and found him leaping over the carcass and rending the flesh from the bones and dividing it in pieces. The eagle raged against him in wrath of spirit and smote him; there he established a statute and ordinance for him and there he tried him. From that day forward the raven raised not his voice to make his prey known to the birds abroad.

The parable: Many have stumbled and been ensnared if they were not silent when the season of their harvest fell. Because they did not guard the opening of their mouth, news of them reached the rulers and each roared like a lion. All of them shall be as thorns thrust away, lurking in hiding like a lion, and they bring an evil name upon them until no gleanings are left. Gleefully they seek them that stumble, to get them provision and plunder; the extortioner is at an end; the spoiler ceaseth. By the utterance of the mouth and want of silence hath the spirit of men been cloven. And I said to him the utterance of whose lips is not guarded and restrained that he is a cake not turned. And the Preacher who hath sown understanding hath said: "The wicked is snared by the transgression of his lips." And the Arab hath said in his instruction to his firstborn son: "Thy secret is thy captive; if thou reveal it thou wilt be its captive."

And I plied my poesy and said:

Who stumbleth with foot, little is his stumbling;
Who stumbleth with mouth, loseth his head.
Know that whoso guards his mouth and tongue
Guards his soul from trouble.

99

Fox, Wagon, Fish

HE THAT IS FILLED WITH DECEIT
AND FALSEHOOD INCREASETH HATRED.

A FOX went upon his way traversing the earth in its length and its breadth, and he turned his face hither and yon, and lo, a wagon came upon his way, filled with fish from the sea. He craved them for the delight of his soul and bethought him of a trick to work; and for the longing of his soul he worked it. He made himself as one dead upon the road, though he was sound of body. He spread his palms upward, so that he seemed as one whose knee had stumbled in the wilderness and who had fallen at the crossroads and was lying dead in the roadway. The wagon driver lifted his eyes and saw before him the fox, who had knelt and lain him down and was stretched out as if anguish had come upon him. He lifted him and carried him (the fox rose not nor stirred) and put him in a bag and covered him, for he feared lest his pursuers should recognize him. He hid him under his skirts, lest the inquirer see him, and covered him with garments until he grew warm, and he lay with the fish in the wagon. Them the fox consumed utterly, and he filled his belly with them; his soul took no mercy upon them. When he separated a part and ate it he said in his heart, "Shall I eat and leave behind?—I shall not rest until I engulf all, even the full vessel that is set aside." So he ate of the fish and was sated, taking as many as seven in his mouth, for his satiety ran over. Then he dug through the bag and alighted from the wagon and ran away and entered a stronghold he found and hid him with the prey yet between his teeth. The wagon passed before his face without the driver perceiving that the fox had fled. Quietly the fox went on and stood in a path in the vineyards, for he feared them that might rise against him; his footsteps stirred not, nor was his hiding place discovered.

Now as he remained there hidden, in fear and in dread and in terror, there entered the place a wolf, weary and fordone and sorrowful, for that his soul panted for prey. The wolf lifted his head and came forward to meet the fox and greeted him, and the fox responded in due form, but bethought him of devices to remove the wolf from his boundary, for he feared him, lest he come and seize that which was his. The wolf inquired after his peace and asked what it was he carried in his mouth. The fox answered in a clear voice, with guile and frowardness and deception: "Peace have I and peaceful be thy coming; greatly have I rejoiced at thy speech. Lo, I went forth to yonder water and found it congealed with cold. Upon it I walked, like a strong man that runneth a course; in the ice I made a hole, and in the hole placed my tail for the space of an hour. Around my tail came the fish, and formed a crown about it as if held with fishhooks. I seized them as with a net and made them my provision, whereof I have eaten and am satisfied. Go thou then and do as I have done. I know thou hast labored in vain; I believe thou hast found nought. To restore thy weary soul eat but one fish and it shall refresh thee." The wolf longed for like dainties, but bade the fox farewell and blessed him and said to him: "Be thine that which is thine; I will not trust thee, to thrust my tail into holes, lest the accursed and bitter waters come upon me." The wolf ran to the pool, which was all frozen with the cold of the night. There he observed a hole made by the shepherds to water their flocks at midday, and he said in his heart: "For all my innocence I have sinned grievously in suspecting the fox. Yet hath he not put his hand forth for deceit, but the truth is established in his mouth, and his hands have acted in good faith. I see the pool and the hole in its surface." So he thrust his tail in the hole and sat by to await the hour when the fish would be gathered in his snare. The sun passed over and was gone and the cold waxed stronger, until the tail was frozen in the pool. But the wolf was filled with joy, for he imagined that he was catching fish with his tail. Said he: "My tail is exceedingly heavy; I know that my seat is strong. Better is this than gain of silver, if all the fish of the pool be gathered. Now shall I be the diligent one that profiteth. But I am fearful of the sons of strangers, lest they see me and slay me and turn me back empty." Then the wolf collected his strength to arise from his place, but could not, for the cold had fallen upon his bottom. His tail, which was in straits, pained him sore; and he cried a great and bitter cry, for that he could not rise to his feet, for the joints of his ankles gave way. The shepherds heard his voice and were astonished, and they went to see what had befallen him. They sought their dogs to urge against him, each man tarring his own dog on, and the dogs attacked and bit him. They surrounded him on all sides, while he perforce remained fixed, and they smote and pounded him to desolation. In the anguish of his spirit he took courage; but his force was spent in vain, for his tail was held fast in the ice. The sun shone upon him, and the shepherds multiplied their blows. They embittered his life; the archers hated him and shot their arrows at him, and discharged upon him every missile that wounds, for he was their enemy from of old. Said they, "Come and let us destroy him." Because he had not guarded his way the shepherds dealt violently with him; all shouted against him, nor were they afraid to come nigh him. With the passion of his strength he persisted in his choler, though his eye was dimmed and his moisture desiccated, until the ice was broken. In their company then he did not tarry, but ran to the forest in a windy storm. Even there he found no respite, for the strong-spirited dogs ever clove close to him. Loudly men called: "Pursue him speedily, and ye will overtake him"; and the dogs gave voice and barked at him. He escaped from his pursuers, for the forest wearied them so that they returned from pursuing after him; to enter the forest they were loath. The wolf hid under a bush, beaten and bruised and subdued; all alone he grieved, and found no helpmeet to console him. And he said: "Surely the bitterness of death is passed. The fox made my way crooked and thought to kill me; I was foolish to believe him when he guilefully bade me seek prey in the pool."

The parable is for a man filled with deception and falsehood. He plots hatred against his neighbor and makes of himself an ambush; he conceals a gin upon his path and rejoices at his great cheat. Woe to the rogue, woe to his neighbor! Ever doth he seek an occasion against him. Upon his lips there is no truth; his ears he maketh heavy and his eyes, blind. Out of the wicked issueth wickedness; against his neighbors he speaketh iniquity. Hatred maketh the line crooked.

And I plied my poesy and said:

I that speak am innocent of deception, pure and guiltless;
Pure be he who beareth the mien of one that kisseth.
He that compoundeth iniquity is as chaff within grain;
Lips of grace make strong the heart of the pure and blameless.

100

Demon & Ship

THEY THAT INSTIGATE QUARRELS
DESTROY STRENGTH AND MIGHT.

THE DEMON walked in company with his mother over a large expanse, going to and fro in the earth and walking up and down in it, until they came to the shore of the sea, where they lifted their eyes and saw a ship filled with horses and men. The ship was on the point of foundering, for the sea and its waves stormed and roared. The passengers cast all the vessels in the ship into the waves to lighten it; their flesh trembled for fear of the sea. One called to another and bade him cast into the sea his adornment and all that his eye coveted and to confess his transgressions and his rebelliousness; then did they empty all their precious things from their bags. The sailors too were affrighted and cried out, and every man shook his treasures from out of his bosom, for the storm waxed greater. Said the demon to his mother: "If thou hadst been with them this day they would have said that by thy hand had this befallen them. So have they done many times over; they utter slander against thee when the day of turmoil and confusion comes upon them, though thou hast committed no violence nor deception." The mother made her reply forthright; she hardened her face and said to him: "Though I be not there, many have I found among those I have raised and swaddled and made great who are willing agents to do my desires. From my hand hath this befallen them; they will lie down in sorrow. Upon earth men shall fear my deeds, for from me issue destroyers and desolators."

The parable is for those who instigate quarrels, for slanderers and maligners. Of their tongue's wrath they sow seed among the wise; their hearts and their lips are eager to do evil. They prophesy false burdens and causes of banishment. Each of them intrigues against his neighbor. They make kings rejoice by their evil, and princes, by their falsehoods; and when their slander succeeds they boast in the midst of their congregation and declare that their agent slander hath done prosperously. But the sage hath said in his wisdom that a man's agent is accounted as himself.

101

Merchant, Robbers, Knight

THE TREASURERS AND JUDGES

ARE FLED AND WANDERED AWAY;

NEW ONES FROM NEARBY HAVE COME.

A MERCHANT walked in company with wicked men. And it came to pass at midday, when they entered a forest, that they observed his clothing was desirable. The men of deception hastened upon him and, like emptiers, emptied him out wholly, and smote him and spoiled him and bruised him, so that he was left stunned and confounded, plagued and bruised and battered. With the string of their bow was he bound and tied. Naked he went forth, without a garment; he wished to go and heal himself of his wounds, but had no strength and fell to the ground and spilled his blood upon earth's bosom. There was none to help him. The flies gathered upon his flanks and arms and encamped round about all his wounds, to pluck and lick the blood from his gashes, like a swarm of sucking bees. They ate and were abundantly satisfied, and because of their satiety rested there and remained. Now a knight was riding by that way, and he turned and saw a man lying with his hands tied behind his back, likely to be consumed in a day, for all his body was bare and insects after their kind lodged upon it, and his belly was lying in the dust. The knight had pity and dismounted from his horse and cut the man's bonds. With branches and leaves from the forest he brushed the insects away and made them

all flee, until none was left and the body of the wounded man was exposed. The man cursed the knight with a mighty curse, reproaching and reviling him with a voice like a ghost's issuing out of the earth. He said to him: "Why hast thou chased the flies away? May he that troubled me trouble thee. Wherefore hast thou troubled me? What have I done to thee and how have I vexed thee? Surely out of the wicked cometh forth wickedness. I am mortally wounded, though I have not transgressed; lurkers have surrounded and set upon me, and have beaten and battered and bruised me. Woe and lamentation have they that plundered me inflicted upon me; they took my veil from upon me. And now hast thou arisen after them to bring anguish to my heart, for thou hast added pangs to my pangs." The knight answered: "Nay, but from thine afflictions have I redeemed thee. What have I done to thee and how have I vexed thee that thou slanderest me like a fool? Did I fear the great multitude that was destroying thy body and cutting it off? Thy soul was brought nigh to the pit and thy life to the slayers. Them that were upon thy naked flesh I cast down to waste and desert ground and removed their burden from upon thy shoulders, so that thou wilt nevermore see them and no more be pained. Wherefore hast thou repaid evil for good, and for my blessing a curse, and for my benefaction destruction?" But the merchant answered the knight with harsh words and said to him: "He that exacteth vengeance shall never remain silent. Thou hast scornfully entreated me and with thine outstretched arm troubled me when thy hand chased from upon me the flies who were already sated with my blood. My body they covered like a garment, but after thou hast put them to flight strangers will come and draw my blood and afford my sinews no rest. Better for me to endure fly and wasp that have eaten to satiety and drunk to drunkenness than to endure those not yet sated. Therefore are my words harsh."

The parable is for treasurers and bailiffs which the folk change and replace when they have emptied our purses of silver. Those men are at peace with us, for we have sated their bellies with dainties and filled their purses and their cups to overflowing; with our silver has their anger been muzzled. But in their place they have installed others, who are not wearied with robbery—new men that come from anigh—wherefore they draw as the lodestone draweth. The young lions do lack, and suffer hunger, and turn them toward gain. The principal folk they judge with bribes, they deny knowledge of their acquaintances; they leave a man no livelihood, no man is free under their power, and they transmit their commandments to a second and also to a third. Therefore give ear to my saying and bear away my counsel: Dismiss not the old judge from before the new. Time prevaileth over a man who hath dealt harshly with his neighbor twice or thrice. Therefore should a man during the span of his life love the judges whom he already knoweth, for the new shall receive of you his standing. Be thou vigilant to aid in his rule that he be not removed from the city.

102

Camel & Mountain Goat

WHOSO IS NOT SATISFIED WITH WHAT SUFFICES HIM WILL LOSE EVEN HIS DAILY BREAD.

BACK of the desert a camel saw mountain goats. Their young ones were in good liking; they grew up with corn. By their side lay he-goats with horns upon their heads; there all the beasts of the field disported themselves. The camel entered the camp and came nigh a goat with horns. He vaunted himself upon his form and image, upon his strength and lofty stature, and that all that walked on fours before him were as grasshoppers in his sight. Answered the goat: "Verily thou art desirable and pleasant, and if thou but hadst horns like mine thou wouldst be very strong." These words the camel took to his heart, and he went to the master who ruled over him and said: "Though size and strength have fallen to my lot, all this profiteth me naught when I see animals with horns upon their heads. Though my little finger is thicker than their loins, they gore west and north and south and malign my tallness of stature and let their bridle loose before me, saying they would gore even me. And now, my lord, hearken to my voice. Cut me mine ears off, and make thy latter kindness loftier than thy first: Give me horns for my forehead." And he importuned him sore. Said his master to him: "Wilt thou then constrain me? Wherefore hast thou made thine asking stubborn? Better hadst thou kept silent in thy petition." His master dealt bitterly with the camel and cut his ears off to their midpoint; he turned not back his hand, nor did he show pity. Therefore hath the camel small ears.

The parable is for one who has sufficient for his needs yet asks for more than his regular provision and says to his neighbors that he cannot live with what is in his hand. His root shall be like chaff and his bloom ascend like dust. In an instant his wealth will be consumed, for at the appointed time a sword is whetted like a razor to destroy and extinguish what greatness he has remaining. And I have found in the book of memorable wisdom, "Greed is partner to blindness." And the Preacher hath written in the proverbs of his wisdom [Proverbs 25.16]: "Hast thou found honey? Eat so much as is sufficient for thee, lest thou be filled therewith and vomit it."

And I plied my poesy and said:

When the camel asked for horns they cut his ears off;
Thus ever doth it befall the greedy if he possess wealth
and flocks.

103

A Man Ploughing His Tilth

BETTER TO SEEK AND SEARCH
IN ONE'S HEART WHO IT WAS
THAT HATH PASSED HIS GOODNESS
BY HIS FACE.

A MAN was ploughing his tilth and with his mattock cleaving the earth and crumbling it, when he found a hoard of precious stones, gold, and silver. Thereupon did he burn incense to his drag and sacrifice to his net; and of the sheep and oxen which were with him he offered holocausts to that place. He honored it with all his might, and he called to his people to do honor to the place. "Do ye as I do," quoth he. "Him that sacrificeth a thank offering will I honor; all of my days will I honor him with my praise. Verily, I am rich; I have acquired strength for myself." No more did he plough or sow or reap, no more stitch together or rip, no more cast manure upon the furrows of the field; his yoke was taken off for fatness. But he kissed that place and honored it with his praises. And lo, the voice of fortune spake unto him: "What doest thou here that thou bowest down and worshipest thy land? Is thy reverence not thy confidence in the store of silver which thou lovest, in the hewn pits which thou hast not digged? Me hast thou not remembered in thy thoughts, though I caused the treasure to fall in thy way. Therefore will I return and take from thee my gold and my silver, and in their place I shall awaken mine anger against thee. No longer shalt thou honor the earth with thy praises, with my gold and my silver which I have given thee. From that day hast thou lifted thy head and bestowed thy silver upon all that thy heart desired. I shall no longer take mercy upon thee; in the sweat of thy brow shalt thou eat bread, until thou return to earth. Naked camest thou forth from thy mother's womb, and naked wilt thou return thither. The pride which hath burgeoned in thy heart is a bud that yields no meal." And he let him go, and so it befell him; when he came to count the treasure and set it in order, though he had but just come forth, he sought but found it not. And he returned him to his station as it had been aforetime, to the ploughs and coulters, the forks and the axes, to reap his harvest and plough his tilth, and his soul was humbled with toil.

The parable teaches a man to search and seek out in his heart who it was that passed his goodness before his face, to requite him according to his beneficence and to praise him according to his deserts, to fulfill his request and do his petition. Let him not change or supplant him, to praise another in his place; but him shall he honor and his people. His mouth nor hand shall fall short for him, as befell the man of the treasure trove, who had honored not him that had exalted his honor and his majesty, but embraced and kissed him that did him no honor.

104

The Ape, His Two Sons, a Leopard

THOUGH A MAN DIFFERENTIATE
BETWEEN TWO SONS, IN THE END
THE DIVERSE WILL BE MINGLED.

UPON a rock near a bush were an ape and his two sons, of whom he loved the younger and hated the elder. When a watchful leopard descended from his lair the ape trembled for himself and the son he loved, for he saw that he was come from the mountains of the leopards. In great fury the leopard came on to destroy and lay waste; he roared over his prey and made a way for his anger. Said the ape: "Of him that I hate I shall know how to be bereft; I shall hide my face from him and he shall be for devouring." And he took him and cast him over his back, intending to present him to the leopard first. But the younger, upon whom he took pity, he carried between his legs as he ran. When he saw that the leopard was approaching nearer he wished to hurl the ape upon his back to the ground, but that one perceived his willfulness and in his desire to deliver his soul grasped hold of the fringes of his hair. When the ape saw that he could not throw him down and the leopard was drawing very nigh, he forsook the one he loved and himself escaped with the one that held sway over his back. When the ape saw that his scheme was frustrated, his reins and heart clove to the one he hated, and his hatred was turned into love; he took pity upon him as a man takes pity upon the son that serves him.

The parable: A man should love his sons in equal measure, for him that he loves best and in whom he reposes his hope the wheel will suddenly ravish away; shut thine eye upon him and he is gone. But him that he hated and kept afar will restore his soul and sustain his old age.

105

Boar, Lion, Fox

WHO MAKETH HIS HEART HARD FOR AN OCCASION, ALWAYS IT WILL BE ILL FOR HIM.

A BOAR came and went as was his way in the court of King Lion. The lion said to him: "What business hast thou near me? Come no more into my boundary and render not the habitation I take delight in unclean." The boar answered him: "My lord, I have heard." And it came to pass in the morning and lo, the boar walked round about the lion's lair, and the lion waxed angry and cut off one of his ears. He called to the fox and said to him in the boar's presence: "If this swine shall not depart from me, show him no mercy and no compassion. This boar out of the wood doth waste my lair, which is my shelter from tempest and stormwind. His is a strange work; now hold him not innocent but slay him." But the boar made his heart hard and his neck stiff, and the lion in his furious wrath cut both his ears from his head and pierced his eyes. But the boar still enraged him with the turds of his dung and made the surroundings of his lair unclean, wherefore the lion said to the fox: "Attack and slay him; his head and knees and entrails, the goodly portions of shoulder and thigh, put thou in my way upon the road." The fox butchered the boar and separated his parts. But when he saw that the heart was fat he took it to see what might become of it; he could not refrain him but ate it. All of the members he arranged in order. The lion came to see the pieces of the boar and observed that not one was withheld; of all the bones not one was broken; he found them all in a row, the head and the fat. But when he came to the entrails, he did not find the heart, and said to the fox in anger: "How didst thou deal deceitfully with thy lord? Where is the heart of the boar which thou didst wound? How couldst thou desire to conceal it from me? And now I shall requite thee according to thy deed; as thou hast done so shall it be done unto thee." The fox answered in his wisdom: "My lord, not against me falls this complaint. Incline thine ear to my saying: Herein art thou not right, and I shall refute thee. Thou didst perceive the boar's rebelliousness and discern his folly; there was no heart within him. When I arranged his members before me, I sought it but found it not. Therefore was he not instructed by the words of the king. It was for want of heart that the fool walked according to his folly, and for want of heart thou didst take his ears and eyes when he hardened his face against thy commandments. My lord the king is wise and will walk in uprightness; he will not frame an accusation against his servant." The lion answered: "I have heard thy voice. If thou be wise thou shalt be wise for thyself. Thou art more righteous than I, therefore shalt thou sit at my right hand all my days. There is none so wise as thou; I will call thy name 'My delight.' Thou shalt be over my house, and according to thy word shall all my people be ruled."

The parable: If thine inclination constrain thee to commit an impropriety, seek among the roots of thine imaginings to deliver thee like a man armed. Envy not men whose hearts and ears are uncircumcised; from what time they went forth from Egypt have they been uncircumcised. A man whose heart and ear are uncircumcised, his evil thoughts are fringes which prevent circumcision. But look thou to a way by which thou mayest go forth from thy sins to enlargement; then wilt thou establish thy soul that it may live. Wisdom giveth its possessors life and provideth healing for great sinners. And I have found in the book of the princes: "Kings judge the earth; the wise judge kings."

106

The Lion & His Son

IT IS GOOD TO BEWARE OF THE WICKED IN EVERY WAY, FOR SONS DO THE DEEDS OF THEIR FATHERS.

THE LION, who is king of the beasts, dwelt in the habitations of lions and followed the usages of his people; with the peril of his life he got his bread, as his fathers had done. He tore in pieces enough for his cubs and strangled for his lionesses. Now when he fell mortally sick and his own soul abhorred him he called to his firstborn son, who was in his city ruling over all that was his, and the young lion responded to his voice. He called to him "My son"; and he said, "Lo, here am I," and he knelt and bowed down before him. He commanded him and said to him: "My son, keep the commandment and live. Govern thy sheep and be thou strong and soldierly. Lamb and ram shall be for treading under the sole of thy foot when thou art yet young and tender; when thy strength waxes great thy hand and spirit shall not fall short. Thou shalt crouch and lie down like a young lion to seize prey and overtake it. Thy foot shall be fleeter than theirs. To the young of kine and to ass colts thou shalt leave no rest, for thou shalt pounce upon them in anger according to thy pleasure. From thy lair thou shalt go up like a lion, and all that rebel against thy lips shall not live. Thou wilt then be king over all that walk on fours. Over the sending forth of the feet of the ox and the ass thou shalt rejoice and over the keeping of all cattle; their outgoing shall be at the setting of the sun. Always for food shall they be, not for merchandise, only for the possession of a heritage. And when thou goest down and reclinest at thine ease, be not wanting in prudence. Of all the beasts and cattle the clean is forbidden thee, but with the hare and the coney thou shalt laugh at destruction and famine. Neither from the swine shalt thou abstain, for its flesh is fat. Thou shalt answer and say Amen. Nothing shall be wanting to thee, but thou shalt eat flesh to thy heart's desire. From all cattle shalt thou draw it forth with a high hand, and over all beasts thy hand shall prevail and thou shalt destroy their majesty.

But of the sons of man beware, for his devices are many. He will ensnare thee in his gins. Though thou be stronger than he, in craft thou canst not evade him, for he arms his hand with a bow as with a grate network to put thy foot in the stocks. For him a precious cornerstone is the pit and the snare and fear, and thou wilt descend to the abyss of destruction. Thou wilt not prevail against him, for none upon dust is his like. Who indeed is his equal? All cattle, every one, are slaves to man, both horses and mules; he desires them for his seat and harnesses them to his chariot. Day after day he lays his burdens upon asses; he ploughs with oxen and slaughters them for food. He is strong in the shearing of sheep. The souls of ox and lion and sheep sorrow, and the lamb is led to the slaughter. Therefore do I bid thee hearken to my counsel and keep my commandment, lest after my death thou be destroyed if thou violate words of truth. Lo, I shall die, as is the way of all the earth, and thou wilt break forth this breach upon thee. Be not afraid, neither be thou dismayed. But guard thy soul that thou go not down to the pit. Be thou strong and of good courage."

Thereafter the king commanded that his son be seated upon his throne in the sight of all his officers, that so they might be among his helpers. And after he had given his commandments he fell upon him and kissed him, and after he had spoken his spirit departed and his eye was dimmed and his moisture fled and his heart was poured out and his majesty was turned to destruction and he was gathered in to his people. The son's mercies waxed warm and he cried out: "My father, my father—thou that didst hold sway over ram and hart—majesty of royalty, chief of battle hosts, woe unto us, woe, that thou art enclosed in desolate land." And he lifted his voice and wept over him and kissed him. At his sound his family trembled and all his ministers with him, and all came to lament the king: "Alas for our lord, alas for his majesty! If the boldness of his face be changed, what shall his orphan children do? After him we shall grope like men blind; wherefore is his chariot so long in coming? He hath fled into concealment. Wherefore hath our shade departed from us? Would that he even hate us and return upon us all the evil that we wrought him. Woe is us that we have sinned; we are perished, lost are we all if our king who was celebrated among the nations hath fallen." And the peoples lamented him, but the son would not be comforted. He enjoined a mourning of seven days, and when the mourning passed, when the strength of the burden-bearer was decayed, and his place knew him no more, they took the dead up and buried him in the rock of his lofty mansion. They called its name High Place, for it was to be a monument whence to behold the carcass of the lion. And it came to pass after they had buried their glory and their treasure that the people turned and departed. And they brought the king's son back and comforted him in his house, and gave their pledge that they would love and serve him.

And when the king returned to his house, he sat upon his throne according to law and statute, and the kingdom prospered in his hand. He turned hither and yon in his roaring, and no beast could stand before him; all were unstrung and confounded at his rebuke. And when the heart of the king was glad in his joy, and his spirit was greatly exalted, he opened his hands wide and made a banquet for all his servants; the drinking was according to the law, none did compel. They raised an ensign to the mountains to satisfy every living creature with favor, with the butter of kine and the milk of sheep. They covered their face with fat until their hearts were appeased toward their king. During the days of the banquet the king called to his ministers and enjoined the chiefs of his soldiery to make the young men rejoice and give the stalwarts confidence, to make them officers over the host, captains of thousands and captains of hundreds. All gathered together and formed a united band—bears and leopards, lions and swine, horses and elephants, dromedaries and camels; the foxes hastened to join the assembly, and there were unicorns and monkeys by thousands of thousands, until there was no place to stand. The camp was exceedingly heavy, and the king was eager to behold it. He made a pavilion there and called to his ministers and household and said to them: "Choose ye out the heroes that ye see before me to be officers in the host and devastate city and province." And they did according to the words of the king; they made the leopards generals and the bears lieutenants and the wolves prefects to fight against the dogs. The deer were runners, and the foxes counselors, for these were clever when they emerged naked from their mother's womb. They arose with a high hand and rejoiced and sang and made their voices heard, crying "Long live our lord the king!" And the people saw and shouted and fell upon their faces, and the king rejoiced over them. To his tent then went each man from the treasure-house, for in the month of spring he had opened his father's stores and multiplied his gifts and made presents to all that came thither, and blessed them, and they went in peace. The people went upon its way, and the king remained in his pavilion with the flowers of his family who made his kingdom strong.

And he went to his stores and brought forth all the treasure of his fathers; but when he saw that what had been hidden away was reduced, he couched in his den and said: "I will clothe me in strength and pass through the wilderness and awaken all my wrath upon any that encounter me. I will avenge me upon mine enemies and fill my lairs with prey. And if I encounter man—though my father bade me beware of him, for that his eyes shine bright and he sees from afar, oppresses him that is beneath him and envies him that is above—may he so do unto me and more also, I shall transgress my father's commandment. As the man is, so is his strength; if his strength prove as unstable as water and he calleth understanding his mother, yet the utterance of lips is a superfluity, for mine is greater wisdom. Before he show his cunning I will smite him with the plague and humble him; his bones will I break."

Ere he was done speaking these words to himself he girded on his sword and issued forth from the forest, his mouth gaping wide. Upon his going out he found a wild ass, at home in the wilderness, and roared toward him; but the wild ass that confronted him was seeking an occasion against him and was not humbled by his roaring. In the eyes of the king this was astonishing, and he said: "Who is this that goeth, and turneth not back at my voice, but abideth before me? Is this the man, of whom my father spoke? Now shall I do that which is in my heart." And he came upon him and smote him, but the wild ass did not recognize him. Ere the lion withdrew his hand he spilled his liver to the ground, and ere he was dead he set about devouring him. Then the wild ass cried out: "Help me, King Lion, our lord. Where art thou and where thy goodness and loving-kindness to deliver thy servant from the hand of his smiter? He is a mighty warrior." And it came to pass when the lion heard him that he knew he had wounded him, and he said: "Who art thou that thou hast rebelled against me? Am I not King Lion, who walks with the eagle?" When the wild ass heard his words he fell before his feet and bowed down to him, for that he was his lord, and he said: "I the wild ass am thy servant; do thou spare me. I have sinned, for I recognized not the king and his roar." The king swathed his face, which was defiled with blood, and said: "Hast thou seen the son of man? What are his deeds and his ways? His expectation shall be shamed." Said the wild ass: "I know not. His voice have I not heard nor have I passed through his land nor have I come to the lodging where he lies, for I know not where it is. Never have I seen him, to know whether he be esteemed or contemptible. But do thou go hence and come to a plain where thou wilt find ass and ox; they know him for they have served him from of old. My words are finished in thine ears; understand well what is before thee." Thus far he spake, and the lion went upon his way.

He found a wild mule and an elephant and laid their lofty stature low. Thence he went forth to break breaches as he walked abroad in the land. And it came to pass as he issued forth from the forest that he saw a horse; strong was he, of handsome stature, clothed with high spirit, sleeker than perfumer's oil, swifter than lightning, and without blemish from his feet to his back. When the lion saw this spectacle envy burned within him, but the horse clothed him in awe for the day of wrath, saying: "Who is this man?" One called to the other, shouting bitterly with all their might, so that the earth was cleft by their voices. And when the lion approached near, the horse reared up on his legs to fall upon him and destroy him; but the lion nimbly leapt aside and escaped, so that the horse had no power over him. The lion took position to the rear of the horse, to harass him, himself being very wary. The horse in his great pride thrust backward, not forward, and clothed him with zeal as with a mantle. He waxed fat and kicked with his hind legs and smote the lion in his loins so that the blow descended even to his arms. When the lion saw that he had wounded him, he grasped his tail, and his wrath burned within him; he ran against the horse in fury and stretched out his right arm and requited his enemy to his face. Terror encompassed his fangs, and he crushed him like a bruised reed. Then did the hooves of the horse grow faint, and before he turned from his wrath the lion roared over his prey and tore at the horse's arm and even his head. The horse fell and knelt, doing obeisance upon his knees, and he cried out: "Help! Lo, I am thy servant, for thou art stronger than I; let thy breath not grow noisome." Said the lion; "Art thou man, whose might is great?" And he said: "Nay, I am horse, and there is none like me. But thou who art so strong, who art thou?" And he said: "I am lion. But where is man? If thy soul is weary of him, wherefore hast thou not smitten him to the ground?" And he said: "Prithee, my lord, I am my master's carrier, to do the desires of himself and all the people of his land." Said the king: "Where is he?" And he said: "Lo, he is in his field, gathering up his work. If it be to battle thou hast gone forth, go hence and thou wilt find him; lo, he is at his tilth; man abideth not in honor."

The lion came to the plain and saw the man binding sheaves to complete his work. And at his coming he saw the ass perishing and lying down under his burden, and the sheep were there also. Dread fell upon them, and they said: "Where is our master?" When the lion heard, he approached them and saluted them in peace. He asked them what their work was and who was their master. Said they: "We are slaves of the man who owns us, and each receives his rations from him. We know not what we shall do. Our soul loathes bread other than his. It is better for us to serve him than to be thy slaves." Said the lion: "Whither hath this great people gone?" Said they: "The man fared hence to the forest to hew wood; of his own rede doth he take counsel. His household hath ridden forth with him."

While they were yet conversing, lo, the fox approached, and the king was pleased to see him. Said he: "This one bringeth tidings; I shall not doubt them." When the fox reached him he knelt at his feet and said: "Is it peace with my lord?" And he answered, "Peace, my son." Said the fox: "I went forth and ambushed a bird's nest and its chicks; I left the winged folk no branch." The king answered and said: "And was not man on guard? Was he not there, or didst thou prove stronger than he?" Said the fox: "It was by lurking I took my prey, not by strength; for who am I and who my people?" Said the king: "Abide with me until I find him; surely I shall smite him in my wrath, a single stroke—I shall need no second. This place is a place of cattle; thou shalt graze in fat pastures." Said the fox: "So be it, my lord king, according to thy words; I shall follow after thee. But beware of snares; the man thou seekest thou shalt find in the thicket of the forest, for he has but now gone forth from his house. Thou shalt approach him to do battle with him and take much booty." So the lion walked with a high hand, and the fox remained in that place.

The parable: Beware of the wicked in every way, for sons do the deeds of their fathers, just as the lion who slew oxen and slaughtered sheep, whether by his nature or by his will.

107

Elephant & Hunter

THOUGH HIS BEGINNING BE STRAIT,
MUCH WILL HE ATTAIN IN HIS END.

THE ELEPHANT is remarkable among the beasts for his figure, his stature, and his aspect, for he is filled with bones and his tusks are encompassed with dread. His neck is two hundred cubits long and issues from his midst, from his breast, between his thighs; it ascertains the what and wherefore of things, and gathers his food into his mouth at a single sweep. It is a full wagon, laden with destruction. His rider is a city and its inhabitants. His maw gapes wide and ascends to his back; he is able to bear burdens, and his stride is exceeding broad.

An expert hunter of the field was tracking and hunting game when lo, an elephant with all his figure and stature and aspect came toward him. The man approached ever nearer, his sword girt upon his thigh. And it came to pass when the elephant came nigh him that he gnashed his teeth against him and opened his measureless maw and hurled him far off. The man was weary and fordone, and his hams touched one another as he walked; he desired to tar his dogs on to bite the elephant—blood is not atoned but by the blood of him that shed it. The man took thought against him: perhaps he could cast him down into his gin. He spread his snare and his ropes and made toils and snares in the forest and chased the elephant until he came thither, but the elephant broke and tore them and destroyed them utterly. Then he whetted his sword; perhaps he could do battle with him. And he went and attacked him and strove to slay him, seeking an opening against him. But when he lifted his hand against him and gathered his strength, his sword was broken and crumbled like potter's ware.

When he saw that he could not prevail against him, he cried for all the people to assemble and said to them: "Mine is this elephant; I have desired him and cast my face upon him. By my cunning I have not availed to capture him in my net and snare, nor yet by my sword and bow; as I am bereft so am I bereft. Do ye pursue after him; perhaps ye will overtake him. When terror and trembling seize him ye will confound him and the mixed multitude which is in his midst; be ye zealous to master him." Quickly they cast him in their pit and captured him in their zeal and wrath and brought him to his master, the hunter of the field. His master said in his heart that he would lord it over him with hard labor and humble his heart with toil. He mounted upon his back and said to him: "Wherefore hast thou so done, to walk frowardly with me, in furious anger and rebelliousness? Me didst thou hurl behind thy back; therefore art thou encompassed with gins and snares."

When he saw that there was no stranger with him he wrapped his face in his cloak and rode upon the elephant until the setting of the sun. As the sickle was raised against the standing grain the reapers saw him and hid from him in the forests; the sinews of their stones were wrapped together in their fright, for they imagined that the demon had invaded their field. Each man said to his fellow: "We have seen the demon upon his horse." And they cried and wept all the night with the voice of great consternation, for lo, a dark dread had fallen upon them. Lamentation waxed strong among them, until they reached an inhabited city, and they said: "Bring forth every stranger and sojourner to make the demon flee from before us. Art thou for us or for our adversaries?" All the city was in tumult over them, and they said: "Against ghoulies and ghosties we shall not do battle, lest we become a laughing-stock and a disgrace." So they forsook their tents, their cattle and their asses, and men and women fled from that place. The man with the elephant came and found their tents as they had been left, filled with precious treasure, gold and silver, sheep and oxen. He sent and fetched them he loved, and summoned all his kinsmen, and he brought forth from the city every desirable thing, whether in chest or tower or press. Over the excellent sheep and oxen and fatted bulls, mother and children rejoiced; but the city was a desolate waste, without man or cattle, without sheep or its multitude of oxen. Even as the king had come upon it to waste it, so he came upon another city and did unto it as he had done to the first, which was left desolate; and so to the third and fourth, to the fifth, sixth, and seventh, and to the eighth and ninth; and so to the tenth also, wherein all he had ransacked was for devouring. And he returned to his house in peace and enriched. He informed them what his hire would be for exorcising the demon which had devastated the land, and they vowed to give him half his plunder, half to be returned to them. So did that man do, and they forgave him that which he had already done.

The parable is for a calculating and wise man who is ready to pursue after his provender. Every day is he weary and fordone, and he finds no respite for his soul nor gains aught by his toil, as befell that man who was alone with the elephant. But when the word of the king touches him so that his fortune waxes strong upon him and raises him ever higher, as when the master of the elephant was enlarged, he must keep his hand from rapine and theft and from the deeds he had wrought, as did that man with his booty. Like a lion he strengthened himself to return the half. If his beginning were strait, much did he attain in the end. Upon savory fare does he dine, and his righteousness stands forever.

108

Cat, Bird, Fox, Hare

A MAN FILLED WITH EVIL AND PERVERSION CAUSES DISSENSION AND BLOWS BETWEEN BRETHREN.

A CAT dwelt in the ruins of houses. From their windows sprouted wheat, of which a few grains were pecked by a bird. The cat thought to hold the bird fast, and said: "Wherefore is my soul straitened, while this bird hath much wheat and barley and liquors of banqueting and joy? Its days all pass without breach or plaint. I said of laughter, It is mad; my soul and my flesh are for a prey. At my soul's desire I shall eat flesh, and in famine I shall not lack food." So the cat went toward the bird privily; but the bird escaped from the spread snare and flew a short space away, lest it be a target for the arrow; it kept a distance of two bowshots. But the cat called to it and pleaded: "Why hast thou fled from me? If thou desire a wife such as I, spread thy wing over thy maidservant. I love the habitation of thy house; upon thee have I reposed my trust, and I have called thee unto me in love. Thou shalt rule my every limb. Come, my beloved, let us fare forth into the field. I shall trample and devour, and thou rend and rieve, and our prey we shall divide by lot together; better are two than one." But the bird made its reply: "Lo, the rains are over and gone, and the time of the singing of birds is come. I shall not alter or change my good wife for a bad. I will not add to her, nor from her diminish. Mine eye is single upon the life of my spouse, no less than hart and doe, and I shall enter no conspiracy. Speak to me no more." Answered the cat: "I am bereft and desolate; of me thou shalt not be afraid, for in my house have I brought thee persuasive gifts. Thou knowest not my lowliness, for I know and shall say after my death that the mouth of strange women is a deep pit." With her large discourse she inclined him to approach nearer, but for her it was confusion and shame, for as they were still conversing there came from the thickets of the forest a fox and a hare and they smote the cat unto death. The vulture escaped from all harm, for he was its enemy and had done no evil; but the cat who had thought to take its soul, her deed was requited upon her head, and it was done to her as she had schemed to do. Afflicted and tempest-tossed was she, and not comforted.

The parable is for a man filled with evil and perversity, who causes dissension and blows between brethren; he lays his friends and comrades low with gins and snares and the prancing of his mighty ones. You will find that it shall be done to him to the full as he had schemed to do to his fellow men.

109

Crab, Frogs, Crane

A RULER WHO HEARS LYING WORDS INQUIRES AND SEARCHES AND INVESTIGATES WELL.

A CRAB grew up in water. Out of his hands he had horns, he was all turned black, and he went not forward but backward. A frog stood at his side and croaked in his ear to frighten him. Said the crab: "What is this sound in my ears? Woe to all my neighbors for the noise of the ravaging host! I have heard and have aroused me to betake myself to the fish for refuge, lest the frog master us." Said the fish to him: "Gird the remnant of thy wrath to follow the counsel of the crane. His beak is narrow and sharp, and he eats frogs altogether; his neck is exceeding long; who can stand before him?" The crab came to the crane and said: "At my terror at the voice of the roaring of the frog my hair trembleth; I am the witness that knows. Prithee, my lord, hear me; have mercy upon me for I am cut off. Deliver me from this fury; enough of the thunder which the raging frogs croak in my ears with their gaping mouths." Answered the crane: "Lo, I dwell in the covert of reed and fens to cut off thence every creeping abomination. Whence hast thou come in thy bereavement? Tell me what my hire shall be and put thy price down in my hand, lest I swallow thee at a gulp." Said the crab: "I am hard and I am small. I am lacking in limbs and in fat and flesh; what savor canst thou find in me? In the day thou confrontest me, know what is before thee. Set thy face toward the frogs; put not a knife to thy throat. Of the frogs thou canst eat thy fill as thy soul desires." The crane answered in a soft voice: "There is none wise and understanding as thou. Thou shalt be over my house all the days of my life, until the day of my death." So the twain concluded a covenant against the frogs to cut them off from the marshes and the rivers and the seas. And the crab and the crane rested without fear—for not one frog was left—as brethren that dwell together. And from their enemies the frogs, who croaked aforetime, there was no utterance and no speech.

The parable is for a man full of wisdom, without deception or falsehood. Slanders that are framed against him are disdained along with them that walk in crooked ways. As a ruler who hears lying words inquires well and searches out and investigates, in order to abolish afflictions abroad, so shall he be diligent and vigilant lest from the granary and winepress, from his household and family and native place, they enlarge their stride against him. He shall do well in his actions and in his words, as he had done with his fathers, and he shall pay his neighbor his hire, upon that day or the morrow, as the crane requited the crab—and the name of his brother was Joktan.

110

Ant & Mouse

LIKE FIRE UPON A LEAFY TREE
IS THE FLAME OF SCORN
FOR THE BOLE OF THE CONFIDENT.

THE ANT, not a strong folk, was scornful of the mouse. As she gathered her bread in summer she came to the edge of the heap at the beginning of barley harvest to glean among the sheaves; it was in compassion for her soul that she toiled, to prepare her food in harvest season. There she saw many mice making free of wheat and barley; six measures of barley they meted out to themselves to bring to their holes, until they had enough and to spare. The ant was filled with wrath and addressed them with contentious words and uttered stinging reproaches: "Wherefore have ye presumed to do so unto me? Have ye no fear of my furious indignation? I am the ant; I am a prince, for I have a garment. I am ruler and I am overseer; I remember injuries and avenge them. For me and over me, there is no king, of all the creeping creatures that walk upon the belly. Why have ye vexed me to take of my granary and my threshing?" Answered the mouse: "Mine is the granary and mine the grain. Wherefore hast thou slandered me? For me it was ruin. Surely thou art despised before me; how canst thou learn to do battle with me? Stay, arise out of the dust, awaken thee; dwell wherein thou dwellest; tread not the strength of my soul. I have eaten of my honeycomb and my honey, and my labor has sufficed for them. Who shall pass over the sea for us?" The ant returned her sayings; her strokes were from sea to sea. Her stings she dispatched against their nobles, against the mice according to their families and against their toil wherewith they toiled. In the days of snow they robbed their water. She returned to her companions to relate to them all that had befallen her, and she said: "I have labored and succeeded; I have tasted and eaten and been satisfied with bread and dainty viands upon the mountains of spices. But the evil mice, those wicked vermin, have reached to my very soul, so that I cannot lift my head. They have gleaned among the sheaves and the provender; the little foxes have spoiled our vineyard. Come ye forth with me to encounter them; I know their battle encampment." The ants hearkened to her, and with them came the cats, to be their auxiliaries and lurk for their blood in their coverts. They came to their place and there encamped until they had consumed them. The ants entered their holes and smote their soles with shoes and mounted upon the backs of the mice as do the bees. They stung them to the quick, to their very souls, until they came forth from their place. Then they brought forth the wheat and the barley and heaped it in heaps. The cats filled their belly with the mice and worked their will upon their enemies; and the ants, not a strong people, but one despised, destroyed them and dwelt in their place until this day.

The parable is for a man poor and humble by the side of a man rich and proud. The pauper speaks pleadingly with him, for he sues for his love, but the rich man answers sternly: "Who has heard the like?" He invents slanders against him to drive him from his livelihood, and his stench rises over him like a fire upon a leafy tree, a flame of scorn upon the thought of him that is at ease. His feet are ready for the appointed day. So is the rich man with his snares. Every driven leaf drives him forth, but God seeks out the driven.

And I plied my poesy and said in my response:
God judges the righteous;
He impoverishes the rich and the poor he enriches.

III

Spider, King, Slave

THOSE UPON WHOM THE RICH TAKE
NO MERCY ASCEND UPWARD,
WHILE THE RICH DESCEND
DOWNWARD TO THE PIT.

THE SPIDER is in the palaces of kings. Her hand holds the distaff, to weave and attach webs to level surfaces and to any beams of walls from houses and tents. The king built a house of great hailstones, but the spider made a web inside it to where the king sat at his table, and the king's anger burned within him. The servant approached, as was his way, to cleanse the house in its breadth and length, and he looked at the spider's web on the beams which went up to the four corners, east, north, west, and south, and he said to the spider: "We cannot dwell together, with the king and his servants. I shall sweep thee out with the besom of destruction." The spider proceeded to the wine and the water and the mead, to cast her poison into the liquors. And the man did not get off innocent; his belly swelled and his thigh rotted. The servant went weeping to his master to tell the tale of the accursed water turning bitter. The king commanded that the beverages be poured out in the streets and in the market places. The servant said: "A bitterness greater than death's do I pour forth." The matter was searched into, and it was found that when the sheep and the swine came from forest and field they drank of their mingled drink, and their bellies swelled and their thighs rotted of the liquor which had been poured forth. They drank and swilled it down, and were quenched like flax. Men sensed the thing which had befallen in the past: By means of a small insect a man big as a giant had been strangled—by draining the cup of poison for which there is no cure or remedy or relief. When the king saw this miracle his heart was jubilant, for he had been saved from great calamity, from a loathsome death to life; his life was in the balances before him. He made a banquet for all his friends, his household, and his kinsmen, and he said: "Better is it for me now to convert the spider from her evil."

So he came to her tent and commanded his servants to enjoin her to come at the king's bidding. Then he said: "I have established peace in thy boundary. I had dealt rebelliously with thee, I had decked my bed with coverings of tapestry were I not afraid of thy destruction and devastation. Now make broad the place of thy tent and the curtains of thy dwelling. Come and lodge where I lodge. How beautiful are thy feet with shoes! Lo, this house have I built thee to live in in return for the evil I did thee. Thou shalt no more sorrow forever, and no more shall evil or deception against thee enter my heart, for thou hast brought me so far as this and hast made my remembrance peace, if thus thou do to me and thine anger against me is abated." The spider answered with harsh words: "There is a time to speak and a time to be silent. Thou hast driven me out from abiding in thine inheritance; lo, I shall send against thee and thy houses a heavy plague of flies. Thou shalt not avail to stand before me, nor yet to be healed, for thou wilt be destroyed by death." And she went and collected all the spiders from houses and valleys, and they all gathered together to attack the king and his servants, and they assailed them to confound and destroy the men until they were consumed. They set watchers and taskmasters over them, and when deep sleep fell upon the men they fell and died in multitudes and not one was left.

The parable is for the poor and needy, upon whom the rich take no mercy, but instigate others to injure them, as though they had been their enemies from of old. But the poor take thought for their latter day and make bands against their death and shrewdly take vengeance to requite them for their treacherous dealing against them. They become pricks in their eyes and thorns in their sides, until they come and kneel and prostrate themselves at their feet to forgive their transgression and remit their sins. And they are humbled and return to the heel of their shame, and they descend lower and lower, down to the pit; and the poor ascend higher and higher. And Solomon in his wisdom hath said: "There is one that maketh himself poor yet hath great riches, but he turns his ear aside from hearing the poor man when he cries."

112

Man, Rock, Mouse

MEN WHO CANNOT ATTAIN FIRM
TRUTH WEAVE A SPIDER'S WEB.

THERE was a man who boasted of his shrewdness and cunning and ingenuity and declared that with his blade he could impregnate the great rock which was in the wilderness and within a month without deception bring to birth and release a living creature. The people of the place went astray after him and hearkened to wizards and magicians. The man kept a big mouse, and at the season he appointed he placed the mouse in a crevice of the rock, where it was held prisoner until the folk came there. The cracks of the rock the man stopped up, and he went and gathered the folk, saying: "Hasten, come ye after me and I will fulfill my saying." Those that doubted, together with those that believed, journeyed forth as one man, and said with mocking lips: "Who hath heard such a thing, who hath seen such a thing? Shall earth travail and a mountain bring forth? But this man hasteneth to verify his word." The man who boasted of his handiwork took in his hand a staff, which he raised against the rock, and he said: "Hear ye, my masters; shall I bring forth a living creature out of the rock and produce it before you?" And he smote the rock with his staff to cast down from it all that he had placed over the opening, and the mouse emerged, all black. Said he: "The mouse was born, and lo, he hath come forth; of all my words none hath fallen to the ground."

The parable is for those who hearken to falsehood and walk in darkness. They believe in words of those who daub with untempered mortar and work in miry clay. They conceive mischief and bring forth iniquity. They put their trust in falsehood and vanity. Any who joins them shall be even as they. Those that play the harlot after them, away from the path of the sensible and the seemly, vanity are they and the work of errors. For that they do not attain the right they weave spider's webs. But their wiles cannot serve for a garment, nor can they clothe themselves in their deeds. They think to lead people astray by their devices, by their visions and falsehoods and shakings; but foolish indeed are they, for they stumble in the snare of their folly. Help they cannot, nor can they deliver.

113

Man & Wolf

A MAN WHOSE EYE AND HEART ARE BENT ON GAIN, HIS MOUTH DECLARES HIS WICKEDNESS.

A MAN taught the letters of the alphabet to a wolf. He said to him, "Say *aleph*," and the wolf answered, "Aleph." Then he said, "Pray say *beth*," and the wolf guarded the utterance of his lips and said *beth* and *gimel* after him. Said the man: "Now listen to what I set before thee, so that thou mayst recognize the letters and put them together and so be able to pronounce what thou wilt. When thou combinest the letters together, we shall be one people. Put *aleph* and *beth* together as I do." The wolf responded "Sheep!"

The parable is for one whose eye and heart are bent

upon gain. His mouth will declare his wickedness and his lips will testify against him to reveal the frowardness of his heart. Wickedness will issue from his belly when evil is found in his mouth, and his thoughts can be recognized from his deeds. He despises Jacob and chooses Esau. His righteousness goeth before the righteous but the perverseness of transgressors shall destroy them. Solomon's proverb [Proverbs 14.22] retains its force. "They that devise evil go astray."

114

Chameleon & Merchants

HE WHO IS FILLED WITH TAINT
AND ABOMINATION AND FRIVOLITY
IS ACCOUNTED BY MEN AS UTTERLY VILE.

A CHAMELEON rooted with her teeth after the roots and shrubs which were under her feet. She threw the dirt over her as she went hither and yon to spread her rooting, and the field was filled with many mounds. There came thither merchants to seek roots for medicines, and they searched for them until the chameleon came out of her place toward them. Said they: "Upon the testimony of two witnesses shall the culprit be put to death"—and they pursued her as far as the mound. Into the mound the chameleon escaped, and she laughed at them and called out: "Why have ye chased after me? I know my house, wherein I may hide to deliver my soul from death and keep me alive in famine. I shall walk in the land of the living and shall not be for a laughingstock. Never again shall ye see me. The roots which ye are seeking, I have uprooted all, for in my heart is the day of vengeance. Ye shall return empty-handed, shamed and discomfited and disgraced among the physicians and among the people. Healers of vanity are ye all, with your charlatanry and your wiles. Depart from me quickly; let not the light of day shine upon you. Everyone will whistle at you, and I shall not spare you my spittle. Baser and viler are ye than all men who have exchanged their honor for shame." The men turned away thence to seek roots in another place, and the chameleon sent her daughter after them to carry out her devices and uproot the roots from the earth. Said she: "Whoso breaches a wall, may a serpent bite him;

these men menace our lives by taking provender and sustenance for their souls from us." The daughter went according to her counsel and did all that her mother commanded her. She came to the place of their sojourn and returned not until she had destroyed all the roots in the ground. She destroyed them forever, so that not one root was found. The men went from that place together, and the chameleon ran after them to tell them that she had done this thing. Said she: "Wherefore have ye toiled for vanity? Who is he and where is he that durst presume in his heart to do so? There is not a wise man among you. I am blind and ye have eyes, yet from me do ye take spices and medicaments. Mine is counsel and wisdom to recognize all the roots of the earth, which of them are good for plaisters, and also all species of dye—white, red, green, and black. But ye walk backward; day and night ye weary yourselves, but find no root." The men did not know at all where her place was under the ground, for the battle is not to the strong nor the race to the swift to reach their goal. These men came to the camp, but there was none to heed their voice and none to answer.

The parable is for a man who boasts of his great wisdom, of his beauty and comeliness and stature, saying there is none like him on earth—who is he and where is he? His heart is emptier of understanding than all men of good faith, but he is filled with taint and abomination and frivolity and folly and is accounted among men as the exaltation of the vile. Out of his vaunted wisdom he will go bowed down; instead of wheat there will come forth a thorn. In all labor there is profit and smoothness, but the talk of the lips tendeth only to penury. And the Preacher hath said in the proverbs of prophecy [Proverbs 17.10): "A reproof entereth more into a wise man than a hundred stripes into a fool."

115

An Old Man & His Sons, a Captain & His Men

HE WHO HONORETH HIS FATHER
EVEN IN DRINKING, HIS
REWARD WILL NOT BE FALSE.

THERE was a man in the land, old and richer than any creature; his wealth extended everywhere, and his sons were with him in his house. He called to them to declare his will: "Hear, my sons, the commandment of your father, for I am old and know not the day of my death. Pray, give ear to me, ye princes, and hear whether my words be just. Hearken to me, my sons all: I have money in my treasuries; take it all for yourselves and divide it among you. Leave not anything with me, but only give me wine from year to year." The old man finished his injunctions, and his sons did for him as he had said. Every day they found wine for him, until after many years they grew weary. They took counsel among themselves and made their father drunk with white wine and red, until he fell asleep before them. Then they summoned their neighbors and said: "Come ye hither, ye that pursue after rewards, and see what hath befallen us; for our iniquities our father hath died." And they went and wept for him and performed the customary usages. The sons dressed him in shrouds and carried him to a cave which he had got ready. And it came to pass that a captain came upon that day; his retinue was large, and there was the noise of a multitude. They sat them in the cave by companies and began to eat and drink. The man awoke from his wine and arose to go to his home; the feasters saw him from afar and left off their eating. The captain said to them: "Truly, this man is dead." The men arose in great fear and departed and left all their possessions; and when the sons came to the cave to see him they found great wealth with him. There they rejoiced mightily, and the favored people went to their house.

The parable is for a man who fills his belly and bowels with dainties, and to the drinker gives wine.

116

An Old Man, His Son, a Fish, the Leviathan

HE WHO DOES THE COMMANDMENT OF HIS FATHER, EVEN THE LEVIATHAN WILL FORGIVE HIS SIN.

THERE was an old man devout and humble whose eyes had grown heavy with age. He put his trust in the Rock who created him. As he lay sick upon his bed he yearned for his elder son, and in view of his approaching death commanded him: "Cast thy bread upon the waters, for thou shalt find it after many days." And it came to pass after the old man died that the son sat upon his father's chair and did as he had commanded him; he walked in the way his begetter had led him and cast his bread into the sea without stint. God caused a great fish to eat his bread until he was satisfied. One greater than his neighbor swallowed him; the great fish proclaimed a day of slaughter for the fish round about, and in sorrow they went to the Leviathan, who was chief of them that handle the oar. The great fish trod his bow in strength against the fish; he wrought destruction among them without mercy and cut their branches off. The Leviathan commanded that he be summoned: "Let him not stand, though his host be great, lest the glory of his nostrils lose their terror. I shall slay him in battle." The great fish came bellowing and lamenting and storming mightily because of his strength; with a great trembling did that fish tremble, for he seethed in his depths like a pot. The Leviathan kindled his anger against him and his eyeballs gleamed like the dawn. Said he: "How couldst thou presume, how could thy heart embolden thee, to do such a thing? Who hath made thee ruler and judge over us? Art thou the man who hath consumed us?" The great fish drew near and confessed: "Let not thine anger kindle if I tell thee the truth. I did in mine iniquity murder, and this thing and that have I done." The Leviathan answered: "From whose hand hadst thou thy repast, who hath fed thee to this point?" And he said: "There is a man whose way it was to sustain me with daily rations; in truth he is responsible for his own injury." Answered the Leviathan: "If thou wouldst atone thy sin, violate not my commandment. Go thou to thy haunt, where thou hast affirmed the man's habit of casting his bread to thee; when he seeks thee do thou swallow him, but keep his soul alive. Thereby wilt thou save thy life, for that thou hast slain without mercy." All answered, "This is appropriate," and the thing was determined and the great fish did so. He swallowed the man within his gullet and spewed him forth before his master. The Leviathan asked the man in anger: "What is this and why is this and wherefore hast thou given the fish thy food? It is not for thee to maintain him; but if it be so and thou art obliged to keep him, then must thou be destroyed for his sin." The man prostrated himself before him and said that he had done this thing in the innocence of his hands and by the commandment of his father. The Leviathan raised his hands and swore by his life that no hair of his head should fall: "Thou shalt not be judged by analogy, for thou hast kept a commandment, and art not responsible for its anomalous outcome. Open thy mouth and I shall fill it with the spirit of wisdom. Thou shalt be clever in all things and wiser than Darda and Chalcol." The saying of Leviathan was established; he was brought out from the sea, and his coming forth was very swift; none was found so wise as he. His history is duly recorded in a book of chronicles.

117

Wolf & Fox

ALREADY HATH SOLOMON IN HIS WISDOM SAID [PROVERBS 11.8]: "THE RIGHTEOUS IS DELIVERED OUT OF TROUBLE AND THE WICKED COMETH IN HIS STEAD."

A FOX went strolling by a fountain and saw the shadow of the moon cast upon the water. He thought in his heart that it was a cheese and greatly desired to eat of it. There before him were buckets hanging in balance, and he looked at them with his two eyes. He put forth his hand and grasped the cords to divide the cheese into portions. As he entered one of the buckets he went down with it into the water; he cried a great and bitter cry and waited there for some man to come and help him. There came to the fountain a wolf, who saw the fox lurking there. Said the wolf: "What art thou doing there? Tell me what mark that is in the water." The fox answered and said: "I have eaten much cheese and am sated; more I could not eat. Some I have stored away for thee. Come hither now, as I advise thee, and eat it, and we shall be comrades together; better are two than one." The wolf hearkened to his counsel and said in his heart: "I will go with him." He put his hand to the bucket which was near him and grasped it and nimbly sate himself within it. Quickly he descended to the fountain, and by the pressure of his weight the fox ascended. The wolf opened his mouth to the shadow to swallow it, but saw that he could not. Said the fox: "By the life of my head, thou shalt not eat of it." The wolf seized the cord in his hand to pull it, but saw that all was vanity. He lifted his voice to the fox in lamentation and said: "Wherefore hast thou dealt treacherously with me?" The fox answered him: "Let be; the wicked cometh in place of the righteous. For such a case hath Solomon in his wisdom said: 'The righteous is delivered out of trouble and the wicked cometh in his stead'."

One day the man went to the fountain, and with him were his wife and daughter and son. The maiden came after them slowly, with her pitcher resting upon her shoulder. In this manner they all went onward until they stood by the fountain. The man drew up the bucket, which showed him the wolf. Said he: "From the water have I drawn him forth." All looked upon the wolf, and the man desired to smite him. All surrounded him and began to beat him with their sticks, until they were wearied. The wolf ran, and they all came after him and pursued him to the place of his dwelling. Then they all returned to the fountain to draw water for their need. The maiden hastened and filled her pitcher and took it in her hand; then the girl lifted the pitcher and returned it to her shoulder, and they went and came to their house, and there they rejoiced with their fathers.

118

Youth, Rogues, Woman, Judge

WHOSO IN HATRED SEEKS A ROD
FOR THE BACK OF HIS BROTHER
WILL BE DESPISED FOR HIS ROD
AND CLOTHED IN SHAME.

A TRAVELER who could make music on any instrument came to a rich man. The rich man was handsome of figure, as though designed with compasses. His stature and the length of his limbs made him handsome; his fathers had exalted him as one chosen among the people. He asked the traveler: "Whence comest thou and whither goest?" And he said: "I come from a distant land. I have seen nobles riding upon horses. The land was good in my eyes; its merchandise is better than the merchandise of silver; and there is no lack of silver in it." Said he to him: "What is the city and what its name, from the time thou wert there?" Said he to him: "It is beyond Aram of the two rivers; it is Alexandria of Egypt." Said he: "So have I heard men say. I shall gather me comrades and go thither for trade, with cloth of goats and precious stones and with colored garments dyed in scarlet. I shall go to Egypt by boat upon the sea, with scarlet and purple and vesture and precious vessels of weight beyond calculation." He prepared all things, omitting none, and when the rainy season was past, he loaded his ship until it was full and overflowing and put in it shield and spear and armor. The sailors put out to sea and were carried forward by an east wind and made land, happy and joyful. They came before Alexandria, and the city was astonished at the sight of a mighty caravel, unparalleled for majesty at the haven of sea or the haven of ships; compared to it, all strength was trivial.

The young man disembarked from the ship and took a mule richly accoutred with bit and bridle, which he found in it, and rode to find entertainment. His report went forth in the streets and marketplaces, and certain rogues fore-gathered and formed a conspiracy to inspect the ship and its riches for the sake of combining against the young man to assault and fall upon him, and to seek a pretext and plot against him, for they were men of guile. The young man went hither and yon to see the city and the region, and a passerby encountered him and said: "To me shalt thou come. The Rock hath caused thee to meet with me, for we are both men of merchandise. If thou wilt, I shall buy all thy goods, for I have ships of Tarshish as well as lighter craft." The young man answered: "If thou hast leisure I shall gladly sell thee all. If it is thy will to purchase, what wilt thou give of all that is in the ship?" And he said: "As thou sayest and as thou choosest; I will fill thy vessel with goods of all sorts." And he said: "As thou sayest; the ship is before you; draw from it and make your purchase." So he bought the merchandise from him, and they separated, each man to his own house.

And it came to pass early on the morrow that he went to see his ship, and a man before him looked upon him, at the girdle upon his loins and the sword at his side girt over his garment. The man said: "Turn aside to me, turn aside, for the sword which is in thy girdle thou hast stolen from me, and also all my money." And he cited him to court to testify before the judge on an appointed day. The young man was meek, and he looked and his face fell. And it came to pass on the third day when it was morning that the young man arose to seek some helper. There met him a solitary man who was maimed; his right eye was gouged out. The man seized him and held him fast, so that he panted within him, and he said, "Why hast thou taken hold of me?"—"Because thou hast robbed mine eye; I will wager my soul against thine that that is mine eye which is in thy head." He found a guarantor for the judge, to be prepared for the day of strife, that he favor not the face of the poor but commit them to judgment. The law of the judge must be upright; he must not have respect to the rich. The man went upon his way, and the young man went on his way, weeping.

And as he went on in search of mercy there found him an old woman and said to him: "Why is thy face, which is handsome, sad?" He told her all that had befallen him and begged her to teach him what to do. Said she: "I shall not inquire or investigate but reveal their secret to you. All their glory and excellence is by the instruction of a very wise old man. With him they share all the profit they gain. They consult with him a day before their appointment and recount to him all their discussion and he writes their words down. They are afraid lest he tell their opponents, and they have nought to answer, and so they share their possessions with him. The old man lives in an upper chamber, and I in the house beneath. By the mercies of the Rock I will place thee at the crevice in the fortress and hide thee from them, and thou wilt hear all their words. And it came to pass on the day they came to take counsel that she hid him in the flax of the wood. They revealed to the old man the secrets of their houses and he considered them and determined the men to evil. The young man heard what was said and gave ear to the old man's speech, and his heart was cheered. They said: "Our lord is understanding and wise, but that young man is a fool and hath no wisdom." They went then to their house, and knew not that the interpreter had been between them.

Upon the day appointed they came to stand in judgment, and there were assembled smiths and hewers of wood and workmen of all kinds to make the day a blessing for the young man and deliver him and reward him for his deeds. Said the judge: "Let all who have suits stand and state their case." The first merchant whetted his tongue with pride: "Make thy demands great and I will give them; I will fill thy ship with all thou wilt say." The young man answered and said: "I desire of thee nought of gold and silver and broidered garments, nor perfumed essences of rich aroma; only fleas do I pursue; my request and my petition is that you fill my ship with them." Every man looked staring at his brother and said: "Hath a man so understanding as this been found?"

Then the second arose and said: "My lord judge, prithee hear: In my house I was quiet and serene from what I gathered and gleaned until I accumulated great wealth. This man came to my house and lay in wait and stole and took all for himself, even the sword which is upon him, and silver and gold and dyed garments. I call to testify against him faithful witnesses who identify the sword. Determine his penalty and sentence him. Let him pay me from his house, and if he have not wherewithal let him be sold for his theft." Then the young man arose before the judge and said: "My lord, I come from the land of Canaan and from France and Spain. In all this my heart hath not trembled nor hath my way been perverse, until I came to the land of Ararat. From there I went to Ispahan, and now am I come to Alexandria to display the sword and see whether a man can be found who will be willing to recognize and acknowledge it. Blessed be the Rock and his mindfulness, for he hath prospered my way. I have labored, and I have succeeded. Lo, with this sword was my father slain, to my great sorrow, and it was found stuck in his belly. My lord judge, here he is in thy hand; do but keep his soul until I ride upon the ass and bring witnesses to the matter; it shall not be forgotten."

Then the third rose in anger, panting to slay the young man, and he spoke against him proud words which were astonishing in the eyes of all: "My lord, this is the man who came to rend me like a lion, and he surpassed me in strength and gouged out my right eye and by his magic and wizardry put my eye in his head. And now if he do not confess I will prevail over him with hard labor. I shall do battle against him and overcome him. I shall sling a stone into his forehead. Do determine my case; let him indemnify me for my eye and for my pain and medical fees and unemployment and incapacitation, for it was in violence that he came against me." Said the young man to the judge: "Prithee, my lord, thou knowest that I am from a distant land and remote from father and brother and sons. Hear if my words be just, if the law of my land is upright and approved in thy sight. Gouge out that man's left eye and also my right eye which he claims was his. Put the two eyes in scales; if they balance and are equal, then is his claim correct. But if one outweighs the other, then shall they see to it that judgment be executed upon him in the view of all, in the vale of Jehoshaphat. With me he shall not fight, but if he confesses and forsakes his evil he shall be pardoned." And so the deceivers were defeated and remained vanquished. They gave the young man all their wealth, and their strength and might were forsaken.

This my parable is an allegory of a man filled with
  iniquity and deception,
Who sought to injure the innocent by working guile
  and fraud.
His day of retribution will come, and his measure
  will be very full;
Into the pit he delved and dug, will he fall in
  trembling and consternation.
There is a man who seeks a rod for his brother's
  back in frowardness and hatred,
But a time will come when he is despised with his
  rod and swathed in shame.
There is a man who breaches his neighbor's hedges
  for reproachful deeds and devastation,
But there will come a day when the serpent will bite
  him and exact vengeance.

Attend to this my parable, ye sons of man, and
multiply not vanity and guilt
As did the three in the story; but they were overturned and left empty-handed.

Go, my parables, to a man whose understanding
Perceives that my words are true and upright,
To be collected with those tested and tried.
If ye have truly found favor in his eyes and no
recrimination,
Then shall I pray the Blessed to make you lie down
in mansions.
Similarly, if he find and point any frowardness in you,
I pray he will hide your manuscript away,
That the memorial of iniquity be nevermore seen.

119

The Envious Man & the Covetous

THE COVETOUS AND THE ENVIOUS
TOGETHER WILL BE CLOTHED
IN CONFUSION, AND IN THE END
BOTH WILL BE MULCTED ALIKE.

HEAR ye the matter of Rabbi Crispia ha-Nakdan, who did judge the heart of an envious man and a covetous and adjudged them to sword, slaughter, annihilation, and the corruption of eternal loathing, and thereby subdued and humbled him who would subvert weight and measure and whose wrath was kindled at the strength of justice and the force of the decree. So hath it befallen man

—aye, men froward and passionate, one covetous and the other envious.

Each hated his brother, and they uttered many recriminations against their Creator, who knoweth the evil of their inclinations, and wickedly they murmured against him. The covetous man would speak as follows: "See how evil and bitter are all the works of God! He has brought the lofty low; why am I poor and indigent, whereas that man, mine enemy and neighbor that dwelleth at my right hand, is rich? He resteth under his standard; why doth he lift his foot to horse and chariot? My soul longs and yearns for his lot, for it is wholly desirable, and my heart turns toward him, to rest in his place." Said the envious man with his wonted hatred: "God will not turn toward thee nor hearken to thy voice to make thee a prince over people. Let me die if thou grow rich or if thou avail to be as I am, clothed in scarlet. I say to God, Make me not guilty. Who can hasten more than I, or who live? I would not that all sons of man possess wealth; enough for thee the livelihood of flesh and blood. I shall walk alone all the days of my world in my riches and my glory, for my hand hath found might. If the time come when I am poor and needy, let my neighbor be even poorer, and all they that pass before me, that they be as grasshoppers in my eyes and all walk in darkness."

And it came to pass as they were walking and talking as they walked that the wrath of the speaker who wished to make a name for himself kindled; he was knowingly sinful. An angel of God found them in the wilderness of Leshem, and when the angel saw them he called to them and said: "What have ye seen and what have ye sought and what have ye inquired of passersby? Know ye your Creator?" And they said: "We know but shall not speak of him, for his doing is strange, so that none can abide it. To my neighbor hath he given all that mine eye desires, and me he hath made to lack all things. His kindness hath he removed from me until my soul is oppressed with much jealousy and vexation, which beseemeth me not." Such was the response of the covetous man in his singular folly. May the form of the envious man's envy, the object of his desire, never come about: "If a man as rich as I shine forth at my side, better for me then is death than life, and rotting of bones for envy. If thou heedest his prayer and he ascend upward then shall I ascribe folly to God, and slander rather than praise him." So they quarreled together and emptied their sacks. Said the angel: "Be silent and wait for your deliverance. Surely ye will be ashamed of speaking against your Creator. Why do ye all quarrel with me? Lo, I am sent before you to give each of you this day his request and fulfill his petition. He is adequate to your demands. The Almighty will vouchsafe you your deserts; raise not your contention against me. He will speak, and it shall come to pass. Suddenly it will come upon you, with strength greater than any people. This is what I grant you: One of you two shall have whatever his mouth utters; it shall come upon him in an instant. And a double portion of what he asks shall accrue to his fellow, who is last in order. This shall be the covenant which ye must not violate. Pass ye over and go upon your way; all that ye shall choose shall come to pass for you." They hearkened to him and said: "Lo, we are thy servants, and thou shalt be our lord; be thy loving-kindness upon us, for we have repented."

And it came to pass as they spoke their words that the angel departed from them, for the spirit bore him off; no eye saw him, nor were his footsteps perceived. Then did they understand and perceive that he was an angel of the Lord and that the law of truth was upon his lips. Spake the covetous one, who lusted for a double portion because his uncleanliness was in his skirts, and said: "Do thou ask." And the envious one answered him: "How shall I ask for a thing when thou wilt emerge stronger than I and double thy dominion and take the share of the firstborn? Thou art the last, and therefore the profit will be thine and the loss, mine. I come first, and how can I request some good thing which will make thy lot better and broaden thy boundaries? Is this a just sentence?" Said the covetous man to the envious: "Art thou envious of me? Make thy request deep or raise it so high that thou wilt have nought to lack and wilt not be taken away from being a city; why shouldst thou be envious when thy soul is filled with all good things? Thine expectations are realized, and thou canst put them in thy basket." Answered the envious man: "If it is truth thou speakest, do thou ask first, in accordance with thy logic, and I will come after thee. Do not thou lust for a double portion. I shall not stand, I shall not avail to lift my head, my soul shall choose strangulation, if thou make thy portion greater than mine, if thou be the last in order." The covetous man grew wroth in his heart and his anger burned within him. He turned upon the envious man in fury and smote him with a high hand; with stone and fist and with the staff in his hand, he belabored his back, and he said: "Ask thou straightway, and my redemption shall come after thee. If not I will destroy thee and slay thee forthwith." And it came to pass when the envious man saw that his hope was lost, that he still clung to his uncleanliness. Since he could no longer hope to make the other ask first he made oppression his level and crying his plumb; he trepanned his skull and battered his head, beating and bruising it. When the envious man's might prevailed, the covetous man was in straits and implored and supplicated him, saying: "My lord, let go of me; I shall ask first and do thou receive a double portion in the end, that there may be peace between us." So he let him go, yet did not release him wholly but held him by his skirts, lest he seek an occasion to flee hither or yonder.

Then spake the envious man, saying: "Prithee, Lord, do unto thy servant the reverse of thy kindness, to requite his deeds upon him. Blind me of one of my two eyes, but mine enemy, of both. Make one of my hands to fall, and double this measure for mine enemy." And it came to pass as he was thus speaking that an awful darkness fell upon them and smote them both with blindness. The profit of the second exceeded the weight of the first, so that he had double his fellow's measure; his words were fulfilled. He turned his face to his fellow, and lo, both his eyes were darkened and his two hands remained in the skirt of his garment, so that his strength departed from him. And lo, his two feet were cut off. And so the two remained there, for shame and disgrace. Their lust was removed from them and also their hatred, for the covetous man desisted from his covetousness; he was content with his livelihood and did not malign his wealth, nor any more covet the possessions of a lordly house, but only the grave. For now he could not avail to put food into his mouth, but only to lick up porridge, as an ox licks grass. Want of eyes resulted in bareness of teeth, nor could he perceive the goodliness of taste. Nor did he stir from his place; his feeding and evacuation were in the same spot, so that he was reckoned as an animal; better for him death than such confusion.

Nor did the envious man who hated his brother any longer begrudge others. His envy had departed at the ends of the members he had lost in his willfulness and had forfeited in his envy; he was smitten to destruction. For this hath Wisdom made her proverb, saying of the envious man [Proverbs 26.24]: "He that hateth dissembleth with his lips and layeth up deceit within him"—and poureth wrath over him. But justice observes measure, and thus it befell the man that was covetous. Covetousness closes the Ten Commandments, and envy closes the Song of Songs, which calls it cruel as the grave. It hath no redeemer to redeem it nor any good at all save envy of wisdom—envy of the works of the pious, not of the works of sinners. It is only wicked, not good. Out of envy cometh covetousness, for envy comes first, but its end is bitter as wormwood. Bitter will be the covetousness which ensues, for its rise is inevitable. It is all a single malady; the leprosy blooms and waxes great until it is sovereign and draws the heart of man to within the veil. In the end it will cast him down and abandon him in the field in disgust. For that he envies the money of others, his friends will dig a pit to snare him. Such is the judgment of the envious; surely whom God hateth, I hold in abhorrence.

Crispia ha-Nakdan petitions his Creator to guard him from envy and deliver him from covetousness. And him who transcribes Crispia's work may the Lord shield from covetousness and envy, from the pit and from hatred, and may no evil thing befall him. Let him not covet the wealth of others, among the youthful; and in old age let him not envy his neighbors their money and property but only their wisdom and their contemplation and their good deeds, which stand forever—to observe them and do as they do. They that do their deeds are like unto them. Envy like this is filled with all goodness, and so said the prophets [Proverbs 23.17]: "Let not thy heart envy sinners, but be thou in fear of the Lord"—and in the words of Mount Sinai, and in the zeal for retribution. He that giveth peace in his high places and in his innocent sheep Israel which is sealed with the eternal covenant, the Rock, whose name is forever, He will bless his people Israel with peace.

AMEN.

Done—praised be the Sovereign!—are the parables of
Berechiah,
His proverbs are his allegories.
Wisdom he gathereth like gold and silver,
Folly he heweth apart and its lovers rejects.
His poesy strengthens the meek, abases the proud,
And causes haughty heads to stumble.
Pure sayings he gathers like herbs,
Bestows them in pots, readies them for cooking;
The wise esteem them as the chiefest spices,
Though to scorners and evildoers they are but broom.

Ended are all the parables,
Praised be the King of all the world.